The Jharro Grove Saga: Book One
Tarah Woodblade
A Bowl of Souls Novel
By Trevor H. Cooley

Trevor H. Cooley
Copyright 2013 by Trevor H. Cooley

The Bowl of Souls Series:

The Moonrat Saga:
Book One: EYE of the MOONRAT
Book 1.5: HILT'S PRIDE
Book Two: MESSENGER of the DARK PROPHET
Book Three: HUNT of the BANDHAM
Book Four: THE WAR of STARDEON
Book Five: MOTHER of the MOONRAT

The Jharro Grove Saga
Book One: TARAH WOODBLADE

Dedication

This book is for my daughter, Paige. The best and brightest up and coming writer I know.
Remember
No matter who you think you are. No matter who you think you should be.
No matter what other people say you are. These two things are true.
You are you, and you are what you do.

Acknowledgements

I have so many people to thank with this one. My wife and editor, Jeannette, who has been extremely patient with me as I wrote throughout our moving process while she packed the house. Also my friends and family who have been so supportive.

Finally I would like to thank my cousin, John. He has been one of my best friends since I was a child and many of the characters and story ideas from the Bowl of Souls series started with games we would play together. The character of Tarah Woodblade came about through a series of conversations John and I had as he was reading my book series. Many of John's ideas and thoughts became part of Tarah's background and personality. As I wrote the book, he helped to proofread it as well. Thank you, buddy.

Author's Note

The story of Tarah Woodblade's creation is a complex one. It started with a game.

While I was writing Mother of the Moonrat, my friend Michael Patty, a lifelong gamer and creator of games, suggested the idea of a Bowl of Souls role playing game. Michael was the designer of my maps for the series and I knew he would be great to work with, so I went forward with the idea.

As we designed the game and built it to a playable stage, I did some play testing with my cousin, John. Now John, being the unique soul he is, decided that, instead of playing as a dwarf blacksmith or a mage or Battle Academy graduate, he wanted to play as one of the most basic character options out there. A woodsman. Basically just a frontier farmer that lives off the land. He became excited with the idea of being a character that was a tracker and guide.

So I came up with a scenario and we started to play. As we began talking about the character, a young woman named Tarah, I became more and more interested. We spent hours talking about Tarah's background and about the dwarf that would become her traveling companion.

As I came closer and closer to the end of Mother of the Moonrat, I knew that beginning the next series was going to be a challenge, especially since I intended for my main characters to take some time off from the adventure while evil started brewing elsewhere. Slowly, as I outlined the series, I realized that there was a large hole in the story. I had a couple ways I could go about tying things together, but none of them quite worked the way I wanted to. Tarah Woodblade's character kept coming up in my mind.

I made my decision. Tarah Woodblade's adventure would start off the next series and lead right into the main thrust of the action. As I wrote this book, I fell in love with the story of Tarah and Djeri. My wife was more hesitant. Would the readers be disappointed with the fact that Justan isn't the main character in this book? I just quit my day job. What if they leave bad reviews and the book sinks? But the more she read the more she was won over and now she says it is is in the top two favorites of all the books I've written. I can only hope that you are won over too.

I know the idea of the Jharro Grove series starting off without Justan and Jhonate may be hard to swallow. Just know that they aren't gone. (and they have a small role to play here too) Justan is back in action in full force with book two. All I can ask is that you trust me. Stick with me. I promise you that if you loved the Moonrat Saga, you will love this book too.

Thank you,

Trevor H. Cooley

Table of Contents

Prologue	11
Chapter One	23
Chapter Two	34
Chapter Three	46
Chapter Four	62
Chapter Five	75
Chapter Six	87
Chapter Seven	102
Chapter Eight	113
Chapter Nine	129
Chapter Ten	143
Chapter Eleven	159
Chapter Twelve	172
Chapter Thirteen	183
Chapter Fourteen	197
Chapter Fifteen	211
Chapter Sixteen	224
Chapter Seventeen	238
Chapter Eighteen	253
Chapter Nineteen	260
Chapter Twenty	269
Chapter Twenty One	283
Chapter Twenty Two	291
Epilogue	301

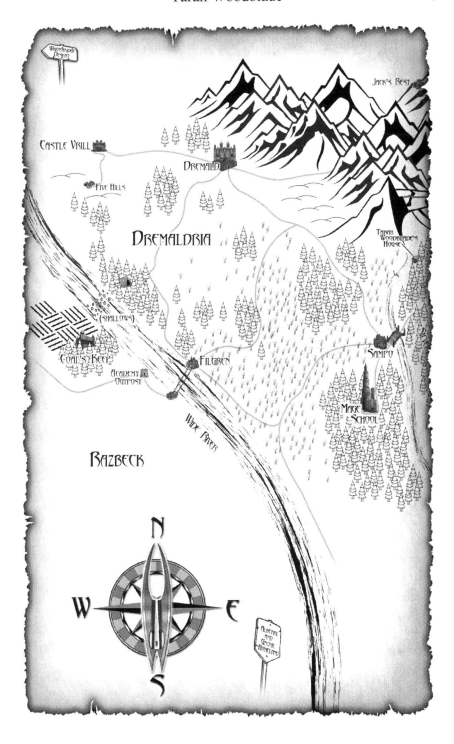

Prologue
227 years ago

"Shh. Yer gonna be alright, Puppy," said Lenui Firegobbler softly as he stood in front of the rogue horse, its bridle in his hands.

It whimpered and he took off his hat, ignoring the rain that soaked through his red hair. He'd learned that Puppy responded better to him when he wasn't wearing the hat. It'd been around the smugglers so long it identified their wide-brimmed hats with rough treatment. The rogue horse calmed and licked his face in response, but it continued to give him the sad doggy eyes. The poor thing was dripping with water and had been whining all morning. Puppy hated being wet.

The team of dwarf smugglers had been standing in the hills outside the Gnome Homeland for hours waiting for their buyer to arrive. The storm had started as a drizzle when they arrived, but now it was torrential. Lenui had dismounted to comfort the rogue and was the only one standing. The other dwarves stayed mounted on their horses, their wide-brimmed hats keeping the rain off their faces.

"You listen to Lenui, boy," Lenui patted its neck and hoped the rain was pouring too loud for the others to hear. "Yer gonna be a lot happier after today. Yer gettin' new owners."

"Dag-blast it, Lenui! I done told you a hunnerd times, its name's just Gold. That's all the durn animal's worth to us!" shouted his uncle, Blayne. He always shouted when he was talking to Lenui, rain or no rain. The dwarf smuggler's black handlebar mustache twisted as he scowled. "That's Cragstalker rule number three. Don't go and get yerself attached to the critters!"

"I ain't attached, dag-nab it! He just looks like a puppy so I been callin' him Puppy!" Lenui barked as he scratched under its chin. It was a lie, of course. Not that he'd admit it, but he'd come to like the dag-gum thing. The two rogue horses they had may have been uglier than sin, but they were also the sweetest critters he'd ever known. The rogues loved to play and loved to be ridden and they'd do just about whatever a dwarf wanted them to do. "'Sides, he likes it. Ain't that why you brought me anyway?"

Normally a dwarf needed to be in his fortieth year at least before he was brought along on an important sale like this one. But when his momma had suggested he go along, the others hadn't resisted. She wanted him to go so he could learn what a smuggler's business deal was like. The others let him come because the rogue horses were calmer when Lenui was around and they knew it.

"Yer a corn-tootin' idjit, Babyface!" yelled his cousin Donjon from atop his chestnut bay. The dwarf had been miserable all day. Not only were his clothes soaked through, he had taken lashes for neglecting to shave his jaw that morning and his rear end was sore. Shaved jaws and handlebar mustaches were the traditional look of their people. The Corntown Smugglers saw those traditions as part of their brand. Nonconformity had consequences and Donjon's punishment had been all the worse because his father was second in command. "It don't look like no puppy!"

"I ain't no babyface, you tender-arse!" Lenui snapped as he fingered his own mustache, pitiful and thin as it was. At twenty-four-years-old he only needed to shave his chin every three days or so and his mustache was just starting to fill in. He couldn't get it to curl up at the ends like the others, but he was sure it would in time. His daddy's mustache was legendary, stretching from ear-to-ear and curling up higher than his eyebrows. "And he does look like a puppy. His head's a puppy head."

Donjon scowled at the rogue horse. "It's a friggin' freak if'n you ask me!"

Lenui disagreed, but he knew what his cousin meant. The rogue was an unnatural looking creature. It had the head and rear quarters of a shaggy dog, but the rest of it was horse, from its neck and forelegs to its back. The end result was that the rogue horse looked awfully awkward, but Lenui had ridden it many times and it rode smooth as silk.

"It's alright, Puppy," he whispered, patting its neck. "Just as soon as yer new master gets here, you won't have to deal with these mean ole dwarfs no more. No sir, you won't."

Lenui didn't know very much about their buyer except that he was a gnome scholar, a fact that had relieved him when he had heard it. The dwarf smugglers usually dealt with the most dark and devious of clients. At least with a gnome scholar, he knew that the rogue horse wasn't likely to be harmed.

Puppy let out another nervous whimper and Lenui wondered if the rogue might be bothered by more than just the rain. He dug his hand through the thick fur on its head, but it didn't seem to be feverish and its sad eyes were clear and focused. He didn't think it was sick, but it kept its tail between its legs and shivered.

"The rain'll stop soon, boy," he promised and as if on cue, the rain slowed to a drizzle. Within a few minutes the clouds opened up, letting the sun shine through. Not long after that, one of the smugglers scouting at the top of the hill called out. The buyer was approaching.

Donjon moved his horse up the hill to get a better vantage point and pulled a peering stone from within his jacket pocket. Peering stones were one of the Corntown Smugglers little secrets; flat river stones that had been magically charged and runed with air. A hole was carved in the center and when a dwarf peered through it, they could see a great distance away.

"Yeah, they're comin' all right," Donjon said. "Buyer's ridin' a camel and there's three stewards on horseback with him. Also, four guards joggin' on foot and . . ." Donjon's jaw dropped. "Aw, hell. They brought a gnome warrior with 'em."

Lenui's eyebrows rose. He had never encountered one of those before. Gnome warriors were the most dangerous fighters in the known lands. They were selected and tested at a young age and spent their entire lives focused on nothing but training for battle. Since they were longer lived than dwarves, they became very skilled indeed.

"Lemme see that," Blayne snapped, bringing his horse up next to Donjon's. The dwarf handed the peering stone over and Blayne looked through it. "Gall-ram it, yer right. Ain't run into one of them in a while. Still, nothin' we should worry about. Just means that our particular buyer is highly regarded 'round these parts."

"But what if the gnome decides it'd be better just to kill us than pay us?" Lenui asked, warily.

Blayne snorted and shook his head. "Son, there ain't no gnome scholar, don't matter how scatterbrained, that's gonna make an enemy of Corntown. Their blasted stewards wouldn't let 'em. 'Cides, if they attack, we'll just freeze 'em," he said, pulling his overcoat back to show everyone the handle of the paralyzing rod protruding from his inner pocket.

The other dwarves nodded. Not many buyers knew the dwarf smugglers methods of capture or understood how to counteract them. Even a gnome warrior would be helpless before them if hit by the magic of that rod.

"Now, listen up, boys," Blayne said while the approaching party was still out of earshot. "Y'all keep yer mouths shut while the buyers are here. Don't talk 'less yer spoken to. 'Specially you, Lenui. I don't care what yer momma says. However Maggie treats you, yer still a dag-blasted baby far as I'm concerned. Keep your gall-durn face closed 'round the buyers, hear me?"

"You s-. . . I got you, uncle." Lenui said, barely stifling a curse. This wasn't the time to talk back to Blayne. His momma had taught him the rules. Still, he couldn't keep a frown off his face. It riled him that his uncle gave him orders about how to talk to clients when he himself was so lousy at it. The other dwarves treated him like a child, but dag-nab it, he was old enough and smarter than most of them. If he'd been a human, his parents would have expected him to move out and have a family of his own by now.

Puppy whimpered again and Lenui rubbed its head. "It's okay, boy. They're here. Soon you won't have to hang 'round us no more." The rogue horse licked his face.

The approaching party neared and as they crested the hill in front of them, Lenui was able to see them for himself. The gnome warrior led the procession and he didn't look anything like Lenui had expected. Gnomes were tall, lanky folk with long droopy ears and noses, but he had been expecting the warrior to be more bulky than the other gnomes he had seen.

The warrior was nearly seven-foot-tall and wiry and walked in a near crouch with one hand on the hilt of a long and slender sword that hung at his waist. His head was shaven and he wore no armor, just a loose fitting pair of pants and a voluminous shirt. Perhaps strangest of all were the wide-lensed spectacles that he wore. They did not sit on the gnome's ears like most spectacles, but were attached to a wide leather band that was tied around his head, likely so they wouldn't fall off.

The guards that ran alongside the party looked like average human soldiers to Lenui. All four wore chainmail and carried shields with an unfamiliar crest on them. The gnome's human stewards were on horseback and wore gray robes and colored sashes. Two of the stewards wore green sashes while the other one, a woman, wore a black sash. Lenui didn't know much about the culture of the Gnome Homeland, but Blayne had told him to treat the stewards with great respect. They were the human caretakers of the gnome scholars and were highly regarded in the gnome community.

The buyer himself was perched on the back of a camel, gazing into a book that he held up close to his nose. The gnome scholar had a shock of white hair that sprouted from his head and wore silken robes; light blue with purple embroidery. Lenui didn't like camels. The ungainly things were temperamental and uncomfortable to ride. He couldn't imagine trying to read while riding one, but the gnome seemed unbothered by the sway of the camel as it walked. He didn't bother to look at the dwarves as their party arrived, chuckling to himself as he read.

"The girl with the black sash will be the one to speak to us," said Donjon with a smirk. "She'll be the one in charge of the gnome's money. The green sash boys are just here to make sure the gnome don't forget to eat or trip over his own dag-gum feet." He snorted. "Probably wipe his arse for him too."

"Shut yer yap," Blayne growled, glaring at Donjon. "Gnomes' got good hearin'. If you ruin this deal, I'll drag you all the way back to Corntown behind my dag-blamed horse!"

Donjon's eyes went wide and he nodded. "Sorry, daddy."

Lenui rolled his eyes. It wasn't fair that Donjon was treated as a full member of the group and he wasn't. Donjon was four times his age, but the dwarf was still dumber than a bag of road apples. Of course, though Lenui wouldn't say it aloud, Blayne was nearly just as bad. Lenui had never seen Blayne leave a sale with

the buyer in a good mood. The dwarf hadn't been put in charge of
the sale because of his diplomacy. He was only there because he
was Pa Cragstalker's oldest son and second in command of the
Corntown Smugglers. Lenui's mother was much better at sweet
talking clients but Pa liked to send his boy, thinking it would be
more impressive to the clients.

Donjon had been right about the steward, though. The
human with the black sash was the one who dismounted first and
approached them. The dwarves dismounted and Blayne walked
forward to meet her, removing his hat as was proper for business
deals. The gnome warrior kept pace with the steward, his eyes
darting around as he watched each of the dwarves looking for the
slightest sign of trickery.

As he did so, one of the green-sashed stewards sidled his
mount up to the gnome scholar and nudged him. The scholar
blinked, looking up from his book in irritation. Then his gaze fell
on the rogue horse and he gave the steward a nod. He handed the
book to the human and climbed down from the camel.

"Good day," said the black-sashed steward.

"Yer late," grumbled Blayne. Likely he was hoping to use
the buyer's tardiness as a means to drive up the price.

"Ah, yes. Many apologies, gentlemen," she replied, giving
him a practiced smile. "We would have left the city sooner, but
High Scholar Abernathy does not like to be out in the rain."

"Don't you think he's livin' in the wrong dag-gum place
then?" asked Blayne with a guffaw. The steward frowned and
Lenui shook his head at his uncle's foolishness. Blayne's face went
red and he cleared his throat. "What I'm sayin' is, don't y'all get
flooded 'least twice a year out here?"

"That is true," said Scholar Abernathy before his steward
could reply. "For now."

The gnome approached Puppy, his nose wrinkling at the
rogue's musky wet dog smell. He lifted its chin and looked into its
sad eyes. The rogue wagged its tail hesitantly and licked the
gnome's wrist. He grimaced and let go of the rogue's head, then
wiped his wrist off on its horse-like flank. "Hmm . . . it does seem
authentic. I must admit I was suspicious when I heard you still had
a rogue horse in captivity."

"We done got two, yer scholarshipness," said Blayne and

though he held his hat in his hands, his demeanor was firm. "We ain't told no one 'bout 'em fer a long while 'cause Pa wanted to hold onto 'em fer himself."

"No one was willing to pay the sum you wanted, you mean?" Scholar Abernathy asked walking along the side of the rogue, examining its flank.

Blayne wasn't about to admit that. He blinked and said, "Naw, it ain't 'bout the money. Pa's fond of 'em and he didn't want to sell 'em to no wizard that'd just accidentally melt 'em to goop. When he heard you was a scholar, why he said, 'that Abernathy'd be just the right sort for our . . . Puppy'.'"

Lenui gave his uncle a scowl.

Abernathy snorted, but continued to examine the animal, walking around to the other side. He kept a slight distance to avoid touching it again, a look of distaste on his face.

"The High Scholar is not fond of dogs, dwarf," said the steward with the black sash. "If you had two rogue horses, why did you not bring them both and let him choose the one he wanted?"

"My dislike for canines will not matter in this case," the gnome said, waving his hand absently. "However, I must wonder why this one was chosen. It is shivering. Is it ill?"

"Would you like us to have it examined first, High Scholar?" the steward in the black sash asked.

Blayne sputtered in offense. "'Course it ain't sick. What're you tryin' to imply? We ain't gonna bring no sick goods to our-!"

"Puppy's fine," Lenui interrupted, hoping to keep his uncle from screwing things up too badly. "Pa Cragstalker just chose him 'cause he's the calmer of the two rogues. The other'n gets excited too easy."

Blayne shot him a glare that promised him a whupping later and Lenui winced. His arse would be just as sore as Donjon's after they got back to camp. He vowed he wouldn't show it like Donjon did though. He might be young, but he wasn't like these Cragstalkers. He was a Firegobbler and tough as iron. Just like his daddy.

"Bringing the calmer animal was likely for the best, considering its purpose," said the gnome. "But why does it shiver?"

"The durn thing don't like bein' wet," Blayne explained. "It hates the water so much it don't even like drinkin' from the pond back home." His eyes widened as he realized the gnome might consider that a bad thing. "But that don't matter. It's a rogue. It'll do whatever you tell it to, whether it likes it or not. You could tell it to swim 'cross the Wide River'n it'd do it."

The gnome didn't glance at the dwarf, but he smiled to himself. "Even better." He held out his thin arm and one of the green-sashed stewards rushed forward with a towel and wiped the gnome's hand clean. "I think I am ready. Pay the dwarf."

The black-sashed steward hesitated. "Are you sure, High Scholar? Do you want to pay full price for this animal?"

"Do it," Abernathy said.

"Yes, High Scholar," she said and gestured. Two of the guards rushed over and retrieved a wooden chest from the back of the steward's horse and brought it over. They set the chest down in front of Blayne and she handed him the key. "You will find your payment in full within the chest."

The dwarf opened the chest and Lenui caught a glimpse of gold before his uncle shut it. Blayne smiled and gestured to Donjon, who carried the chest back to their horses. He looked back to the steward. "You realize we'll be countin' this when we get back to camp?"

"I counted it all myself, sir," said the steward with a slight frown.

"Alright, then," Blayne said. "A few things you'shd know bout this rogue. It's a meat eater so it don't much like grains. It's smart as a reg'lar horse, but not much smarter. Also like all rogues, if you let some wizard pry too much into the magic holdin' it together, it's liable to die on you."

The way the rogue horses had been created was a great mystery and the reason they were so rare was that most of them had died in the hands of wizards. Once again Lenui was glad Puppy was going to a scholar. Even if the gnome was curious about how it was made, he wouldn't be likely to kill it with magic. Especially after Blayne's speech.

The gnome didn't even look at Blayne. He simply shrugged and said. "I won't need it for that long, I'm afraid. Anne, would you bring me the implements please? The animal's odor is much too strong to bring it all the way back to the stables."

"Yes, High Scholar," said the steward with the black sash. She ran to the camel and unstrapped a long cloth-wrapped bundle from its side.

When she returned, the gnome withdrew a golden chalice from the bundle and handed it to her. Then he unwrapped the rest of the cloth, revealing a peculiar scepter. It was three-feet-long and made of polished copper. The length of the scepter was covered in intricate runes and its end was shaped into the likeness of a gnome's head. The look on its face was joyous and its mouth was open as if it were singing.

"Hold the animal still," Abernathy commanded.

The four guards surrounded the rogue horse, each one grasping a leg. Puppy didn't like this treatment. He struggled and whimpered. The men had difficulty holding on. The gnome approached the rogue and wrapped the arm holding the scepter around its neck. Then he reached into his robes with his other hand and pulled out a wicked looking knife.

Lenui's eyes widened. "Hey, what're you gonna-?"

In one smooth motion, the gnome scholar drew the blade across Puppy's throat. The rogue horse staggered as blood spewed from the wound. While one of the stewards caught some of the blood in the chalice, the scholar held the scepter underneath its neck, letting the blood soak into the runed length of it.

"Puppy!" Lenui ran towards the rogue horse, but the gnome warrior darted in front of him. Lenui froze as he felt the cold of the gnome warrior's blade against the skin of his throat. It gave him a warning glare. Blayne and Donjon grabbed Lenui by the arms and yanked him back.

"What're you doing, you blasted idjit!" Blayne snapped in his ear. They dragged him over to his horse. Blayne reared back and punched him in the mouth. Lenui fell backwards, his vision blurring. "Get up and get on your garl-friggin' horse!"

Lenui rolled to his knees and looked up in time to see the black-sashed steward hand the blood-filled chalice to Scholar Abernathy. The gnome drank deeply, then grimaced and handed it back to the steward. One of the other stewards rushed over to hand him a towel. The other held out a waterskin. The gnome rinsed out his mouth and spat, then began to clean the blood off of his face and hands.

Puppy fell to his knees and shuddered, then the guards let go and he rolled onto his side. By the time the gnome handed the towel back to his stewards, the rogue horse had stopped breathing.

Blayne kicked Lenui in the side. "I said, 'on your horse'!"

Lenui stood and spit out the blood that filled his mouth, noticing that one of his bottom front teeth came out with it. Numbly he realized that Blayne must have landed a knuckle right on it. Only twenty-four-years-old and he'd already lost a tooth. Maggie wouldn't be happy about that. He climbed the set of stirrups and swung his leg over the saddle.

"I told you not to get attached to them critters!" his uncle said, then walked over to talk to the steward.

Lenui swallowed and ignored the snickers of the other smugglers as he looked at Puppy's unmoving form. He clenched his fists. This was wrong. This was all wrong. He knew what his mother would have said. Maggie would have called this business. What the scholar did with his property was none of his concern. But his daddy would've seen things different. He would have told Lenui that your animals needed to be treated with kindness and respect. He wouldn't have sold any animal to someone that would mistreat it. He wouldn't have allowed what just happened either. But there was nothing Lenui could do about it now. Puppy was dead. If he tried to go after the scholar now, the gnome warrior would kill him and the other dwarves wouldn't lift a finger to help.

Scholar Abernathy lifted the scepter and Lenui noticed that it looked completely clean of blood. The gnome nodded and handed the scepter to a steward. "Remove its ears and tail and bring them back with us," Abernathy instructed, then wiped his face and hands with the towel. "The rest can be left to rot."

The scholar retrieved his book from the steward and hummed to himself as he walked back to the camel. He opened the book, already reading as he climbed into its awkward saddle. If Lenui had a bow he would have shot him, consequences be damned.

"Uh, you sure you want to just leave the rogue there?" Blayne asked the black-sashed steward, one eyebrow raised. "Wizards'd pay good money fer a whole rogue horse carcass."

"Would you like to buy it back from us?" asked the black-sashed steward.

Blayne frowned and rubbed his chin as he thought about it. "Well, uh . . ."

One of the other stewards whispered something in her ear and she shrugged. "It seems that the High Scholar may be interested in your second rogue horse. Would you tell Pa Cragstalker we will be contacting him soon in regards to the beast?"

Blayne eyed Puppy's corpse. "Well, I dunno. Pa's got other buyers interested-."

She reached into her robes and pulled out a bulging pouch. "If Pa promises to hold it for the next six months in case High Scholar Abernathy wants it we will include a fifty gold bonus."

"Fifty gold, huh?" Blayne mused.

"And you can keep this one's corpse to do with it what you will," she added with a roll of her eyes.

"You got it," Blayne said with a smile and took the pouch from her hands.

The buyers soon left. Lenui stared hollowly as he watched the others make a litter to drag Puppy's remains on. He was glad they didn't tell him to help. He would have punched all of them.

Blayne saw the look on his face and sidled his horse next to him. "Yer lucky Maggie's my sister or I'd kill you fer the way you acted back there."

"I ain't surprised," Lenui said. "Hell, maybe you should just kill me now and deal with momma later."

When they got back to the camp, Blayne had Lenui stripped and bound to a tree and lashed him bloody. Lenui refused to cry out or apologize and was quiet for most of the three-week trip back to Corntown. Blayne thought him sufficiently cowed, but Lenui was spending the majority of his time trying to figure out what he was going to do when they got home. He finally made his decision the day before they arrived.

Lenui put on a brave face when they got back. He laughed about the incident with Pa Cragstalker and his mother. He waited a few days before he snuck over to the rogue horse's pen in the middle of the night.

"Hey, Monkeyface!" Lenui whispered.

"Wee!" shouted a rough voice from the darkness. Monkeyface was smarter than Puppy. It couldn't pronounce many words, but it did remember the last part of his name.

A few moments later, the rogue horse approached the side of the pen where Lenui stood. It had the front end of an enormous gorilla, the mid section of a horse, and the rear end of a mountain cat. Its huge face stretched unto a toothy smile. "Wee!"

Lenui hopped over the fence and scratched behind its horse-like ears.

"Come on, boy," he said. "I think it's about dag-gum time we set you free."

Chapter One

"You got money on ya?" asked one of the scruffy men, an evil gleam in his eye.

Tarah fought down her nerves and breathed in the situation using all the training her papa and grampa had given her. She sensed three men altogether, but the two standing in front of her were the immediate threat. They were unshaven and filthy and wore cast-off armor that had been badly damaged and messily repaired. She couldn't see the third man, but she could hear him shifting his feet behind the bushes.

"Money? Why, are you beggars?" Tarah asked, arching one eyebrow coolly. This wasn't good. These men were likely leftovers from the war. They wore swords, but didn't move like trained soldiers so that meant they were probably Ewzad Vriil's men.

"Beggars?" said the man, frowning. He wore a leather half-helm and his eyes were as yellow as his teeth.

"You asked for money," she reminded. Tarah forced her body to remain relaxed. She planted her quarterstaff in the ground casually as if it were no more than a walking stick, but she knew that it was imposing. The wood was red as blood and the runes carved into it suggested unknown magic. "Strange. I wasn't expecting any beggars this far from Sampo. I didn't bother to bring any coppers to throw to you."

The man's sneer turned into a snarl and he drew his sword. The weapon was a longsword and of a much higher quality than she had noticed before. The pommel was worn and dirty but the blade was polished and there were a series of runes impressed along its length. It could have magic. "Does a beggar carry a sword like this?"

Tarah's hand tightened slightly on her staff, but otherwise

she didn't allow any of her anxiety to show. She just wanted to get to Sampo. Why couldn't they have been bears? She could handle three bears. Wild beasts were predictable. It was men she had difficulty dealing with.

"So not beggars." She shrugged and rubbed her chin, giving them a look that suggested mild curiosity. All the while she kept her ears open for sounds of an arrow being drawn from the bushes. "Maybe you're tax collectors then? Funny, you don't smell like tax collectors."

"Yeah, that's right," said the second man. He had a thinning mop of greasy hair that had probably been blond once. A cruel scar ran across his forehead. He laughed, but Tarah noted that his laugh was forced. He wasn't as confident as the first man. "We're tax men. Here to collect our fees."

"You accept broken bones as payment?" she asked, giving him a bored look. Tarah twirled her quarterstaff with her right hand and planted it in the ground again. Inwardly she calculated how long it would take her to get to the man in the bushes. She hadn't heard the creak of a bow being pulled back, but he could be readying a throwing weapon.

"You? Break our bones?" said the man with the fancy sword. He wasn't as impressed by her act. "You're big for a girl maybe, but no match for us." He looked her up and down. "Least you sound like a girl. Wouldn't know it by looking at you."

Tarah's jaw clenched. She knew what she looked like well enough. She was indeed tall for a woman, and her frame was more muscular than feminine, especially in her armor. At least he hadn't made fun of her face yet.

"Ugly though," the man continued with a snort. He looked at the thin-haired man. "What do you think, Hal? This a girl?"

Tarah's hand tightened on her staff further, her arm muscles stiffening. She didn't like that his words bothered her. She should have been used to the ridicule by now. She had always been plain, even as a child, and that was before the fight that bent her nose. Still, being called ugly always riled her up. She refused to let her feelings show and forced a yawn instead.

The first man's flippant attitude had put his friend at ease. Hal smiled. "Hard to tell what she is under that leather armor of hers, Eddy. It looks nasty. What's it made of? Dirty dog hides?"

"Moonrats," Tarah replied and both men's eyes widened as they looked at it closer. These men were a bit thick. Most recognized it right away. The dead gray color of the fur was one giveaway. Not to mention the moonrat tails that hung at her waistline, the shriveled hands on the ends of the tails were still intact. "They ain't good eating so I had to do something with 'em."

The men took a step back. Moonrats were feared, especially as their numbers had grown during the war. But the shock on Eddy's face didn't last long. His sneer returned. "I know who you are. You're Tarah Woodblade aren't you? That *hero*?"

The sarcasm in the man's voice shook her. She knew just how little of a hero she was. She had come back to face her actions and had been expecting the ridicule, but to hear it from this bandit . . . She made herself give her grampa's teachings one last chance.

"That's right," she said confidently.

"Too bad. See, we got a special hero tax," Eddy said. "Give us your money and weapons and we'll let you leave . . . unmolested."

"Unmolested?" Tarah sighed, shaking her head. "If you know who I am and you're determined to be bandits, I guess I've got no choice."

She shrugged the small pack she carried off of her shoulders. She set it onto the ground next to her, then removed her bow and quiver and laid them on top of it. Eddy grinned, thinking he had cowed her, but Tarah gripped her red staff in both hands and assumed an attack posture.

She gave him a menacing grin of her own. "I'm glad you decided not to be beggars. See, Tarah Woodblade doesn't kill beggars. But I have been thinking of making my next set of armor out of bandit skin."

Hal took two more steps back, his face white, but Eddy's smile broadened. "You know, by what I seen, moonrat skin is pretty thin. I bet it makes a terrible armor."

The man gave a slight nod and there was a rustle in the bushes. Before Tarah could turn, she felt a thump in her back. It had been a throwing knife after all. She heard the blade fall to the leafy ground. Eddy had been right about the thickness of moonrat skin. That was why her grampa had reinforced the leather with treated fiber mesh. Luckily the blade hadn't hit a seam.

Tarah turned and ran for the bushes. The hidden man stood up in surprise and drew his sword. Tarah leapt and swung her staff down at his head. The man was able to bring his sword up in time to block, but the strength of her swing, assisted by her staff's weighted core, slammed the man's sword blade into his forehead and he crumpled to the ground.

Tarah didn't have time to wonder if he was dead. She heard a roar behind her and twisted around to find Eddy bearing down on her, his polished longsword swinging. She swung one end of her staff up under the blade, knocking it high. Its keen edge missed her head by inches and she brought the other end of her staff down low, catching the side of Eddy's right knee.

There was a faint popping sound and the knee bent in a way it shouldn't have, but the man didn't even wince. He spun around on his left leg, swinging his sword in a heavy two-handed slash. She blocked the attack, but the strength of the blow quivered through the wood.

Tarah's eyes widened as she saw his face. Eddy's mouth was twisted in a snarl, his eyes burning with anger. In her experience, most bandits gave up after a blow to the knee, but this man fought like a berserker. She had seen that same look in the eyes of her papa when he fought. Could this man have been one of them?

The thought slowed her reaction time and she didn't make a counterstrike. He spun again, bringing his sword around at her other side, but as he swung, he shifted his weight to his right knee. His leg gave way and he stumbled to the side, crying out in pain. Tarah took a step back, letting the blade cleave the air where she had been standing. He fell to his side.

No, she told herself, this man wasn't like her papa. He fought with rage, but not with skill. Her eyes darted towards his companion, but Hal wasn't attacking. He was backing away, fear in his eyes. She gave him her best glower and he turned and ran. She took a deep breath and looked back to Eddy.

"Do you consider your knee payment enough?" she asked. "Or do I need to keep breaking you?"

"I'll kill you!" he shouted and tried to climb back to his feet.

"I wouldn't do that," she warned. "You got some torn

ligaments. You try to fight on that knee and you could do permanent damage."

He roared and stabbed his sword into the ground to help him push to his feet. He stood, heavily favoring his right leg, and pulled the sword back out of the ground. She shook her head. She was no longer afraid, but she was still unsure how to deal with him. She thought on it as he limped towards her.

Her papa wouldn't show mercy to a bandit. He'd say it's best to kill the man. That way he could never be a threat to her or anyone else. Grampa Rolf would say leaving dead bodies behind was to be avoided. It would be better to knock him unconscious and take his sword; teach him a lesson.

Eddy reared back and as he swung his sword at her again she made her decision.

She swung one end of her staff up, knocking his attack to the side, and brought the other end around, connecting with the side of his knee again. This time the joint gave way completely. He screamed but refused to fall, she twirled her staff and connected with a blow to the back to his head that silenced him and dropped him to the ground.

She stood over his unconscious form and frowned. Why had she seen her papa in this man? They were nothing alike.

Tarah crouched beside him and removed his leather half-helm. She felt the wound behind his head and nodded. The helm had done its job as she had hoped and his skull was intact. She hadn't killed him like her papa would have done, but with that knee, the man wouldn't be accosting people in the woods again.

She pulled the sword belt and sheath from Eddy's waist and glanced at the sword still clutched in his hand. Now that she looked at it, she could tell that the sheath didn't match the blade. Likely the blade had been stolen and Eddy had just found a sheath it fit in.

Tarah pried the hilt from his fingers and her breath caught as a brief vision passed through her mind. There was an intense battle. Men were falling everywhere, some of them on fire, some even melting. Eddy was terrified. He saw the sword's shining blade laying on the bloodied earth and picked it up as he ran . . .

Tarah blinked the thoughts away and shivered. She didn't usually see visions like that unless she was tracking. She looked

over the blade closely, impressed by its workmanship. Too bad it
was of no real use for her. Her papa had taught her a bit of
bladework, but she wasn't a swordsman. She slid the runed blade
back into the man's ugly sheath and belted it around her waist. She
would take it back to town with her and see if there was a reward.
Surely a runed blade like this was worth something to someone.
Maybe people were looking for it.

She took a deep breath and headed back to the bushes
where she had struck the man who threw the knife. She winced as
she peered over his unmoving body. The blade of his sword was
wedged in his skull. She reached down and felt his neck but there
was no pulse.

Tarah shivered. This wasn't the first man she'd killed, but
she hadn't killed many. Papa had told her that there would be times
when killing was necessary. Grampa had taught her that if she was
smart, she shouldn't have to.

"Grampa, your way didn't work this time!" she grumbled
aloud. She knew what he would have said. 'Come on, Tarah, you
know there are no guarantees. Even the best salesman in the known
lands can't dissuade a man determined to die'. They'd had that
conversation the first time she'd been forced to kill a man.

She looked down at the corpse and shook her head. She
refused to feel guilty. It wasn't her fault the man didn't know how
to block a staff blow. Still, she couldn't avoid a bit of sadness as
she checked his pockets for coins. Grampa had taught her not to
waste an opportunity to make money.

The man didn't have much, just a few silver pieces. His
sword was rusty and plain, but the brace of throwing daggers he
wore across his chest was in good condition. There were slots for
five knives and the four remaining blades were oiled and had a
decent balance. She took the brace and walked back to retrieve the
knife that he had thrown at her earlier.

She lifted her pack from the ground where she had left it
and pulled out a notebook. She tore a scrap of paper from the back
page and scribbled a note on it, then walked back to Eddy's
unconscious form and tucked it into his pocket. She didn't know if
the man could read, but she felt it was sound advice. The note
simply said: *Become a farmer. Sincerely, Tarah Woodblade.*

There was no reason to stay any longer. The third man had

run, but for all she knew, he could have gone for help. Tarah collected her things and headed on through the trees. She followed Hal's tracks for a few minutes just to be sure. He was headed north and east, out of the woods and into the plains. She didn't think it likely that a large group of bandits would be confident enough to camp this close to Sampo and the Mage School, but if there was such a group, it was probably best to find out so she could warn people.

She crouched and gripped her red staff tightly as she touched a few of the tracks. As she did so, a series of images flashed through her mind. They weren't strong visions like the one she had seen when touching the sword, but more like brief emotional glimpses. Hal was afraid of her. He was determined to leave the area. He didn't expect the other two men to survive. His intention was to keep running.

She sat back on her haunches. It didn't seem like he was going for help. She could keep tracking him and learn more as she went, but in reality, she knew he wasn't a threat. Following him further was appealing only because it would help her delay her return.

Tarah turned and looked up through a clearing in the trees. In the far distance, she could barely make out the tip of the Rune Tower disappearing into the clouds. She knew exactly where she was. A few hours of hard walking and she would arrive in Sampo. She felt trepidation rise within her, but she grit her teeth and quelled it. She'd hidden away long enough. It was time to face her actions and pick up the pieces.

She walked through the fall leaves to the northeast until the trees gave way to vast grassy plains. The grasses were waist high and yellow and Tarah kept her practiced senses open for signs of hidden creatures. A short time later, she avoided a wasp mound that was hidden in the tall grass. This time of year they were dormant, but many people had learned the hard way that they could still be riled if you put a foot through their nest.

A grin played across her lips. She had tracked and guided people through these plains many times and the dangers were as familiar to her as the trails around her woodland home. After so long being away, she found them comforting.

She climbed a large grassy hill, knowing that she would be

able to see the city when she reached the top, but when she crested it her smile faded. The familiar skyline of Sampo sat in the distance but, between the hill where she stood and the city, the landscape had changed.

The plains on this side of Sampo should have continued all the way to the city's edge, interrupted only by the occasional road and a few small farmsteads. Now the plains were gone; burned away or churned underfoot. This was where Ewzad Vriil's army had camped during the war.

Tarah swallowed as the anxiety she had been feeling for the last several months crept back into her chest. She tried to remind herself that there was nothing she could have done to change things. The good people had won without her help, but there was one fact she couldn't avoid. Dremaldria had been forever changed by the war and while everyone else had fought, she had run away.

She hiked down the hill and made her way across a stretch of blackened earth to the Grandriver Road. This was the main route from Sampo to the great city of Gladstone at Dremaldria's southern border and to her relief, there were still signs of constant use. She reached down to feel the tracks, but it was impossible to make sense of the jumble of emotions that filled her mind. Too many people traveled this road.

Tarah continued towards the city, glad to see that the last mile or so of the road had been leveled and the ruts filled in. This told her that the people of Sampo were getting back to life as normal. The final stretch was well-trafficked and had even been graveled.

As she neared the outskirts, she passed a large merchant caravan headed south. A dozen guards rode with it, Battle Academy soldiers by the look of them. That was a good sign. Perhaps the rumors of the Battle Academy's destruction during the war had been false after all. If so, the region wasn't as bad off as she had feared.

Sampo was the third largest city in Dremaldria, its streets sprawling over several miles. It was a major trade hub for the kingdom, sitting on the junction of the roads to Dremald, the Battle Academy, the Mage School, Malaroo, and Razbeck. As a result, the city was populated by a variety of races and cultures. This was immediately evident in the hodgepodge of buildings that lined its broad streets.

Tarah's anxiety deepened as she approached. She had been in Sampo hundreds of times, but she had never been comfortable in the city. There were far too many people. She preferred the peace of the countryside. The city was blanketed with the dull roar of human activity.

The scars the war left on the city were evident the moment she walked in. Some of the buildings were fire blackened and many of the windows were boarded up. But the city was fast recovering. Building crews were hard at work repairing the damage and their hammerings and chiselings were drowned out by the calls of the merchants and hawkers that lined the road.

With this many people, she should have been able to pass through with some sort of anonymity, but her armor and red staff marked her too well. She saw stares from many in the crowd and a few even pointed. Tarah swallowed. Evidently news of her cowardice had spread.

She felt like cringing and running away, but she shoved those feelings down and called upon the litany her grampa had taught her. She was Tarah Woodblade. Tarah Woodblade didn't cringe. She kept her back straight, shoulders up, her face calm and collected, and walked with purposeful strides, staff in hand, keeping her eyes forward and ignoring the passers by.

Her destination was on the northernmost side of the city and it would have been much faster to take side routes, but she stuck to the main streets. To take the quieter path could be seen as hiding from her shame and that would be counterproductive. Grampa Rolf would have told her to start rebuilding her reputation right away. Let the word spread that she had returned. The people may have heard Tarah Woodblade was a coward, but those that saw her now would have a hard time believing it. Or so she hoped.

Despite her outward show of confidence, her guilt weighed on her and all the looks she was getting made things worse. By the time her destination came into view the stress of it all had given her a throbbing headache. Lines of pain crept from the base of her neck up across the back of her head.

The Tracker's Friend was a two story tavern and inn. To Tarah's relief it looked to have survived the war with little damage. This was the place she stayed in Sampo when she had to remain in the city for awhile. It was also the official guild hall for the Sampo Guidesman Guild.

Tarah stepped up to the door, smelling the familiar scent of ale and wine that emanated from within. She reached for the door handle and saw that her hand was shaking. She tightened her hand on the handle and took a deep breath to steady herself.

The other guild members would be waiting inside. It would be up to them if she were to be kicked out. She was the best tracker among them. The problem was that few of them had wanted to let her join in the first place.

The Sampo Guidesman Guild was the premier tracker and guide guild in the region. Eastern Dremaldria was a dangerous place. The academy patrols kept the goblinoid population down, but even the main roads weren't safe to travel alone. For people who couldn't afford to pay for academy guards to escort them through hazardous areas, the guild was the next best thing. Most of Tarah's jobs had come from the guild. If they dropped her, the task of rebuilding her reputation would be close to impossible.

Tarah pushed the door open and stepped inside. The common room of The Tracker's Friend was rugged, but clean. The proprietor, Sly Milt, was a guild member himself, though retired. He kept the central area and bar well lit so as to be inviting to potential clients and unlike most taverns in Sampo, the place was free of tobacco smoke. Milt never liked the stuff.

Usually the place was full of patrons and guildsmen, but it seemed strangely quiet. Most of the tables were empty and Milt wasn't at the counter. Instead there was a buxom woman in a clean white apron cleaning out tankards. Tarah frowned. Milt had never hired a tavern wench before. He felt they were a distraction.

Tarah looked around the room, gauging to see if she had any supporters present. No one looked up at her entrance, but the few men she recognized were just townsfolk. None of them were guild members. Had the war decimated the ranks of the guild?

"Why it's Tarah Woodblade," said a surprised voice to her left.

Tarah swore under her breath at having overlooked the man. It was Bander the Nose. He was one of her biggest detractors and, in Tarah's opinion, a real jerk.

Bander wore a wide grin under his bulbous nose as he

stood from his table by the door. "Holy hell, girl. We weren't sure you were alive."

"Yet here I am," she replied, her expression giving away nothing.

"Well come on over to the bar. I'll buy you a drink!" he replied loudly and everyone in the common room looked her way.

Tarah had to force her jaw not to drop. Bander never bought drinks. This was bad. He was smiling too hard. He was setting her up.

Bander turned and raised his tankard to the room. "Hey, everybody! It's Tarah the Hero! She's returned!" There was a loud shout of approval and men all around the room raised their tankards and called her name.

Chapter Two

"The hero?" Tarah mumbled in shock as she glanced at the cheering men in disbelief. What was this about? Tarah was unable to keep the surprise off her face as Bander led her to the bar.

The tavern wench gave her a wide grin and handed her an ale-filled tankard. "Wow, Tarah Woodblade. So good to meet you."

Tarah simply frowned at her and looked back to Bander. "What's this about? Where is everyone? Where's Milt?"

"The war hit the guild hard, Tarah," Bander said, the smile sliding from his face. "Tolbo and Zeem are dead. They were killed by Vriil's men while trying to get folks out of the city. Gerrat the Owl and Jared are still missing. We think they're dead. Heck, we thought you were dead until just now. Everyone else is out on jobs including Milt. He had to come out of retirement until we can get more members in. He hired Sara here in the meantime."

Tarah's frown deepened and she looked down at the frothy ale in her tankard. So that was it? Their ranks were decimated so they were willing to overlook her cowardice? She heard her grampa's voice excitedly telling her that this was an opportunity. Yet she felt her guilt swell. These men hadn't exactly been her friends, but what if she had stayed and fought instead of running away? Could she have somehow done something to save them?

"But at least you're back," Bander said, a reassuring smile on his face. He slapped her back. "Why, with Tarah Woodblade as a member, we'll be just fine."

Tarah knew she should be relieved, yet her unease grew. This was too good to be true. This had to be a set up. Bander was acting too nice. Bander was never nice.

She slammed her tankard on the bar and grabbed the front

of his shirt, jerking him close. "What are you up to? Patting my back? Talking nice to me? Usually all I get from you is, 'Hey, Ugly'."

Bander's face reddened and he looked away. "I-um. I'm sorry about that. You didn't deserve it and . . . that was before."

"Before what?" she said with a glower.

"Before I learned about you," he said, then lowered his voice and gave her an apologetic glance. "Listen, I admit that I used to think you were just a braggart. Then, once I saw you in action, I was a bit jealous that you were a better tracker than me."

Tarah's eyebrows rose and she let go of him. Bander the Nose admitting she was better than him? He had been the guild's best tracker before she'd come along.

He straightened his shirt and cleared his throat. "But hey, that was before I heard what you did during the war."

"And what did you hear?" she asked. Surely this was where his ridicule would begin.

"Well," he said. "The rumors started spreading around right after the war ended, and at first I didn't believe it, but I just got back from a trip guiding some of the Pinewood refugees home and the stories they told . . ."

Tarah steeled herself for the punchline, expecting him to bust out with a laugh and call her a coward to her face.

"I gotta say, that was some amazing stuff you pulled," he said with an amazed shake of his head. "Guiding fifty villagers to safety? In the dark? In the middle of a full-on invasion by the moonrat witch? I never could've done it."

"Fifty?" Where had he gotten that number? That night was a blur to her, but surely there hadn't been that many.

"Was it more than that?" The same awed smile she had seen on Bander's face when she first entered the inn reappeared. "All I can say is wow. You really are a hero."

Tarah cocked her head at him in surprise. The man actually sounded genuine. She didn't know how to respond at first, but then Grampa Rolf's training took affect.

Tarah cleared her throat. "Fifty does seem like a small number. But then again, that was a crazy night. I would've saved more if I hadn't been so busy fighting monsters off so the others could escape."

Bander laughed. "That's what they said you were doing. Unbelievable! I mean that's the kind of thing you hear about the academy greats, but you're a woodsman. One of us!" He lifted his tankard to her and raised his voice. "Here's to Tarah Woodblade! Making the Sampo Guidesmen proud!"

The common room erupted in shouts of agreement as everyone lifted their tankards. Tarah blinked and took a drink along with them. Usually she hated ale, and the ale at the Tracker's Friend was fouler than most, but she barely noticed the bitterness. When she slammed her tankard back down on the bar, she noticed it was half empty. The tavern wench promptly filled it back to the brim.

Tarah couldn't believe her good fortune. That night in Pinewood had been over six months ago, just before the war hit the Sampo area. She was relieved that Bander hadn't asked where she'd been since.

"So," Bander said, putting his own tankard down and smiling at her. "Where have you been? Most of us thought you were probably dead."

Tarah repressed a wince and lifted her tankard to her lips again while she thought of how to answer. She had intended to come clean about running away, but the situation had changed. She took a few swallows and realized that the ale was less bitter than usual. This didn't seem like Milt's regular recipe.

Don't get drunk, warned her papa's voice in the back of her head. Grampa Rolf's voice agreed. *Drinking ain't for you. When you're in a tavern, let the others get tipsy. Tarah Woodblade keeps her mind open for opportunities.*

That's what I'm doing, she replied and set the drink down. "I nearly did die, Bander." She needed to distract him from his question. "Uh, got in a bit of a rumble on the way here, in fact. Ran into some bandits on the edge of the Mage Woods."

Bander frowned. "Vriil's men?"

"That's what I figure. They looked the type," she replied.

"We've had problems with them ever since the war ended. I hoped they would just go back to wherever it is they came from, but lots of them have been hanging around the area, harassing folks." His frown deepened. "Did you leave them alive?"

She looked away. "Tarah Woodblade does what she has

to."

He nodded approvingly. "Good riddance. I hope the whole lot gets themselves killed. The academy's been sending out patrols, but thousands of those dirt-eaters ran off after their leader was killed. The jail's full of them."

"So the academy is still around," Tarah said. "I'd heard rumors that they were destroyed."

Bander shook his head. "Well, the academy itself was destroyed. But everybody got out before it blew up. Where have you been? I thought everybody knew that."

Tarah's face reddened and she came up with something quick. "After what happened in Pinewood I had moonrats and monsters chasing me all the way to the border." As soon as the words left her mouth, she regretted it. Stupid! That story left too many holes. Before Bander could process what she'd said, she added. "You know, those bandits I ran into had something on 'em."

Tarah slid the polished sword from the ugly sheath at her waist and set it on the bar top in front of him. "It looks like a magic blade of some kind to me. Is anyone looking for swords lost on the battlefield?"

Bander's brow furrowed as he looked at the runed surface of the blade. He ran a finger along one of the runes and let out a low whistle. "Yeah, I'd say you're right. I don't know what it does, but I can always tell when something's got magic in it. It has a certain glow to it, you know? As far as lost swords, we don't have any jobs posted about any. You could take it to the academy post down at the Mage School and see if anyone recognizes it."

"I was hoping to head home." Tarah hadn't seen her house since running away and she was worried that something might have happened to it.

"I heard one guy say a guard gave him five gold for a fancy spear he found," Bander added.

"Five?" Tarah's brow furrowed. That was a more than decent finder's fee. The best reward she'd had was two gold and that was the day she had tracked and returned the mayor's prized pony.

"You know what, if you wanted to head to the Mage School, you could also make some extra money on the side,"

Bander said. He gestured to the wench. "Sara, can you hand me that job? The one that I posted this morning?"

"Sure, love," Sara said and headed over to the job board on the far side of the bar.

Tarah gave Bander a disapproving look. "Love?"

"That's . . . that's just what she calls everyone." Bander laughed nervously. "Hey, don't get the wrong idea. I'm a married man."

"Most of you are married. That's why Milt never hired any serving wenches before," Tarah said shaking her head as the buxom wench returned, paper in hand. "I'm surprised he did it now."

"You want anything else, *love*?" Sarah said, slamming the paper on the bar top and giving Tarah a flat look. Evidently she had overheard.

Tarah ignored her and picked up the paper. She glanced at it and looked back at Bander. "A guide job? Just taking a family to the Mage School?"

"A couple and their son," Bander replied. "They think he has magic talent and want to take him to the school to get checked out."

"That's more like guard work than guide work," Tarah said. Most people didn't bother to hire a guide from Sampo to the Mage School. It was a well traveled road, impossible to get lost on. It had been a few years since the last time she escorted anyone there. "Is the road still that dangerous three months after the war?"

"Of course not," said Bander. "And I told them that. But they're insistent and paid up front. I was going to do it myself, but I really shouldn't leave. Milt asked me to stay behind and watch the place until he or one of the other senior members got back."

"I don't know." Tarah rubbed her face. She really wanted to check on her house and heading to the Mage School would delay her return a day or two. Tarah thought about the drawing sitting in her pack and realized she had a third reason to head to the school. It was possible that there were three ways to make money in that short trip . . . Grampa would never forgive her if she passed up a deal like that.

Bander smiled urgingly. "Come on. They paid full guild rate. This little job will net you five silver dremals. That's good money. I've never known you to turn down work."

"You're right," she said, stepping back from the bar. "Tarah Woodblade doesn't turn down a good job. I'll do it."

"Good," Bander said. "They're staying at the Birch Inn. And they want to leave right away."

"I can read the instructions, Bander," Tarah replied, shaking the paper at him before tucking it into her waistband.

He nodded, his smile fading and Tarah realized that she was acting incredibly rude. Bander usually deserved such treatment, but not today. Besides, Tarah Woodblade was stern. Not rude. She cleared her throat.

"Thanks for the job, Bander. And, uh, for being nice." Tarah lifted her tankard from the bar and raised her voice as she turned to the sparsely filled hall. "To Sampo and the Guidesman Guild!"

Bander smiled again as shouts of agreement echoed through the hall. This time Tarah only allowed herself one swallow of ale. She slammed the tankard onto the bar and forced herself to give the tavern wench a nod of thanks, then headed for the door.

After the dark confines of the guild hall, the light of mid-day stung her eyes but Tarah blinked away the discomfort and strode down the street with a slight smile on her face. That had gone better than she could have imagined. No one knew what she had done. Tarah Woodblade was bigger than ever.

Once again she noted the stares of the passers by, but this time she recognized them as stares of awe. She gave a slight nod to each of these admirers and for a time she allowed herself to enjoy the looks. It was good to feel the hero. Tarah turned down a side street, hoping to make a stop before picking up her clients.

Her steps slowed as the burned-out facade of Ollie's Bookstore came into view. She stopped in front of the once familiar entrance, one hand rising to her open mouth. Through gaping holes in the building's outer walls, she could see blackened timbers and the ashy remains of books.

She stepped back and looked around. It seemed that the fire had been started in the bookstore itself. The stores on either side of the building had been freshly repainted as if they had only sustained minor damage, but there were no signs that Ollie's place was being rebuilt.

Tarah swallowed and she hurried on, eager to put the building far behind her. She wondered what Ollie had done to anger the occupying forces. Had they burned it as an example to others? Ollie's had been her favorite bookstore in Sampo and she knew that if Ollie was still alive, his store wouldn't be sitting like that.

Someone in the crowd called her name as she walked past, but Tarah didn't acknowledge him. She couldn't. The feeling of guilt had come rushing back. The people of Sampo may not know what she had done, but Tarah did.

Back straight! Tarah Woodblade doesn't slouch, Grampa Rolf reminded her and Tarah realized that she had lost her composure. She straightened her back and wiped away the tears that had begun to well in her eyes. *That's better. Tarah Woodblade doesn't cry. Tarah Woodblade is tough as iron. Tarah Woodblade is confident. Tarah Woodblade fears nothing.*

Tarah nodded and continued towards the Birch Inn. Though she was grateful for her grampa's support, she couldn't shake the guilt that gnawed on her. Her face impassive, she whispered quietly, "But I ran. People died and I wasn't here."

People die all the time, Grampa Rolf said. *You can't be responsible for other people. Worry about taking care of yourself first.*

You can't save everyone, her papa's voice agreed.

Tarah didn't reply. This time their assurances sounded hollow. She might not have saved everyone, but she may have been able to save Ollie.

The Birch Inn had the reputation of a middle-quality establishment, but it aspired to higher clientele. The boards that covered the building were white washed and the wooden roof tiles painted red. A stable boy stood out front to take horses and a greeter wearing only mildly stained finery stood at the front door.

Tarah didn't want to go inside. The stench of whisky and cleaning solvents that came from the common room was too strong. She motioned to the greeter and handed him the job posting, telling him that she was there to pick up the family.

She didn't have to wait long. A few moments later, the door burst open and a boy burst through the doors. He had light brown hair and freckles along with the gawky thin body of a young teen. He looked around excitedly and was followed shortly by a flustered-looking overweight woman. She wore a fur cloak that seemed much too heavy for the fall temperatures.

"Berty!" she called. "Never go running off alone. Especially in an uncouth foreign town!"

"But mom, one of the Sampo Guidesmen are here for us! I'm perfectly safe," the boy whined.

The woman glanced around. "I don't see anyone."

Tarah cleared her throat and the woman swung around to face her. "I'm Tarah Woodblade of the Sampo Guidesmen Guild. I'm here to take you to the Mage School."

The boy's face fell. "A lady?"

The woman's brow furrowed in concern. "There may be a mistake."

"I promise you there's not," Tarah replied with a good natured smile. Usually this sort of reaction put her on edge, but after the events of the day she found it almost refreshing. This was the attitude she had been trained to deal with. "I'm the best guide in the guild."

The door opened again behind the woman and a tall man with graying hair and a thin mustache stepped out, the job sheet in hand. The woman clutched his arm. "Derbich, dear. This 'woman' claims to be our guild guide."

He turned his gaze on Tarah, one eyebrow raised. "Don't worry, Anna, the young man inside told me she's quite good." He handed her the paper. "I am Derbich Furley of Razbeck. This is my wife, Anna, and son, Bertwise. I have signed the document and I believe all is in order."

From the fine look of their clothing and the way Derbich had introduced himself, Tarah surmised that these people were minor nobility. Or at least they wanted to be seen as such. She hadn't heard of house Furley, but Razbeck politics weren't her specialty. Tarah looked at his signature on the paper, then nodded before folding it and tucking it away. "Very good. You ready to leave right away?"

"Are you sure, dear?" the woman said to her husband, distrust on her face. "She looks . . . uncouth."

Don't show anger, but be firm, Grampa Rolf's voice said. *Increase your client's confidence.*

"Tarah Woodblade is never 'uncouth'." Tarah replied, keeping her expression neutral. "As for my appearance, I've been on the road for a long time and had to fight off beasts and bandits on the way. I would've stopped to clean myself up, but I was told you were eager to get to the Mage School."

"Beasts and bandits?" the boy said, his eagerness reappearing.

"We are pleased to have your services," the man said, ignoring his wife's concerned look. "The stable boy should be bringing our horses around any moment."

"Good," Tarah said. "I'll have you there by nightfall."

The stable boy came from the back of the inn a short time later leading three horses that were laden for travel. They looked to have come a long way. Tarah saw a flash of silver as Derbich tossed a coin at the stable boy.

"Hey lady, don't you have a horse?" Bertwise asked as he mounted his own.

"Not for this trip," Tarah replied and looked to his father. "The roads will be pretty congested until we get out of town. Keep close."

She led them to the main square where all the major streets joined and took them down the Mage School road. Several people in the crowd waved at her and she nodded back at them. Tarah hoped that the family was seeing the interaction. Perhaps the respect the crowd was giving her would ease the woman's mind.

Like the Grandriver Road, this one had also been recently maintained. Tarah kept a swift pace and as the family followed behind, she mulled the day's events. The sight of Ollie's shop kept coming up in her mind. If she had stayed in Dremaldria, would she have saved him?

What you should be wondering about is your pay, Grampa Rolf suggested.

That was true. Derbich had tossed the stable boy a silver piece as a tip. These people would have paid better than guild rate. Was Bander ripping her off? Normally that wouldn't have surprised her, but after the way he had acted in the guild hall . . . She shook her head. Perhaps not much had changed after all.

Tarah pushed the thoughts away. There was no use worrying about it now. She focused on the road ahead, noting the various scars in the landscape that told of the battles fought along the way.

The family kept to themselves for the first two hours and Tarah enjoyed the quiet. Then the boy rode up to Tarah's side. He brought the horse uncomfortably close to her so that he could speak without his parents hearing.

"So why do you wear that ragged armor?" he said. "Momma says it doesn't even look functional."

"It works fine, thank you." She was well aware that it needed repair, but there was nothing she could do about it until she got home. "It stopped a throwing knife just this morning."

Bertwise wrinkled his nose at her in disbelief. "Why is your staff painted red?"

"It's not paint. It's a rare type of wood." She paused for effect. "Dipped in the blood of many monsters."

"No way," he said in awe. He reached out. "Can I see it?"

"No," she said and continued to walk forward, her eyes moving back to the woods around them. There was something in the air. A strange scent.

"Okay, fine," the boy said, his voice oozing irritation. He sounded like someone who wasn't used to being refused. "What happened to your nose?"

Tarah was quickly remembering just how much she hated teenage boys. She let out a calming breath. "I got in a fist fight with a giant."

"Right," the boy said in disbelief. "Looks like you lost."

"Tarah Woodblade doesn't lose." She gave him a wicked grin. "The giant might have bent my nose, but I took off its head."

The boy snorted, but she saw a hint of belief in his eyes. "Is that a true story?"

"My stories are always true," Tarah lied. Her stories were only partially true. "What about you? Why do your parent's think you have magic?"

"I was real mad at my mother one day and I don't know how I did it, but the wall in my bedroom turned to mud and melted," the boy said, his voice proud.

Tarah nodded. She could believe it. A picture formed in her mind of Bertwise throwing a rich-boy tantrum and melting a wall. Papa had told her that magic could do strange things when its power was first awakened.

"And that's not all," Bertwise added. "Mom thinks I got that new spirit magic stuff too."

"Never heard of it," Tarah said. She suppressed a frown and jogged forward a bit, looking into the bushes to the side of the road. Something was bothering her about the area and she wasn't sure what it was.

Berty pulled up next to her again "Yeah, spirit magic is a kind of magic no one knew existed before. The Mage School just announced it a few months ago." He gave her a proud grin. "And I have it. Mom says I'll be one of the most important students at the school."

"And what does this new magic of yours do?" she asked.

"I can read a person's mind," he said confidently.

"Oh really?" Tarah closed her eyes briefly, extending her other senses. She didn't hear anything out of the ordinary. What was it about the road that was bothering her? "What am I thinking then?"

"Well, I can't tell unless I'm touching someone," Bertwise said. "Actually it works best if I put my head against their chest."

Tarah snorted. "Well that ain't happening."

"I don't want to put my face against your nasty armor!" The boy said, his face red. "I was just saying my magic works best that way."

"Right. I'm sure that line works great with the maids in your castle," Tarah said.

"Look, if you don't believe me, just let me hold your hand," he said. She snorted again and he blinked. "I mean, grip your hand. Sometimes I can tell what people are thinking even from that."

"I don't think so," Tarah said.

"Come on," the boy said. He leaned out of his saddle stretching one hand out to her. "Let me prove it."

She glanced back at his parents but they were deep in conversation, looking at each other. She sighed and moved her staff to her left hand and reached up to him.

The moment the boy grasped her fingers, she felt a strange tugging sensation and the boy's eyes widened. Tarah jerked her hand back. "What was that?"

"You're frightened," Bertwise said in surprise.

"Tarah Woodblade fears nothing," she replied coolly, but her heart was thundering. What did he see?

"No. You act tough, but inside . . . you're afraid of everything." A grin spread across his face. "Dad, you hired us a coward!"

"Don't be stupid, boy! I-." Tarah caught a whiff of that strange scent again and this time she identified it. She swallowed.

"You what?" he said.

"Shh!" Tarah said, one finger to her lips. "Stop your horse." She waited for the boy's parents to catch up.

"What were you two talking about?" the woman asked.

"We need to pick up the pace," Tarah said. "I think there's danger nearby."

"On this road? Don't be ridiculous," Anne replied.

Derbich wasn't as foolish. "What is it?" he asked, his eyes focused.

Tarah knew better than to tell them, especially the woman. It was okay for a guide to make people wary; a wary client stayed close and obeyed. But scaring clients was a no-no. Scared people do stupid things. "Just keep close, but don't ride past me unless I tell you to."

Derbich nodded and Tarah ran ahead and the family urged their horses into a trot, keeping close to her. The smell grew stronger as they went and Tarah's concern grew.

"Please don't let there be more than one," she whispered.

They came around a bend in the road and Tarah saw them. Standing in the middle of the road swaying slowly were two trolls.

Chapter Three

Tarah raised her arms, signaling a halt. The nobles jerked back on their reins, causing one of the horses to give out a nervous whinny. The trolls stopped their swaying and sniffed the air, saliva dripping from their open mouths. Luckily their eyesight was poor and the wind was blowing in Tarah's favor. Like all common trolls they were tall and thin, with long wicked claws and large mouths full of razor-like teeth. Their skin had a greenish tint and extruded a glistening slime that had pooled on the ground around them.

Trolls are hard to kill, warned Tarah's papa. *Best to avoid them whenever possible.*

"I know," Tarah whispered, a shiver of fear rising up her back. Unfortunately, the creatures were standing in the middle of the road. She pulled her bow from its place over her shoulder and turned to Derbich. "Keep your voices low. They haven't noticed us yet. Do any of you have a way to make fire quickly? Magic fire starters?"

"No." Derbich answered, his eyes concerned.

"What are those things?" Bertwise whispered.

"Trolls," Tarah said, but kept her focus on Derbich. "How bad do you need to be at the Mage School today?"

"Let's go back to Sampo, Derbich," Anna said, her voice a bit too loud. One of the trolls cocked its head and took a few steps in their direction. "We can come back tomorrow with armed guards."

"Be silent, Anna." Derbich turned a frown at Tarah. "I would much rather be there this evening, Miss Woodblade. That's why I paid your man more than the standard guild rate."

Tarah's lips tightened. So her suspicions were right. She would have a nice chat with Bander when she got back to Sampo.

"I can take you around 'em. There is a ravine not far off the road. We'll have to lead the horses."

"I demand we go back to Sampo!" Anna protested. "I am NOT traipsing through the underbrush with creatures around!"

The trolls screeched at the sound of her upraised voice and began to run towards them. Tarah swore. "You three stay where you are. Don't run unless they get past me."

The trolls were coming fast. She would only have time for one shot and she had to make it count. Tarah reached back to her quiver and ran her fingers quickly over the fletchings, selecting an arrow she knew was steel-tipped. Gathering her concentration, she drew the arrow back and fired.

 The arrow struck the lead troll between the eyes and drove deep into its skull. Tarah nodded in satisfaction as it tumbled to the ground. The other troll ran on heedless of its downed companion, its claws outstretched. Tarah dropped her bow and ran to meet it, her red staff in hand.

A troll fights without strategy, her papa said. *Hunger is the only thought in its head. It'll charge and swipe with its claws, trying to pull you in and bite you.*

Yeah-yeah. Thanks a lot, Tarah replied. She was scared enough without the reminder. The thing was at least a foot taller than she was and by the way it barreled towards her Tarah knew that standing toe-to-toe with it wasn't going to work.

Soon it was almost on her. Tarah darted to the side, just under it's wicked claws, and swung her staff down low, using it's momentum against it. Her staff cracked it across the shins and the troll fell forward.

It crashed to the ground so hard that Tarah heard the snap of breaking ribs, but the troll scrambled to its feet, heedless of pain, and turned to face her. Tarah planted her feet and the end of her staff met its face, striking it across the upper jaw and nose. The troll stumbled backwards as blood, teeth, and slime flew from its mouth.

For most creatures, such a horrendous blow would have ended the fight, but Tarah didn't dare let up. Before the troll could right itself, she shifted her hands on her staff and swung again, her weight distributed perfectly to lend the blow as much power as possible. The staff struck its temple, shattering its skull.

The troll fell convulsing and Tarah struck again. Three more times, she bashed its skull, softening it up. Then, when its movements had stopped, she pulled an arrow from her quiver and stabbed through its fractured skull, pinning it to the ground.

Breathing heavily, she turned to see if the other troll was back up yet. When she saw that it hadn't moved, she let out a sigh of relief and turned to face her clients.

Anne was staring at her, wide-eyed, her hand raised to her mouth in horror. Derbich gazed at her with respect, one eyebrow raised. Bertwise, on the other hand, wore an eager grin.

"That was amazing!" the young noble said and spurred his horse forward to get a closer look at the downed troll. Tarah raised her hand and opened her mouth to tell him to stop, but she was too late. As his horse lunged forward, she heard a loud snap.

"No!" she cried and rushed past the confused boy. A lump rose in her throat as she picked up her bow from the ground where she had dropped it. The impact of the horse's hoof had split the wood down the middle. She glared at the boy. "You see what you did?"

"I'm sorry," Bertwise said, confused by her reaction.

"Don't worry, Miss Woodblade," said Derbich. "We'll buy you a new one."

"M-my papa made it for me," she said, her lips quivering. "It's . . . not replaceable."

Tarah Woodblade doesn't cry. Tarah Woodblade doesn't mourn. Not where she can be seen, Grampa Rolf reminded. Tarah swallowed her sorrow and swung the broken bow back over her shoulder.

"I insist," Derbich said. "We can make an arrangement of some kind."

Tarah shook her head, but felt an insistent nudge from her grampa and said, "We can settle up when we arrive at the Mage School. For now, I need to burn these things. Come on. Follow me." She led them down the road and stopped them at the body of the first troll she had downed.

"It's moving!" cried Bertwise.

The troll raised its head and began to push itself up from the ground. It opened its mouth and gurgled, releasing a rivulet of slime. Tarah could see the arrow slowly being pushed out of the wound as the creature's brain healed. She swung her staff in a precise strike, smacking the end of the arrow and driving it back into the troll's head. The steel arrowhead popped out through the back of its skull.

Anna yelped as the troll convulsed, then laid still. Tarah grabbed it by the leg. The troll's skin was slick and rubbery and she fought a grimace off of her face as she began pulling it down the center of the road towards the second one.

"What are you doing?" Anne asked from atop her horse. "Let's ride on."

"We can't, Madam Furley. They heal too quick. If we leave 'em here, they'll just attack the next person that comes down the road," Tarah said, dragging the heavy troll past their horses.

Bertwise didn't believe it. "How can it heal an arrow through the brain?"

"They don't have much to heal," Tarah replied.

"Troll brains are simple, Berty," Derbich explained. "All they think about is eating. Besides, even if you cut their head off, they'll just grow a new one and walk around as if nothing happened."

"And the head you cut off will grow another body if you let it," Tarah added, grunting as she pulled its body on top of its friend. "Once saw a troll cut into ten pieces. Two weeks later, came back to find ten trolls." That was actually one of her papa's stories, but Grampa Rolf would say telling tales was a good idea, whether the story was true or not. That's how you grew your legend.

"The best thing you can do is leave something stuck through its brain until you can burn it," Tarah continued. She looked down at the troll whose head she had smashed. The bones of its skull were already re-forming. She set down her pack and reached into the front pocket for her flint and steel. "Now hold tight while I set these things on fire."

"Right there in the middle of the road?" Bertwise asked.

"Don't want to burn down the forest," Tarah said.

"I don't like standing around here," Anne complained. "What if there are more of those things around?"

"This won't take long," Tarah said through gritted teeth. If these people weren't clients she would have chewed the woman's ear off. Instead she kept her voice even.

"Don't worry, dear," Derbich said. "Trolls burn quite quickly. Their slime is flammable."

"How efficient of them," Anne grumbled.

Tarah turned her back on the woman and struck her flint against the steel, sending sparks onto the trolls' glistening bodies. It only took a few strikes before there was a soft whoosh. The flames came up so suddenly that the horses shied away.

The trolls began to squirm as the fire ate into them and one of them jerked spasmodically, sending strings of burning slime across the road. One string landed on a slime trail the trolls had left earlier and Tarah rushed over as fire began to spread. She was able to kick dirt over the trail to stop the flame's spread just before it reached a pool of slime at the forest's edge.

"See, lady?" Tarah said. "That's why I wanted 'em in the middle of the road. Who knows how long they've been in the place leaving their slimy tracks every. . ."

Tarah's voice trailed off. She walked to the edge of the road and crouched down. "No way," she mumbled to herself, gazing at several slime-covered impressions in the ground. Their pattern was quite distinct.

"Do we really need to wait around here until those things stop burning?" Anne said.

"Just a minute longer," Tarah said. She opened her pack and reached deep inside to pull out a piece of folded parchment. She opened it and compared the ink drawings on the page to the impressions in the ground. They matched perfectly.

Gripping her staff tightly, she tucked the parchment under her arm and reached down with her free hand to touch the tracks. A deep hunger flashed through her mind and she snatched her hand back, frowning slightly. She couldn't sense the mind of the creature that had left the track. The troll slime was in the way. She sat back on her haunches and looked at the piece of parchment again, her brow furrowed.

"Miss Woodblade? Is there a problem?" Derbich asked. The man's voice was tinged with concern.

She shook her head and tucked the parchment back into her pack, then stood and turned to face them. "It's nothing of importance, sir. We should move on." He raised an eyebrow but nodded and Tarah added, "I'll pick up the pace. We'll still make it by dark if we hurry."

She started on down the road towards the Mage School at a brisk jog, leaving the smoldering remains of the trolls, and the curious tracks, behind. The nobles had to urge their horses into a trot to keep up. To Tarah's relief, they kept a slight distance, giving her time to mull things over.

When the drawing of the strange tracks had been given to her, Tarah had scoffed at the idea that such a creature existed. But now she had seen real proof. The tracks had belonged to a large beast with the front end of an ape and the rear end of a great cat.

She could feel her grampa's smile. There was a lot of money to be made if she could track that beast down. Too bad the tracks had been so old. From the state of them, they had been left in the mud two rains ago and from the looks of the forest around, it hadn't rained in quite some time. She bit her lip. The creature could be anywhere by now.

Tarah Woodblade doesn't turn down an opportunity to make coin, Grampa Rolf reminded.

It's too much of a stretch, grampa, she replied. Still, it was a lot of coin. She shrugged the thoughts away. She could worry about that later. The most important thing at the moment was to deliver the nobles to the Mage School.

Tarah kept up her pace and soon she was breathing heavily. She shook her head, refusing to slow. Three months of hiding had weakened her. Tarah Woodblade didn't get winded. Not after a mile run. Besides at this speed, none of the nobles had bothered to speak with her.

The enormous Rune Tower loomed ahead and she ran on, her eyes taking in the scars of war all around her. The fighting had been heavy along this last section of road. Trees were broken, many of them charred, and huge sections of the forest had been torn up. Tarah didn't let guilt touch her this time. This had been the result of battling with magic. Surely there was nothing one person could have done to help.

Tarah's legs were burning by the time the walls of the Mage School came into view. She slowed to a walk, her jaw dropping. The walls had shrunk.

The walls used to be a marvel. Raised by powerful earth

wizards, they had been fifty-feet-high and made of a single sheet of black rock and used to hang out overhead far above the ground, giving the oppressive feeling that they could collapse on her at any moment. Now, though they were made of the same black rock, the walls were maybe twenty-feet-tall at most. Tarah swallowed as she thought of the sheer amount of power that would have been necessary to bring those walls down.

The Furleys hadn't seen the walls in their previous state. Anna gave out an awed gasp and Bertwise hooted in excitement. They urged their horses forward and soon passed Tarah in their rush to get to the gates.

Derbich let them race ahead, slowing down as he came next to her. "I must talk to the wizards, but I would like to speak with you afterwards if you don't mind waiting, Miss Woodblade."

Without thinking, she nodded and he hurried to catch up to his wife who was already at the front gate speaking to a guard and gesturing excitedly. Tarah walked on, watching as he caught up to them and calmed his wife. Before she reached them, another guard came from inside the wall and ushered the family through. They didn't look back.

Tarah stopped and grit her teeth in consternation. Why had she agreed to wait? There was nothing to do outside but stand in the dirt and they could be gone for hours.

She looked up at the darkening sky. Surely there was no real need to stay. The Furleys had already paid the guild. If she started back to Sampo now she would be back at the Tracker's Friend to throttle Bander by midnight.

She turned around, intending to do just that when she heard her papa's voice chastening her, *Be responsible, Tarah. If you see something dangerous in the woods, you got to warn folks.*

Her shoulders slouched and she mumbled, "I know, papa." Tarah looked back at the guards standing by the gate. There were two, one standing on either side of the wide gate, and both were looking her way. She headed towards one of them. He was a big man wearing a breast plate and carrying a spear.

"Hey you!" Tarah said and the man's eyes widened in surprise. His face was weathered and a long scar wrinkled one cheek. "You in charge here?"

"Me? No. I'm just a student," he said with a voice Tarah

found high for a man his size.

"You're a student?" she said, puzzled. "At the Mage School?"

A hesitant smile appeared on the man's lips. "Naw. At the Battle Academy, Ma'am."

"What's an academy student doing standing guard at the Mage School?"

His smile faltered. "It's a big place. Everybody helps with guard duty."

Tarah frowned. The academy didn't send students on guard assignments. More had changed than she'd thought. "I don't have time to talk to a student. Where's your guard captain?"

"Uh . . ." The student took a few steps back from the wall and looked towards the top of the wall. "Jerry!"

A helmeted head appeared at the top of the wall and peered down at them as it shouted back, "What?"

"This . . . lady wants to talk to someone in charge!" the student replied.

The person on the wall let out a sigh. "I'm coming down!"

A few moments later a guard dressed in full polished platemail walked from inside the gate, his helmet held under one arm. He was short, perhaps a full foot shorter than Tarah, but he had a wide-bodied frame. His shoulders were as wide as a man half again his size and his arms were huge. He approached them and Tarah realized from his stride that he was a dwarf. She hadn't noticed right away because, unlike other dwarves she'd seen, his hair and beard were cropped short and neat. It reminded her of the way her papa kept his beard trimmed.

The student saluted him but the dwarf just scowled. "You call me captain when you're on duty, kid," the dwarf snapped. "And my name's 'Djeri', not 'Jerry'. understand?"

The man's face reddened. "Yes, sir."

Tarah found it strange to see such a young-looking dwarf addressing that grizzled man as 'kid'. But then again the races with blood magic lived a long time. For all she knew, he could be hundreds of years old.

"Alright, Yerd, back to your post," the dwarf said in dismissal and turned his eyes on Tarah. He raised one trimmed eyebrow at her armor and red staff, then met her gaze. His eyes were green. She'd never seen a dwarf with green eyes. "And what can I help you with?"

"You're the guard captain?" she asked.

"No. Riveren the Unbending is in a meeting right now," the dwarf said, his voice a deep baritone. "But I'm one of his sub-captains. You can speak to me."

So Riveren was still in charge. The 'Unbending' moniker was new, but at least someone she knew had survived the war. "Okay, captain. I wanted to tell you that you guys have problems. We ran into trolls on the road here from Sampo."

The dwarf didn't look surprised. "How far from here?"

"About half way," Tarah said. "There were two of 'em."

"Two trolls," Djeri said, nodding. "Thanks for telling me. I'll send some men down to take care of them."

"Those trolls are dead," she replied. "I burned 'em and left 'em in the middle of the road. The reason I'm warning you about 'em is because there could be more. There was a lot of slime in the forest around the area. I had folks to guide so I wasn't able to stay around and count tracks."

"You killed them?" The dwarf looked her over again, his face thoughtful.

"Tarah Woodblade won't be slowed down by a couple trolls."

Djeri smiled. "You're Tarah Woodblade? The hero of Pinewood?"

"I am," she said and though she injected pride into her voice, something about the dwarf made her feel a little guilty saying it. "But I'm not from Pinewood itself."

"I heard about you." He gave her a respectful nod. "Most people thought you were dead, but the Pinewood folks said you were too tough to die. Where have you been?"

"It's a long story," she said quickly. "And it's getting late. I really need to get heading back. I just wanted to warn you before I left."

"Come on. There's no need for you to leave just yet. Not when it's just getting dark," the dwarf replied and Tarah wondered where he was from. She had never met a dwarf that sounded so . . . human. "Why don't you stay here for the night? Dinner's just starting back at the barracks and there is a guest house open that you can sleep in."

"I-I don't know."

"I insist," he said with an encouraging grin. "Listen, the food here might not be dwarvish, but it's way better than the turd soup they serve at the inns in Sampo. And I hear the beds at the houses are really nice."

"Well . . ." Tarah hesitated. A bed sounded wonderful, but Tarah really didn't want to spend the evening trying to explain where she'd been during the war.

Djeri took her hesitation as a yes. "Good. Yerd! Send a message to Wizard Beehn that we have a guest." The big man nodded and ran through the gate. Djeri put an arm around her shoulder and urged her inside. "Thanks for warning me about the road. I'll tell Riveren about it as soon as he gets out of the meeting. I'm sure we'll send a patrol out at first light."

Tarah sighed in acceptance and allowed him to lead her through the gate. The view inside the walls was pretty much the way she remembered it. The main road continued through vast manicured lawns to a cluster of class buildings and a clock tower at the center of the school. The enormous Rune Tower rose up behind it all, stretching endlessly into the sky.

That was the home of the wizards, the home of the Bowl of Souls, and more importantly to Tarah, the home of the greatest library in Dremaldria. Tarah had never been inside, but her mother had told her tales of it. She had always dreamed of roaming the library, reading the tales of the great adventurers of days gone by. But the wizards would never let someone like her in there.

Djeri paused to let her take it in, but he didn't stop talking. "I'm sorry you had to deal with those trolls. We've had difficulty keeping the area clear. Ewzad Vriil and the moonrat mother left a lot of turds behind for us to deal with."

Djeri led her to the left, away from the main road and towards the guard barracks. This area was much bigger than Tarah remembered. There were two new buildings and several neat rows of tents spread in the grass beyond.

As they came closer, Tarah could see men milling about as they came on and off the wall and heard the sound of sparring coming from the training grounds behind the buildings. "You seem to have a lot more guards than before," she observed.

"Most of the men you see are students," Djeri said with a shake of his head. "The majority of the graduates are either out on assignments or helping with the rebuild so our forces are stretched pretty thin. The wizards are letting us teach the students here until the new academy is complete." The dwarf brought her to the largest of the buildings and Tarah caught the first scent of the food being served. "There's so many of us here right now that the Mage School set us up our own dining hall. We've found it best to keep our students separate from theirs as much as possible."

Tarah's mouth watered and she realized she had hardly eaten all day. They entered a wide and open dining hall packed with tables and the clamor of talking men. At the back of the room, several servers wearing white aprons were standing behind tables laden with food, dishing it onto plates for the guards.

"The food line's right here," Djeri said, taking her to a group of men that were waiting to have their plates filled. "I'm sorry, but I'll have to leave you here. I have other duties to attend to."

Tarah frowned. "What am I supposed to do?"

"Just get your food and sit anywhere. No one will give you trouble," he assured her. "I'll tell Riveren you are here. I'm sure he'll want to talk to you. One of us will return to show you to your guest house in a little while."

The dwarf patted her shoulder and left and Tarah's anxiety rose. As she watched the dwarf walk out the front door, she had to force the frown from her face. She replaced it with an expression of confidence and waited for her turn at the food, ignoring the curious stares of the men all around the room.

Her palms were sweating by the time one of the workers placed a large plate in her hands. She turned her attention on the food and gave nods to the workers as they piled various meats and vegetables on her plate. Each dish looked like a delicacy to her, covered with herbs and cooked to perfection. The last worker topped her plate with a large yeasty roll and Tarah stepped away eager to get started.

Now the question was where to sit. There wasn't a completely empty table in the whole hall and the number of men watching her had increased. Sweat beaded on her forehead as she looked around the room and Tarah finally selected an empty spot on a table along the back wall.

There were four other men at the table, but none of them were looking her way. She sat at the end farthest from the men, setting her pack down next to her so that no one would try to sit there. The four men must have just finished a long shift, because they barely glanced at her with sleepy eyes before returning their gazes to their plates.

Watch and learn, Tarah. Watch and learn, said her papa's voice and Grampa Rolf agreed. *The best salesman is observant. Keep your eyes and ears open in every situation. You never know what opportunities may arise.*

She didn't care about opportunities in this place, but Tarah tried to listen to the conversations at the tables around her. Then she took her first bite and their advice was forgotten.

These academy men ate like kings. The roast beef was covered with gravy and fell apart in her mouth, the ham was smoked to perfection, and the roast duck had a sweet and slightly nutty flavor that made her wish she had the whole bird on her plate. The roll was soft and buttery, but the food that impressed her the most was a strange vegetable she had never tasted before. It was yellow in color and looked like a mix of tomato and squash, but had a smooth texture and a peppery tang to it.

As she ate, the weariness left her body and she realized that these academy men weren't eating like kings. They were eating like elves. There was magic in this food. She felt like she could run all the way back to Sampo without stopping.

She was sopping up the last bit of gravy from her plate when she felt a tap on her shoulder. She looked up to see a guard in bulky plate armor standing beside her.

"You Tarah Woodblade?" asked a female voice.

"Yeah," Tarah responded hesitantly.

The guard took off her helmet and Tarah saw a pretty face and a head of short-cropped blond hair. A horizontal line of black paint covered the guard's face from nose to eyebrow. "I'm Kathy. Djeri asked me to take you to your guest house."

"The dwarf sent you?" Tarah stood to find that this woman was almost as tall as she was and by the size of her plate armor, Tarah knew she must be very strong.

"He asked me," the woman clarified. "Djeri's a friend, but

he's not my boss. He was called into a meeting or he would have come himself."

Tarah picked her pack up off of the bench beside her and shook her head as she shrugged it on. "You academy guards sure have a lot of meetings."

Kathy smiled. "That's what happens when you're posted at the Mage School. Wizards love to talk. Come on. Follow me."

They left the dining hall and walked back across the main road to the far side of the gates where a row of small houses stood. There were horses tied in front of one house and Tarah saw Derbich Furley standing next to them talking to a woman wearing mage robes. Tarah's shoulder's slumped. She had been hoping they would be staying somewhere else.

"This'll be your place," Kathy said, pointing to the house nearest the gate. She handed Tarah a key. "The wizards keep the place clean. We eat at dawn, but there's always food in the dining hall, so you can sleep in if you want."

"I don't know if I'll be able to sleep at all after that meal," Tarah said. "I can't imagine what it'd be like eating that food every day."

Kathy gave a half chuckle. "Yeah, you feel amazing the first few times, but you get used to it after awhile. I hardly notice it anymore. Anyway, it was nice meeting you."

"And you," Tarah replied. The woman nodded, then turned and walked back towards the barracks.

Tarah glanced quickly over at Derbich and was relieved to see he was still talking to the mage. She hurried over to the door of the small house and unlocked it, hoping to get inside before he noticed her.

"Miss Woodblade!" Derbich called and Tarah winced. He said one last thing to the mage before jogging over to talk to her.

Tarah frowned inwardly, but said in what she assumed was a polite tone, "Hello, sir."

"So you are settling in, then?" he asked.

"I'll be staying the night," she said. "But I plan on leaving in the morning."

"Ah, we may be here a week or so," he said, looking slightly disappointed. "Would you consider staying and escorting us back?"

There was nothing she could think of that she wanted to do less. "Sorry, I can't. I've got other things I need to do back home."

"Ah, I understand." Derbich hesitated a moment. "Miss Woodblade, I feel I must apologize for my family's behavior."

Tarah blinked in surprise. "Not at all. They were, uh . . . fine, sir."

Derbich shook his head. "Nonsense, I know how horrible they were. I must ask you to forgive them. They are out of their element. You see my wife is, shall we say, sheltered. This trip is her first time out of Razbeck. In fact, it's her first time to journey anywhere outside the city by any means other than coach. As for Bertwise," He let out a regretful sigh. "I've tried to imbue that boy with common sense, but the noble court has corrupted him. I'm hoping life at the school will be good for him. Perhaps the wizards will teach him some humility."

"I'm not sure the wizards have any," Tarah replied.

Derbich chuckled. "Well, at least this talent of his means he won't be taking over the family lands when I am gone. His younger sister is much more of a leader."

"I see." Tarah nodded in understanding. People with magic talent weren't allowed to rule. It was a law established by the prophet long ago and the Mage School itself enforced it. "Well, I wish your family well." She turned to head into the house, but the man cleared his throat.

"Wait, I still need to settle up with you," he said.

"Settle up?" Tarah said, unsure what he meant.

"Yes, I paid your man earlier, but there is the matter of your broken bow to attend to."

Tarah had been trying not to think about it. "I've told you it isn't replaceable."

"Surely there's something I can do to help," he insisted.

Tarah had the urge to yell at him. What was he going to do, bring her papa back from the dead to make her another bow? But at her grampa's silent urging, she said instead, "What do you propose?"

"I've been thinking on that." Derbich pulled a coin purse out of his coat pocket and fished around inside. "I know that the bow was an heirloom, but perhaps this will help."

Tarah frowned slightly. "Even if you gave me a handful of

gold pieces, it won't buy me a bow better than I can make myself."

Derbich's brow furrowed and he placed four gold pieces in her hand. "I don't know about a handful, but this should at least help with material costs."

Tarah swallowed. That was more than she had expected. "It will help. Thank you, sir."

Derbich gave her a calculating look. "But you saved our lives today. So perhaps I can offer you something better."

"Better than gold?" she asked.

"How about steady employment?" he suggested.

"What do you mean by steady?" Tarah asked.

"As long as you wanted it," he said. "From what I saw at your guild house, it seems the Sampo Guidesmen have come under hard times. Come work for me. House Furley may not be the highest house in Razbeck, but I could use someone with your talents. I can provide you with steady work and good pay."

"Leave the guild?" If she had been asked the day before, she would have been tempted to take it. "I . . . appreciate the offer, sir, but-."

"It is a standing offer." Derbich reached back into his purse and pulled out a type of coin Tarah had not seen before. It was slightly larger than a standard gold piece. The outer portion was made of silver while a golden disk sat in the center. "This is a Furley House mark. If you are ever in the City of Beck, come to my estates. Show this to the house guards and they will let you in to see me."

Never close a door, Grampa Rolf said. *Any business contact is a good business contact.*

"Thank you, sir," Tarah said. She took the coin and deposited it along with the gold in her pocket. "I will think on it."

He patted her shoulder. "That's all I can ask. Now, I must wish you a good evening. I hope we can do business together again."

Tarah considered his proposal as he walked away. A steady job with a noble house? There could be worse ways to live. It was the kind of life her papa would have wanted for her. But that would mean leaving Dremaldria for good. It would also mean dealing with people every day. Tarah shuddered and turned back towards the cottage door.

She stepped inside to find a tidy living space. The arrangements were nicer than any inn she had ever stayed at. There was a central area with a table, two chairs, and a small cupboard and two identical bedrooms sat at either side of the space. A vase of fresh flowers sat in each room, filling the house with a fresh scent.

Tarah picked one of the bedrooms and threw her pack down just inside the doorway. She glanced at the intricate pattern on the quilt covering the bed. The wizards sure did their best to make the place inviting to their guests. Tarah frowned. This place made her feel like even more of a fraud.

She sighed as she unlaced and removed her armor. The sweaty stench of her underclothes made her wince. Tarah used the washbasin by the bed to clean up as best as she could and pulled a somewhat cleaner set of underclothes from her pack. Oh how she wished she were home. To have clean clothes and sleep in her own bed would have been so nice. She pulled back the quilt on the bed and looked at the clean white sheets, sure that there wouldn't be much sleep for her here. Then she sat on the bed.

Tarah let out a sigh of a different kind. This was no straw mattress like at the inns she frequented. It wasn't even stuffed with cotton like the mattress at home. She laid back into the luxuriant softness and smiled as she pulled the silky quilt over her. This had to be stuffed with down of some sort, though she couldn't imagine what kind of bird had feathers that soft. And the pillow . . . she rubbed her head into it and smiled at the faintly floral scent. No she wasn't sleeping tonight. This was far too comfortable to miss by indulging in something as ordinary as sleep.

She was snoring softly within minutes.

Chapter Four

Knock, knock, knock!

The sharp rapping shook Tarah from her slumber. She opened her eyes to find that sunlight was streaming in from the small bedroom window. How long had she slept?

Bam, bam, bam!

"Just a minute!" she shouted and hurriedly threw on pants and a shirt, not having time to strap on her armor. Tarah left the bedroom and moved to the front door just as whoever was there beat the door loudly again. She frowned and cracked the door open, peering outside. "What do you . . ?"

There was no light outside, just the deepest darkness. And two eyes; two glowing yellow eyes like luminous orbs. Tarah's heart jumped. Those were moonrat eyes. Just as she made the realization it let loose a chittering moan. It was a haunted and penetrating sound, both sorrowful and hungry.

Tarah slammed the door shut and took a step back, her hands shaking. What was a moonrat doing here?

"They'll never truly be gone, Tarah," said her papa's voice and Tarah turned to see him standing in the doorway to the second room, leaning against the doorjam. He was just as she remembered, tall and handsome with a muscled frame and an easy smile above his stubbled jaw. "But come on, you don't fear moonrats, do you? You've certainly killed enough of them."

"N-no, papa," she said, then jumped as something heavy slammed against the front door, rattling it in its frame. "B-but-."

"Of course you ain't afraid. Tarah Woodblade fears nothing," Grampa Rolf lectured. Suddenly he was sitting at the small table beside her, a steaming mug of tea in one hand. His eyes twinkled under their bushy brows and his thin gray mustache stretched as he gave her a reassuring grin of his own. "You can take that thing, girl. Tarah Woodblade can handle any situation."

Tarah nodded and her staff appeared in her hands just as the door to the outside shook again. This time great cracks appeared in the wood. She looked to her papa for assurance, but he was gone from the doorway and the bedroom beyond was enveloped in blackness.

"Papa!" Tarah called, but there was no answer. She looked to Grampa Rolf, but he was gone too, his cup left steaming on the table.

She took another step backwards and the front door exploded inwards, shards of wood scattering into the room all around her. The moonrat eyes still glowed in the night beyond, but they were now at equal height with hers. A hand reached out of the darkness and gripped the doorjam. It was a human hand, each finger glistening with jeweled rings.

A man slowly pulled himself into the room, straining as if the darkness was trying to pull him back. A long black wizard's robe enveloped his form and the glowing eyes came into the house with him, glaring at her from within the thick hood that covered his head.

Tarah held back a scream as, with a grunt, the figure tore free of the night and pulled a jagged dagger from within its robes. A horrible voice echoed from within the hood, "Uglyyy Giirrrl."

"Tarah Woodblade is no girl!" she snarled and swung her red staff at his head.

The man lurched backwards and the end of her staff caught only the fabric of his hood. The hood tore free, revealing a head that was a hideous mix of moonrat and man. The moonrat eyes bulged out from the sides of a skull covered with mangy gray hair and a shortened snout was pulled back in a toothy snarl. Saliva dripped from its jaws as it said, "Youu are nooo Wooodblade!"

The creature surged forward. Tarah swung her staff in an overhand chop, but the tip struck the low ceiling and the creature's dagger slashed under her upraised arms. Its wicked blade cut across Tarah's chest, scoring deep.

Tarah stumbled back, clutching the wound. It was bad. It was real bad. She was pretty sure it went all the way to the bone. Hot blood poured down her belly and her vision swam. If only she had been wearing her armor.

The moonrat man chittered in triumph and licked its bloody blade. "Youu feeaar me. Youu are scaaared, uglyy giirrrl!"

"No," she gasped. "Tarah Woodblade fears nothing."

"Youu are scaaared and youu wiill looooose."

"No!" It was wrong. She refused to lose. She refused to die.

She let go of the wound, gripping her staff with both hands. As her blood touched the wood, the runes carved into it glowed with a blue light and the pain and fear were sucked away. With a cry of defiance, she thrust with her staff as if it were a spear.

The tip of her staff burst its right eye and exploded through the back of the creature's skull. It dropped its knife and clutched at the staff. Steam shot from the wood as the runes seared its hands and the moonrat man collapsed.

Tarah pulled her staff free and the creature reached a quivering hand towards her. Its jaw worked as it said with a weak gurgle, "Uglyyy Giirrrl . . ."

The moonrat man fell still and with a soft pop, its left eye fell free from its skull and rolled towards her. Tarah stared down with horror as it came to rest at her feet. The yellow light in the eye grew until it filled her vision and an awful but familiar voice echoed in her mind.

"Tarah Woodblade, you are marked for death."

Knock, knock knock!

Tarah sat up in the soft bed gasping and drenched with sweat. The morning sunlight from the small bedroom window hurt her eyes and she looked around, momentarily disoriented. She clutched at her chest and was relieved to find that she wasn't wounded.

The loud knock rang out again and Tarah threw back the quilt. She grabbed her staff and ran to the front room. She threw the door open, her body in defensive posture, her staff at the ready.

A graying woman wearing kitchen livery yelped and backed away, nearly dropping the large covered platter she held. Her mouth dropped open. "Wh-why young lady! I-I! Please cover yourself. There are men out and about at this hour!"

Tarah's face colored as she realized she was standing in her underclothes. She kept her expression calm and fought off the instinct to slam the door. Instead, she set her staff just inside and folded her arms. "I don't see any men here now. Just us girls. What do you need?"

The woman cleared her throat. "The Captain Commander noticed that you did not make it to breakfast this morning." She gestured with the platter. "I was asked to bring you some food."

"Thanks," Tarah said and took the platter from the woman. The savory smell of sausages and freshly baked bread filled her nose and the warmth of the platter reminded her just how chilly the morning air was. "Uh, tell the captain I appreciate it."

The woman curtsied and, giving her one more scandalized glance, scurried away. Tarah swung the door shut with one foot and sighed as she sat the platter down on the table. Her eyes were drawn to the chair across from where she stood.

In her dream, Grampa Rolf had been sitting in that chair. He had looked just like he had when he had first come to live with her, proper and full of vigor. Her eyes moved to the doorway of the far bedroom where her papa had stood looking strong and healthy. How had she dreamt this room in so much detail? She had barely been in it the night before.

"Oh how I miss you, papa," she said, tears welling in her eyes. "Oh how I miss you both."

The image of the moonrat man flashed through her mind and Tarah shivered. She ran her hand back across her chest, tracing where the creature had cut her. What a vivid dream that had been. The way its face had looked, part man, part moonrat . . . was her imagination that good to come up with something like that? And the voice that had spoken in her head at the end, it was the mother of the moonrats threatening her just as she had the night Tarah had run away.

"But she's dead. Destroyed," Tarah said and was frightened at how unsure her voice sounded. *They'll never truly be gone, Tarah.* That's what her papa had said in the dream. What had he meant?

Dreams are just dreams, Tarah, Grampa Rolf reminded her.

"Right." She shrugged away the sense of dread that boiled in her chest and focused on the smell of the food the woman had brought her. She lifted the cover on the platter.

Slices of sausages and that strange vegetable from the night before were piled on one side of the platter, while a half loaf of bread sat on the other. Tarah tore off the top of the bread and wrapped it around some of the sausage and vegetable, then took it with her into the bedroom to eat while she dressed.

It was delicious. The sausage was spicy, but the vegetable had a mellowness that tempered the heat. Energy flooded her limbs and with each bite the feeling of dread faded. By the time she started buckling on her armor, Tarah had pushed the dream away. She was eager to get going. She could be back in Sampo by mid day, or if she pushed it, back home by nightfall. Home was what she really needed right now.

She pulled on her quiver and regretfully strapped her broken bow to her pack. Just as she was about to leave the room, she saw the sword on the floor by the bed. Tarah put one hand to her forehead. How had she forgotten about the sword? She should have shown it to that guard captain she'd met the day before.

"I'll have to find him on my way out." Tarah picked the sword up and laid it on the bed, then headed back to the table to wrap up the rest of the food for her journey. She was just piling the last of the sausage on the remaining bread when there was another loud knock. Tarah felt a slight jolt of fear at first, then chuckled at herself as she answered it.

"Tarah Woodblade! So good to see you again!" said the broad shouldered man standing at the door.

"Captain Riveren," Tarah replied, shaking his hand. The man had fiery red hair and a pointed beard and wore a leather vest over a short-sleeved chainmail shirt that exposed his heavily muscled arms. Tarah would have been freezing wearing that garb in the chill morning air, but he looked at ease.

"That's Captain Commander Riveren," Djeri reminded. The dwarf was standing beside Riveren and was wearing the same suit of polished platemail as the day before. His green eyes were filled with energy this morning.

"That's fine, Jerry," Riveren said offhand as he looked Tarah over with penetrating blue eyes. "How long has it been?" His smile was infectious and Tarah couldn't help but return it.

"Nearly two years," she replied. "I ain't been back here since Captain Alphonze died."

Riveren's smile faded slightly. "That's right. I saw you at

the funeral. Wow, it has been a long time."

Tarah nodded. "I guess I just haven't had many reasons to come back since then."

"I see," he said. "Well, it's good to see you anyway."

"Yeah. You too," she said and had to force her eyes away from his. Riveren was one of the reasons she hadn't been back to the school since Alphonze's death. The captain was too handsome. She couldn't think straight when he was around and Grampa Rolf had told her not to let boys be a distraction.

A good looking man can turn a young lady's mind to mush, Papa agreed and Grampa Rolf added, *Tarah Woodblade is never infatuated.*

"I heard about what you were up to during the war," Riveren said, his grin returning to full force. "Fantastic work, that. Some of the Pinewood refugees you saved stayed with us during the siege. They told us about how you led away hundreds of creatures so they could escape."

"Yeah, how did you survive that?" Djeri asked.

"Skill," she replied. Tarah's guilt rose at the lie and she added, "And luck, I suppose. My memory of that night's kind of a blur."

"Never let it be said Tarah Woodblade isn't humble," Djeri remarked with a twinkle in his eye and Riveren elbowed him.

Tarah Woodblade is never humble, Grampa Rolf agreed. *Not unless you think it'll help you look good.*

"Well, thanks for coming to see me off," Tarah said. "I was just packing some lunch for the road home."

"About that," Riveren said. "I was actually hoping you would delay your return for awhile."

Tarah paused, "Why's that?"

"We want to offer you a job," Djeri said.

Tarah's business sense perked up, but with it came a strange uneasiness. "You two?"

"Actually, the Battle Academy," Riveren said and his smile was gone, replaced by a businesslike seriousness. "We have a contract to complete, but our available personnel roster is really thin. Jerry and I think you would be perfect for the job."

Tarah blinked. Surely he wasn't serious. "The academy wants to hire me to complete one of their contracts?"

"No! Well, not exactly," Djeri said. He paused as some students wearing mage robes walked by. "Can we discuss this inside?"

"Okay. Come in," Tarah said and that feeling of uneasiness grew as the two guards stepped in. What was it they didn't want anyone to hear?

Riveren sat down at the small round table and Djeri stood next to him, gesturing for Tarah to take the other chair. The two of them were so wide-shouldered that the area around the table looked quite small. Tarah hesitated for a moment before pulling the chair out a few feet and sitting down.

She leaned back and folded her arms, fixing them with a calculating stare. "So from the way you're doing this, I take it the academy wants to hire me to complete their contract, but they want me to do it quietly."

"No." Riveren chuckled uncomfortably. "It's not like that. We don't pawn off our contracts on others. We just want to hire you as a . . . specialist to assist one of our own."

Tarah's reluctance increased at the thought of working with others. "How many other 'specialists' will be on this job?"

"None," Riveren assured her. "It's a two person job."

"And why do you need my help?" she asked dubiously.

He leaned forward and rested his elbows on the table. "We need a tracker."

"You guys don't have enough trackers?" The academy trained some of the best trackers and scouts in the known lands.

"Not here at the Mage School," Djeri explained. "Most of them are already out on assignments and the rest are helping with the rebuild. Besides, our client suggested you specifically."

"Your client suggested me?" Tarah said, baffled. "How did they know I was here?"

"Our client is one of the wizard high council," Riveren explained. "The job came up in our meeting last night and when Djeri mentioned you were staying the night, they wanted you to be part of it."

Wizards are crafty folk, her papa warned.

Wizards have money, Grampa Rolf rebutted.

"Which wizard is this?" Tarah had met only a handful of them in her lifetime.

"Wizard Valtrek," Djeri said and Riveren winced.

"We're not really supposed to reveal the identity of the client until the job is taken," Riveren said, giving the dwarf an admonishing look.

Tarah frowned. "I've never heard of this Wizard Valtrek."

"Well, he's heard of you," Djeri said. "He was quite excited when he heard you were on the grounds."

"I don't know . . ." she said and the two of them stared at her, Djeri's green eyes pleading and Riveren's handsome face beseeching. Tarah realized that she wore a scowl on her own face and quickly smoothed her expression. "What's the job?"

"Well," Riveren reached into a pocket in his vest and pulled out a folded page of parchment. He opened it and slid it across the table to her. "Before we can tell you, you'll need to sign this."

"You're kidding," she said and quickly read the verbiage. "You can't tell me what the job is unless I sign an agreement saying I won't tell anyone I was offered the job?"

"Wizard Valtrek is very thorough." Riveren said with a shrug.

"He thinks the contract is sensitive in nature," Djeri explained. "Look, I know this must stink like turds the way we're doing this, but trust me, the academy doesn't take dark jobs."

Secret jobs can mean big coin, said Grampa Rolf excitedly.

"Yeah, but that's usually because they're dangerous," she mumbled, her skin crawling.

"What?" Riveren asked.

"I'll need a quill and ink if you want me to sign this," she said, pushing the feeling of uneasiness away. After all, what could it hurt to listen?

"Here, use this," Djeri said. He handed her a narrow metal tube with a wooden cap on one end. "It's called an ink cylinder. One of the wizards brought them back from Olivera. Everybody at the Mage School is using them now."

She raised an eyebrow as she pulled off the wooden cap. A tiny brush stuck out from the end of the tube, glistening with ink. *Grampa Rolf would have loved this*, she thought as she signed the bottom of the parchment. *He could have made a fortune selling these*. She slid it across the table to Riveren. "So what's the job?"

"Have you heard of rogue horses?" Riveren asked.

"Yes," Tarah said. "Magic beasts. But aren't they just legends?"

The two guards looked at each other and Djeri chuckled. "They're real enough. I've seen a few of them up close over the years. In fact, we had two staying here at the Mage School during the siege."

"You had two rogue horses here?" she said. Evidently fighting wasn't all she'd missed during the war.

"Those two have nothing to do with this job." Riveren said. "There's another one out there. Wizard Valtrek has received reports from both Razbeck and Dremaldria that there's a man traveling around hiring trackers to try and track this particular one down."

Tarah nodded slowly, thinking of the man that gave her the drawings that sat in her pack. "And what does the wizard want me to do?"

"He wants you to find it first," Djeri said.

"There are actually several parts to the job," Riveren added. "Your first priority is finding and tracking this rogue horse. Secondly, he wants you to destroy any tracks you find so that this man or any of the people he's hired don't find it. Third, you should keep an ear out for this man while you search. Any information as to who the man is or what his intentions towards the rogue horse are should be reported back to Wizard Valtrek."

"What do I do with this rogue horse when I find it?" she asked.

"You do nothing with it," Riveren said. "You simply report back to Wizard Valtrek when you find it."

Tarah ran one hand through her hair. "How am I supposed to do that? This thing could be anywhere. By the time I came back to the Mage School it could be long gone."

"You let me take care of that part," Djeri said.

Tarah raised an eyebrow and pointed at the dwarf. "You're coming?"

"That's right, just the two of you." Riveren answered with a smile. "Tarah Woodblade and Jerry the Looker on an academy mission. I'm getting chills."

Jerry the Looker? Tarah snorted. "Yeah. Sorry, but lugging

around a dwarf in full platemail ain't gonna make it easy for me to track this thing down."

Djeri's face reddened. "You won't need to 'lug' me anywhere."

You need to be nice if you want to get along with people, her papa chided.

Tarah ignored the voice and gave the dwarf a frank stare. "Look, this ain't meant to offend, Jerry, but I gotta keep a certain pace while I'm tracking and you'll slow me down. Besides, the clanking of your armor will scare any beast, rogue or not, away."

Djeri's eyes narrowed, but before he could respond, Riveren said, "Just a minute, Tarah. Jerry is a veteran member of the Defense Guild. He can keep any pace you can set. As for his armor-."

"Have you heard me 'clank' even once?" Djeri interrupted and as Tarah thought about it, she realized that she hadn't. "And this isn't even my traveling armor. The suit I'll be wearing is padded for stealth. As for any other objections you can come up with, girl, they're not worth turds. I've been adventuring for a hundred years. I know what I'm doing."

"Turds?" Tarah said, then shook her head. "Fine. If you say you can keep up, I'll believe you."

"Does that mean you'll do it?" Riveren asked with a hopeful smile.

His blue eyes glinted charmingly, but Tarah wasn't quite ready to answer that question. "Do we have a description of this rogue horse?"

Riveren nodded. "One of Valtrek's sources saw it briefly. The front end of it's some kind of ape-like thing and its rear end is like a mountain cat." He pulled out another sheet of parchment and slid it towards her. "The tracks look like this."

Tarah struggled to keep her gaze indifferent. The drawings were very similar to the ones in her pack. How much should she tell them? "I've . . . seen these tracks before."

"Where?" Djeri asked in surprise.

"On the way here from Sampo, right by the place where I burned the trolls," she said. "They'd been there for a long time, maybe a few rains, but it was hard to tell. They were covered in troll slime."

Djeri rubbed his beard musingly. "It has only rained a couple of times since the end of the war."

"But it's a starting point," Tarah said.

"The report Wizard Valtrek had is more recent than that," Riveren said. "He says that his source saw the rogue horse two days ago just east of Pinewood. He has a map I can give you. That is if you're taking the job."

"Just east . . ." Her house was in that area. Tarah felt a strange certainty that this was something she was supposed to do. Still, she resisted. "How much will this pay?"

"Two gold dremals a week," Riveren said. "That's nearly full graduate pay."

Gold is gold, said Grampa Rolf.

"I'll do it," Tarah agreed.

"Good!" the Captain Commander said with a wide smile and stood. "I'll grab the contract while you two gather the provisions you need. I'll meet you back at the gate in an hour with your horses."

"Horses?" Djeri said with distaste.

"You'll need them if you want to get there quickly," Riveren said.

"I'd rather ride a turd," the dwarf grumbled.

"I don't think that's physically possible, Jerry," Riveren said with a chuckle.

"I'm not much for horses, Riveren. You know that," Djeri said.

"I agree with the dwarf," Tarah said. "Can't tell you how many times I've been tracking something for folks and we get to a tight squeeze or a steep climb and they're like, 'What the hell are we supposed to do with the horses?'."

Djeri laughed and Riveren sighed. "You're going to need something to help with your provisions at least. I'll talk to the stableman." He stood to leave, but Tarah reached out to stop him.

"Wait, there's something I wanted to show you." Tarah walked to the bedroom and retrieved the sword, then brought it back to the table. "I found this sword in the hands of a bandit northwest of here." She unsheathed the blade and laid it on the table in front of them. "Do you have a way of knowing if someone is looking for it?"

Riveren froze, the smile falling from his face.

Djeri's eyes were wide with recognition. "That's Tamboor the Fearless' blade."

"He's called Master Tolivar now, Jerry," Riveren corrected, his voice sounding haunted as he reached one hand out to touch the hilt.

"Right," the dwarf said.

"Tamboor's . . . This is Meredith?" Tarah asked, swallowing at the thought that she'd been carrying such a legendary sword.

"Yeah," said Riveren, sadness in his eyes. "I was there on the last day of the war when this sword was lost on the battlefield."

"Is he dead?" she asked.

"No," Djeri assured her. "He's fine."

Tarah's brow furrowed in confusion. If he was alive, then why was Riveren's attitude so solemn? "Then I guess he'll be wanting it back," she said slowly.

"I don't know." Riveren said. He slid the sword back into the ugly sheath and picked it up. "But that's his decision to make. I'll send it to him." He turned his gaze on her. "I suppose you're wanting a finders fee."

"Well, I-." Her grampa's training screamed yes, but she found herself saying, "'Course not. I'm just glad to return it."

Riveren gave her an appreciative nod and placed a hand on her shoulder. "Thank you. I'll-um, be seeing you at the front gate in an hour then. Jerry will help you get the supplies you need." He gave her a brief smile, then opened the door and left.

Tarah stared after him in puzzlement. "What was that about?"

"His friend died while wielding that sword," Djeri said somberly. He gave her a calculating look. "I'm surprised you didn't ask for a reward."

Without knowing why, Tarah said, "My papa told me all about that sword. Tamboor the Fearless used to be a friend of his."

"Oh?" the dwarf said, he looked like he wanted to say more, but he didn't.

"Well I guess we should get our provisions together, eh Jerry?"

"Yeah." The dwarf started to leave but paused in the

doorway. He sighed and turned around. "Listen, girl. We're going to be working together for awhile and there's one think I want to get clear before we get any further. My name's not Jerry. It's Djeri."

"Oh," Tarah said. "But Riveren was calling you Jerry."

"Yeah, I have to put up with it from him because he's the captain, but I'm not putting up with it from you." Tarah's mouth tightened and the dwarf raised his hands defensively. "Look, I don't mean any offense. It's just that I've seen some relatives of mine put up with it and next thing you know, no one says your name right."

"I guess I can see how that would get annoying," she said.

"Okay?" he said. "So again, it's Djeri."

"So . . ." She squinted as she sounded it out. "It's kind of like Jerry, but not quite?"

"It's really not that close," the dwarf insisted and spoke his name slowly. "It's Djeri."

"Okay, but," Tarah frowned. "Do I really have to roll the R? I mean, I don't want to insult you or nothing, but I always feel dumb trying to roll my Rs."

He stomped his foot. "Blast it, girl, it's not that hard. Djeri! It's not a full roll of the R. More like a half roll."

"And there's a duhjuh at the front?" she said. "So . . . Djeri?"

"Good. Well . . . close enough. It'll do," said the dwarf. He shrugged and shook his head as he walked out the door. "This could be a long trip."

As Tarah followed after him she couldn't help but agree.

Chapter Five

Arcon sipped the watery ale in his tankard. His eyes scanned the the tavern for any hint of his pursuers. Mallad was a dangerous place for him to be. Of course all of Alberri was dangerous for him right now. He just hoped that his pursuers wouldn't think to look for him in the heart of their domain.

He had picked a perfect spot to wait, a booth near the side exit, slightly hidden in the shadows, but with a clear view of the front door. There were three such spots in this place, a fact that had first attracted him to it the week before. The roughly carved sign hanging outside the tavern read, 'The Mallad Duck'. Arcon knew the name was a bad pun, but that was unimportant. This was a place to hide from the eyes of the city and that's what Arcon needed the most right now.

"You aren't the only one 'ducking' here."

Arcon ignored the voice in his head. She knew that he was aware of the tavern's other occupants. Magic was highly regulated in this city and the authorities had ways of knowing when spells of power were used, but there were ways to hide magic. Arcon could sense the low thrum of hidden spells in several areas of the tavern. He couldn't see the composition of the spells with his mage sight, but they were there.

Arcon had several spells going himself. One darkened the shadows around him while the other disguised his face. Neither spell would be noticeable by any but the most experienced of wizards. Arcon knew more about hiding magic than most. After all, he had been doing it for a long time, ever since he first picked up the moonrat eye.

"You had an excellent teacher," the female voice reminded, her deep and throaty voice as loud as if she were speaking right in

his ear.

He snorted softly. Her statement was true enough, but only because he had spent a lot of that time hiding his magic from her. *Leave me alone, Mellinda. None of the magic here is being directed on me.* He had protective magic of his own. He would know the moment someone tried anything.

She fumed in silence over his casual use of her name and Arcon smiled. As far as he was concerned, being able to needle her without punishment was the one perk he had with their current . . . situation.

Arcon's thoughts were interrupted as the front door to the tavern opened briefly. A shaft of sunlight penetrated the darkness, highlighting the figure of a lone man wearing a long tan coat with a high collar. The man paused in the light for a moment, his head moving back and forth as he scanned the dim confines of the tavern. Then the light vanished as the door shut behind him and he walked down the stairs to stand in the shadows by the bar. Arcon couldn't see the newcomer's face, but he wasn't too worried. His pursuers always ran in groups of three or more.

"*You don't know that for sure,*" Mellinda said. "*We should leave.*"

They know what I can do, he reminded her. In fact his pursuers knew too much about him. The last two times they had come close to finding him, the dark wizards had been accompanied by either archers or dwarves wearing some kind of charm protecting them from fire magic. Fire was his main talent. *Besides, I can't spook every time someone enters. It's more dangerous out in the streets where I can't keep track of everyone.*

The newcomer left the bar and moved to a table not far from where Arcon sat. He held a drink in one hand and didn't so much as glance in Arcon's direction. He sat stiffly in a chair facing away from Arcon and took sips from his drink as he moved his head, scanning the darkness on the far side of the bar.

"*Staying on the move has its own benefits,*" she urged.

He let out a small sigh and took another swallow of the weak ale. *Don't worry. I only have to wait here one more hour and then we can go back to the scholar's estate.*

"*And wait there for how long this time?*" she grumped.

As long as it takes. He is our way out of this, remember?

This was your idea.

"*Of course I remember. It's just that this waiting is tedious.*"

Arcon didn't disagree. Over the last week, they had spent over six hours a day waiting at the scholar's estate in hopes that he would deign to see them. *The stewards assured me that today would be a better day to gain an audience.*

"*Of course they did.*" Sarcasm dripped from her voice.

The newcomer had stopped drinking. His tankard was laying on its side on the table in front of him and he was sitting completely still, his back arched as if he had been straining at something. Arcon began to wonder if he were dead. He reached out with a tiny trail of air magic, searching for a heartbeat, but then the man cocked his head and Arcon saw his shoulders move slightly with the inhale of a breath.

Arcon shook his head slightly. Everyone acted strange in this place.

Even if the stewards were lying, you know it's much safer inside that estate than anywhere else in Mallad. The scholars were the real power in Mallad and no one dared to cross them. Even the dark wizards left them alone. *You know this is our only way out of this.*

"*Of course, dear one,*" she replied, her voice was deep and throaty again. "*You know best.*"

Arcon felt a rush of pleasure rise within him at the sound of approval in her voice. Bile rose in his throat at the unwelcome feeling. He hated the fact that she was able to manipulate him even without her powers. He had let his guard down again.

"*Don't react like that, my dear. I was being quite sincere,*" Mellinda cooed. "*You have grown much since we first met. The ordeals you have been through made you stronger.*"

The ordeals you put me through, he growled mentally and slammed his tankard down on the table top. The rap of the metal against the wood was loud enough to cause a shifting in the shadows at the other tables. *Leave me be, you dead witch!*

"*Arcon-.*" Mellinda's voice sounded concerned.

No! Arcon raged. *You stay silent unless I ask to speak with you. I won't hesitate to lock you away in the darkness again.*

"*Look at the newcomer,*" she insisted. There was a quiver

in her voice.

A surge of fear rose within Arcon's chest. The man was looking right at him. His body was still facing away from Arcon as stiff as ever, but his head had somehow swiveled all the way around. His eyes were large; too large for his face.

"Don't look too close!" she shouted. *"Look away. Don't let on that you noticed!"*

Arcon did his best to keep his expression blank as he forced his eyes to slide away from the man's face and focus on a point in the darkness beyond. The man blinked once with enormous eyelids and his nostrils flared. Then a laugh rang out a few tables over and his head swung back around to follow the sound.

Arcon swallowed. *How did he do that? How did he swing his head around like a . . . blasted owl?*

"Because it's not a man, you idiot!" she spat, her tone full of panic.

What is he? Arcon asked.

"Just get out of here while it's not looking!" she shouted. Arcon began to slide out of his chair. *"And don't let it hear you!"*

Arcon muted his magic as much as he could, then quickly spun threads of air around his body and the chair beneath him, creating a sound-proof cushion as he slid the chair back and slowly made his way to the nearest exit. He spun another thread of air to absorb the light around him, giving him a protective blanket of darkness as he paused in the shadows by the doorway and peered back at the newcomer.

"Get out!" Mellinda demanded.

But Arcon didn't dare open the door. The light would give him away and whatever it was had already noticed his absence. It stood, its head swiveling as its overlarge eyes scanned the room.

Its bizarre behavior didn't go unnoticed this time. A loud crash rang out as a table was overturned near the front of the tavern and two men bolted for the main entrance. Arcon could sense the muted cloud of magic surrounding them. The thing darted after the two men. Cries of outrage filled the air as it threw chairs and the people occupying them aside in its haste.

Light flooded the room as the two men threw open the front door and Arcon slipped out the rear. He stepped into the alleyway beyond and let the threads of air fall away as the door shut behind him. Another spell shifted his disguise, changing his hair to a deep red and turning his cloak gray. He ran towards the busy street ahead, not slowing until he reached the edge of the alleyway.

He blended into the crowd, walking away from the tavern as swiftly as he dared. Shouts rang out from the front of the building and the people around him slowed down, turning to look. Arcon kept walking and the shouts turned to screams. To Arcon's relief, the people of Mallad weren't stupid. Most of the crowd began to run away from the screams and he ran right along with them.

What was that? he demanded.

"*That,*" Mellinda said. "*Was a basilisk.*"

No. Arcon paled. He resisted the urge to turn and look behind him.

He had learned about them at the Mage School. Basilisks were creatures with the ability to mask the true shape of their bodies. No one was quite sure how they did it, but they were adept at blending into their surroundings and the wealthy sometimes used them as assassins. Fortunately they were very rare. Arcon had never considered that one would ever have a reason to hunt him down.

Surely you're mistaken.

"*There's no mistaking what I saw. Blast it, I should have noticed right away. The way the thing was turning its head to look around instead of just moving its eyes. They have a bird-like way of moving if you know what you're looking for.*"

The screams had faded into the background and Arcon was able to slow down, breathing a little easier. *Its eyes were all wrong.*

"*Yes. They are good at hiding but have difficulty copying the human body. Their true form is too different. They can never get the faces quite right,*" Mellinda said. She chuckled darkly. "*People used to send them after me quite often during the height of my power. Luckily I was hard to kill.*"

Arcon suppressed a shiver. In a very real way, the witch that shared his mind was far more frightening than any creature he could come across. At least for the moment she had no choice but to be on his side.

At the next major cross section, he turned the corner and headed towards the scholar's estate at a leisurely walk. *Perhaps it was after those other men. The ones that ran.*

"*I doubt that. We were simply lucky that they ran. The low levels of magic in the place may have confused it momentarily, but you didn't fool it with your sly 'look away' maneuver. It was going to follow you the moment you tried to leave.*" She sighed. "*In fact, I would say it's already figured out its mistake. It is likely that it's on our trail right now.*"

Should I run again? he asked. He was only a half mile or so from the entrance to the Gnome Homeland. The scholar's estate was just inside and no dark wizards dared operate inside the homeland.

"*It wouldn't do any good. The dark wizards might not enter, but a basilisk wouldn't be afraid. It would just sneak up and kill us while we waited to see the scholar, then take the rings and be gone.*"

Arcon clutched the secret pocket that had been sown to the inside of his shirt, feeling the lump that was the Rings of Stardeon. *I'll hide my trail then. What spell do I need to use?*

"*It's not as simple as hiding your tracks or disguising your body,*" she said. "*Not now that it's seen you. Once a basilisk has identified you, it's over. This thing has more than your scent. It has your magical essence in its mind and probably that of the rings as well.*"

"But-." Arcon said aloud, his mind in a panic. *So what are you saying? We're dead? I should just give up now?*

"*No, you fool, but there's no use hiding. We need to find a place to fight,*" Mellinda said, her voice determined. "*And we don't have much time. We need to find it quick.*"

Arcon glanced around, looking for a vacant alleyway. Alleys were less frequent in this part of the city. The tall buildings were stacked right next to each other, several in a row sharing walls. *Fight a basilisk? And in the city? How do I do it? Any magic I use powerful enough to fight with will alert the guards.*

"*Very true and it will take a lot of magic to kill this thing. They are more resistant to elemental magic than dwarves. If you kill it, every magic user in miles will know it.*"

I don't have that much magic. Admittedly, he was well above average in fire and his air and water talents were decent, but he wasn't on par with the greats.

Arcon turned down a long alleyway that looked perfect for his needs. There were no vagrants and only a few windows faced inwards. It would have to work.

"You must put on the rings," she said.

Arcon froze. *No. We'll have to fight it without them.*

"You know it's the only way. When you kill the basilisk the surge of power will alert the watchers in the city, but once you take the rings back off, they will have no way of tracing that level of magic to you."

Her logic was true, but Arcon hated the rings. He'd been forced to wear them twice before, each time to fight off whatever force the dark wizards sent against him. The surge of power was tremendous, but in his mind the power was far overweighed by the hungry essence of the things, sucking at him, draining his vitality and leaving his body and his fingers . . .

"Ewzad Vriil found the way around that," Mellinda reminded him.

Arcon was well aware. The wizard had overcome that problem by turning the power of the rings inward and becoming one with them. But that situation was permanent. The only way to remove the rings after that had been death.

"Never that," he said aloud.

"Then you'll have to put up with their hunger," she replied in exasperation.

Arcon stopped half way down the alley and pressed himself against the wall at the joining of two buildings. He reached out with air magic and pulled the shadows around him, absorbing the light, then reached under his shirt and opened the secret pocket, letting the rings spill into his hand. He shivered at the weight of them.

There were two sets of five rings, one for each finger, and every one of them fixed with a different precious gem. Each set was linked together by gold chains. When they were worn, their wielder's magic was boosted exponentially and in addition would give him the power to manipulate the body of any creature, man or beast.

"Put them on!" she urged.

They're tangled. The chains had wrapped around each other. He began untangling them, but the magic he was using made it hard for him to see the rings in his own hands.

Mellinda gasped. Someone stood in the mouth of the alleyway. This person was shorter and thicker than the man in the tavern and he wore a different coat, but the way he scanned the alley, moving and cocking his head, was the same. *"That's it! Put on the rings!"*

Arcon had the first set untangled and began shoving them on each finger. The rings moved, becoming larger or smaller in order to conform to the size of his fingers. As the rings went on, each finger began to twist and writhe bonelessly as if each digit was an individual serpent with a mind of its own. A rush of power accompanied the change, but Arcon could feel the rings feeding on him as the flesh of his body withered, tightening on his bones as if he hadn't eaten for weeks.

The basilisk started moving down the alleyway towards him, its steps slow and methodical as if it didn't see him in the shadows.

"Put them on faster or both of us are dead!" she commanded.

You're already dead, he pointed out. Putting on the last set of rings was the hardest part. The writhing fingers on his other hand didn't want to obey and it took a large amount of concentration to get them to hold still while he put the last rings on. The creature was only a few steps away when he finally got the last ring on.

The enormous surge of energy that accompanied that last ring made Arcon forget his fear. His puny masking spells melted away and he extended one squirming hand towards the creature. His fingers undulated in unison as a pillar of fire erupted from the ground under the basilisk's feet.

The fire roared upwards in a column thirty feet high. The sudden heat caused the windows facing the alley to crack. A squeal ripped from the creature's engulfed form, but it continued towards him.

Arcon formed a wall of solidified air between him and the basilisk, keeping it at bay while he increased the intensity of the fire. The city's watchers wouldn't be able to ignore a surge of magic of this magnitude. Arcon knew he had to end this quickly.

The basilisk only slowed. One singed hand began to push

into the wall of air, its digits thinning and sharpening into talons. There was a sharp crack as the rocks making up the walls of the buildings around them exploded, peppering the alley with heated shards of rock.

"*That won't stop it,*" Mellinda warned. "*You're killing it too slowly!*"

"What do you suggest!" he snapped. The basilisk continued to push its arm through the wall of air. Its claws were only a foot away from his face.

"*Reach into its body with the magic of the rings!*"

"I don't know how," he shouted back.

"*I do. Let me take over!*" she suggested.

Arcon laughed. "Never. I'd rather die right now."

"*I don't have my powers and this is your body,*" she urged. "*You could always wrest back control.*"

"Yeah, right," he said. He took a step back and increased the thickness of the wall of air. The basilisk pushed its head out of the blaze and into the wall. The burnt remains of its face reformed into a bird-like beak. Arcon winced. Even so, it wasn't as frightening as the prospect of Mellinda taking over his mind. *Just tell me what to do.*

"*That could take too long. We could die while I try to explain!*"

Then talk quickly, because I wasn't joking when I said I'd rather be dead.

Mellinda snarled in anger and said, "It's similar to healing magic. Reach into its body as if you wanted to probe an injury, just try to send your magic through the rings themselves as if they were a tool."

Arcon blinked as he processed her instructions, then did as she said, picturing the magic flowing through the rings and out of the undulating fingers at the end of his hands. His energy pierced the basilisk's flesh. What he found was confusing. The thing had no organs, just unformed tissue, except for the muscle and bone in its spine and limbs. The intense heat of the fire spell ate away at its form, but at a slow rate.

"*Don't try to make sense of its body make-up. Just paralyze the thing!*"

That was a spell Arcon understood. He expertly wove an

intricate latticework of air and water and sent it through every fiber in the creature's strange body, holding it in place. It stopped pushing through the wall of air, but the basilisk immediately fought at the spell, its very flesh rejecting the magic.

"Blast! I'd forgotten. Stardeon had the same problem with the creature. Find its brain. It won't look like a human brain but it's a cluster of nerves inside the thing. It's the only part of a basilisk that never changes, no matter the form."

It took Arcon a moment to find it. The creature's head was filled with unformed flesh, as was its chest. He finally located the knot of nerves that Mellinda had described deep in the creature's hip, one of the places least likely for an attacker to target.

"Destroy it!"

Arcon's paralyzation spell had deteriorated to the point that the basilisk was pushing through the wall again. Only its rear leg was still engulfed by his pillar of flame. Quickly, he tried to burn the area, but its flesh was too resistant. Finally he simply latched onto the nerve cluster and pulled as hard as he could.

The basilisk's brain shot out of its body and ricocheted down the alleyway, a pulsing lump of pink flesh. Its body trembled, then froze. Its tissues began to harden, stiffening until they were solid as rock.

What the?

"You did it," Mellinda said with a laugh of triumph. Arcon found a smile of his own creeping along his pale face. *"That's what happens when a basilisk dies. They turn to stone, statues of their own moment of death."*

The creature's final form was quite hideous, part man, part beast. Its twisted head was frozen in a soundless screech, a forked stone tongue escaping its open beak. It's clawed arms were extended, the joints on one of its legs bent in the wrong direction.

Mellinda chuckled grimly. *"I used to keep them around as decorations in my main palace."*

Arcon's smile faded.

"You! Stop!" came a gruff voice from the far alley exit.

Arcon turned just in time to throw up a spell deflecting several ropes of air that had been cast around him. Several guards and a man wearing wizard's robes stood blocking his way. They wore the livery of the Mallad guard.

"*Just kill them*," Mellinda commanded. "*Best do it now before more arrive. They won't be able to trace it back to you once the rings are off.*"

Arcon wasn't so sure. He gestured and another column of fire rose, blocking off the rest of the alley and obscuring them from the armed men at the entrance. Another wall of air went up, holding back the heat of the blaze. Several arrows thumped into it, hanging in mid air while their fletchings burned.

"*That was foolish*," she growled. "*Now you've trapped us here. There are probably even more guards.*"

Arcon turned and faced the wall of the alley, then gestured with a slicing motion, sending a razor thin blade of air through the stone. He made two vertical cuts, then one horizontal one into the wall, then pushed it inward.

No one was inside the building as the rectangular block of wall crashed down. The people inside must have evacuated. It was a workshop and the fire outside had heated the room, causing several tables and some shelving to start on fire. Arcon built a shield of cooled air around himself and stepped into the room, leaving the alleyway blazing.

"*Very well. So you're not always as foolish as you seem*," Mellinda said.

Arcon walked deeper into the building and cut a similar rectangle through the far wall. Shouts rang out as the stone crashed down. It was another shared wall and this building was full of people. It looked to be an eating establishment. Arcon caught a glimpse of several tall gnomes and stewards wearing green sashes before he sent multiple weaves of air into the room, absorbing the light and turning the room pitch black.

While people yelled and stumbled around in surprise, Arcon made his way to the front exit and stood just to the side of the door as he began removing the rings from his fingers. As he did so, the vitality returned to his body, filling out his flesh and returning the health to his face. The power also faded. The roaring pillars of fire in the alleyway vanished. So did the walls of air. The last thing to go was the blackness that enveloped the building Arcon stood in. Light returned to the room as he removed the last ring from the thumb on his left hand.

While people looked about in shock, some of them picking

themselves up off the floor, Arcon placed the rings back into the hidden pocket inside his shirt. He wasn't worried that he'd be recognized. The man that stood next to the door looked very different from the emaciated mage that had burst into the room. His clothes were a different color and his hair was a deep auburn.

Nevertheless, he quickly exited through the door and walked into the street beyond. The road was filled with guards and Arcon did his best to look dazed as several of them pushed past him into the building. He joined the crowd of onlookers watching as Mallad's official mages put out the fires.

Chapter Six

Arcon watched with his mage sight as the mages, their robes emblazoned with the Mallad crest, worked efficiently. They had the fires on the exterior of the buildings extinguished within seconds, one of them sending gouts of water into the burning sections while another pulled the very oxygen out of the air around the blaze. They were well-trained, but the way they cast the spells was different than Arcon was used to. This likely meant they were from Alberri's mage school.

"*What are you doing? Just get out of here*," Mellinda urged. Arcon obliged her, turning away from the scene and continuing on his way towards the section of the city known as the Gnome Homeland and the scholar's estate.

He kept his jaw clenched nervously for the first few minutes, but to his relief, no guards shouted at him. *I was gauging how strong they were. I need to know what I'm up against if they're going to be after me as well.*

"*Don't be ridiculous. They don't know who they're after*," Mellinda assured him. "*Besides, the basilisk statue in the alleyway will just confuse them further. All they'll know is that the dark wizards are somehow involved.*"

Right, he replied. She had a point. Alberri's constant problem with dark wizards was the reason they kept such a close watch on magic in the first place.

Still, he waited until he was sure that he was too far for the wizards to sense it before he sent a muted spell through his clothing, deflecting all dirt and ash as he walked. By the time he approached the gate to the Gnome Homeland, he looked as clean and immaculate as if he had come fresh from a bath.

"*You cast that spell differently from the way I learned it*,"

Mellinda remarked.

The spell they teach at the Mage School takes much longer.
Arcon replied. *I learned this version from watching Ewzad Vriil.
The man never truly bathed.*

The capital of Alberri was in actuality one enormous city
split into two very different sections. Mallad was the eastern half
of the city. It was elevated above the other, covering the top of a
raised plateau in the desert highlands. The western half consisted
of the Gnome Homeland and it covered the plateau's slope and the
lowlands below.

Mallad was the newer, but more run down section of the
capital. This was where the tradesmen, the nobility, and the palaces
of Alberri's human king were located. The King of Alberri was
little more than a figurehead, though. Everyone knew that the true
authority of Alberri came from the gnome scholars in the
homeland.

Arcon was relieved to see that the line at the gate was only
ten people long. On past days, the line had stretched a block. If
only he had a steward's sash or scholar's badge he wouldn't have
had to wait at all. But there was nothing to be done about that so he
stood and waited his turn at the guard station. He put on a calm
face, ignoring the sounds of commotion down the street. The
wizards had put the fires out, but smoke still filled the air as the
onlookers were questioned.

Finally it was Arcon's turn at the gate. The homeland
guards were very thorough, forcing him to remove his cloak and
making a close inspection of the dagger he wore at his waist. Still,
it went relatively quickly compared to the first time he'd been
through. Arcon had learned quite quickly what was and wasn't
allowed in the Gnome Homeland. The guards gave him a
temporary pass and let him through the gates. He slid the paper
into his pocket and hurried on his way, knowing it only gave him
leave to stay in the homeland until dark.

"*They are a lot more particular now, than when I was last
here,*" Mellinda remarked.

"Yeah I know. You say it every time we come through," he
mumbled. "It's been a thousand years, what do you expect?"

"*It doesn't look much different, though,*" she said and he
could tell that the reminder of her age stung her. "*The gnomes*

haven't changed much."

Arcon shook his head. *Of course not. Some of them were probably around before you were imprisoned. Do you see any familiar faces? Gnomes you tortured, perhaps?*

She slipped into a sulky silence as he came upon the huge entrance to the estates of scholarly house Mur. Arcon smirked, knowing that her silence wouldn't last long. The longer they were stuck together the more talkative she got.

"What do you expect?" she snapped. *"There's nothing else for me to do, but talk to you. My mind used to be vast, my thoughts endless. I could speak with hundreds of servants at once. Now it seems like I can barely hold two thoughts together."*

Arcon raised one eyebrow, surprised that she had admitted it. He took no more than four steps into the gardens at the front of the estate before a green-sashed steward was standing in front of him.

"Oh, it's you. The mage," the steward said. She was a sour-faced human woman, but Arcon thought she had likely been quite a beauty in her younger days. He guessed she was now somewhere around her fortieth year. Like all stewards, her attire was plain, just a white robe and her long brown hair was tied up in a bun. A green sash crossed her body starting at her right shoulder, designating that she was one of the stewards whose job it was to take care of the physical needs of the scholar.

"Good afternoon, Steward Molly," Arcon said, giving her the most charming smile he could muster.

"You don't give up easily, do you?" she replied, and his charm must have worked because a slight smile of her own curled the corners of her lips.

"I believe that once all is said and done Scholar Aloysius will be quite glad that I have been this persistent. I am bringing him an offer that falls squarely in the realm of his focus," he said.

She folded her arms. "So you say and yet after a week, he still hasn't found the time to call you in."

"He also hasn't told you to send me away," Arcon reminded.

"That could mean that he has a vague interest in you," she admitted with a shrug. "Or he simply forgets you're waiting."

Arcon's smile faded only slightly. That was one of his

fears. Gnomes were known to be forgetful.

"No, I'm sure about this one," Mellinda prodded. *"Especially after what we learned last night."*

You had better be, Arcon said. *When word of that dead basilisk reaches the dark wizards they will know I'm in the city for sure.*

"Come then," Molly said, turning her back on him. "Follow me to the waiting area. You're not the only one here today."

She led him down a marble path through beds of exotic flowers and sculpted greenery until they came to the intricately carved front steps of the manor. As she had on previous days, the steward avoided the stairway, instead taking him through a side door.

The interior of Scholar Aloysius' residence was lit by orbs of light. The floors were polished stone covered with fine carpets and the walls were lined with fine wood panels and shelves laden with scholarly work. The place reminded Arcon of the Rune Tower. It reeked of pretentiousness parading as functionality.

"All scholars surround themselves this way," Mellinda commented with a snort. *"As if merely surrounding yourself with books makes you smarter."*

For our sakes, I hope he's genuine, Arcon replied.

"Oh he is," she assured him. Their research had been exhaustive. *"He's of House Mur. The frauds don't last long in Mur. They get parsed out to the lesser houses."*

Among the gnomes, heritage was less important than accomplishment. Scholars were shifted from house to house depending on the prestige of their published work. Mur was one of the highest houses and from the information Arcon had gathered, Aloysius had been with them for well over two hundred years.

The waiting area was actually an atrium in the middle of the residence with a large fountain in the center that spewed various colors of water depending upon the hour of day. A stone obelisk stood in the center of the fountain and was marked with lines denoting the time. As the sun passed overhead, the shadow cast by the rooftop would climb the obelisk and once it reached the uppermost line, all those waiting for appointments with the scholars had to leave. Arcon had learned to hate the thing. Winter was nearing and the shadow climbed faster each day.

"Here you are," Molly said, gesturing to a stone bench facing the fountain. "If the scholar wishes to see you a steward will let you know."

Arcon's eyes focused on the two others that were already waiting near the fountain. One was a tall gnome wearing a set of somewhat natty scholar's robes, while the other was an overweight male elf wearing fine silk robes. He was sweating profusely, shading himself with a lacy parasol while he read out of an ancient-looking book.

"*You don't see many of those,*" Mellinda commented, adding the mental equivalent of a surprised shake of her head. "*Fat elves.*"

Arcon was concerned. These other visitors would likely prove to be of more interest to the scholar. His chances of being seen that day had plummeted.

He reached out and caught Molly's arm as she turned to leave. Her arm was surprisingly muscled under that robe. The green-sashed steward turned on him a surprised glare and Arcon was quick to let go. It was considered a crime to accost a steward. One word from her and he would be kicked out of the homeland.

He smiled apologetically, giving her a short bow, "I'm sorry, Molly. I shouldn't have touched you. I was-uh hoping you might pass a message on to Scholar Aloysius for me if you could. I have some information that might hasten his decision to see me today."

"*What are you doing?*" Mellinda asked.

Molly's glare only lessened slightly. "You are lucky that I like you, mage. What could you possibly say that would pique his interest?"

"*You better not give too much away,*" Mellinda warned.

He leaned towards the steward and lowered his voice, at the same time sending out a muted thread of air to muffle their conversation and keep the others in the room from hearing. "Please tell the scholar that in addition to the prior information I had for him, I also have knowledge regarding the whereabouts of a certain artifact of power he would be interested in."

"*That's exactly the information I didn't want you to tell her, you fool!*" Mellinda growled and from the rage in her voice Arcon knew that if she still had her power, he would be bleeding from the eyes.

Molly pursed her lips, her glare fading altogether, "I can get him that message, but do understand it means nothing unless he's truly interested."

"Of course. Thank you so much, Steward Molly," Arcon said, this time deepening his bow.

She nodded and continued on her way through the doors into the scholar's apartments. Arcon sighed and dropped the spell as he took a seat on a bench near the fountain to wait. The two other occupants of the atrium didn't seem to have noticed his interaction with the steward. The fat elf merely turned a page in his book, while the gnome took a small notebook out a pocket in his robes and scribbled in it, muttering to himself.

"That information was for the scholar's ears only! What if she tells other stewards or another scholar with a similar focus?" Mellinda demanded.

I had to risk it, Arcon explained. He leaned forward, resting his elbows on his knees while he rubbed his eyes with the palms of his hands. *We have to see him today. If the dark wizards were willing to go so far as to send one basilisk after me, what's to say they didn't send two? You yourself said that they'll know we're here now. We could come back to our room tonight and find an assassin waiting.*

"You had better be right," she said, her tone threatening.

Or what? What are you going to do? Nag me some more? he snapped. *Don't forget I can easily lock you away again.*

"I haven't forgotten," she mumbled.

The first few days after she had returned to his mind had been hellish for Arcon. When he had felt the eye turn in his chest and her voice had filled his mind, raging over the attackers that had destroyed her, he had groveled before her voice. He had done her bidding exactly as asked for fear that she would punish him. Then he made a realization. There was no weight to Mellinda's voice. That feeling of heaviness and power was missing.

Oh how she had howled once he realized that her threats were impotent. He had ignored her for a while, trying to close off his mind while she shouted and cajoled and pleaded. Finally he had figured out how to quiet her. He shoved her presence into his hiding place, the tiny pocket within his mind he had used to store his secret thoughts when she had controlled him. It worked perfectly. Rail as she might in that tiny space, he didn't have to hear her and better yet, she couldn't hear him. In that place, she was completely isolated.

He had left her locked away for weeks at a time, only letting her out when he had need of her knowledge. She had been a beast to deal with at first, but the punishment was effective. For a creature who had once been able to probe the minds of hundreds at a time, the complete silence of the little room was the worst torture he could have given her. Finally she had learned to behave, leading to the uneasy truce they had now.

"You do realize that if you had just listened to me in the first place, we wouldn't be in this situation," she reminded him.

Now is not the time to bring that up, he said. It had been during one of her stints locked away in his secret room that Arcon had tried to sell the rings to the dark wizards. *If I had listened to you in the beginning, I would be trying to become the next Ewzad Vriil. No thanks.*

"We would be in a seat of power aiding the Dark Prophet's return," Mellinda reminded him. *"And no one would have sent a basilisk against us."*

Yeah, instead we'd have the entire Mage School against us. Besides, I want nothing to do with the Dark Prophet's return, Arcon said, glaring. He glanced at the sweaty elf, who looked away quickly, returning his eyes to his ancient book as if he hadn't been watching. *I'm tired of being under the thumb of some evil power.*

Mellinda snorted. *"Some freedoms have to be sacrificed if you intend to climb the rungs of power."*

I'm done with that. Power is never really what I wanted anyway. Arcon stood and began to pace around the fountain. No, he was in this position because of blind lust. He had wanted Mellinda, or at least the form she had sent his mind glimpses of. He had let her seduce him into becoming her spy at the Mage School, betraying the wizards and eventually even killing his friend.

The dead witch laughed at the bitterness in his mind. *"Well you got what you wanted in the end, didn't you? You and I, your true love, together forever."*

A shiver crawled up Arcon's spine at the thought. He had been hoping for a way out of that possibility. *Do you really think this is permanent?*

Mellinda sighed tiredly. *"My only hope for true freedom was my blue-eyed child, but his eyes were ruined somehow. Then my enemies destroyed my forest and that filthy Roo girl cut my soul in two. The vast majority of my powers disappeared and I fled. I only had seconds before I would have evaporated into nothingness. The only reason I survived was because they didn't know about the orange eye I placed in you. It was just strong enough for me to transfer my thoughts and memories into. The rest of me is gone."*

What about your other orange eyes, the ones you sent off on Ewzad's errands? Arcon's brow furrowed. *If we found another one, couldn't we perhaps transfer your mind into someone else?*

"They're all gone, you fool. Those wizards destroyed all the orange-eyed children within my reach. Besides, even if we did find one, I no longer have the power to transfer my mind into it. No, we're stuck together, you and I. Until those dark wizards kill us anyway."

Arcon grimaced and looked at the obelisk. The shadows had climbed over half way up the stone. He had less than two hours before the stewards would turn him out and he'd be forced to leave the homeland for the night.

"Scholar Tobias," said a young male voice. Arcon turned to see a green-sashed steward walk into the atrium and stand beside the gnome with the natty robe. "Scholar Aloysius will not be able to see you today."

The gnome sat up and shut his notebook, vague irritation in his voice as he protested, "What is this you say, Reggie? That scallywag refuses to see me?"

"That is what his stewards inform me, sir," the young steward said calmly. From his oily brown hair and pimply complexion, Arcon reckoned he couldn't have been more than seventeen or eighteen.

"That gnome must be from a middle house," Mellinda remarked. *"Prestigious enough to have a steward, but low enough that he was assigned one just out of diapers. That's a slap in the face to a scholar."*

The gnome sputtered. "Did you remind them that I'm the

gnome that wrote, 'The Tactics of Scivaldoon'? Hmm? Or, 'The High Treatise on the Siege of Beck'?" He poked the steward in the shoulder with one long index finger. "I won a three-decade grant for that one."

"Of course I did, sir," the young man assured him, his polite expression unchanging. "His stewards were quite impressed, I assure you. They suggest we return tomorrow. For now, you must come with me and ingest your evening meal."

"Oh, must I?" the gnome said, blinking, one bushy eyebrow raised in confusion. "Surely I just ate."

"Not since this morning, sir," the young steward said. He grasped the gnome's forearm and helped him to his feet. "You sat with Scholar Bernadette and ate a salad, remember? It was covered with smoked salmon, your favorite."

"Ah . . . Yes, well I suppose I must do as the stewards suggest," Scholar Tobias said, letting the young man lead him out of the atrium. "Just make sure that Aloysius knows I'll be back tomorrow. I won't allow him to continue brushing me off like this."

"Of course, sir," the steward said.

The fat elf snorted, rolling his eyes and shaking his head before returning to his ancient book. Arcon had to agree with the ridiculousness of the conversation he had just overheard. This gnome, Tobias, led about by the young steward as if he were an elderly man in the care of a grandchild.

"*You're not far off,*" Mellinda agreed. "*Gnomes are the smartest of all the races and yet so woefully unable to take care of themselves. Why my own Dixie . . .*" Her voice trailed off.

Dixie? Arcon asked. *What were you saying?*

"*Nothing,*" she mumbled, a note of sadness in her voice. "*Nothing of note.*"

Time crept by and Mellinda stayed silent, mired in her own thoughts. Arcon watched the stone obelisk and tapped his foot nervously while he watched the shadow's inexorable climb towards its peak. The chance that the scholar would see him grew slimmer every moment. By the time the shadow reached the edge of the top mark, Arcon was so busy planning out how he was going to survive the night that he barely noticed the next steward enter the room.

"Elder Qelvyn," came a female voice from behind Arcon and he turned to see Molly aiming a polite smile at the sweating elf. "I am sorry, but Scholar Aloysius will be unable to see you today. If you would like, you are welcome to return at noontime tomorrow and try again."

The elf raised one finger at her while he finished reading his page, then he set a ribbon in the book to mark his place before looking up at her. His voice sounded high and regal as he spoke, "My tribe has often dealt with your master, child." He stood, tucking the book under his arm. "But that may not always be the case. He is not the only one who can cater to our needs. Remind him of that if you please."

"Of course, elder," Molly said, giving him a slight bow. "Scholar Aloysius has nothing but respect for your people."

The elf grunted and took his leave, stepping lightly as if his extra weight meant nothing. Another steward met him at the door to guide him back through the house.

He must be one of the High Desert Elves, Mellinda mused. *Not many tribes dress so flamboyantly. I wonder what business that tribe has with our scholar.*

Molly kept her eyes on the elf as he left, smiling with her teeth clamped shut. "Oh they threaten, they threaten. Always they threaten." She turned her gaze to Arcon. "You come with me, mage."

"*Finally.*"

Arcon sighed with relief. "So you gave the scholar my message?"

She inclined her head slightly. "He must have been quite intrigued by your message to see you today. He has been quite busy."

"Then I am honored," Arcon said. "How may I ever thank you?"

"Perhaps a way can be found," she replied, arching one eyebrow before turning and walking away. "In the meantime, follow me. If we don't hurry, he may turn his thoughts elsewhere."

Arcon hurried after her, "Of course, Steward Molly."

"*Keep sharp. This gnome will be crafty if I have correctly guessed his focus,*" Mellinda reminded him. "*You do realize you may have to . . . dally with this steward later, don't you?*"

I have 'dallied' with far worse, Arcon reminded her as he followed the steward through the door at the back of the atrium. *And I'm ready for the gnome . . . I think.*

Molly led him down a corridor decorated differently than the front of the residence. The book shelves were much sparser here, the halls instead lined with suits of armor and portraits of great leaders and scholars of the past. Here and there strange old weapons were mounted on the walls. If Molly hadn't been walking so fast, Arcon would have stopped to stare at some of it. After a few turns, they arrived at the door to the scholar's office.

"This is where I leave you," Molly said, standing in front of the door. "I must warn you that Scholar Aloysius can be quite abrupt. If you begin to prattle, he will send you off."

"I understand," Arcon said.

"Do you?" She shook her head at him. "Have you known any gnome scholars, mage?"

Arcon thought for a moment. "I knew librarian Vincent at the Mage School and I have met several gnomes since coming to Alberri."

She gave him a brief snort. "Scholar Aloysius is not like other gnomes."

"This is good."

Arcon wasn't so sure. Something about Molly's expression had caused a nervous knot to well up inside him. "I will be . . . concise."

"See that you do. The two men he keeps inside are quite adept at tossing out the unwanted." The middle-aged steward took a step towards him and traced one manicured finger along his jaw. "If this goes well for you I'll be seeing you later."

She walked on down the hallway and Arcon swallowed. He looked at the ornately carved wooden door in front of him. The carved scene was of marching armies and banners. Taking a deep breath, he raised his hand and knocked on the door.

The door was opened by a large beefy man wearing steward's robes. A wide red sash crossed his chest and there was an sheathed sword attached to his waist. He gave Arcon a brief glance and beckoned him inward.

"A red sash," Mellinda said excitedly. *"And he's wearing it openly. This is good for us!"*

Arcon didn't see how. Gnome stewards were supposed to wear green or black. Red sashed stewards were supposed to be a myth.

Another human came from his left and stood in front of him. He was of a smaller build than the other stewards, but his face was harder and he seemed more dangerous. He frowned at Arcon. "Wait. You are using magic. Drop any spells if you wish to enter the scholar's presence."

"Another red sash! And this one has mage sight!"

"Of course," Arcon said and he let his magic fade. His cloak faded back to brown and Arcon's hair became its original blond. "Is that better?"

The steward narrowed his eyes, but gave a brief nod and Arcon stepped into the room.

Unlike the rest of the residence, Scholar Aloysius' office was decorated in stone. The floor was polished marble and green pillars sat at the corners of the room. The walls on Arcon's right and left were covered with weapons and scepters and various other items, each one with a small placard underneath. He shifted to mage sight and saw a soft glow of elemental magic around most of them.

Mellinda chuckled.

At the back of the room was a row of bookshelves made from black onyx and in front of them was an enormous desk of dark mahogany. Scholar Aloysius sat behind the desk, his eyes perusing a scroll that he held in veiny hands.

The gnome was hunched over, but he had a youthful look to him as far as gnomes go. He had a full head of glistening black hair and his large ears only drooped slightly. As Arcon moved to stand before him, he rolled up the scroll and turned his eyes on the mage. He didn't wear spectacles and his eyes were sharp and focused.

"Mage Arcon," the gnome said, gesturing with the scroll in his hand. His voice was deep and clear. "You have been patiently waiting to see me for some time now, I hear."

"It was worth every moment, Scholar," Arcon said with a bow.

"I was quite surprised you used your real name when you put in the request," Aloysius said, his dark eyes gauging Arcon's response.

"*Go on. As you rehearsed,*" Mellinda prompted.

"I wanted you to look up my credentials, sir," he replied.

The gnome raised a trimmed eyebrow. "Did you now? A mage on the run? A fugitive from your own school and a known associate of the deceased dark wizard Ewzad Vriil? I could have met you with the Homeland Guard."

Arcon cleared his throat. "I wanted you to know that I could be useful to someone with your particular focus. I did some research on you as well, you see." *Be right. Be right.*

"*Stop questioning me and focus,*" Mellinda reprimanded.

"Useful to me? I am a high scholar of house Mur. Your very presence in this room could sully my reputation. And . . ." Aloysius unrolled the scroll and gestured to the flowery writing on the parchment. "I understand that you are in quite a bit of trouble with the Night Clan. It says here that they sent a basilisk after you."

He knows a lot. "True, sir, but I have taken care of that problem."

"By creating such a commotion that half the capitol's wizards were called out after you?" The gnome waved his hand dismissively. "Far too noisy for my tastes."

"My hand was forced, sir," Arcon replied. "But might I point out that the mere fact I killed the basilisk is proof of my usefulness?"

Aloysius pursed his lips thoughtfully. "True, killing such a beast is nasty business and your survival is commendable. But why would I want someone with that much trouble around me?"

"We both know the dark wizards wouldn't dare go after you, Scholar. Besides, as I told your steward earlier . . ." Arcon reached into his shirt and opened the compartment. The red-sashed stewards at the door saw the movement and started towards him.

"*Don't!*" Mellinda shouted.

"Because I have these," Arcon said, extending his hand. The Rings of Stardeon glistened in his palm.

The stewards grabbed Arcon's arms, jerking him back. The rings nearly slipped out of his hand.

"Stop!" Aloysius demanded. The stewards stopped pulling on Arcon, but they didn't let go of him.

The scholar stood from behind the desk, his narrow seven-foot-frame towering over the mage. His dark eyes gleamed down at Arcon and the mage noticed that the gnome's posture was not that of a dusty bookworm, but that of a person used to command.

"Why show this to me?" the scholar asked, his gaze focusing on the glittering rings. "You are no fool. You know that my focus is items of power. I could easily take them from you."

Arcon didn't let his fear touch his face. *You had better be right about him.*

"*He's wrong. You are a fool,*" Mellinda replied and her voice sounded worried. "*And I am right, but there is something strange with him that I can't figure out.*"

Her hesitation was uncharacteristic which unnerved him, but he plowed on anyway. "Because simply possessing an item of power isn't enough for you. You're a scholar. A gnome that wants to leave his mark on the world. You could take the Rings of Stardeon, but what's groundbreaking about that? What you want is to make an item of your own." He paused for effect. "You want to be the next Scholar Abernathy."

"Abernathy?" The gnome's face twitched and his eyes became filled with anger. "You know nothing about me, mage. Abernathy was little more than a book sniffer that got lucky. I am so much more."

"*Oh, this is better than I hoped. Look at his gaze. Look at his stance!*" Mellinda's voice was filled with excitement again. "*Listen to me. Get down! Bow your head to him!*" Arcon hesitated. "*Now, you fool!*"

Arcon did so, ripping his arms free from the stewards' grip and smacking his knees to the marble floor. *Why?*

"*This is no regular gnome.*" She shoved ancient memories into his mind and Arcon understood.

Scholar Aloysius walked around his desk and moved to stand over the mage. He stood there for a moment and Arcon said nothing. When the gnome finally spoke there was a hint of pleasure in his voice. "You grovel? Are you so desperate for my money?"

"I don't want a job, great one. I just want to serve at your side." Arcon bent lower and pressed his forehead against the cool stone. The stewards grabbed his arms. "I, Arcon, mage trained at the Dremaldrian Mage School, and former servant of King Ewzad Vriil pledge myself to your service."

While the scholar pondered this, the stewards pulled at Arcon. He resisted, struggling to stay prostrate before the gnome. He tore free from their hands again, smacking his head on the floor. His vision swam as they pulled on him again.

"Stop!" Aloysius commanded and the stewards released him. "I am finding myself amused. Tell me, Mage Arcon. Why would you pledge your service to me, a scholar?"

Arcon did not remove his head from the marble. "Because one day you will rule this land."

Chapter Seven

"Come, you stupid mule!" Djeri said, fuming as he tugged on the animal's lead. The mule didn't want to keep up with their quick steps. The stableman had assured them that the beast was well trained and Tarah could tell that it was. It didn't wander. It obediently followed their lead, but for some reason it seemed determined to plod along at a wagon's pace.

"Still griping about that dumb animal, dwarf?" Tarah replied, several steps ahead of him. They had been on the road for nearly a full day and grumbling about their traveling companion seemed to be the dwarf's chief source of entertainment. Tarah wasn't sure what to think of him yet. He was so unlike other dwarves she'd met. "It ain't gonna dissipate into nothingness from the sheer force of your complaints, you know."

"Dissipate into nothingness?" The dwarf laughed. "You puzzle me, Tarah. Most of the time you talk like some back-woods girl, but every once in a while you come out with a turn of phrase that throws me off. Where do you get that talk from?"

"I might be back-woods raised, but Tarah Woodblade ain't uneducated, Dwarf," she replied, her brow wrinkled in irritation. She glanced back at him. "And if we're talking about strange, what about you? You talk straighter than any dwarf I ever met."

"Straighter?" he said, one eyebrow raised. He had decided to wear a half-helm for the journey, but she had seen a full helm strapped to his pack on the mule. Djeri's travel armor looked well-worn and had been painted a muddy green. As the dwarf had promised, the armor made very little noise as he walked. The enormous two-handed mace he wore rattled in its sheath from time to time but that was it.

"Yeah. You talk all high falootin' like a human lord," she

explained.

"Oh. So you expect dwarves to sound uncouth." His statement was loaded, but there was a hint of amusement in his eyes.

Tarah was confused. "No. Not uncouth. Just . . . like folks, you know?"

"Do you know many dwarves?" he asked.

"Of course I know dwarfs," she said with a snort. "How could I be from this area and not know dwarfs? I've worked for dwarfs out of Wobble lots of times." The statement was mostly true. She had worked for dwarves before, but this was her first time partnering with one. It had nothing to do with them being dwarves, though. She avoided working alongside anyone as a general rule no matter what their race was.

Dwarves can be rough around the edges, but they usually make great companions, her papa said.

Dwarfs are greedier than most. You're better off working alone, Grampa Rolf's voice disagreed. *A salesman often finds that his partners are more fond of the money than they are of them.*

I'm not sure how your salesman talk helps in this case, Grampa, Tarah replied. Aloud she said, "So what makes you different from the other dwarfs I've met, Djeri?"

"Good, you said my name right," the dwarf remarked, then lapsed into silence for a moment as he mulled over what to say next. "I suppose I just have a fondness for proper speech. I don't see any need to muddy up my language just to fit in with my peers-. Come on, you no-good turd-machine!" he snapped, jerking on the lead as the mule slowed down once more.

"You can blame your buddy Riveren for that one," Tarah reminded him for the third time that day. "I didn't want to bring any animal on this mission."

"Neither did I!" Djeri argued.

Tarah shrugged. The dwarf had argued against bringing the mule along, but Riveren had insisted. Evidently Wizard Valtrek had specified in the contract that they take this particular mule with them. Tarah didn't understand why. Sure, it allowed them to bring more supplies along, but they were perfectly capable of finding their own food along the way. On top of that, there was something strange about the animal that Tarah couldn't put her finger on.

Best to be wary when dealing with wizards, Grampa Rolf said. *There is money to be made but whenever a wizard's willing to pay, they're gonna have some broad plan that they're not gonna tell you about.*

"Yeah, yeah, Grampa," Tarah replied. "I know."

"What are you mumbling about?" Djeri said in response. His armored boots squelched in a patch of soft mud as he strained with the animal.

"Stay on the grass," Tarah warned. "The mud on the bank here will take the shoes right off you."

They had passed Sampo earlier that day and were now traveling north along the western bank of the Fandine river. The prairie grass grew all the way to the water's edge in some places, but where the water had worn the bank down there was nothing but pebbles and mud. The mud wouldn't be a problem much longer, though. The first hard frost of winter would come any day now. Then the banks would be hard as rock.

"I see that," he said, yanking a foot out of the mire. He moved back to solid ground. "When do we cross the river? Our destination is east of here."

"There's a stretch of shallows just a mile or so ahead," she said and looked to the far side of the bank where tall trees grew at the river's edge. The last time she had been this way the forest had been filled with the bobbing glow of moonrat eyes. It seemed empty now.

"Ugh," Djeri said, shivering as he looked at the swirling water and anticipated having to wade across. There were small pieces of ice bobbing from upstream. "You know, we could still head back to the Sampo Bridge and cross there."

Tarah had considered crossing the bridge at Sampo. It was the most direct route, but in the end she had decided against it. The trees had grown tight together in that stretch of the forest and there were some steep hills. The way the mule was laden would make for tough going.

"Nah, there's a board bridge at the shallows that we can use. Or at least there was last time I came through."

"I've never heard of any other bridge across the Fandine. How long ago was the last time you saw it?" Djeri asked. "Are you sure this bridge of yours is still standing?"

"I last crossed it just after Pinewood was attacked," she admitted, but didn't share that the moonrat mother's forces had been right at her heels at the time. "But it should still be there. Come on, I'd like to cross it before nightfall."

The dwarf eyed the lowering sun. "I'm not sure we'll get there in time. This mule is slowing us down too much." Tarah sighed and he added defensively, "Look, you try dragging this thing around if you think it can be done faster."

"No. You're the muscle," she said. "I'm the scout."

Djeri laughed. "And here I thought you were the hired help. Now you're the scout, too?"

Tarah rolled her eyes then turned and walked towards the animal. "Just keep moving forward," she instructed and passed them, heading back the way they had come.

"What are you doing?" Djeri asked, though he continued forward as she had asked.

"Finding out what this dumb animal's problem is," she replied. "I'll be right back."

Tarah continued south for about a hundred yards, retracing their steps, then knelt down and inspected the mule's tracks. She touched the impressions of its hooves and a picture began to enter her mind. Hmm, this thing was smarter than she had given it credit for. She headed back towards the dwarf, running her fingers along each track as she went. It took her several minutes to catch back up to them, but by the time she got there, Tarah understood why the beast was being difficult.

"Hold up for a second," she told Djeri, then moved to stand in front of the animal. "I've got something to say to you, mule."

It snorted, giving her a dull look. Tarah responded with a glower and swung down with her staff. The red wood struck the beast right between the eyes. The mule stumbled in surprise, its eyes widening at the stinging blow.

"Whoa!" Djeri cried. "Killing the thing won't help."

Tarah ignored him. She hadn't struck it that hard. But she had gotten its attention. The animal was glaring at her, trying to decide whether or not to bite.

"Listen to me, Neddy," she snapped, using the name its masters had given it. "I may not be a wizard, but I am in charge. You follow me and you'd better keep up. I won't put up with no

orneriness from you. We'll take you back to your masters when
we're done, understand?" The mule's eyes narrowed, but it gave
her a snort of understanding. "Good! And stop tormenting the
dwarf. As funny as it may seem, he can hit you a lot harder than I
can."

The mule gave Djeri a bitter look, then bent down to bite
off some grass.

"He understands," Tarah said with a nod. She turned and
walked upstream, continuing towards the shallows. The short delay
had been worth it in her mind. Now the beast wouldn't be such a
burden. She reminded herself to give it a treat the next time they
stopped.

"What was that?" Djeri asked as he followed after her, his
brow raised in wonder. The mule came obediently behind him,
keeping pace with Tarah's long strides.

"I was just getting his attention. He's not really hurt," she
assured the dwarf.

"But why?" he said.

"Neddy here's well trained. He knew to follow us because
the stableman told him to," Tarah explained. "But he doesn't want
to be with us any more than we wanted him along. He'd much
rather be with the wizards he usually goes out with. So he's been
sulking. Also, he thinks it's funny messing with you."

The dwarf glared back at the mule, then gave her a
quizzical look. "And you knew all that by looking at its tracks?"

"Tarah Woodblade's the best tracker in the known lands. I
can tell an animal's mood by the way it steps," she lied. "He was
having a great time at your expense. The rest of it I just figured out
from what Riveren told us about the animal."

"And how did you know its name?" Djeri pressed.

Tarah blinked. With each track, the name had been clearer
in her mind. Neddy was the name the mule identified with. The
wizards called it that all the time. "The-uh, stableman called him
that as we were leaving."

"No he didn't," Djeri said. "He never called it by name. I
would have remembered that."

Tarah swallowed and increased her pace. Stupid! She
should have been more careful with her mouth. "That's where I
heard it. You must not have been paying attention."

"I always pay attention," the dwarf said with a slight frown, but to Tarah's relief, he didn't question her further.

Be careful not to give too much away, Grampa Rolf reminded.

Yeah, might be a little too late for that, she replied.

Grampa Rolf had taught her to show off her tracking skills to clients whenever possible. That was how she grew her reputation. But they had both agreed that it was best to keep the magic ability of her staff a secret. If people found out that her prowess was due to a magic item, her mystique would fade. People might even try to take the staff for themselves. As a result Tarah often found herself walking a tight line between showing off too much or too little.

Still, she decided that it would be best to keep theatrics to a minimum with Djeri. He was too observant and if he suspected anything magical about her abilities he might talk. Dwarves had a reputation for being loud mouthed and from what Tarah had seen it was well-deserved.

They increased their pace along the riverbank and to Djeri's relief Neddy was well behaved, keeping up without complaint. As a result, the sun was just beginning to set when the river widened and the shallows came into view. The light caused the river to gleam with a red hue, making the waters look a lot warmer than Tarah knew they were.

"The bridge is still here!" she looked back at the dwarf, a smile on her face.

Djeri squinted at the water. "I don't see it."

"It's right there," she said, pointing. "See that first board right off the shoreline?"

"That's your 'bridge'?" he said, with a frown. The board extended from just above the waterline and ended at a wide flat rock. Another board continued from there to the next rock and so on across the shallows. From their angle it looked like there was an unbroken line across.

"It's a board bridge, like I said," Tarah explained. "It's just there so we don't have to wade across. My papa and I built it years ago with treated boards we got in trade from Pinewood."

"Treated boards . . ." He eyed the construction distrustingly. "Even if these boards can hold my weight I don't see how we're getting the mule across."

"He'll be fine wading. The water might be deep enough to reach his belly at times, but nothing so deep he'll get our stuff wet. The bridge is for us." She raised an eyebrow at him. "Or more specifically for you. You're tall for a dwarf maybe, but belly high to a mule is chest high to you. And in that platemail-."

"I understand you," Djeri interrupted. He was glaring at the boards now.

As if in response to their conversation, Neddy walked to the waterline next to the first board and bent to drink. After one swallow it shivered and took a few steps back, giving them a derisive snort.

"You'll cross!" Tarah barked, shaking her staff at the mule. It shivered again and looked down in acquiescence. Tarah felt a little guilty about bullying the beast, but reminded herself that it knew very well when it wasn't doing its job. "That's better."

You should always be kind to beasts, Tarah, said her papa's voice. Tarah pursed her lips at the admonition. She resolved to make it up to the mule later assuming it behaved.

Tarah walked across the pebbled ground to the first board plank. The wood had grayed with age and greenish algae clung to the edges. She nudged it with her foot and smiled when it didn't budge.

"See, Djeri? Treated lumber. Pinewood's finest!" She stepped onto the board and strode confidently up its angled surface to the first large rock. The board gave only the slightest of creaks.

"What's to keep it from sliding off the rock?" the dwarf asked.

"Papa anchored each board into the rock with heavy steel spikes." She knelt down and touched one spike, focusing on the power of her staff. Many years had passed and yet she was able to just faintly feel the purposeful thought of her papa as he had driven the spike in all those years ago. A lump grew in her throat as the memory of that day rose in her mind.

It had been the fall of her fourteenth year. Her papa had picked out the site over the summer, choosing a place just north of where the Pinewood folk sent their logs downstream to the sawmill in Sampo. He had traded several large furs and deer skins for the wood. It had been a few months before the rot hit her father hard and he had been as hale and strong as ever. She remembered the ease in which he had dragged the heavy load through the forest.

At the time, Tarah had felt the board bridge to be a waste of time. Sure the trip to the Sampo bridge from their home was a tough one, through thick undergrowth and the edges of the dark forest's taint. But that was nothing she couldn't handle. Her papa had been insistent, though. He had been watching the increase in the size and strength of the moonrats as well as their numbers and had wanted an easy escape route in case there was ever a need to flee.

In retrospect, his forethought seemed almost prophetic. The bridge had saved Tarah's life multiple times in the last few years. She thought back to his behavior that week and wondered if he had already noticed the first sign of the rot. Had he foreseen the possibility of his death from the disease?

"Are you sure about leaving that thing to cross without us? What if it bolts and takes our packs and supplies with it?" Djeri asked, still standing at the shoreline. He was eying the mule warily. "Look at the way it's hesitating at the shoreline."

"He'll be fine," Tarah assured him. "I trust him."

Djeri's eyes narrowed. "I wouldn't trust that thing further than I'd trust a turd in the hands of a monkey."

Tarah turned and pointed her staff at the mule. "Go on, Neddy. Cross! Show the dwarf!"

Shuddering, the beast stepped into the shallow water and began its way across, picking out a path among the rocks. Tarah could almost sense its discomfort as the icy water deepened, but soon it was half way across.

Djeri rested one hand on his helmet and shook his head. "You surprise me once again, Tarah Woodblade. How did you make it do that?"

"I didn't do nothing. I told you he was well-trained," Tarah replied. She started across the next board. It was just as firm as the last, even if a bit slick. She glanced back at him after reaching the next rock. "What about you, Djeri? Too scared to cross or are you as well-trained as that mule?"

The dwarf let out a low chuckle, then took a deep breath and stepped onto the first board. When it didn't immediately buckle under his weight, he continued along, shuffling his feet sideways. The wood creaked, but held and he made it to the first rock. He stayed there for a moment as if taking strength from the solidity of the rock before shuffling onto the next board, his arms held out in an attempt to steady himself.

By this point, Tarah was moving with confidence. Soon she was half way across and paused as she watched Neddy reach the far shoreline. She had been fairly accurate with her estimate of the water's depth. The mule's belly was wet and dripping with slushy water, but their packs and supplies were dry. He stood on the bank and looked back at them, miserable but relieved.

"Good boy!" she called and started across the last stretch of boards.

This was where the crossing got a bit tricky. A tree had fallen into the river just south of the bridge, changing the course of the current. The water here had deepened and two of the boards sat just an inch or so above the water line. The water churned and swirled around the anchoring rocks causing occasional spray to coat the boards with a fine sheen of ice.

Tarah didn't notice just how slick the boards were until her feet began to slide out from under her. She reacted quickly and contorted her body, her staff held out to help her regain her balance.

"Woah!" she said, her heart racing as she navigated the last slippery board. She was now nearly at the shore's edge. "Watch your step, Djeri."

"What's this you say?" said the dwarf in a panic and Tarah realized that his crossing had not been going as smoothly as hers. He stood at the half way point with his arms held straight out and quivering. His face was pale, his teeth clenched in an anxious grimace. "It gets worse?"

"A little further down it gets a bit icy," Tarah admitted with a wince. She had crossed this bridge so many times in the past that she hadn't considered that the dwarf would find the crossing difficult. "But don't worry. I'll let you know before you reach that part."

"I hate to tell you this," he said, slowly edging out onto the next board. "Dwarves aren't made for this kind of bridge." He swallowed as the board let out a loud creak. "We need a bridge made of stone or one with-!" Djeri gasped, windmilling his arms a bit. "One with at least a railing of some sort."

Tarah put her hands on her hips. "How can you be afraid of heights after working the Mage School wall?"

"It isn't heights, Woodblade," he snapped. "This isn't high! My problem is with these narrow blasted boards!"

"Well it's too late to do anything about it now," Tarah replied. "You should've said something to me before now. I would've made you cross on the mule."

His fear turned to a frown as he made it to the next rock. "I would much rather swim this river than ride that beast."

"He's already on the bank waiting for us," she pointed out.

He eyed the next two boards with trepidation. "Taking the Sampo Bridge would have been the better route."

She could see that now. "Okay, you're at the slick part now. Just keep your feet squarely in the middle of the board and shuffle sideways."

"That's what I've been doing the whole time!"

"Good. Then you've got practice," she said. "Just know that now there's a real reason to be careful."

"Shut up!" he said, edging onto the icy board. It bowed a little under his weight and water lapped around his boots. "This isn't a bridge anymore. Dag-blast it! What am I saying? This never was a friggin' bridge!"

"Now you're sounding like a dwarf," Tarah remarked. "There. You're at the rock now. One more board and you're out of the slick part."

"One more board?" He stepped onto the rock and turned his glare on her. "Who told you you were a good guide? I see four more boards until I'm off this ri-!"

He lifted his right foot to step onto the next board and his left foot slipped out from under him. His back struck the icy rock and he slid head first into the slushy water.

"Djeri!" Tarah jumped onto the board sliding across to get to him. The dwarf came up briefly, sputtering and scrambling to find a hand hold, but the current pulled at him. The weight of his platemail and great mace drug him under.

Tarah thrust her staff into the water. "Grab on!" The back of the dwarf's hand brushed the staff, but he couldn't latch on. Tarah froze, her eyes wide. He was right. What kind of guide was she? "Come on!" But his hand didn't come back up.

    "Papa! Grampa!" She begged, but no advice was forthcoming. The dwarf was going to die and it would be her fault. "Oh blast it all," Tarah said with a growl and jumped in after him.

Chapter Eight

Tarah gasped as the freezing water enveloped her, but this wasn't her first time in the currents of the river and her papa had taught her what to do. She ignored the shock of the cold and found her footing quickly. The pool created by the downed tree reached half way up her chest. The swirling current pulled at her and Tarah dug in with her feet as she searched for the dwarf.

He found her first. Djeri's powerful hands latched onto her legs, threatening to drag her under. She grit her teeth, straining against the current and Djeri's weight as he pulled himself out of the water using her armor as handholds. He wrapped his legs around her in his haste to get to the surface and her armor threatened to tear at the seams.

"Just a blasted second!" she shouted and thrust her staff into the river bottom for extra leverage.

The dwarf's head broke the surface and he sputtered, "C-cold!"

"No kidding! Just stop struggling or you'll pull me under with you!" She glanced around. They had been pulled out towards the river's center and there weren't any large rocks for her to grab onto. She had to get the dwarf thinking instead of reacting. "Listen, we're gonna have to let the current bring us back towards the shore. Can you see the way the water's flowing?"

Djeri turned his head and looked at the surface of the pool, gauging the circular pattern of the water's flow. "Y-yeah. It could pull us that way if we don't d-drown first."

Tarah grunted. "We'll be fine. Just . . . for nature's sake, put your feet down! It ain't that deep where we're standing!" Djeri's legs became untangled from hers and he found that he was able to just barely keep his head above water. "Good, now work with me. We'll make our way there one step at a time."

It was slow going and the intense cold made it seem like it took forever. Tarah's limbs were numb by the time they reached the pool's edge and they weren't finished yet. There was still a quarter of the shallows yet to go. They continued on, dragging themselves through the last stretch. Finally, they collapsed onto the pebbled ground of the shoreline, icy water pouring from their armor.

The dwarf turned pained eyes on her, his beard coated in slush. "I'm c-colder than a witch's tur-tur-tur-!"

"Yeah-yeah. I get it," Tarah said, breathing heavily, her eyes closed. Oddly, the air entering her lungs felt warmer than her internal temperature. So tired. It would feel so good to sleep. Yes, sleep would be nice . . .

Get moving or the cold will have you, her papa instructed. His voice was forceful, just as it had been on the day he first said the words.

Tarah's mind drifted into the memory. She was little then, but she couldn't remember how old. She was kneeling by the river's edge, one small hand plunged into a gap in the ice just as her father had instructed. The pain had been excruciating. Her papa stood next to her and as she looked up at him pleadingly, his expression had been kind, but amused.

"Just leave your hand in a moment longer, Tarah" he said, his voice encouraging.

Tarah grimaced. She could barely feel her hand anymore, but the cold had turned into a deep ache that ran up her arm towards her shoulder. It was as if her very bones were turning to ice. She fought back tears. "It hurts, papa!"

"Yes, the cold hurts, Tarah. Remember that," he said. "You can take your hand out now."

Tarah removed her hand from the water and stood. She stared at her hand, expecting her skin to be blue, but it was flushed red. It was difficult to move her fingers.

Her papa knelt beside her. He had seemed so huge to her then; a hulk of a man. He was wearing his enchanted leather armor, left over from his academy days. It consisted of a leather breastplate and shoulder pauldrons, but left his muscular arms bare.

He reached out and took her frozen hand in both of his. His hands felt like hot coals as he looked at her with serious eyes. His eyes were so blue. His familiar voice was deep and comforting. "If you ever fall into water cold like this, your whole body'll feel like your hand just did. If that happens, get out quick as you can. Just keep your head. Swim the same way you would if the water was warm. Lots of folks panic and drown in the cold. That ain't happening to you."

"Yes, papa," she said.

"Good. Now get up and get moving," he said, giving her an approving smile. "Come on. You can't lay there and expect to survive."

"What?" Her nose wrinkled. What was he talking about? She was standing already. Or was she? She felt hard earth beneath her back. When had she laid down? Her papa's face began to blur. The world around her faded until all she could see was his blue eyes.

Get moving, Tarah. Get warm! Her father's voice commanded, but it was as if he were far away. What was wrong? Something wet and hot slid across her face. It hurt. Was her face on fire?

Her mind was jolted back to the present and her eyes fluttered open to see the mule's breath steaming in front of her face. "Gah, Neddy!" He licked her again with his fire-like tongue and she frowned at him, sensing his amusement. They had made him wade across the cold river, but the people were the ones that laid frozen on the ground. "It's not funny."

She struggled to sit up. Her papa was right. She needed to get moving. Her limbs protested, but she forced her body to stand, using her staff to keep herself propped up. Blast, but her armor was heavy!

She looked back at the dwarf. He was lying on the bank, still breathing heavily, his eyes droopy with exhaustion. She didn't blame him, but he needed to get moving too.

"You strong enough to get up, dwarf?" Tarah asked. "Or do you need me to toss you on Neddy's back?"

Djeri scowled and rolled over. "I'm fine," he said, his lips pressed to the mud. He slowly shoved against the pebbled ground and pushed himself to his knees. "I'm a dwarf. I'm finer than fine.

I could carry that mule if I had to." He winced as he stood, then folded his arms and gave her a firm look. "How about you, Woodblade? You look like you're about to fall over."

"Tarah Woodblade doesn't fall over," she replied and at just that moment her legs wobbled. She clutched her staff, hoping fervently that the dwarf wouldn't end up having to carry her. She told herself it would be okay. Surely her blood would warm once she started walking. "Come on. There's gonna be a freeze tonight and we need to get dry. I know a good spot close by."

Close by was a bit of an exaggeration. The sun had slipped below the tree line and the spot Tarah hoped to reach was almost a mile away, which in her condition might as well have been ten. She started down the narrow trail she and her father had used so many times over the years, grateful that this part of the forest was so familiar to her, because it was hard to think. Neither of them bothered to lead the mule anymore. Neddy followed behind them on his own.

Tarah's boots sloshed as she led the way. Djeri walked right behind her, grunting, his suit of armor sounding like it was full of water instead of a dwarf. Tarah shook her head. She could only imagine how much heavier his armor had gotten with all the padding soaked. Her own armor felt like it had absorbed half the river. She kept a steady pace and some strength began to return to her limbs, though she was shivering uncontrollably.

Tarah Woodblade doesn't shiver, said Grampa Rolf.

"Shut up," she mumbled.

"You said we were close," Djeri reminded her. The dwarf wasn't shivering anymore, but he swung his arms about constantly as he walked, clenching and unclenching his fingers to keep his blood flowing. "How much further?"

"It's just over the next hill," she lied. It was a common guidesman trick. As long as the client thought they were near the destination, she could keep them going twice as long.

"Yeah, right. How far is it really?" the dwarf asked. Tarah looked back to see he had one eyebrow raised. "Come on. This isn't my first journey. How long until we reach the camp?"

She berated herself. He was an academy veteran. Of course he'd know the tricks. "A half mile. There's actually about three more rises to go."

"Then let's pick up the pace," he said. "The light's almost gone and if you're right about the chill, you're going to need a fire soon."

He was right and if her mind hadn't been so numbed, she would have recognized it. Dwarves were tough by nature, part of the magic in their blood. He could probably go on for miles. She was the one fading fast. Tarah forced her numb legs into a light jog.

That half mile felt like five miles. Tarah found it hard to keep her balance and her breaths came short and fast. Her vision swam and as she topped the second rise, one of her boots caught on a tree root. She nearly crashed to the ground, but somehow Djeri was at her side, steadying her. He said something to her about getting on the mule, but she shook her head and kept on.

Climbing that last rise felt like the most difficult thing she had ever done. Every step was torturous. A sigh escaped her lips as she arrived. Tarah pushed through the thick pine boughs on the side of the trail and stepped into the small clearing she had been heading for.

The campsite was surrounded by thick pine trees that protected it from the wind and did a good job of hiding the light of a fire. The lean-to she and her papa had made there so many years ago still stood, taking up a good portion of the clearing. A ring of blackened stones sat in front of it, ready to be used.

Tarah smiled in relief. Just standing in the place helped bring vigor back into her limbs. She immediately began pulling at the laces of her armor, eager to get the icy clothing off.

There was a grumble behind her as Djeri shoved his way through the trees, pulling the mule behind him. He paused, the frown fading from his face as he looked around the campsite. He nodded approvingly. "This could work."

"Hurry and get a fire going," Tarah instructed. The laces were hard to undo with her numb fingers, but at least her mind was working again. "I left some dry wood stacked under the lean-to last time I was here."

"Right," Djeri said. He began hauling dry branches and logs out from under the shelter. He cursed. "Uh, there's a big hornet's nest in here."

"It's too cold for 'em to stir. Just clear it out of there. Toss it in the fire if you want," she said, sighing as she was finally able to pull the heavy soaked armor off over her head. She began pulling off her boots.

"I hope you're right," Djeri said. After a worried grunt, he tossed a large paper nest into the center of the rock ring and began laying firewood over the top of it. He chuckled. "What am I worried about? I don't know if I'd even feel a sting right now, I'm so numb all over. I . . . Uh . . . Tarah?"

"What?" she said, laying her underclothes on the dry ground beside her. Even the cold air felt warm on her skin after those wet clothes.

"Uh . . ." He averted his eyes, his cheeks flushed red. "You're naked."

She frowned. Why should that concern him? "Wet clothes will kill you in this weather. Come on. Get that fire started. Where's that academy training of yours?"

"R-right." He walked to the mule and opened his pack, then began searching for his fire kit.

He was taking too long. Tarah rolled her eyes and by the time Djeri finally found his kit and pulled it out, light flared behind him. He turned in surprise to find Tarah, still naked, crouched by the lit fire shivering. The wasp's nest had gone up quickly.

"You were moving too slow," she explained as she rose and walked to the mule. She began untying her pack from Neddy's saddle. Djeri was standing next to her, blinking stupidly, the fire kit still in his hand. That cold must be affecting him more than she'd thought. "Go on, dwarf. Get that armor off."

Djeri cleared his throat and turned his face away from her. "How did you get that fire started so fast?"

"I left some flint and steel next to the wood pile just in case." Tarah replied. She briefly considered putting on the filthy set of underclothes remaining in the pack, but instead just took a dry shirt out and pulled it on. She glanced back at the dwarf and saw that he had turned his back to her, but he still hadn't worked on that armor. "Hey, you okay? Snap out of it and take that armor off!"

"I'm not taking this armor off," he said. "I told you. I'm a dwarf. I'll be fine."

"Go stand by the fire at least," she commanded. He did so

without a word and she pulled on a pair of pants and stockings. Each new piece of clothing helped, but she knew it wasn't enough. She was still shivering violently and the temperature was dropping by the moment. She pulled a wool blanket from the mule's back and wrapped it around her shoulders. She would feel much better if she had her winter cloak. Hopefully Djeri wouldn't mind stopping by her house on the way.

Tarah returned to the fire and stood opposite the dwarf, watching him add a few branches to the burning pile. Water still seeped from the padding under his armored plates. She shook her head. There was no way he was getting any warmth through that.

"Why're you being so stubborn? Even dwarfs can die from cold." Tarah was pretty sure that was true.

"I'm in the Defense Guild. We don't take off our armor," he said, his eyes not leaving the fire.

"Come on now. I know about your guild's 'rules'," she replied holding her hands out over the flames. She wished she could hold her whole body out over the flames, like on a spit. "My papa told me all about 'em. He said you only had to keep your armor on during training."

"I'm on a mission, girl," he said. "I will not remove my armor."

"Hey!" Tarah scowled at him, "What did I tell you about calling me 'girl'? I've been trying to use your name right."

He gave a short sigh. "I apologize."

"And what does your academy training say about falling in freezing water? What are you supposed to do then?" she pressed.

"I told you I'll be fine," he said, raising his voice. "Just leave me be!"

"I ain't gonna!" Her voice rose to match his. "Tarah Woodblade don't take no guff from a client! When I'm guiding you, you run by my rules!"

"You're not the boss on this mission!" Djeri shouted.

Tarah wasn't having it. "You get that armor dried out, Djeri the Looker! Stout Harley himself would tell you the same. We ain't in a battle. The mother of the moonrats is dead. There's nothin' nearby for you to fight!"

As if in response, a moonrat moan rose from the forest behind them.

"Oh really?" Djeri said. "Did you hear that?"

Tarah lowered her voice. "That moonrat is far off to the south. It won't be any trouble to us." The dwarf gave her a wry look and she added, "What? You telling me that you, a guard captain, couldn't fight off a single moonrat without your armor on? 'Cause if that's the case, let me know and I can protect you."

"Blast it, Tarah, it's not that!" he said.

"Then what's your problem?"

His lips worked in frustration until he finally said, "I . . . I'm just not comfortable undressing in front of you."

A laugh escaped her lips. "Really? That's what this is about? Look, I was raised by men. You ain't got nothing I ain't seen before. Besides, you're a dwarf." She paused. "Wait. Dwarf parts ain't different are they?"

"No!" he said, his face red. "That's not the point. I'm just saying I don't feel comfortable."

"Okay. I promise not to look!" Tarah said, her hands raised defensively. She laughed again. "Sheesh, go over there and change into something dry. You do have something dry, don't you?"

"Just some long underwear," he admitted.

"That's all you brought?"

Djeri noted her smirk. "Look, that's what I wear under my armor and I wasn't planning on changing out the padding unless the weather turned really cold."

"Then what's taking up all the space in your pack over there?" Tarah asked. "It's swollen like a tick."

The dwarf sighed. "Fine. I'll go over there and change. You . . . keep your eyes on the fire."

While Djeri grumbled and walked over to the mule, Tarah took some rope from her pack. She had never before met a male that was so self-conscious. What was the dwarf so worried about? Did he have some kind of deformity or nasty scarring? Now that her curiosity was piqued, she wanted to look.

She resisted the urge and began stringing the rope between the trees, setting up lines as close to the fire as she dared. Then she wrung as much water as she could from her wet clothes and hung them to dry. Her leather armor was so heavy it bowed the rope until it nearly dragged on the ground. She sighed. There was no way it would dry overnight. She wasn't looking forward to putting the damp armor back on in the morning. As it was, she barely felt as if she had warmed up at all.

Djeri eventually finished changing and slung his own dripping underclothes over the line. He had dressed in a fresh set of long underwear and had a blanket wrapped around him. Saying nothing to Tarah, he dragged his bulging pack over to the fire. Then he pulled his armor next to him and sat cross-legged working on it.

Tarah found his appearance surprising. With his neatly trimmed beard and without his bulky armor, she could have mistaken him for a short human man. He was perhaps a bit overly wide and burly for a human, but he didn't look very dwarf-like to her eyes. She watched him take his armor piece-by-piece and remove the soaked padding attached to it. Soon he had a rather large and spongy pile.

"What're you doing?" she asked, concerned that he might decide to wear it without any padding. That armor would make a racket.

"I'm changing out the pads," he said, then gave her an assessing glance. "How are you warming up?"

"Slowly," she said. It truly did seem as if the firelight was bouncing off of her instead of infusing her with its heat. She still felt chilled to the bone.

A moonrat moan echoed through the night once again. Tarah listened intently and a few seconds later heard an answering moan, though this one was much softer.

"They still sound far away to me," Djeri said.

"Still far to the south," Tarah agreed. "The second one was even further away, perhaps on the far side of the wizard's road. Those were mating calls, though. Not hunting calls." She stared into the fire. "It's strange just hearing two moans. The forest hasn't been this quiet since I was a little girl."

"Yeah, well most of the moonrats are dead now. And without the witch leading them, they're just animals like any other." Djeri pulled the last piece of wet padding off of his armor and began rummaging through his pack, pulling out large wads of white fur.

"Were you there?" Tarah asked. "When the moonrat mother was killed?"

"No, but my uncle told me all about it. When the great Wizardess Darlan ignited her spell, it wiped out most of the dark forest, killing all the orange-eyed rats in the process." He shook his head and threaded a long curved needle with some kind of metal thread. He started attaching the white fur to the underside of the armored plates. "I was part of the clean-up afterwards, though. We marched through the elf forest, killing any moonrats or trolls we found. They really weren't much trouble."

"Then the elves got their homeland back," Tarah said, relieved.

"You know the elves?" he asked, his voice surprised.

"Well. I can't exactly say I'm friends with 'em, but we got a healthy respect for each other," Tarah replied. "I've always done my best to warn folks away from their land and every once in a while they've helped me out when I needed it."

"Huh," The dwarf said, sounding impressed. "Well, the witch had made quite a mess of their place. All the green trees were scratched up and gnawed on and much of the soil had been dug up and strewn about. Also there was something wrong about the dead moonrats. Where they rotted, the plants died. Even their turds were toxic. We had to gather them all up in a pile and burn them."

"Yeah," Tarah had first hand experience with the foulness of moonrats. "Tell me about it. We had a hell of a time making my armor. Their leather kept rotting away the binding straps. Finally we had to use moonrat intestine to tie it all together."

Tarah looked at the dwarf's new padding. She couldn't quite place the origin of the fur. It looked soft, somewhat like rabbit, but was too long and stringy. "Say, what's that new padding of yours made of?"

"Snow fox," he said, laying one completed leg piece aside and picking up another. "It's a family secret on my mother's side. Does a great job of keeping the heat in. I was going to wait and put it on in the dead of winter, but I guess my hand has been forced."

"Why wait?" Tarah asked.

"The stuff works too good," Djeri explained. "On even a slightly warm day I'll be sweating barrels." He shrugged. "Oh well. I guess I'll just have to deal with it."

Tarah nodded and watched him for a few minutes longer.

Suddenly her body broke out in a fresh round of shivers. Tarah's teeth chattered. Why didn't she feel any warmer yet? She had always prided herself on her cold resistance. While other women were shivering, she was usually quite comfortable. It was one advantage that came from being big-boned, a legacy from her father.

Eat, Tarah, her papa said. *Your body needs fuel to stay warm.*

You always forget to eat, Grampa Rolf agreed.

They were right. Maybe food is what she needed. "I guess it's dinner time. You hungry, dwarf?"

"I am," he said without much enthusiasm. "I wish we had some meat to cook, though."

"Me too," Tarah said. A sizzling spit of anything sounded good right then. Unfortunately, she still needed to replace her bow and she was too cold to hunt in the dark anyway. "So what's in your academy supplies?"

"Ugh. Some bread, hard cheese, dried fruit. Maybe even some peppered beef." He rubbed his hands over his face. "I've got some spices and stuff too, but we'd need to get some water boiling and I'm not heading back to the river."

"Bread and cheese it is, then," she said, heading to the mule's side. He was just standing there looking miserable, his eyes glimmering in the firelight. She ran an arm down his front leg, concerned that he was still chilled from the river, but his skin felt quite warm to her cold hands. "What is it, Neddy? You hungry too?"

"There's some grain and a feed bag on his saddle," Djeri said. "Just go easy. We don't know how long this trip is going to take."

Tarah poured some feed into the bag. Then she realized that she hadn't given the mule that treat she'd promised and tossed in a handful of dried fruit as well. She mixed it together and put the feed bag over his mouth, then rubbed his ears. "Sorry, guy. I know it's not much. I'll get you something better tomorrow."

She handed the dwarf some food and sat back down at the fire to eat her own. It may have been standard trail rations, but to her it tasted quite good. The bread was tough, but flavorful and the cheese had a perfect blend of saltiness and sourness. The food must have come from the Mage School stores because she immediately felt it flooding her body with energy.

"You still cold?" Djeri asked, his brow furrowed in concern.

Tarah realized that she was still shivering despite the magic in the food. "I don't know why."

He put down the piece of platemail he was working on and reached out his arm. "Give me your hand."

Tarah frowned a bit, but scooted closer to him and held out her hand. When he grasped her fingers, she nearly gasped. His hands were hot. That dwarven constitution was truly remarkable.

"You're not recovering fast enough," he said. Then his cheeks colored and he released her hand. "I-uh have something here that might help." He dug into his bag and brought out a bottle filled with clear liquid. "This is pepperbean wine. It should warm you up."

"Drinking when you're this cold don't really help," Tarah said, shaking her head. "You may think it makes you warmer, but really it makes things worse."

"This stuff is different," Djeri insisted. "It's a special recipe. The elves call it 'firewater' and it will definitely banish the cold. This is how I was planning to make it through the night before you made me change out of my armor."

Don't let men get you drinking, her papa reminded. *You never know their intentions.*

"I'm not one for getting drunk," Tarah said.

"Neither am I," Djeri said, looking slightly offended. "I didn't bring this for getting drunk on. It's too precious for that. I use it for medicine. One swallow only. That's all it'll take. Trust me."

Tarah cocked her head. She looked into his eyes and saw only earnestness, but how well did she really know him? To her surprise, she found herself saying, "I trust you, Djeri."

She took the bottle and pulled out the stopper. She raised it to her lips.

"Wait!" he said. "You should know that it's not just called firewater because it makes you warm. Pepperbeans are hot. I mean spicy hot. It'll burn going down. More so if you aren't used to it."

She snorted. Her father had kept a small pepper garden and

she had eaten a lot of spicy food growing up. "Tarah Woodblade ain't afraid of hot."

She was wrong.

This wasn't like chunks of peppers cut up in the stew or even the spicy sauce her papa liked to put on his meat. This was pure fire. Liquid flame.

To her credit, Tarah didn't spit the liquid out, but gasped mid-swallow despite herself. A tiny trickle of the molten liquid went down the wrong pipe. She went into a coughing fit. It hurt. It hurt bad! Her lungs burned like she had inhaled live coals. Tears streamed down her face. Her nose ran.

She barely noticed Djeri take the bottle from her hand and put the stopper in. Then he was pounding her back. "You alright?"

"Y-you son of a-!" Tarah hacked. She coughed. She retched. She turned on the dwarf and began pounding him with her fists. "You trying to kill me?"

Djeri raised his arms defensively, absorbing the blows. "I didn't say inhale it!" Finally he wrapped his powerful arms around her and held her still while she struggled. "Just calm down. Breath easy. The burning will fade, I promise."

She stopped struggling and forced herself to breath easier. He was right. After a few moments, the burning in her lungs faded. She was left with a molten sensation that went down her throat into her stomach where it burned like a blacksmith's forge. "You can let go of me now."

Djeri released her and backed away. "Do you feel warmer now?"

"Of course I do!" Tarah spat. She was sweating and her cheeks were flushed. "Anyone would feel warmer after going through that! I feel like I ran friggin' five miles!" Then she laughed.

"That might have worked too, but not as fast," Djeri said, laughing along with her. "I'm sorry, I wasn't expecting that to happen. For a moment I thought you might pass out."

"I nearly did!" she said, then coughed again. She stood, breathing heavily. "Why in nature would anyone drink that stuff on purpose?"

"I tell you, it's a delicacy," he said then picked up the bottle and released the stopper to take a swallow for himself. He stopped the bottle and whistled. "You shouldn't feel bad. I've been drinking this stuff my whole life and still it gets me." He sucked cold air in through his teeth as he put the bottle back in his pack. "Uncle says it's the human side of my heritage."

"You're heritage?" Tarah said, confused.

"Yeah, my daddy was half-human," he said, then frowned, looking embarrassed. "I don't know why I just told you that. I never tell anybody that."

"Your papa was?" Tarah asked. "I never heard of a half-dwarf before."

He swallowed and sat back down next to his armor. He picked up his needle and wire thread. "There aren't many. Dwarves and humans don't tend to . . . like each other in that way. It happens, but not often." He began stitching more pieces of fur into the armor. "Life can be hard for a half-dwarf. Other dwarves are usually nice about it, but you can't avoid the looks and whispers. To make things worse, my daddy's family was more rough on half-breeds than most. He ended up moving away from them as soon as he was old enough."

"But how would being half-human affect his blood magic?" Tarah wondered.

Djeri shrugged. "In that way it's the same as being a half-elf or half-gnome."

"There's half-gnomes too?" Tarah said, her jaw dropping.

"Yeah. It happens," Djeri said. "As far as their magic goes, you never know what a half breed will end up like until they're fully grown. Some take more of their human side; some more of the blood-magic race. For a half-dwarf, for instance, they might have a varying amount of the dwarf toughness. My daddy looks mostly dwarven, but his magic is weaker than other dwarves. He doesn't heal quite as fast as regular dwarves do."

"And what about you?" Tarah asked.

Djeri smiled. "Well, my momma was full dwarf and of a proud heritage, too. I'm full dwarf as far as anyone can tell. I'm tough as any of them."

Tarah nodded, but she knew he wasn't saying everything. She could see his human part in him, even if it wasn't obvious at first. She didn't press him on it, though. That was his business. Djeri didn't say anything further and they sat in silence for awhile.

Then Tarah stood.

"Well, I think I'll try and get some sleep," she said.

"I'll stay up awhile," Djeri replied. "I need to get my armor finished."

"Right." Tarah walked over and removed Neddy's feeding bag, then brought one of the bedrolls over to the lean-to and laid it out. She pulled her quarterstaff next to her and slipped inside. This was her first time in an academy bedroll. It was thicker and made of a stronger material than the one she usually brought on long journeys. The inside was quite cold at first, but the pepperbean wine was still working strong and her body heat warmed it up quickly. Soon she was completely comfortable and her tired body seemed to melt into the fabric.

Tarah's eyes rested on the dwarf. He was still working on the armor, though the pile of unfinished plate was fairly small. Every once in a while he would stop and look in her direction, a slight crease in his brow as if his thoughts were troubled.

Djeri was a mystery to her. For some reason she felt oddly comforted by his presence. It was so strange. She had never felt comfortable in the company of anyone besides her family. Not even the people she guided. Not even after weeks of travel with them. And here she was after one day of knowing him, at ease with the company of a dwarf- well, three quarters of one anyway. She had even gone and . . . she had . . .

Tarah swallowed. She had actually stripped naked. Had she really been so brazen as to stand there in front of him as if such a thing didn't matter? Not that a dwarf, or any man for that matter, would feel attraction to someone that looked like her, but why had she done that? She would never have stood naked in front of anyone else she could think of, so why had she felt no shame over doing so in front of Djeri?

She pursed her lips at the frustrating train of thought. Surely papa wouldn't have approved of her behavior, but he and Grampa Rolf had remained silent. Hmm. She nodded curtly. That in itself was a good enough answer. Why should she feel shame or embarrassment if they had no problem with it? Getting out of those wet clothes had been a necessity. After all, it had been about survival. Tarah Woodblade did whatever was necessary.

With that comforting thought, she let the troubling

questions go and allowed her body to fade off into sleep.

Chapter Nine

It was dark. Dark and warm and to Tarah's discomfort, the air around her was also moist. Moist like the inside of someone's mouth. She was fully clothed, wearing her armor and boots.

Blast, it was stifling. She sat up and her head hit something soft and rubbery. And wet. She reached up and her hands slid along a slimy surface. Where was she? The floor underneath her undulated and rose up slamming her against the soft ceiling. Then it fell back down again and Tarah bent, reaching for a wall or a doorway, anything. Her hands encountered something hard and unyielding. The walls were made of large interlocking plates of some kind. They were like . . . Teeth! She was inside a mouth.

She shouted. She kicked. She pried at the enormous teeth, but the mouth wouldn't open. Finally she pulled out her belt knife and began stabbing.

With a hideous creak, the jaws began to open. Sunlight poured in and Tarah's wincing eyes saw blue sky. The tongue beneath her moved forward and Tarah slid out under the teeth and past huge lips into open air. She got to her knees and stood to find that she was far above the ground. The forest seemed to be a hundred feet below.

She turned to see an enormous hooked beak of a nose and two enormous eyes. She was standing on the tongue of a giant. How could this be? Did a giant this large even exist?

The tongue stretched out further and propelled her upwards. The giant's lip was curled in a snarl. His brow was furled. There was hatred in his eyes. Why hadn't he chewed her up? Why hadn't he swallowed her?

Because I wanted to feel you suffocate on my tongue, said a voice from deep within her mind. **I wanted you to drown in**

my saliva. She cowered in fear as a building-sized hand rose up from below, forefinger and thumb extended. **Perhaps I'll just settle for popping your head**.

Tarah screamed and her staff appeared in her hands. She lashed out at one of its enormous eyes. The tip of her staff changed, transforming into an arrowhead, and pierced the black center of his eye. She twisted. The giant screamed. Its fingers clutched at her, but in its haste it knocked her aside instead.

Tarah fell from its hideous tongue. She plummeted towards the trees below as the giant roared in anger. Saved from the beast, now she would die from the fall. In desperation she clung to her staff, willing it to save her.

As if in response, her staff grew rapidly. It lengthened and its end shot towards the ground beneath her. Suddenly her descent halted. Tarah clutched her staff, suspended just feet above the treetops. The red wood expanded until it was the thickness of her arm.

You think to escape? Foolish girl! The giant's head descended towards her, its face contorted with rage. Enormous hands reached for her.

Tarah slid down the staff as fast as she dared. Soon she was surrounded by the branches of the trees. The staff lurched and Tarah leapt away, clutching a thick branch. She turned her head in time to see the staff tear from the ground and disappear into the sky above.

Downward she climbed from branch to branch until her boots touched the forest floor. A roar of anger echoed from above and she heard a crash in the forest behind her. Tarah ran.

She was disoriented at first, but soon she realized she was not far from Pinewood. A strange certainty entered her mind. If she made it to her house, she would be alright. Her papa would protect her.

She fled through the trees, knowing exactly where to go. This forest was familiar territory. She had been traveling it all her life. The trees called out to her as she passed with whispered greetings. She continued to hear crashing in the forest behind her, but her fear was gone.

Tarah enjoyed the run. Soon she would be home. Her papa and grampa would welcome her with open arms and she would be safe. The crashes faded behind her. Then the path leading to her home came into view.

Tarah stumbled to a halt. The stone pathway leading to her door had been torn up. The flat stones her father had so painstakingly carved lay broken and cast aside. Where the stones had been the ground was wet and red, as if moistened by blood.

She walked to the side of the curving path until her home came into view. Tarah's heart sank. The facade of her house had been painted the rusty brown of dried blood. Staked up around the perimeter of the house were the heads of Pinewood townsfolk. She recognized them. These were the people she hadn't been able to save.

Tarah ran to the door and tried to open it, but it was locked. She pounded on it, ignoring the sludgy redness that came off on her hands. "Papa!" she cried. "Grampa Rolf!"

"They'rrrre deaad," said a horrible voice and a face appeared in the window beside the door. It was the deformed face of the moonrat man.

"No!" shouted Tarah. "They're not dead. Papa!!"

"He's rigghht next to youuuu, girrrll." The moonrat man hissed.

Tarah turned her head and saw her father's face. His head was mounted on a pike next to the door. His proud jaw hung open and his eyes stared at her unblinkingly.

"No." She backed away in horror. "Papa!"

On the other side of the door, mounted on another pike was the head of her Grampa Rolf. A sheet of parchment had been nailed to the side of his head. Scrawled on the parchment was a long list of crimes, each one attributed to different versions of her grampa's name. Some of the names she had heard before, but all of them were written in her grampa's own handwriting.

Thievery – Rolf the Pincher
Lying – Ramshackle Rolf
Assault – Rolf of Pinewood
Adultery – Rolf, son of Ben Yelloweed
Murder – Rolf Beraldi

"No," she said, shaking her head in denial. A crash echoed from behind her and she turned to see the approaching form of the giant's torso above the treeline.

The door to her house creaked open and shadowy creatures flooded out. Each one of them had a face like a mix of moonrat and goblin and each one carried a wicked sword.

"No," Tarah sobbed. The goblin-moonrats streamed towards her. Tarah backed away, her boot's squelching in the bloody mud.

She called out for help and suddenly her staff reappeared out of nowhere. The red wood was stout and firm in her hands. Tarah gritted her teeth and stopped, facing the goblins, her weapon at the ready. She wasn't about to be slaughtered. The creatures hissed and slowed warily.

Unfortunately, her triumph was short-lived.

The area around her grew dark. The moonrat man stood in the doorway of her house and laughed. The staff drooped, its wood becoming soft in her fingers. Tarah looked up and saw the rapid fall of the giant's enormous foot overhead.

WHAM!

Tarah swore as her head struck the roof of the lean-to. She flailed about for a moment, disoriented. Then the top of her bedroll fell away and she caught a glimpse of the familiar clearing in the pale morning light.

"You alright?" Djeri asked. The dwarf was propped up on one elbow, looking at her bleary-eyed from his bedroll. He had evidently decided not to sleep next to her under the lean-to because he was laying next to the smoldering remains of the fire.

"Uh, yeah," Tarah said, blinking for a moment. The inside of her bedroll was sweltering and a thin sheen of sweat covered her body. She climbed out, momentarily grateful for the icy chill of the morning air.

The dream still sat heavy on her mind. She wanted to dismiss it, but it had seemed so real. She felt a gnawing certainty that this was different from her usual dreams. For two nights in a row now, her dreams had been vivid, but this one was more so. This one meant something.

She fixed the dwarf with a worried gaze. "Djeri . . . I got a favor to ask you."

"Huh?" Djeri pulled an arm out from under his blankets and scratched his head. His arm was covered in platemail and Tarah understood that he had put it back on before going to sleep.

His boots and gauntlets were the only parts of his armor sitting outside his blankets. "What are you talking about?"

Tarah pulled on her boots, ignoring the cold wetness that still lined the inside. "I want, no, need to go by my house right away."

"You mean now?" Djeri asked, sitting up all the way.

"Yes. Right away," Tarah said. She stood and lifted her armor off the line with a grunt. It wasn't as heavy as it had been the night before, but it was still damp. Putting it on wouldn't be pleasant.

Nothing like cold wet armor in the morning, said her papa dourly.

No kidding, she thought as she pulled the leather cuirass over her head.

Djeri threw back the cover of his bedroll and began pulling on his own icy boots. He looked an impressive sight. Tufts of snow fox fur hung out from under each individual plate and Tarah figured his suit would make great camouflage in a winter campaign.

"Son of a turd, these boots are cold!" he griped, then returned his eyes to hers. "Just how far away is this house of yours? Will it take us out of our way?"

"No. Not at all," she said, her face earnest.

Djeri gave her a dull look. "Come on. Be straight with me. How far out of the way is it?"

"Tarah Woodblade is always straight," she said automatically.

He rolled his eyes.

"What? It's just-. It's . . ." Why couldn't she get anything past him? Tarah sighed. "It'll take us about a half day off course if we leave straight from here."

He frowned thoughtfully. "Wizard Valtrek was pretty insistent we get to these tracks quickly. Why is it so important we go to your place now?"

"I got clean sets of clothes and winter gear there," she said, which was true enough. "And I need to replace my broken bow." She finished tightening the bracer on her right arm and nodded, feeling more like herself, despite the cold.

"That's all?" he asked.

"Yeah," she said. Then added, "Well that and besides, I ain't been back there in months. I really need to check up on the place. I . . ." she nearly said more, but stopped herself.

Never tell your clients more than they need to know, Grampa Rolf said approvingly. *It's never good to air all your secrets.* The image of Rolf's impaled head flashed though Tarah's mind and she shivered. What was the reason for that list of crimes nailed to his head? Could they have been real? Had her grampa really done all those things? Surely not.

"Hmm," Djeri said. His eyes bored into her, his expression skeptical. Finally he shrugged and slid the handle of his great mace through the harness on his back. "Well, I guess those tracks have waited this long. What's a few more hours delay?"

She gave him a relieved smile. "Thank you, Djeri."

He smiled back. "We should hurry, though. Let's get going."

Tarah quickly began taking the camp down. While she did so, the details of her dream kept replaying themselves over and over in her mind. The moonrat man had been in her dream again; this time in her house. Why? And what was the reason for that giant? What had it all meant?

There was no need for them to cook, so she buried the coals and took down the clothes lines. Most of the clothes were still a bit damp, but not too bad. She packed them away, knowing that she would be able to replace them once she arrived at her house. Or at least that's what she hoped.

While she worked, Djeri fed the mule and put the bedrolls away. Several times she turned her head in his direction and caught him giving her a calculating look. It was obvious that something was still bothering him, but she decided not to worry about it. Get home. That's what was important.

They ate a quick breakfast of dried meat and fruit and set out. Tarah took them further down the path she had used the night before, heading deeper into the forest. A few miles later, she led them down a narrow fork in the trail.

Neither of them spoke for most of the way. With Neddy being so well behaved, Djeri didn't even have anything to gripe about. Tarah knew she should have been happy with the quiet. After all, this was the way she preferred to travel. The thing she found most annoying about being a guide was talkative clients. But for some reason, with Djeri nearby, the silence was awkward.

Tarah found herself looking back at him often. The whole time they walked, the troubled look never left his face. To her chagrin, she had a rising urge to break the silence. She ignored this feeling for awhile. She told herself to focus on what they would find when they reached her house. The silence stretched out, seeming more and more oppressive the longer they went.

Finally, Tarah cleared her throat. Djeri looked up at her, but she froze. What should she say?

Tell a story, Grampa Rolf suggested. *A good salesman often finds that a tale or two sets a client at ease.*

"You know, I-uh guided a nobleman through this part of the woods a few years back," she said lamely.

"Yeah?" Djeri replied.

"Yeah," she said. "I took him out here to hunt a moonrat."

The troubled look eased somewhat. "You found a nobleman that wanted to kill a moonrat?"

"Not exactly," Tarah said. "He didn't care so much about the killing of the thing. He just wanted to eat one."

A smile curled Djeri's lips. "Really?"

"Yeah!" Tarah said, encouraged by the dwarf's change in mood. "I met him in Pinewood. He'd been boasting at the local tavern, see? Told folks he was a fancy eater. He said he'd eaten all the good meats of the world. Said he'd try anything that could walk, crawl, or fly. Of course some of the boys decided to call him on it."

"Of course," Djeri said.

"They asked him, 'Have you eaten snakes?'. He says, 'Yes sir I have.' They said, 'You eaten bugs?' He says, 'As long as they aren't poisonous.'"

"He liked eating bugs?" Djeri asked.

"One of the boys asked him that. He said, 'It's true, my good man, that most of them don't taste very good. But crickets are quite tasty. Snails can be quite good too if you cook them just right."

"Snails!" the dwarf laughed out loud.

Tarah nodded. "Hey, don't knock it! My papa was into teaching me how to survive. He made me eat some strange things growing up and I tell you that nobleman was right. Snails can be pretty good."

"No thank you," Djeri said, waving a gauntleted hand. "I don't think surviving's that important to me."

"Yeah, well this nobleman wasn't eating those things to survive. He was just eating 'em 'for the experience', as he put it," Tarah explained. "That's when I heard one of the boys ask him if he'd eaten moonrat. He says, 'Dear sir, I have eaten many different types of rodentia. Each has their own flavor and some are finer than others."

"Rodentia?" Djeri said, laughing again.

"Yeah, that's how he put it," she said. "One of the boys had a clever idea. He decides to play a little trick on the nobleman and goes, 'Yeah, but you ain't eaten moonrat. Moonrat's a delicacy.' 'Course everybody in the room understood the joke and no one told the nobleman any different."

"Who was the prankster?" Djeri asked.

"Jono, son of Pell."

"I thought that might be him," Djeri said, nodding. "He was one of the ones you saved during the attack on Pinewood, wasn't he?"

"Yeah," Tarah said, her smile fading a bit.

"I met him during the siege on the Mage School," Djeri said. "He got himself into some trouble with his antics. I thought he was funny, but the leaders weren't too happy with him."

"Yeah," Tarah said. Jono wasn't one of her favorite people. "Sounds like Jono."

"What was the nobleman's name?"

"He was from House Stots," she said. "I think it was Wilson Stots, or something like that. It was a long time ago."

"Oh. I haven't heard of him, but go on," the dwarf said.

"Anyway, so Stots says, 'If anyone here has some moonrat I can try, I would be most happy to.' Jono says, 'Well the thing here is we have a local tradition regarding eating moonrat. See, you gotta hunt one down and eat it yourself."

"No," said Djeri, his eyes wide with amusement.

"Stots seemed kinda flustered. He says, 'Well, I would do so if I knew how to obtain this beast.'" Tarah's lip curled mischievously. "That's when I decided there was an opportunity to make some money and I spoke up. I said, 'I'll tell you what, mister nobleman. I'll take you out and help you find a moonrat to hunt.' The boys went crazy laughing. Jono says, 'Yeah! Take Woodblade! If anyone can find you a moonrat to eat, it's her." In truth that wasn't the way he put it, but Djeri didn't need to know all the details.

"Of course at this point, the man couldn't turn you down," Djeri surmised.

"He had no choice," she said. "His very pride was on the line. So he hired me. I took him out that very night. It was just me, him, and a couple Stots family guards. Now I could've taken him across the wizard's road and found him one right away, but he was paying me hourly and like my Grampa Rolf always says, 'Don't let an hourly hire off early.'"

Tarah paused, her cheeks reddening. Why had she said that? She knew better. Never say anything to a client that could make it sound like she'd cheat him.

To her relief, Djeri just chuckled. "Sounds like something my uncle would say."

She cleared her throat. "So anyway, I took him out in this direction. It was a good area mainly because the moonrats were much fewer on this side of the road and I didn't want to end up surrounded. You know, for his safety."

"Right," Djeri said knowingly.

"Well, we weren't one mile from town before Stots hears his first moonrat moan. That noble went so pale, he nearly glowed in the moonlight. Let me tell you, he was ready to abandon the whole hunt then and there. But I promised him I knew a good spot right close where we could find a rat and do it safe."

"Yeah right. Probably five miles away," the dwarf surmised.

"Hey, let me tell the story," Tarah said, then shrugged. "But you're not far off. I didn't find him a good one until I'd say maybe two hours after midnight or so. At that point, the moonrat moans had been echoing pretty steady for a long while and all three men were shaking in their boots. Now he didn't know it, but I'd been doing my best to steer us around all the big groups of rats. This was my first chance to get him one all alone.

"When he saw those glowing yellow eyes, I swear he

nearly died in surprise. He wasn't in no shape to battle the thing and I sure didn't want a dead noble on my record. So I whispered to him, saying, 'Hey, you can kill the thing if you want to. But if you'll pay me one extra silver, I can kill him for you and I won't tell anyone it was me who done it.' He says, 'My lady, I don't care how the beast dies. I just want out of here.'"

Djeri laughed again.

Tarah continued, "So I pick off the moonrat with a single arrow right through one of its ugly eyes. Stots has one of his men carry the thing and it stinks so bad, he makes him carry it downwind of us. Now here's the dangerous part. I knew the other moonrats could smell a corpse from far away. So I started leading the men all around the forest looking for ways to get back to Pinewood without being chased by a moonrat army.

"It was a long stroll, I'll say that right now. Stots gets nervous and he says, 'Pardon my asking, my lady, are we lost?' I say, 'Naw, I know exactly where we are.' Which was true. It was sunrise by the time we got back to Pinewood. Stots was so glad to see the place he paid double my asking price." Tarah ended the story with a wink and kept walking, satisfied that she'd changed the dwarf's mood around.

All was quiet for a few moments before Djeri burst out, "Well, did he eat it?"

Tarah nodded. "Oh yeah. He made a big deal of it. He brought out his personal cook and invited all the boys that'd been in the tavern the night before. He bragged about how dangerous the hunt had been and how fierce the battle. 'Course everyone knew it was me that killed it, not him."

"And what did he think of the taste?" the dwarf asked.

"Well it stank bad when they skinned it. His cook tried all kinds of spices and herbs, but when it started cooking over the spit, folks started gagging. Whoo, the smell was so wrong. It smelled like skunk spray mixed with baby poop and garlic."

Djeri started laughing again, this time so hard his face went red.

Tarah found his reaction encouraging and added some detail. "Not only did it smell bad, it looked nasty. The cook left the head and the tail on and everything. Then he started basting it with butter and somehow that made it smell worse. Folks started leaving at that point. I've gotta give it to Stots, though. He was determined. I left before it was done cooking, but Jono swears the noble ate an entire moonrat leg before he started losing it," Tarah said with a disgusted shake of her head.

"Anyway that smell hung around Pinewood for days. Stots got so sick that his guards finally had to take him back to the Mage School to see a specialist, but then he . . ."

Tarah trailed off, slowing her steps. She looked at the forest around them. Djeri was laughing even harder at that point, but something didn't feel quite right. The air smelled funny and there was a sound that bothered her.

"Ugh," Djeri said, wiping his eyes. "I'd feel bad for the poor guy if he wasn't so stupid. That reminds me of the time two dwarves from Wobble tried to cook up a moonrat. Their names were Kharl and Broose. They decided that-."

"Shh!" Tarah said, placing a finger against the dwarf's lips. She crouched, her staff at the ready. Djeri understood. His face grew deadly serious and he reached back and grabbed the head of his great mace, ready to pull it from its harness.

Tarah focused on her hearing and finally she made out the sound she was looking for. Something was running away from them through the leaves. She took off after it, running hunched over, her staff held out parallel to the ground. When she caught up to its tracks, she ran alongside them, her free hand dragging through the impressions as she went.

"It's a gorc!" she said. "And it's heading off to tell others we're coming!" She didn't wait for Djeri's response, but picked up her speed, having a good idea where it was going. The evil thing was headed towards her house!

Tarah had faced gorcs before, but this was the first time she had seen one in her forest. They were nasty creatures; one of the goblinoid races. Gorcs were larger and smarter than a goblin, but smaller and less intelligent than an orc. They were smart enough to make crude armor and weapons, but they preferred to fight with weapons and armor stolen from villages they raided or soldiers they'd killed.

Luckily, Tarah knew the area better than it did. The gorc weaved around trees and plunged through undergrowth, trying to slow down any pursuit, but it couldn't hide its intentions from her.

Tarah took a straighter path. She passed the gorc unseen and stopped to wait for it on the far side of a long patch of tangled briars.

The gorc was quite surprised when Tarah's staff darted out from behind a tree. She struck it in the shins, sending it sprawling into the leaves. It recovered quickly, jumping to its feet and spinning to face her, its sword already unsheathed.

Tarah's staff struck its hand, knocking the sword from its grip, then she swung back around with the other end, striking the gorc's temple. It crumpled to the ground, unconscious.

She stood over it, glowering. The gorc was an ugly thing. It had yellow skin mottled with brown spots. Large bushy eyebrows hung over its red eyes and its face was riddled with various piercings. A tattoo of a moonrat eye emblazoned on its forehead.

Tarah soon heard Djeri churning through the forest behind her. The dwarf plowed through the tangled briars, their wicked thorns doing little more than scratching the paint on his armor. By the time he caught up to her, Tarah had the creature bound.

"Blast you were fast! I didn't think I'd catch up to-." Djeri stood there for a moment, breathing heavy and staring at her captive. "You used the Pross technique for binding goblinoids," he said in surprise.

Its two feet were bound together, pulled behind its back and tied to its left arm, but she left its right arm free. It was an old academy trick her father had taught her. Goblinoids had a terrible command of the common tongue and in order to be understood, they used a lot of gestures.

"Yeah, I hope it gestures good, because I'm really tempted to simply kill it and move on," Tarah said.

"Hold on. Save your threats until the thing's awake," Djeri said. "Tell me, how do you know this technique?"

"Papa taught me," she said quietly, staring at its clothing. Its pants were cobbled together from animal skins, but its shirt was made of fine silk and fastened together in the front with silver buttons. Tarah's lips curled up into a snarl. "It's been to my house."

"How can you tell?" Djeri asked

"My house is less than a mile from here," she said and pointed. "See that shirt it's wearing? That belonged to my grampa."

Djeri's expression turned dark. "Right. Wake it up."

Tarah placed her boot in its belly.

The gorc awoke with a spray of vomit. It coughed and grimaced and spat, then jerked its free arm about in alarm. "My armss! My legs!" It reached back and seemed relieved to find that its limbs were intact. It turned its panicked gaze on them. "Curse you, beasts! Lets Ursus go!"

Tarah poked its chest with her staff. "What have you been doing in my house?"

The gorc snarled at her and then its eyes widened in surprise. Its lips twisted into a grin. "You're-! You're Woodblade!"

"You've heard of me?" she asked.

"You wears the misstress' children. You wields a staff of bloood. It's as foretold! You're Woodblade. You've come!"

"Did you say mistress?" Djeri asked. "You follow the witch?"

It ignored him, its eyes on Tarah. "Youu are marked for death!"

Tarah felt a jolt of fear. "Not any longer. The moonrat mother is dead."

"She can'tss die." Ursus sneered. "The misstress is eternal!"

Djeri gave Tarah a curious look, then backhanded the gorc, splitting its lip. He grabbed its face with one powerful hand and turned its attention to him. "She's right, gorc. Your mistress is dead. She was killed months ago, her dark forest destroyed. The war is over."

"No!" it cried, its eyes wide in denial. "No. She lives still! Clobber tells us the misstress' words." It raised a shaking hand and pointed to Tarah. "Clobber tells us of Woodblade's coming! Tells us of the rewards."

"Who is this 'Clobber'?" Djeri asked.

"He is the mistress' speaker. He has her great eye of command. He is the finders of the great sword, 'Killer', and he tells us of your coming!" It smiled at Tarah, revealing a mouth full of crooked and jagged teeth.

Tarah pushed away the fear. "Tell me about this sword,"

she demanded. "What does it look like?"

"Killer is Clobber's treasure. It shines! It glows in the sun. It cuts and burns!" it said fervently. "It was made to kills you, Woodblade."

Tarah's face paled. She felt light headed with sorrow. "Where . . . did he find this sword?"

"The misstress told him where to finds it," Ursus said, its eyes feverish. "She told him it is his glory!"

Tarah's hand rose to her mouth.

"How many of you are there?" Djeri said, turning its face back towards him.

The gorc refused to look at him, its eyes focused on Tarah. "We have been waiting for your return, Woodblade. Waiting for such a looong time!"

"Well I'm back!" Tarah snarled and thrust out with her staff, crushing its windpipe.

The gorc gurgled, clutching at its throat. Djeri shoved at its chest, trying to help it breathe, but his efforts were useless. Its eyes rolled up into its head and its movements ceased.

Djeri glared at her. "Why did you do that? We could have gotten more information out of it!"

"We don't need his information," Tarah said, glaring back at him.

"He could have told us how many of them there are and where they're staying," Djeri insisted. "He could have warned us of traps!"

Tarah raised one eyebrow at him, her jaw set firm. "You worry about how many of them there are? Traps?" She stabbed the butt of her staff into the ground. "This is my forest and I have their tracks."

Chapter Ten

"Hold on just a minute, Tarah," Djeri said, standing beside the gorc's corpse. "What's going on here? What are we getting into?"

"You heard it," she said, glaring at the gorc, her face twisted with rage. "The mother of the moonrats sent a bunch of goblinoids to my house and they've been waiting for me to come home."

"I heard that, but why?" Djeri asked. "Because of Pinewood?"

"Maybe. Partly." She ran a hand through her hair and began pacing. "To tell you the truth, I was probably a thorn in her side for a long time before that night. I've been killing moonrats my whole life. Disgusting things. I've led folks through her territory a few times, maybe helped the elves a time or two . . . I don't know."

"It said you were marked for death," Djeri said.

"Yeah, the moonrat mother told me that once. The night of the attack on Pinewood." She stopped, her eyes staring into the trees. "I heard her voice in my head promising I'd die. Happened just before I killed an orange-eyed rat."

She opened her mouth to say more, but she stopped herself. What was she about to say? It scared her so bad she ran away? Did she trust this dwarf enough to start blurting out all her secrets? Airing her shames?

Don't tell folks everything you know, said her grampa and papa in unison.

Her eyes locked onto Djeri's. The dwarf was watching her closely, gauging something. She could almost see a set of scales being weighed in his mind.

"How did you know?" he asked.

"What?"

"This morning. How did you know there was something happening at your house?" he asked. "You've been worried about it all day."

"Does it matter?" she said. "We're here now. We have proof that they're in my house, wrecking my stuff, stealing my things!"

"I want to know," he said.

"Why?" she said, throwing her hands up in frustration. "Look, if you don't want to help, that's fine. You're not working for me. I'll clean these things out on my own and come find you when I'm done."

She started to storm away, but Djeri grabbed her arm.

"Let go of me!" Tarah said, jerking out of his grip

Neddy picked that moment to appear, walking around the edge of the thicket. The mule saw their expressions and gave them a reproachful look. He sniffed at the dead gorc, then snorted and kicked dirt on it.

"I'm going," Tarah said.

"Just listen to me for one minute, woman!" Djeri commanded. He fixed her with a focused gaze. There wasn't any anger in his eyes, just frustration and determination and . . . maybe a little of something else? Worry? Tarah wasn't sure. "I am going to help you whether you tell me what's going on or not. I'm not completely sure why. But I am. Just please, as a favor to me . . . give me something, because two and two aren't coming together here."

Tarah wasn't quite sure what he meant, but she found herself nodding. "I had a dream last night. I-I can't explain it, but I had a dream that monsters were in my house and I when I woke up . . . I just knew that it was true."

"Oh," Djeri said, all doubt fading from his eyes. He gave her a relieved chuckle. "Why didn't you just say that this morning? I mean, good grief, I've been feeling led about by the nose all day."

"I don't get you," Tarah said in confusion.

"I knew from the moment you asked me that you weren't being straight with me about why you wanted to go home. But you tried to be convincing and I decided to trust that you had your reasons," he said. "But the farther we've walked away from our mission goal, the more its been bothering me."

"But I couldn't explain that to you," Tarah said. "It was a dream."

"Why not? I would have understood. Dreams are important. My father dreamt of my mother a week before he met her for the first time," he said earnestly. "He taught me that dreams are fate's way of communicating with us."

Tarah cocked her head at him. "But my dreams have never meant anything before."

"They did today," He said, kicking at the dead gorc for emphasis. "So what's your plan now? Did your dream tell you what to do next?"

"Well . . ." She tried to think of any clue in her dream; something that could help. "Not really. Just stay away from giants, I guess."

"Giants?" Djeri said. "Are there giants at your house?"

"I don't think so, but we'll find out soon. First, though." She knelt down and began undoing the buttons on her grampa's shirt. "I'm taking my stuff back from this gorc."

The gorc didn't have much else on him. Tarah found one of her spoons in its pockets, but that was it. When she was done searching it, they tossed the corpse deep into the thickets where it wouldn't be easily found if one of its friends arrived. Then Tarah convinced Djeri to wait with Neddy while she scouted ahead.

She headed on towards her house and saw signs of the intruders right away. She found more of Ursus' tracks, criss-crossed with tracks from several other goblinoids. She inspected the tracks and with each one she touched, more of the situation became clear. She returned to Djeri within the hour, her anger stoked.

"So what did you find?" the dwarf asked.

"There's ten of 'em. All are goblinoids. Two orcs, four gorcs, and three goblins. They've been staying in my house for six months waiting for me to return," she said, her lips twisted in rage. "Six months! Nature knows what they've done to it in that time!" She raised a hand to her eyes, tears flowing. *Oh papa! Grampa. I'm sorry!*

"That's okay," Djeri said, patting her back. "If you can

fight like the people of Pinewood say, we can handle that many."

Her hand creaked on her staff. "Tarah Woodblade can fight," she promised.

"Another thing. You said there were ten of them," Djeri pointed out. "But you counted off nine just now."

"There's nine I know of for sure. Then there's their leader. The one with the sword." Oh how she hoped she was wrong about the sword. "I didn't see any of his tracks, so I'm not sure what he is. All I could tell was that the others fear him." There had been a lot of fear in the tracks, but only brief flashes of their commander, barely enough to tell that he was ugly and muscular. "I think he's big, though. Probably an orc."

"You know that much even though you didn't see his tracks?" Djeri asked.

Tarah shrugged. "I told you I'm good." It wasn't a very good answer, but the dwarf didn't push her on it.

"Okay, so three orcs." Djeri rolled his shoulders. "This could be a good fight, then. Do you know how they're set up?" he asked as he walked to the mule and removed his half-helm.

"I didn't get close enough to see their formation, but their tracks did give me a good idea of their movements." She thought for a moment, trying to decide how much she could tell him. "The three remaining gorcs and two of the goblins are archers. They take turns staying in hidden places around the house for much of the day in case I show up, but they spend the rest of their time wandering around. Hunting mostly."

Djeri nodded as she talked, untying his full-helm from its saddle and tying his half-helm in its place. He turned to face her, his helmet stuck under his arm. "Archers put us at a disadvantage. Do you think you can kill one and take its bow? I'd like to have you on the perimeter, taking out as many of them as you can from afar."

Tarah's nose twitched at the thought of using a goblinoid bow, but she said, "That shouldn't be a problem."

"Good, then here's the plan," he said. "You head out. Get a bow. Kill their scouts and archers as quietly as you can. I'll give you a half hour."

"Then what are you going to do?" she asked.

He reached back and grabbed the head of his enormous

mace and pulled it from the straps on his back. It was a wicked thing, almost as long as he was tall and the head was a spiky octagon. He grasped the handle with one hand and rested the weapon on his shoulder. "I'm going to walk up to the front door."

Tarah smiled despite herself. "You can handle that?"

Djeri chuckled. "I know you've never had the chance to see me fight, so I'll let that remark slide."

"It does seem like a rather incomplete plan, though," she said. "What if we get there and find more trouble than I thought?"

He raised an eyebrow, "Could the great Tarah Woodblade be wrong?"

"No," she said automatically. "But the plan still seems a little bare bones."

"I like to improvise," Djeri explained.

"And what do we do about Neddy?"

"We leave him here and come back for him later," he said. "We'll tie him of course, so he doesn't get lost."

The mule snorted in disdain at the idea.

"I don't think we'll need to tie him," Tarah said. She walked over to the mule and placed a hand on his forehead. "You'll wait for us, won't you, Neddy?" Neddy snorted and pawed the ground. She nodded. "He'll wait."

Djeri shrugged. "Fine, but hear me, mule. If you take off with our things, we'll hunt you down. And I'm not afraid of eating mule steaks."

The mule's eyes narrowed.

"Alright," Tarah said. She took her quiver from the mule's saddle and slung it over her shoulder. "I'm off, then. Head straight north from here and you'll see the path to my house."

"Remember, you have a half hour," Djeri said. He placed the full helm on his head. She could barely see his eyes through the slits in the metal. "Be quick. I don't want to have to take them all on by myself."

Tarah nodded and ran ahead, her staff held loosely. Her thoughts churned. Djeri was putting a lot of faith in her and he barely knew her. She had to take out a lot of the goblinoids before he arrived, or he wouldn't survive. The thought of his death disturbed her more than she expected.

She focused on finding an archer.

The secret to taking out a bowman with a staff is to get as close to him as possible without being seen, her grampa instructed.

"Yeah-yeah," Tarah mumbled and pushed his thoughts away. She knew what to do.

Tarah headed towards her house, keeping her footfalls as silent as possible. At the same time, she listened for movement and looked for tracks. Most of the ones she saw were old and of no current use, but she began to see a pattern. The old tracks were fainter, the footfalls light as if the goblinoids had been more careful about leaving obvious tracks. But the newer the tracks, the sloppier they were.

Tarah touched a few of them and sure enough, her suspicions turned out to be correct. From the flashes of thought that passed through her mind at each track, Tarah understood that the six months of waiting had taken a toll on the goblinoids. In the beginning, all of them had been fervent believers. They were diligent because their mistress had commanded them to follow Clobber to this place and wait for Tarah Woodblade's return. Then time passed and their patience had worn thin.

They had run out of provisions and become unruly. There had been fifteen of them in the beginning, but Clobber had been forced to kill four of them to keep the others in line. The more time went by, the more apathetic the goblinoids had become. Now they had to search farther and farther to find food and they stopped bothering to cover their tracks.

She began thinking of ways to use that against them. Tarah was so focused in her thoughts that she didn't sense the first goblin coming until they were both in sight of each other. They both blinked stupidly for a moment before Tarah darted towards him.

The goblin let loose a short squeak of fear before unsheathing a rusty short sword. The creature was fairly small, perhaps four feet tall, and scrawny, its mottled green skin stretched across a crooked frame. Its baggy clothing was cinched by one of her Grampa Rolf's belts.

Tarah felt a moment of disappointment that it wasn't one of the archers before she swung her staff. She leaned into the blow, focusing her weight onto the tip. The goblin tried to defend itself, but the hard red wood knocked aside its hasty block. Her staff caught the goblin in the side of the head.

There was a muted sound, like a rock striking a rotted stump. The goblin's feet flew out from under it and its head struck the ground with enough force that, if it hadn't already been dead, the impact alone would have killed it.

Tarah didn't bother to check this one's body. There would be time for that later. She dragged it into a bush and kept on, her mind refocused. She had limited time to find and kill the archers before Djeri arrived at her door.

She followed the goblin's tracks for a while and learned that it had been with some others, but had left them to hunt on its own. Evidently the other two were gorc archers. They had shot a rabbit and had refused to share their kill with the goblin. They were going to cook it and eat it far away from their leader Clobber so he wouldn't try to claim a share.

Two archers. Tarah nodded, biting her lip in concern. She headed in their direction, having a good idea where they were from the pictures in the goblin's memory. This could be tricky. To take out both archers she would need to catch them by surprise. Hopefully they were eating next to each other.

The smell of smoke soon caught her nostrils and Tarah slowed down. She moved towards the cook fire on silent feet. The scent of the burnt fur caused Tarah to grimace in distaste. The gorcs hadn't even bothered to skin their catch first.

She heard them before she saw them. The two gorcs were muttering to each other, arguing about how to divide their meal. They were hunched over an impromptu spit, their fire set in the middle of a pile of leaves. Tarah frowned, surprised that six months of messy fires like that hadn't burned the forest down.

She was pleased by one thing, though. The archers were standing close together. Their bows were lying on the ground behind them. Tarah shifted from tree to tree, making sure their backs were to her as she closed in. Finally she was as close to them as she could get. It was time to break cover and attack.

Tarah moved from behind the tree and crept towards them, feeling a surge of fear. She became angry with herself. Why did this happen? Why was it that every time she faced danger, she became a coward? Tarah Woodblade didn't feel fear!

She was almost within striking distance when one of them glanced over his shoulder. Its forehead was covered by a moonrat eye tattoo similar to the one on Ursus. The gorc's eyes met hers and it cried out. Tarah shoved her fear aside and ran forward, her staff in mid-swing.

It raised its arms defensively. Her blow knocked it to the ground and from the sound of its cry of pain, Tarah was pretty sure that she had broken both limbs. She spun, her staff in motion, but its companion had backed out of reach. This second gorc giggled at her, unconcerned for its friend. Unlike the others, its tattoo was on its temple.

"The Woodblade!" it said in recognition, a feverish gleam in its eye. It held a narrow sword in its hand. Tarah felt a chill of warning. She had not heard it draw the blade. The sword was clean and made of good steel, telling her that it was something stolen during the war. It twirled the sword with a flourish, showing practiced hands. "The mistress will be pleased!"

"I'm sure she will be," Tarah said. She spun her staff several times and stopped in attack posture. "You can tell her all about me, soon."

She sent two swift strikes at the gorc, but to her chagrin, it dodged both blows and darted forward with a counter strike. Tarah was barely able to bring her staff back around to block the attack. This gorc was good. She couldn't afford to mess around.

"Oh, the rewards will be great!" the gorc taunted. "When I bring Clobber your head, he wi-!"

Tarah dove forward, her staff a blur. The gorc blocked the first strike, but the follow up snapped its elbow. She pivoted and sent four more strikes in. To the gorc's credit, it managed to dodge one of them, but she scored heavy hits to its hip, its knee, and finally the wrist of its sword hand.

The gorc looked shocked as the hilt of the sword fell from its useless fingers. Tarah spun and swung her staff in one more heavy blow, destroying the gorc's face. It fell dead.

"Die, Woodblade," said another voice. Tarah turned just in time to see that the first gorc was standing. It pulled an arrow back on its bow.

She had been wrong. She had misjudged the blow and hadn't broken its arms. That was the thought that passed through Tarah's mind as it released the arrow. To her relief, the arrow shot out to the far right and she saw that she hadn't been completely wrong after all. The arm that held the bow hadn't broken, but the wrist on its other arm was bent at an odd angle. It was surprising that the gorc had been able to pull back an arrow at all. Perhaps the stress it was under had numbed it to the pain. The gorc reached back to draw another arrow, but its hand missed the quiver.

Tarah didn't give it a chance to try again. She drove the butt of her staff deep into its abdomen. It fell forward and she delivered a finishing blow to the back of the gorcs head, cracking its skull.

"Now I have a bow," she said. But as she picked up its bow, she frowned in distaste. The orc's bow was warped. The stupid thing hadn't cared for the weapon and had let it sit wet. Tarah snarled and cast the useless thing aside, then looked for the other bow.

Fortunately, the other gorc had taken better care of his weapon. The bow wasn't of great quality, but it was at least serviceable. She paused for a moment, looking down at its corpse.

The creature had been exceptional for a gorc. What had made it so? How had it become so skilled with the blade? For a moment she felt compelled to reach out and touch the gorc's ruined face. Part of her wanted to try and absorb memories from its corpse in the same way that she absorbed them from tracks. There had to be a way to understand such a creature. There had to be a way to use it.

Tarah stopped her hand from touching the corpse. That last thought hadn't come from her own mind. Tarah glared warily at her staff. Sure enough, it had absorbed some of the gorc's blood

There were times she wondered about the weapon. It seemed as though it had desires of its own or some unknown purpose beyond tracking. She felt it strongest after a kill. The staff was eager. It wanted something more from the gorc, and drinking its blood was only part of it.

The fire, said her papa's voice and Tarah shook her head, pushing the uncomfortable thoughts aside. He was right. She should put out the gorcs' sloppy fire, but another concern popped up. How much time had passed? Had it been a half hour yet?

With a curse, she tossed aside the half-cooked rabbit carcass and stomped out the flames. It would be best to bury the embers, but she settled for kicking the leaves away from the spot before continuing on.

There were seven goblinoids left and two of them were archers. She needed to find them fast. She touched the tracks of the two gorcs she'd killed, but only felt their desire to eat their kill and hide it from their leader. She circled around towards her house, keeping to the trees.

Her ears caught the sound of running through the leaves and she turned in time to see a gorc running to the north and west of her. There was a bow in its hand and a full quiver on its back. Tarah shoved her staff through the harness on her back and started after it, drawing an arrow.

Djeri paced back and forth next to the mule, grumbling, his great mace heavy in his hands. He hated this part of battle; the waiting. Every moment that went by brought a jumble of emotions: anticipation for the fight, worry, fear of death, relief that the fighting had not yet begun. This time was worse than usual. He was still trying to process the enigma that was Tarah Woodblade.

He kicked at a rock, sending it tumbling through the leaves. They called him Djeri the Looker. It was an odd name, badly worded, but he was proud of it. He was observant. It was a gift he'd always had. He could look at a situation and immediately recognize the intricacies. It was the same with people. If Djeri just spent a few hours with a person, he could usually understand them.

Tarah Woodblade, though. That girl was different. Every time he thought he had her figured out, she turned him on his ear. Mostly she was smart and confident, a seasoned adventurer. But at times she was insecure and frightened, like a young girl out on the trail for the first time. At times she came off as fake. For a while he had been sure she was acting or putting on a show, as if her entire persona was a carnival act. But he couldn't deny her skill. The girl knew what she was doing. She was able to learn things from tracks that Djeri found hard to believe. He needed to know more about the girl's history.

He let the head of his mace hit the ground and lifted his visor, eyeing the mule. "What do you think, Neddy? What's with Tarah?" The mule snorted and bent down, pushing leaves aside with his lips, looking for something to eat underneath.

Djeri narrowed his eyes. Neddy knew what he was asking.

It was smarter than it looked. Tarah had seen that.

He sighed. It was time to go. He patted the mule's neck. "Listen here. You stay like Tarah told you. We'll be back before dark."

He set off in the direction Tarah had shown him, setting the weight of his mace onto his shoulder. His anxiety began to fade. He found the weight of his mail and weapon comforting as he walked. It was a reminder. He had work to do.

That was the thing most people didn't understand about the Defense Guild. Most people thought the armor they wore was about safety. There were even academy graduates that thought wearing platemail was a cowardly choice.

During the war, he'd heard jeers from his friends, saying men in the Defense Guild were just afraid of getting hit. No, it just allowed them to get hit harder. They could take heavy blows and keep fighting, taking down foes that were larger or stronger or even more skilled. In that way, the platemail they wore was just as much a weapon as their swords and axes.

Tarah hadn't understood either. The night before, when he'd refused to take off his armor, it wasn't because of some sense of prudishness. It wasn't embarrassment over her seeing him unclothed, despite what he had told her that night. Why had he told her that anyway? The image of Tarah's body flashed through his mind and Djeri's face flushed. He shoved the thought away. It truly hadn't been because of some insecurity over being in that defenseless state, sitting at the fireside next to a statuesque . . .

Djeri's steps slowed briefly, his mind wandering. Then he growled and strode forward faster. He took the mace off of his shoulder and let the weight of it rest in his hands. No, his reluctance to remove his armor had been about the code of the Defense Guild. He was on a job. His armor was his tool and he had work to do. That's all.

He churned through the leaves, swinging his mace from time to time as he walked. It was going to feel good to crush something again. He came across a large rotting stump and, on a whim, swung at it. With a satisfying thump and a hail of splinters, the mace sunk into the wood.

Djeri nodded in satisfaction, but when he tried to remove it, the head was stuck. With a curse, he pulled on it and worked the mace back and forth, wrenching it free. He looked down at the mace in his hands.

It was an ugly thing. At least that's what he had been told. He understood why people felt that way. The mace was overly large. The workmanship of the haft was sturdy, but not fancy and the octagonal head was just a little malformed, as if the smith had held it in the forge too long. The spikes were of varying lengths and some of them even bent.

Those bent spikes were actually why he had bought it from a trader so many years ago. His friends had laughed, but Djeri saw a history in it. This was a weapon that had seen heavy use and against tough foes. When he carried it into battle, that history was shown to each enemy and he had seen the fear it had caused reflected in their eyes.

Djeri smiled and set it back on his shoulder, shaking his head. Of course that was why he had chosen it for this mission. He had been away from adventuring for a long time and of all the weapons he owned, this was the one that made him feel the most intimidating. This ugly weapon was his declaration to the world that Djeri was back.

It wasn't long before he came upon the path Tarah had described. It was about three paces wide and free of rocks and weeds. He stepped onto it and headed towards her house, wondering if Tarah had obtained a bow yet. Not that it mattered much. He would plow through the goblinoids anyway.

After a short distance, wide paving stones appeared on the path. They looked rough-hewn, as if cut by hand, but they were set well and didn't shift under his feet. It seemed truly out of place this deep in the forest, like something a dwarf would do.

Just then a goblin walked out of the trees not ten yards in front of him. A fur cap sat on its head, partially obscuring a circular tattoo. Its eyes widened in surprise and it dropped the firewood it carried. "A dwarf!"

"Are you scared?" Djeri asked, giving it a toothy grin. He hefted his mace and it turned and ran, shouting. He chuckled and lowered the visor on his helmet as he followed. His other concerns faded altogether. Now there was only battle in his mind.

He followed the panicked goblin down the path through a dense copse of trees. It shouted all the way, warning of dwarf invaders. Then as the path left the copse, Tarah's house came into view. Djeri paused for a moment despite himself, taking it in. The place looked nothing like he had expected.

The front of the house was of log cabin design, with a thatch roof that hung out over a wide front porch. It had a large single front window and a thick front door that was painted red. The strange part was the way the house disappeared into the side of a steep and rocky hill, looking as if it had been half consumed by the earth. He could tell that despite its oddness, the house had once been a tidy place, well taken care of.

The front window had been broken outwards, pieces of a chair still wedged in the frame. The yard was spotted with burnt spots where cook fires had been set and several of the large paving stones had been overturned or broken. Scraps of paper and parchment littered the ground along with bits of colorful fabric, likely the pieces of clothing the goblinoids had decided not to use.

Sitting on opposite edges of the porch were two burly orcs, both with moonrat eye tattoos on their foreheads. They had small knives in their large hands and were carving something into the wooden supports. As the shouting goblin ran up the pathway towards them, they looked up from whatever they were whittling and rolled their eyes as if this was a common occurrence. The goblin stopped half way to the porch and began jumping up and down and pointing.

Djeri's fingers tightened on the haft of his mace. He let his anger build at these goblinoids, these monsters, laying in wait as they defaced Tarah's home. He ran towards them. The orcs froze in surprise when they saw him appear from the copse. He lifted the mace over his head.

"Dwarf! Dwarf, stupids!" The goblin was yelling. It was so focused on getting the orcs' attention that it didn't notice Djeri running up behind it. "I tells you, it's a mean nasty dw-!"

Djeri's mace burst its skull, the force of his blow driving its small body into the paving stones. He jumped over its crushed form and ran on, bits of the creature remaining stuck to the weapon's bent spikes.

The orcs stood and clutched their weapons. One of them, with orange skin and crude leather armor, carried what looked like a woodsman's axe. The other, brown-skinned and muscular, wore no armor, but carried a wide wooden shield and a spiked mace. The goblin's death didn't seem to frighten them as much as Djeri had hoped. Both of them had odd grins on their faces as they started towards him.

These beasts were fanatics. Somehow even with the witch they worshipped dead, they still believed. Djeri planned to disabuse them of that notion. He didn't wish to be caught between them, though, so he angled his trajectory towards the orc without the shield.

Just before he reached the orange-skinned orc, he heard the unmistakable sound of an arrow plinking off his shoulder pauldron. He caught a quick glimpse of a goblin archer standing on the hillside above the house. There was nothing he could do about that. He just had to hope that it wasn't good enough to hit a gap in his armor. Where was Tarah?

The orc, a good foot taller than the dwarf, swung his axe down in an angle aiming for the joint at Djeri's neck. Djeri leaned forward, twisting his body so that the axe missed its mark, glancing off his back plate. At the same time he brought his mace low on a sideways strike that hit the orc in the side of the knee.

Its limb crumpled inward and the orc cried out as it fell to the side. Djeri tore his mace free from its leg and ignored another arrow that bounced off his helmet. He turned to face the second orc.

This one was a bit more cautious. After seeing its friend downed, it stopped and watched the dwarf warily, its shield held in front of it, its mace held back, ready to strike at the right moment.

"Are you scared, orc?" Djeri asked, stepping towards it. The orc took a step back.

"Clobber!" it yelled. "We're being attacked!"

"My leg! Mistress! My leg!" shouted the other, laying on the ground, clutching its ruined knee.

Another arrow zoomed by, this one missing Djeri completely. There was another goblin archer, this one standing on the rooftop. Where was that girl? There was a loud thump from inside the house.

Djeri knew he had to finish the two orcs off quickly before their leader arrived. Well, one was easy. He feinted at the brown-skinned orc, causing it to take another cautious step back, then spun around, swinging his mace down in a back-handed blow that caught the first orc in the face. When he brought his weapon back up and faced the remaining orc again, there were shreds of orange skin stuck in the spikes.

"Blasted dirt-grinder!" the orc spat, a common derogatory term for dwarves among orcs. "Come! I've killed your kind before."

This one did seem to have fought with dwarves before. Or at least it knew what to do. It held its wide shield low to avoid attacks to the legs and its mace was cocked back, ready to strike a downward blow if Djeri came too close. With enough strength behind it, a direct blow would crumple even a dwarven helmet.

Djeri smiled, his keen eyes catching something. If this thing really had fought some of his kin, he hoped that it had fought them with this same shield. Because if it had, they had done him a favor. The wood was chipped and gouged as if by many weapons, but one weapon in particular, likely an axe, had started a fine crack that ran the length of the shield, right along the grain.

"Hurry up, Clobber!" the orc shouted. "Mrag just died!"

Another loud thump came from within the house.

"Are you ready?" Djeri asked the orc. He took one step back and tensed his body, gripping the shaft of his ugly mace with both hands and bringing it into striking position.

He heard the rush of another arrow, but this one came nowhere near him. One of the goblins cursed.

"Come at me, dirt-grinder!" the orc growled, his muscles taught and ready.

Djeri came. His powerful legs churned and he covered the distance between them faster than the orc expected. Djeri put his full force into the swing, putting all his strength into it. The orc lifted his shied into position and Djeri shifted his weight just enough to bring his weapon in line with the perfect spot.

The steel head struck the cracked spot with more of a devastating impact than Djeri had expected. The shield split in two, sending splinters of wood into the orc's face and eyes. The mace drove into the orc's arm, shattering bone and knocking it off its feet. The orc landed on its back, shards of wood scattered all around it.

Determined not to let it recover, Djeri walked to its side

and stomped on the hand holding its weapon. The orc groaned and looked towards him. One of its eyes had been pierced by splinters, but the remaining one focused on him with hatred and disbelief.

"That was a bad shield," Djeri said with a shake of his head.

"Clobber will kill you," it promised.

"Not likely," Djeri replied and swung his mace down again, ending the beast. He tore the weapon free and grimaced at its gory state. The worst thing about this mace was the cleanup.

Another loud sound echoed from the house and Djeri turned to see the door shudder. With a creak, the door swung inward. From the pool of sunlight where Djeri was standing, he couldn't see through the dark interior.

"What's this?" said a deep voice. A hulking shadow stirred within. With loud heavy steps, the leader edged through the doorway. "You kill the mistress' servants, dwarf-dirt?"

Clobber came to the edge of the porch and rose to his full height, nearly seven and a half feet tall. Djeri sighed as the sunlight illuminated his enemy. This was more trouble than he'd expected.

Clobber was an ogre.

Chapter Eleven

Tarah arrived at the top of the hill just in time to see Djeri knock the orange-skinned orc down. The dwarf was brutally efficient. Each blow of his heavy mace not only crushed bone, it tore free chunks of flesh leaving his opponent a broken and bloody mess. Tarah shivered at the savagery of it.

She saw an arrow clang off of the dwarf's helmet and scanned the area. Two goblin archers were on the hillside above the dwarf, one of them on her roof. Fortunately, their bows were small and their arrows crudely made. It would take an amazing shot to injure the dwarf.

Nevertheless, she didn't hesitate. Tarah fired twice in quick succession. The first goblin was just beginning its slow tumble down the hill when her second arrow pierced the other one through the head. It fell just as Djeri charged the second orc.

Tarah whistled softly to herself as she watched the dwarf's swift blow destroy its shield and throw the orc to the ground like a rag doll. She began to pick her way down the hill towards the dwarf, but she didn't make it very far before Clobber emerged, his voice deep and fearsome.

The ogre stepped into the sunlight, and stood to his full height, half again as tall as the dwarf and as wide as two men, with a bulging muscular body. She had never seen an ogre this large in person before. He wore a breastplate made by the crude joining together of two man-sized breastplates and a pair of her papa's breeches strained to fit his legs.

Inset in the ogre's thick overhanging brow, as if pushed halfway into his skull, was a green moonrat eye. The eye was shriveled and veiny and the skin around it was puffed up and enflamed.

In his right arm, he held an enormous iron shield. It was shaped like a long rectangle and had a snarling moonrat face painted on its surface. He took another step forward and Tarah saw that he dragged an enormous sword behind him, its handle clutched in one hand. The blade was sharp and highly polished and two elemental runes were carved into the metal near the tip.

Tarah's jaw clenched so tight that her teeth hurt. It was as she had feared. The ogre carried her papa's sword. A memory came unbidden to her mind of her papa polishing the weapon by the fireside, the soft glow of the firelight making the blade seem to gleam.

Though Djeri must have found the ogre's appearance intimidating, he didn't let on. The dwarf let the head of his greatmace fall to the ground in front of him and leaned forward on its pommel casually, his hands gripping the handle. "So you're the one they call Clobber?"

"You killed my followers!" the ogre accused pointing with a rigid finger.

Tarah couldn't see Djeri's face through his visor, but she imagined a smile on his lips. "I work for the Battle Academy. Killing goblinoids is one of my jobs. As is killing ogres that invade the homes of my friends."

"Friends?" The ogre's wide mouth stretched into a grin. "You are friends with the Woodblade?"

"She's quite upset with you," Djeri said.

"The Woodblade comes?" shouted the ogre. "Bring her here! She must die for my mistress!"

Tarah's first arrow struck the ogre in the base of his muscular neck. "You don't have a mistress! Not anymore!"

"There you are!" Djeri said. He pointed to the hill above her house. "There've been archers firing at me from up on the . . . oh. I see you got those."

He was interrupted by a laugh as the ogre tore the arrow free. Though the wound bled profusely, Tarah hadn't struck a major artery. "The mistress said to wait. She promised you would come!"

"She was right!" Tarah said, firing again. She aimed for the juncture of his jaw line and neck, but this time he brought his shield up and the arrow bounced harmlessly away.

"You can't kill me with arrows!" The ogre bellowed. "The mistress showed me my death and it is glory!"

"Watch me!" Tarah said, firing again. The ogre raised his shield, but she wasn't aiming for his neck. The arrow pierced his calf instead. "Your shield isn't big enough, idiot!"

The ogre grunted, but ignored the injury, stepping forward. "I will kill you after your dwarf-friend is dead!"

Another arrow darted in, driving deep into the ogre's foot. It grunted again and Djeri laughed.

"I don't think you'll make it over to me!" the dwarf said as Tarah fired again. Another arrow plunked into the ogre's calf right next to the first one.

With a growl, Clobber crouched behind the shield to better cover himself from Tarah's bow. He then lifted her father's sword and crept slowly towards the dwarf.

Tarah pursed her lips. The shield hid him pretty well. She reached back and fingered the feathering on her arrows, wishing she had taken some from the gorcs. She had only five left; two steel-tipped, two iron, and one with a stone tip. She moved further down the hill to get in closer range. "Watch out, Djeri! That sword is sharp!"

"This is Killer!" Clobber announced, raising the blade into the air. "The mistress' gift!"

For a brief moment, the ogre's head rose above the shield, giving Tarah a narrow window. She fired for his temple, but the ogre brought his shield up slightly. The steel-tipped arrow glanced off the top of the shield and penetrated the ogre's scalp. It traveled along the top of his skull to stick out the other side like a garish tribal piercing. Blood poured down either side of his face, but the ogre made no sign of his discomfort and continued his slow advance on the dwarf.

"Just back away, Djeri. I'll pin him down!" Tarah shouted.

Djeri didn't move, still leaning on the pommel of his gory mace. "I'm not afraid of his sword."

"Killer will chop you in two!" Clobber sneered. Tarah fired an iron arrow at his foot and cursed as it stuck into the bottom of the ogre's boot heel. "Your armor is nothing, dwarf-dirt!"

"Your face is nothing," Djeri spat.

"Move, Djeri!" Tarah yelled. "I know that sword!"

"Too late!" said the ogre. In one fluid motion, Clobber lurched forward, coming briefly to his full height as he swiped down with his massive arm. The sword, designed to be used two-handed by a human, had a blade that was four-feet-long.

Tarah watched in horror, fully expecting the dwarf to be cleaved in two. But Djeri was deceptively fast. As the sword came down, he leapt backward, jerking his mace with him. The tip of the sword scored the front of the dwarf's breastplate, leaving a long jagged tear, but it didn't slice his flesh.

The ogre quickly ducked back behind his shield.

"Hey!" Djeri said, his anger directed at Tarah. "Why didn't you fire? I just gave you the perfect opportunity."

Tarah's face flushed. He was right. While the ogre had made his strike, several critical areas had been exposed. Why hadn't she fired? Tarah pulled back another steel-tipped arrow. "Sorry! I won't miss next time."

"I hear you!" said the ogre, rage in his voice. "I'm not scared."

"You should be," Djeri taunted. "We killed all your friends. Your mistress is dead."

"No! She lives!" Clobber yelled. He made as if to lunge again, but thought better of it and stopped, remaining crouched behind his protection. "She speaks to me!"

"Liar! You haven't heard from her in three months?" Djeri snorted. "Come on! Come closer so I can kill you too!"

Tarah watched with concern as Djeri lowered his gory mess of a mace. It was as if he was unconcerned with the ogre's next attack. She nearly cried out in warning, but thought better of it. Surely the dwarf was doing this on purpose to draw the ogre out. She began to edge around as they spoke, hoping to get a better angle.

"The mistress talks to me! She's part of me," the ogre declared, shifting behind the shield in a way that Tarah couldn't see. Djeri could see what he was doing though and he didn't seem concerned.

"Yeah, I see that eye in your head," the dwarf said with a knowing nod. "I'll bet it's been hard keeping your friends convinced that you were still in charge. It had to be difficult for someone as stupid as you are to make it sound like you were giving out her instructions."

"She wants you dead now too, dwarf-dirt!" the ogre snapped.

"Is that so?" Djeri said. He let the head of his mace hit the ground and took a step forward, right in the path of the ogre's previous strike. "That eye in your head itches, doesn't it, now that it's started to rot?"

The ogre roared and attacked again, launching his long body forward, his arm stretched out in a mighty swing. This time he brought his shield up with him, protecting his head and neck as he struck. Djeri saw the sword coming, but he didn't jump away. The dwarf leaned into the attack instead, yanking the ugly head of his mace up from the ground just in time to connect with the long blade.

Tarah wanted to scream at him to dodge, but didn't let his opportunity slip away. She launched the steel-tipped arrow into the ogre's lower back just under the lip of his armor, a kidney shot. She ran towards them, knowing that her strike hadn't been enough, sure that Djeri had been cut down.

The ogre gasped in pain and sunk back behind the safety of his shield. To Tarah's surprise, the dwarf was standing unharmed. He was staring dumbfounded at the head of his mace which had been cleaved nearly in two, the halves hanging open like a split melon.

Tarah laughed in relief and notched her second to last arrow. Clobber wasn't doing as good a job covering himself anymore. His wounds were taking a toll.

"Agh!" Clobber yelled. "Go away, dwarf! I must kill the Woodblade."

"My mace!" Djeri said. "You split my favorite mace!" He charged the ogre, his weapon swinging back. The ogre shifted to meet him.

Tarah couldn't allow the dwarf to be struck by that sword again. She fired, her iron-tipped arrow striking the back of the ogre's left leg just above the knee. Clobber reared back, but was unable to stand, his hamstring severed. He fell to his knees and brought up his sword in just enough time to block the dwarf's blow.

Djeri's mace struck the ogre's blade with an audible ring

and one of its hanging halves broke completely free, bouncing off the ogre's breastplate before hitting the ground. The dwarf leaned into the ogre, the remaining half of his mace gripping the sword. Djeri let go of the weapon with one hand and punched the ogre in the face with his gauntleted fist.

"Stop!" Clobber complained and Djeri struck him again, breaking the ogre's nose. The dwarf had him pinned. He couldn't stand because of the wound in his legs. He couldn't move his left arm because it was holding his shield, and the dwarf's weight kept him from moving his sword arm.

Tarah now had a clear shot of the ogre's back. She sank her last arrow into the ogre's lower back beside the other one. The ogre howled in pain and frustration. Djeri's fist struck a third time, catching him in the open mouth.

Teeth hit the ground and Clobber roared, shoving with all his strength. Djeri rolled to the side, allowing the ogre's arm to push past him. Then the dwarf completed his spin and brought the remaining half of his mace down against the side of the ogre's head. Clobber fell to the side with a groan, landing on top of his shield.

"Now," Djeri said. "You big pile of-."

Tarah pushed past the dwarf and stood over the ogre, placing one foot on his chest. "You said I couldn't kill you with an arrow." She grabbed the steel-tipped that still protruded from Clobber's scalp and tore it free. She pulled back.

"M-mercy," the ogre pleaded, tears running from his eyes. "P-please. I'll go back home. I'll leave the little peoples alone."

"Tell your mistress that Tarah Woodblade survived," she said and fired, piercing the moonrat eye in the center of his forehead. Clobber's eyes rolled up and he went still. Tarah stepped back and threw the bow down on top of him.

Djeri stood there stunned for a moment. "That was brutal."

Tarah turned on the dwarf with a snarl and shoved him. "What were you thinking? He could've killed you!"

Djeri barely moved. "Why did you do that?"

"What? Kill him?" she asked, incredulous. "You were going to kill him."

He took off his helmet and looked at her with questioning eyes. "He said 'mercy', Tarah."

You don't kill an enemy that's asked for quarter, agreed her papa.

"Shut up both of you!" she yelled and pointed at the dwarf. "This thing didn't deserve mercy, not after what it did."

Djeri's brow furrowed, "I know that it's been living in your home, stealing your things-."

"Living in my house? This is my papa's sword!" She pried the pommel of the sword from the ogre's dead fingers. Flashes of thought poured through her mind as she touched the weapon; the ogre's triumph at his find, his religious fervor as he slew one of the goblinoids that wanted to leave. She gasped and shoved the sword into the dwarf's arms. "None of his memories remain with it now."

Djeri nodded slowly, "I understand how you feel."

"Do you?" she asked, glaring. "I buried this sword with my papa ten years ago. This isn't theft, this is desecration."

The dwarf had nothing to say to that. There was sadness in his eyes as she turned away, leaving the weapon with him. Tarah walked towards her house, pulling her staff from the harness on her back as she went. She had to see what else the creatures had done. How many of her memories were left?

The scraps of paper lay scattered around her porch meant little at first. Then she bent down and picked one up. Her hands shook. It was a page from one of her books. She scanned over the small amount of writing but couldn't tell which book it was from. She strode up to the porch. It hadn't occurred to her that they might destroy her collection on top of everything else. She rushed through the front door, her heart pounding.

As she waited for her eyes to adjust to the light, the first thing she noticed was the smell. Her house smelled like a wild animal's den; all musk and body odor. And the air was damp. Why was the air damp?

The front room had once been a tidy space. A round dinner table and chairs had sat on one side next to a cupboard, while two more cushioned chairs sat in front of the fireplace. Now the kitchen chairs were broken in pieces and the table stained and covered in vile carvings. The padding on the chairs by the fire had been torn out and shreds of paper were scattered all across the floor. The walls had been painted with strange symbols and representations of the moonrat mother. Each one more vulgar than the next.

She touched her grampa's chair by the fire, hoping against hope that she would feel some remnant of his thoughts. Unwanted memories flashed through her mind instead; the evil thoughts of the goblinoids as they had defaced the room, followed by the ogre gleefully feeding her books to the fire. She withdrew her hand as if stung and moved down the hall, tears streaming down her face. The two doors at the end of the hallway had been defaced with more painting, but remained closed. Tarah paused, afraid to open them.

Her papa had built their house over the mouth of a cave that extended into the hillside. The cave had been converted into their sleeping space. Her parents had built a wall dividing the cave into two rooms, one for them and one for Tarah.

She placed a hand on the doorknob to her room, hoping at the very least that her hiding spot had been undiscovered. Tarah winced as the bloodthirsty thoughts of the ogre entered her mind. She shoved the door open. That musky stench was stronger here.

It was immediately obvious to her that Clobber had taken her bedroom as his own. Her bed frame had collapsed under his weight, her blankets dirtied. Her dresser, something her grampa had brought to the house at great expense, had been emptied, the drawers broken, and vile contorting figures were carved all over it.

The entire rear wall of the room was taken up with a twisted shrine. The moonrat skins she kept for use with armor repair had been laid out on the walls and an intricate representation of the moonrat mother had been painted beneath them. Piled on the floor in front of the shrine were the rotting heads of woodland animals the goblinoids had hunted.

Tarah backed out of her room and looked to the last door. A thick lump stuck in her throat. It had been her parent's room in the beginning and then Grampa Rolf had moved in after her papa died. Tarah reached for the knob but couldn't make herself open it. She backed up and slowly slid down the wall, her face in her hands, unable to face what was inside.

Tarah wasn't sure how long she stayed in that position, but she became aware of sounds in the front room as Djeri moved about. She didn't bother to look, absorbed in her despair. Finally, she heard the heavy clomp of his footsteps come down the hall. There was some shuffling and then a thump as he sat beside her.

He said nothing for a while. Then he let out a long sigh. "I-uh, gathered the bodies out front and cleaned out the front room as best as I could. I looked, but there's not much of use left."

"They're gone," she muttered.

"Who?" he asked.

"My papa. My grampa," she said, her head still in her hands. "Gone."

"I'm sorry," he said softly. "Was your grampa . . . here when you left?"

"No. Their memories are gone," Tarah explained. "I was gonna go in there but I can't."

"Those goblinoids can't take your memories away, Tarah. No matter what disgusting things they did to the place."

"No! You don't understand!" She looked at him, her eyes swollen and red. "I feel memories. When I touch . . ." she shut her mouth. What was she doing? Why was she telling him this? She could ruin everything.

"When you touch?" he asked, his eyes kind.

"I don't tell folks this," Tarah said. But she wanted to. She needed to. She paused, her jaw working, but neither her papa or grampa said anything to help. "W-when I touch something I can feel a residue, the memory of the thing that last touched it."

Djeri's eyes widened in sudden understanding. "Like when you track."

"Yes! I can feel the thought that the animal had when it made the track." Tarah felt a sense of relief as the words came out. This was something she hadn't shared with anyone. Not even her papa. Only her Grampa Rolf knew. "I-I. In this house. I don't move anything. I don't like to clean because . . . because-."

"Because you might destroy the memories they left behind," he said.

Tears fell from her eyes again as she nodded. "This place is ruined! Everything I touch only has the memories of those . . . those monsters!"

Djeri's hand rested on her arm and Tarah turned to embraced him, sobbing into his armored shoulder. What was she doing? She never embraced people. But the dwarf didn't recoil. He brought his arms around her and held her, letting her cry.

Once her tears had subsided, he said gently, "And that

room?"

She looked at the closed door. It had been full of their thoughts. So many memories. She had left it unchanged for years. "It's Grampa Rolf's room. But I can't go in there. I can't! I know they've done something awful to it."

"I'm so sorry, Tarah," Djeri said and Tarah could feel the sincerity in his voice. "Would you like me to go in for you? I can see if there is anything worth saving."

She pulled back, looking at him with gratitude. "Would you?"

"Of course." He stood. "Is there anything in particular you want me to look for?"

There were so many things. "Anything that hasn't been destroyed. Would you check his trunk? And under his bed?"

"Sure," he said.

Tarah stood and turned away as he opened the door and stepped inside. The smell that came out made her shudder. She stumbled back into her room and stood anxiously waiting. She couldn't believe she had actually done it. She had told Djeri her secret. And he hadn't scoffed! If only she had been brave enough to tell him about her staff.

What about your gold? asked Grampa Rolf.

Her eyes moved to her bed. She hadn't seen any gold anywhere in the house. Was it really possible that her hiding place had remained undiscovered? Surely not. It was a ridiculous hope, but she walked to the bed anyway.

Tarah grabbed the broken wooden frame, ignoring the vile memories of the ogre that leapt up at her touch. With effort, she dragged the bed away from the stony cave wall. At the base of the floor was a wide rock, one of the paving stones that her father had used to make the path. It looked like it hadn't been moved!

Good! Grampa Rolf said. *With enough gold, Tarah, you can do anything!* It had been his idea, hiding her gold in case someone came to the house while she was out.

With trembling fingers, Tarah lifted the edge of the stone and pulled, revealing the hollow underneath. Everything was still there. She sat next to it and lifted the two heavy bags of coin out of the hole and held them close in relief. "It's still here, Grampa!" she whispered.

Gently, she set the two bags aside and reached back inside the hole. She pulled out a long cloth-wrapped bundle and opened it hurriedly, revealing a long slender piece of wood; her papa's bow. Her fingers touched it and she immediately felt his presence, strong and focused, as he hunted. Her lips quivered as she wrapped it back up and laid it across her legs.

There was one more thing inside and it was perhaps her most prized memory. Tarah withdrew a leather satchel from the bottom of the hole. Taking a deep breath, she lifted the cover and stuck her hand inside to touch the small book within.

For a brief moment the world faded away. Tarah was small again. Tiny. Not quite six-years-old. She was sitting in her bed, a book open in her lap. One soft arm was wrapped around her, the other pointing out a spot on the page. She listened intently as a loving voice helped her sound out a word.

The memory faded and Tarah closed the satchel. Tears rolled down her face again, but these weren't tears of sorrow. They were tears of happiness. She still had the memory of her mother.

The door in the hallway closed and Tarah heard Djeri's heavy footsteps as he entered the room. His look was dour.

"They didn't find my hiding place!" she said. "My coin was untouched and I have my papa's bow."

"Good!" he said, a smile touching his lips. "I wish I had better luck. I-uh, won't say what they'd been using the room for. I only found these two things."

Tarah stood and walked over to him. In one hand he held a small glass jar. It was half-full of a thick pink substance.

"I'm not sure what this is, but it doesn't look like something a goblinoid would carry around," Djeri said.

"That's Grampa Rolf's," she said, taking the bottle from him. She felt a very faint memory of her grampa's, just an absent grunt as he closed the jar. "Thank you."

"Then there's this," Djeri said. He held out a thin tube of parchment. "The bedpost was broken and I saw this sticking out of the end."

"I've never seen this before," Tarah said. When she touched it, a powerful memory crossed her mind. It was her grampa's, fervent and secretive as he rolled the scroll up tight, fearful of discovery. Strangely she got a sense that he was outside somewhere, standing in the cold. "I need to see this in the light. Would you grab those two bags?"

Tarah quickly picked up her father's bow and the leather satchel and headed down the hallway towards the front door. Djeri hoisted the two bags of coin, grunting in surprise over the weight, and followed her.

She left the house and stepped into the light, briefly noticing the pile of goblinoid bodies in front of the porch before unscrolling the parchment. She squinted at the small fine penmanship. This wasn't written in her grampa's hand.

"Good gravy, Tarah. That's a lot of coin," Djeri said.

"I don't spend much," she said absently. "I never know when I might need it." Except on books. She was going to need to replace her books. "You ever heard of 'Jharro Tree sap'?"

"I've herd of Jharro trees," Djeri said cautiously. "What's on the scroll?"

"It's a list of ingredients and amounts. I think it's the recipe for my grampa's resin." Tarah said. "The stuff he used to make my armor." She rolled the tiny scroll back up and slipped it into the leather satchel along with the small jar.

She turned back and looked at her house. "I can't live here anymore."

"You know, it's not so bad really," Djeri said, rubbing his chin. "After our mission's over, we can come back. I'm sure some of the Pinewood boys would help. We could clean the place up and sand off the carvings, make it good as new."

"No," Tarah said with a shake of her head. "All the memories are gone. This place just ain't my home anymore."

"You know . . ." Djeri paused thoughtfully. "Whatever those goblinoids did, they can't really take your memories away. Even if your magic-."

"No matter what we did with the place, it wouldn't be the same," she said. "They didn't just take away my family's memories. They replaced them with their own."

I'll never truly be gone, Tarah, her papa said. The memory bubbled to the surface. He was in bed. The rot had taken his vitality and he barely had strength to lift the finger he placed on her forehead. *I'll always be with you in here.*

"You can scrub those away too eventually," Djeri

suggested.

"Stop," Tarah said, raising a warning hand.

"Then what do you want to do?" Djeri asked.

Tarah Woodblade takes action, Grampa Rolf said.

Tarah looked back at the house, her jaw set in anger. "We drag those monsters' corpses inside. Then we burn it to the ground."

"Burn down your home?"

Tarah nodded grimly. "If I ever live here again, I'll be starting from scratch."

Chapter Twelve

While Djeri went to retrieve Neddy, Tarah took a solitary trip around the side of the hill to her papa's gravesite. It looked much like she had feared. The ogre had dug it up and thrown aside the heavy stones she'd laid on top of it. Her papa's bones had been piled on the ground next to the grave.

Tenderly, she placed each bone back in the grave. No flashes of memory entered her mind while she did so. Bones didn't keep a memory. It was an oddity with the magic that Tarah had never understood, but she was grateful for it now.

Her trail shovel had been left with the mule, but instead of heading back for it, she used a flat rock and scrapped the dirt back in. It was hard work, but Tarah did it reverently. By the time she was finished replacing the stones on top of the grave, she was sweaty and dirty and her back was sore.

Tarah headed back towards the house feeling worn-out and emotionally drained. The moonrat mother had marked her for death and even though she still drew breath, Tarah felt like part of her had died. She had been uprooted. She had no home. All that was left was to bury that part of her past.

Your survival is the most important thing, Grampa Rolf reminded. At the moment, she didn't know if she agreed.

When Tarah returned to the house, she saw Neddy standing outside. Djeri was having some difficulty pulling Clobber's body in through the front door. The ogre's legs were inside, but his upper body was wedged in the doorframe.

"Hello, Neddy," Tarah said, patting the mule's head before going to help Djeri out.

Together, they got the ogre's body turned and pulled inside next to the others. Once they had finished, they loaded up the front

room with any flammable debris they could find. Then they set to
clearing away all leaves and fallen branches from around the
house. Tarah would have felt incredibly guilty if they mourned her
loss by burning down half the forest.

The sun was fading into the treetops when Tarah started the
fire. She lit a stack of tinder just inside the front door. The flames
spread fast. Soon they poured out the door and licked along the
thatched roof. Tarah found it frightening how quickly her home
burned.

Djeri walked up and placed a comforting hand on her
shoulder as they watched the fire rise. Tarah's face was wet,
though she didn't feel the tears.

"What do you want to do with this?" Djeri asked. He held
out her papa's sword. "I took the scabbard off of the ogre before I
dragged it in. It's in surprisingly good shape considering."

"You mean considering the fact that it spent the last ten
years in the ground?" Tarah reached out hesitantly and touched the
hilt. The memory that flashed through her mind was no longer the
ogre's. This one was more recent, full of Djeri's sadness for her as
she had left the sword in his arms. She gave the dwarf a thoughtful
look.

"I don't know what to do." She had considered throwing it
into the fire and letting it be buried in the rubble, but now she
wasn't so sure. A strange impulse overcame her and she found
herself saying, "Why don't you hold onto it for now?"

"Me," he said in surprise. "I couldn't do that."

"Just until you find a replacement for your mace," she
suggested and added half-mockingly. "You do know how to use a
greatsword, don't you? It's not too big?"

A half smile touched his face. "Woman, I might be young
for a dwarf, but I'm a hundred and fifty years old. I've used about
every weapon there is and I have two greatswords in my collection
at home. Still," he said, turning the sword over in his hands. "I've
never used one quite this nice. Are you sure?"

"For now," Tarah said. She liked the idea of Djeri's
memories washing the ogre's away. "Just until you find a
replacement."

Djeri nodded slowly. "Thank you. I'm honored."

"And you should be. My papa was a legend," Tarah said,

taking the sword from him. "Now turn around and I'll help you belt it on."

Tarah set the scabbard diagonally across Djeri's back. The dwarf was right. It was in good shape. The wooden sheath was uncracked and the leather barely weathered. Her papa had kept it well oiled.

While she adjusted the straps, Djeri said, "Tell me about your papa. Who was he? The way you talk about him tells me he was an academy man."

"His name was Gad the Brawler," she said. "He was Berserker Guild."

"Gad the Brawler?" Djeri said in astonishment. His jaw worked for a moment. "You're kidding! You were right about him being a legend. Why he could have been guildmaster."

"They offered it to him twice," Tarah said. "But papa never liked being in charge. He just wanted to fight. He was happy to serve under Tamboor the Fearless until the berserkers were disbanded."

Djeri reached up and grasped the pommel of the sword. Tarah had belted it on at just the right angle and the blade slid free of the scabbard with one long pull of his arm. The blade gleamed in the firelight as he shifted his body into an offensive stance. "Then this sword is the Ramsetter?"

"Yeah," she said. The sword was huge in his hands and yet somehow it looked right. "Papa got it as a gift from some king or other after a mission. I don't know all the details. He didn't brag about it much. When it came to his academy days, he preferred talking about the other warriors."

"Anyone who's been through history classes at the academy knows about this sword." Djeri said, shaking his head. "Made by a master smith, runed for carving through armor like it was paper. No wonder it nearly cut my mace in two."

"I warned you," Tarah said. "When that ogre swung the second time, I was sure you were dead."

"If that ugly mace of mine hadn't been so thick and stubborn I would have been." Djeri shook his head. "I'm still mad about that, by the way." He slid the blade back into its scabbard. "So tell me. How did Gad the Brawler and his daughter end up living out here all alone?"

Tarah's brow furrowed in indecision as she stared at the climbing blaze. She never told clients about her past. Grampa Rolf had warned against it. Whenever someone asked her where she was from, she'd say, 'I was born in the forest and raised by squirrels until I was big enough to kill moonrats.' Or. 'Tarah Woodblade wasn't born. I just appeared one day, cutting myself free from a bear's belly.' She had a dozen of them and usually she'd just repeat new ones until the client stopped asking. But she'd already told Djeri some of her biggest secrets. Why stop now?

She took a deep breath. "When the academy got rid of the berserkers, papa could've done anything, I guess. He could've stayed and joined the swordsmanship guild like Tamboor did or he could've joined about any army in the world, but he decided to retire. Momma wanted to stay in Reneul, but papa hated living in the city, so they compromised and moved out here, close to Pinewood where momma was born."

She paused, letting the light of the flames create afterimages in her vision. "They were happy for a few years, but momma died when I was real young. Papa decided to stay here and raise me in the woods. He liked living in the country. You know, away from his fame. Besides, he didn't want me learning life from city folk."

"Did you like it here?" Djeri asked.

Tarah looked down, "I loved being with papa. He taught me how to survive. How to hunt. Taught me everything I know about the bow."

"Really?" Djeri said. "I didn't know Gad the Brawler was a bowman."

"Well, there ain't much call for berserkers to use a bow, is there?" she said. "Bow hunting was his hobby. That, and tracking."

"Huh. Well, I guess you can't know everything about a man from his legend," the dwarf said. "Did he teach you staff-work too?"

"No. That was Grampa Rolf. He gave my staff to me as a birthday gift when I turned twelve." She smiled. "Papa didn't like it. Thought it was too fancy. To tell you the truth, he just plain didn't like Grampa Rolf. He was my momma's father, see? Papa thought he was a bad influence on me.

"Anyway, my papa taught me what he knew about staff fighting, which was limited, but when he knew he was dying, he sent Grampa Rolf a message, asking him to take care of me. At least, that's what Grampa Rolf said."

"What happened to your father?" Djeri asked.

"He caught the rot," she said, shrugging.

"Wow." Djeri shook his head. "It seems such a shame a man like Gad going that way."

"Yeah, I guess you dwarfs don't have to worry about that," Tarah said, not noticing Djeri wince. "Seems everyone I lose dies from sickness. I was sixteen when papa died. Grampa Rolf left me about six years ago. He was getting old and got a bad case of red-lung when I was out guiding some folks. By the time I got home, he was too sick to move."

"I'm sorry to hear that," Djeri said, cocking his head at her as if gauging something.

"It's life, I guess. 'Folks come and go and you're left to keep living with what they taught you,'" Tarah said, quoting one of her Grampa's sayings. "Momma taught me how to read. Pappa taught me how to track and how to survive. Grampa taught me staff work and business. Now I'm on my own."

Her house was completely engulfed now. The fire had grown so hot, Tarah had to back away for fear it would burn her skin. She took a few steps backward, bumping into the mule.

"What about the Sampo Guidesman Guild?" Djeri asked. "I hear they're like family."

Tarah snorted. "Yeah, right. The men might be close, but they only put up with me because of my name. A few of 'em are okay, but for the most part, they're like a boy's club that don't really want a woman in their group."

"They can eat turds, then," said Djeri with a scowl. "You should join the academy when this mission is over. You'd get in, I'm sure of it. You're already a better shot than most of our bowmen and your abilities would make you invaluable as a scout."

Tarah looked at Djeri, smiling. "Thanks for that. I've thought about it, you know. Being academy like my papa. But he told me long ago that he didn't want me to be a warrior. He said to stay a woodsman. Tracking and guiding are good, respectable trades."

Djeri looked at her and shook his head. "Well I'm not going to tell you what to do with your life, but I'm afraid your thinking is just a little off. Whether you're academy trained or not, you're already a warrior."

They unpacked their bedrolls and ate dinner. Then as soon as the flames died down enough that they were sure the forest wouldn't ignite, they moved to the other side of the clearing and went to sleep. Or at least that was the plan. Tarah stayed awake a long while watching her house crumble to embers as Djeri's words kept tumbling over and over in her mind. He really thought she was a warrior? Good thing he didn't know how scared she was all the time.

In her dreams that night she fought the moonrat man amongst the burning embers of her house. Her papa and grampa were there cheering her on, but Djeri was yelling at her to get out of there. Slowly she realized that the glowing coals had eaten through the soles of her boots and flames were licking up her legs.

She ran from the house just in time to see dark figures dragging Djeri away. Tarah chased after them as the flames crept higher and higher up her body. Then she saw Djeri fighting the dark figures with the Ramsetter. He hewed them in half with great swipes, but there were too many of them. They were pressing him inexorably towards the open mouth of the giant who was laying in wait on the ground behind him with eager eyes.

Djeri continued to back up, unaware of the giant's oncoming maw. Tarah ran and tried to fight her way through to him. Her staff knocked the dark figures in the air, but she wasn't fast enough. The flames had reached her head.

Tarah woke with a gasp, to find that Djeri was already awake and making breakfast. The morning light was streaming across the hillside and nothing remained of her house but timbers. The cave mouth yawned open to the air, belching the occasional puff of smoke. Djeri had found the well and evidently it was still working because he had a soup boiling, made from their dried beef and grain along with spices of his own.

The meal was good, if a bit hot on the tongue. Then they packed up and readied themselves to leave. Tarah had decided to take her satchel with her, but they were left with the dilemma of what to do with the two large bags of coin. Djeri wasn't comfortable carrying that much money around with them on the mission. They discussed it and finally Tarah and Djeri each took a spade from their supplies and headed to a nearby spot to bury it.

"This really is a lot of coin, Tarah," Djeri said, shaking his head as they arrived at the place. It was under a tall pine tree that Tarah was quite familiar with, its trunk pockmarked by years of target practice.

"Six hundred and forty five gold worth," she said and Djeri whistled. Tarah shoved her spade into the earth at the base of the tree. "Yep, it's just about every penny Tarah Woodblade's brought in since I was eighteen."

"You're kidding me!" Djeri said. "That's a lot of earnings in what, eight years?"

She shrugged. "Grampa Rolf taught me good. I do this for him really. I make the most out of every deal just to make him proud, you know."

"You seriously just go around thinking of ways to accumulate money?"

"I'll spend it one day," she said matter-of-factly. "If I ever have anything I really need."

"You mean like when you have kids of your own?" Djeri suggested.

Tarah snorted. "Like any man would have me! No, I reckon I'll find some use for it. Maybe I'll open up a bookstore some day; one that folks would come to from cities all around."

Djeri was frowning at her in a strange way. "You shouldn't think that way, Tarah. Your future should be more than a job. What's your legacy? What will you leave behind if you don't have children?"

"What?" she asked and then she thought she understood his question. He was worried about all that money going to waste. "I'll tell you what. If I die and I don't got no one to leave it to, you can have it for all I care. You'll live longer than me and you know where I'm burying it."

"Me?" Djeri sputtered.

"What's bothering you, Djeri the Looker? Are you thinking of killing me and taking my money?" Tarah laughed, shaking her head as she continued digging.

Djeri stood and blinked at her for a moment before finally

chuckling. He lifted his spade and helped her dig.

When their task was done, they headed out for the location of the tracks. Tarah gave one last look to the only home she'd ever known and left, not sure how long she'd be gone or even what she would do if she ever came back.

The journey was a long one, and they were quiet for the most part. The weight of the events from the day before sat heavily on Tarah's shoulders and she was beset by a deep melancholy. Djeri understood and let her be. It took more than half the day before they came to the area described on the map.

Tarah knew the area well. Her father had taken her hunting there several times as a child and she had guided a few hunters this way that were looking for deer. It was a lightly forested and rocky place at the base of the mountain slopes. This was the part of the journey which Tarah had most disliked bringing a mule into, but Neddy was stalwart and obedient, making it through the difficult terrain without many issues.

The map wasn't detailed enough to show the exact location of the tracks, but from the descriptions the wizard had given them, Tarah knew that they were located somewhere along a small stream. That narrowed down the search considerably and they found their first track at the second stream they came across.

"Is this it?" said Djeri. "You're sure?"

"Yes," she said. The water had partially filled the track back in, but she was confident of the pattern. "It's a bit old but we'll see . . ." She touched the track and was jolted by the strength of the memory. Gasping, she withdrew her hand.

"What was it? What did you see?" Djeri asked.

She frowned at him, unused to being around people who understood her ability. "It was strong. This track is at least three weeks old, but it felt as new as a track just made yesterday. Even stronger. It's kind of hard to explain."

She followed along the stream, touching each track and being startled by the power of it each time. The beast was strong, confident, and loyal. It was moving with a purpose, but without a clear understanding of where it was supposed to go.

Tarah scratched her head. "You said you met two of these rogue horses, Djeri?"

"Yeah," he said.

"Would you say they're smart?" she asked.

He nodded. "Well one of them was part man and I'd say he was smarter than most. His name was Samson and during the siege he was put in charge of all the stablemen. Uh, the other one, its hard to say. Her name was Gwyrtha and she was part lizard. She was sweet though and it seemed like she knew what was being spoken. Sir Edge talked to her like she was a regular person."

"Well this one seems smart too, but it's like he doesn't know where he's going," she said.

"It's a he, then?" Djeri said.

"Yes, or at least that's the feeling I get. I'll understand more with each track," she said. "We should destroy the tracks as we go, don't you think?"

"It would be better if we didn't have to backtrack to do it," Djeri agreed.

"Right, well the best way to do it in the mud is just to smudge it a bit with your foot and kick some dirt into it. The main thing is to make it unrecognizable," she said.

"I wouldn't have recognized them as they are," he replied.

"You're not a professional tracker. That's who we're supposed to be hiding them from," she reminded him.

They went to work covering the tracks she'd found and then started following them further up the stream, destroying them as they went. Tarah was quite impressed with the beast. The more glimpses she got, the more she got the feeling that the intensity of the memories had something to do with the strength of its spirit. It was like the intensity of five or six tracks all at once.

"You planning to work for the academy forever, Djeri?" Tarah asked at one point.

"What do you mean?" he replied.

"You know, dwarfs live a long time," she said. "Are you gonna work for them all that time?"

He let out a short laugh shaking his head. "I really haven't thought about it. I'm an academy man through and through. I can't imagine working for someone else. But who knows where I'll be a hundred years from now? Who knows where the academy will be?"

"You'll eventually retire, right?" Tarah touched another track and was jolted with a partial thought from the rogue that made her sure he was carrying some kind of load on his back. "I guess what I'm saying is, what will you do when you're no longer a warrior?"

"I don't know," Djeri said, covering up a track with his boot. "It's hard to imagine a different life. I tried blacksmithing once. I didn't have much of a talent for it, but I guess I could see myself doing that one day."

"You could settle down and start a farm," she suggested.

"Ha! I'd rather eat a turd," he said, shaking his head.

"Come on!" Tarah groaned, standing up and facing him.

"What? Farming's not for me. My parents struggle at it every day. It's the same thing over and over." He smudged another track. "I didn't realize you liked farming."

"It's not that," Tarah said, putting her hands on her hips. "It's the word 'turd'. For nature's sake, you use it all the time! It's like it's the only swear you know."

Djeri looked at the ground, an odd smile on his face. "You know I figured this was coming sooner or later. All my friends ask me eventually."

"Yeah? Well what's it about, then?" she asked with a scowl. "Is it some running joke where you just keep saying 'turd' until some idiot asks you why?"

The dwarf laughed. "It's not like that. It's just that when I was young I had a bit of a foul mouth."

"You don't say?" Tarah replied.

"My mother got after me about it all the time until one day my father came to my room and sat me down. He said that since he couldn't make me stop cursing altogether, he'd make me a deal. I was allowed one word only. As long as that was the only word I used, they would stop giving me grief about it," Djeri said. "And I've done my best to stick by that deal ever since."

"And you picked 'turd'?" Tarah said incredulously.

"It's the perfect word!" Djeri exclaimed with a wide grin.

Tarah folded her arms. "Explain yourself."

"It's versatile. I've thought up tons of ways to use it over the years. Also, it isn't so foul you can't say it in front of mixed company." He shrugged. "And it also didn't hurt that it was my mother's least favorite word."

"Yeah, that's the real reason," Tarah said. She went back to

her work, kicking through a track with her boot. "But I wouldn't
say it in front of company,"

"Oh wouldn't you?" he asked, one eyebrow raised.

Tarah smiled slightly, "Well some company maybe, but-."

There was a plunking noise and a small golden orb rolled in
front of them. It emitted a brief flash and Tarah couldn't move. She
could breathe, but the rest of her body was stiff. In the periphery of
her vision, she could see that Djeri was frozen as well.

Tarah heard the stomping of many boots and soon they
were surrounded. Tarah couldn't see them all at first but two of
them came to stand in front of her. They were dwarves. Both of
them wore dusters and wide-brimmed hats. Even more
distinctively, they both had handlebar mustaches, a style Tarah had
never seen on a dwarf before.

"Well, what do we have here, Boss Donjon?" asked one
with a blond mustache.

"I dunno, but they're messin' with our dag-blamed tracks,"
said the other, a squint-eyed dwarf whose mustache was jet black.
He pulled a long cigar from within his duster's pocket and stuck it
in his mouth. "Let's take 'em back to Shade and see what he wants
done."

Chapter Thirteen

"But Molly. It's not about that." Arcon pleaded, clutching the steward's arm. "Just hear me out."

The steward yanked her arm free from his hand, her eyes delivering a warning glare. "We both know that's not true, mage! And just because you have the scholar's favor it does not allow you to molest a steward."

"Come-come, Molly dearest" Arcon said with a pouting lip. "I thought you liked being molested."

They stood near the doorway to her chambers, an austere set of rooms, all white marble with cushioned accents. The place reminded him of what he'd imagined princess' rooms to be like when he was a child. Only the princesses of his dreams didn't have crow's feet.

The steward's face colored slightly. "Arcon, as much as I enjoy our sweet times and as much as I enjoy letting you convince me for minor favors, you go too far. I will not let you interfere with my duties. If you try to press me, I will be forced to report your proclivities."

"By the gods, can't we just kill the woman?" Mellinda complained. Her dislike for the woman had grown with each night he had been forced to spend with the steward.

Tempting, but I don't think I'm in a safe position to start murdering people right now, he replied.

Arcon had been relieved when Scholar Aloysius had agreed to protect him. Molly had told him the dark wizards had been informed that he wasn't to be touched. In fact, one night when she was feeling particularly talkative she let slip that the wizards had recalled two more basilisks that had been searching for him. But the last two weeks had been agonizingly slow.

"Molly, please," he said. "I wouldn't dare ask you to do anything unbecoming of a steward of your stature."

"That's exactly what you're going to ask me," she replied.

"Just listen to my request, please," Arcon said, giving her the smile that had melted her heart so many times before. "If you feel I've overstepped my bounds, go ahead and report me."

"I am a hair's breadth from doing it now," she warned, but folded her arms and allowed him to speak.

"The token Scholar Aloysius gave me has been helpful." He grabbed the pin set in his collar, a square metal carving of an open book with a scroll lying across it. "And it lets me come and go from the homeland, which I am grateful for."

"However?" Molly said with a roll of her eyes.

"My access is extremely limited," he said, his hands up defensively. "I wish to help the scholar! That's why he gave me his protection in the first place. But I can't do the research necessary to help. This thing won't give me access to any of the libraries in the homeland and on top of it all, I still have a curfew at night."

"This is all true," Molly said. "Your pin identifies you as an asset to Scholar Aloysius. Nothing more."

"I understand that, dear one," he said patiently.

"*Dear one?*" Mellinda said. "*Really? Ugh, if I had a body you'd be making me ill.*"

Arcon cleared his throat, "However, isn't there a way that I could get a request in to the scholar to raise my classification? Isn't there something higher than 'asset' which would allow me into the libraries at least?"

"Yes! There's something higher. You could be an official assistant or an honored guest. Both of those have privileges. Indeed, you could even be a steward. Then you would have access to everything!" Molly's face had grown redder with each sentence. "But you're not! Would you like to know why? Because you're a nobody! A peon! Do you know what a peon is?"

"Yes, Molly," he said dully.

"At the risk of being vulgar, I'll tell you," she said with an angry laugh. "A peon is someone whose worth is so low that it is societally acceptable to urinate on them! Do you understand?"

"I know what you're saying," Arcon replied. He kept his gaze down, but his hands were clenched into fists.

"Good!" Molly said.

"*Kill her!*" said Mellinda. "*Please, just put the rings on and explode her from the inside. Better yet, shrink her down to the size of an ant and squish her! No one will ever know.*"

Arcon chose a different tactic, thickening his voice with sadness. "I apologize for offending you, Molly. Please know that I-I'm not from here and I don't understand all of your customs." He fed a small amount of water magic to the corners of his eyes, causing an overflowing of tears. "I just want to help Scholar Aloysius and I-I don't want to be a disappointment to you."

He turned away and sat on the edge of her bed, wiping the wetness from his cheeks. As he did so, from the corner of his eye, he saw a look of guilt upon Steward Molly's face.

"*I can't believe it. That might actually work. Where did you learn manipulation like that?*"

Oh please, he said. *It's how you convinced me to carry one of your eyes around the Mage School every morning.*

"Well-uh," Molly began, choosing her words very carefully. "Now that you understand your place here, I'll tell you this. I informed Scholar Aloysius of your desire to access the libraries a few days ago. He is considering it, but . . ." She placed her hand on his shoulder. "I'll mention it again, though I don't think it will change anything."

"Thank you!" he said, turning and embracing her. He kissed her neck in the way he knew she liked. "Thank you so much, dearest. I know it must be a difficult thing to bring up, but I'm glad he listens to you."

"Scholar Aloysius listen to me?" she said with amusement. "Arcon, you really do know nothing. I may be chiefest of his green-sashes, but I'm no red. He listens to me regarding the care of his household and the occasional visitor, but that is it." She shook her head and walked back to the doorway. "Now leave here discreetly, sweetling. And since I am doing you such a huge favor I expect to see you back here tonight."

"Of course, dearest," he replied. "I wouldn't have it any other way."

The moment she was out the door, he sighed and fell back on the bed. This was truly ridiculous work. Seducing a middle-aged steward had not been on his list of ways to gain power.

"It most certainly wasn't on mine," Mellinda grumbled.

"I'm doing what's necessary," he reminded her.

"Perhaps, but it doesn't mean I like being present for the event."

"Would you prefer I lock you away?" he asked.

She had to think about that one for a moment. *"No."*

"Then stop complaining." He looked in the mirror and used air magic to clean some of the steward's makeup from his cheek. The woman slathered herself with it. Even more so since they had started their dalliance. "What do you think? Will my little performance do any good?"

She gave him a mental shrug. *"I suppose another bug in his ear can't hurt."*

"Hmm." Arcon left Molly's chambers dissatisfied. There had to be a better way to advance his cause with the steward, but what was it?

He checked to make sure that the guards weren't watching as he exited the steward's quarters. What to do next? There wasn't much for him to do during the day. He could go into Mallad and prowl the taverns in hopes of picking up some information. The complaints of the lower inhabitants had proved interesting from time to time. But such endeavors seemed useless now that he had the scholar's protection. With a sigh, he began wandering the gardens.

After a few minutes gazing uninterestedly at the exotic plants, he sat down on a stone bench under the shade of a lilac tree. Arcon rubbed slowly at his temples. He needed access. He needed a way to rise in stature so that he could enact his plans.

I'm just going to have tell him, he announced. *There's no way around it.*

"The scholar?" Mellinda said warily. *"You want to tell him what?"*

I want to go through with our plan, Arcon decided.

"That sounds easier than it is," she said. *"He obviously doesn't want to see us just yet."*

"But why is that?" he asked aloud. *I have skills he can use. I have knowledge that could be helpful. Why is he leaving me sitting here to rot?*

"He's a gnome," Mellinda grumbled. *"He'll live as long as*

he wishes to. This means he has patience. Something I wish I still had. Being trapped in your mind is boring, dear Arcon. Especially when you're just sitting around all the time."

You've changed, Mellinda, Arcon said.

"Oh?"

You were clever once. Calculating, methodical, alluring. You were a planner. You thought up schemes that brought the known lands to their knees. Now you do nothing but make pithy remarks as I go through my day.

She chuckled. *"That's what I've been reduced to. Compared to my old heights, my existence now is just a joke."*

He leaned forward, peering at the well-trimmed grass as if in hopes something would come out and announce the answer. But of course there was nothing. The grass in this place was like the lawns at the Mage School. It didn't serve a purpose except for something to look at. It would be so much more useful out in a field somewhere feeding some sheep.

He snorted. Right now he was just like this grass in Molly's eyes. Pretty to look at but basically useless. Just something to . . .

He cocked his head. Wait a minute. He was being foolish. He had a resource. A good one, even if it was a dangerous one. He just wasn't putting it to use. *Mellinda.*

"What?" she said boredly.

At the height of your power, what was your greatest skill? he asked.

"Plotting," she said. *"Outthinking my opponents."*

I think it was more than that, he said. *It was understanding your opponents. You're ability to read people was what made you so dangerous. It's how you snared me, finding my weakness and then latching on like some kind of unburnable leech.*

"That's not so hard with a thousand years' experience," she said, sounding flattered. *"It's also easier with the mind power of hundreds at your disposal."*

Then tell me. What did you notice during our first visit with Aloysius? Arcon asked. *Figure him out. Tell me what you learned.*

She thought for a moment. *"I've told you this. He is different. Unlike other gnomes, he's not bogged down by his focus. He's intelligent enough to become a top scholar and at the same time able to function without constant hand holding. It's rare. A once in a thousand years oddity."*

That's not what I'm talking about. Something about the way he interacted with me told you that I should bow to him. Why?

"Because of his focus," she said *"He tells the world it's the creation of powerful items, but his every action and the way he surrounded himself showed me that his true focus was just the accrual of power."*

Alright. That's helpful, but there's something else. Something else . . . He stood from the bench and paced, rubbing his chin.

Mellinda stirred in realization. *"He liked you. I saw it in his eyes. He liked your boldness."*

"That's it, then!" Arcon turned and walked towards the central building, crossing the useless grass lawn. *I've got to be bold. He'll leave me sitting here like any ordinary asset unless I can get his attention.* He started up the steps and was met at the top by a steward wearing a green sash.

"Good morning, mage," he said, his expression showing only mild curiosity. "Can I help you?"

"I was hoping to sit in the atrium," he said with a smile. "I enjoy the fountain in there."

"Of course," the man said returning his smile, though the smile didn't reach his eyes. "Please follow me."

The steward led him down the long corridor to the atrium and from the stiffness of his spine, Arcon could tell the man didn't like this part of his job. Serving scholars was one thing, but making pleasantries with nobodies was beneath him.

"Your observational skills aren't bad either," Mellinda remarked. *"Though I must say that I fear your little scheme could fail quite spectacularly."*

Aloysius thinks I'm useful in some way. You even said he liked me. What's the worst that could happen?

"You could end up jailed," she said. *"Or even executed by one of his red-sashes. They take their procedures very seriously. Going around the system is going to make them angry."*

The steward left him in the atrium and strode away, a bored look on his face. Arcon saw Scholar Tobias waiting there with his pimple-faced steward. It was difficult to see why the gnome insisted on coming day after day. Aloysius was never going to see him.

Arcon paced for a moment gathering his courage. *I'm going to be bold.* Let the stewards be angry if they wished. It was the scholar he was trying to impress.

Arcon walked past Scholar Tobias, nodding politely. There were none of Aloysius' stewards in sight, so he strolled through the door at the rear of the atrium and kept on walking. This was working well. The stewards were so used to proprieties that no one expected someone to just walk in. He turned down the corridor lined with weaponry, his pulse quickening.

"Excuse me?" said a perturbed voice. Arcon looked down a hallway to his right and saw a bespectacled steward with a black sash. He looked quite surprised. "What are you doing in this part of the residence, sir?"

"Steward Molly sent me this way," Arcon said.

"She is going to strip the flesh from your bones for that," Mellinda remarked.

The steward narrowed his eyes. "You should not be here unaccompanied."

Arcon lifted his pin so that the steward could see. "It's okay. I know the way," he said and continued his walk down the hall, speeding up his steps.

"B-but that's not . . ." The steward sputtered and turned to rush down another corridor.

Arcon swallowed. Not good but it would be fine. He was almost there. He made the last few turns to the scholar's office. They could all rush after him, but if the scholar was okay with it, he'd be fine.

"What if he's not in there?" Mellinda asked suddenly. *"We have no way of knowing if he's in his office today."*

Don't borrow trouble, he said, pausing outside the door as he realized what a crucial piece of information he was missing. Were boldness and stupidity the same word?

"Back in my day they were. Especially if you were dealing with me," Mellinda said.

He took a deep breath, steadying himself as he readied a few choice spells. Licking his lips, he opened the door and entered the room.

The red-sash stewards were well-trained. Two swords were

unsheathed and arcing towards his neck before his foot touched the marble floor. He released a spell and a dome of air rushed into existence around him, stopping the blades inches from his neck. His eyes swept the room.

Scholar Aloysius wasn't behind his desk, but was lounging in an ornate chair at the side of the room. He held an open book in his left hand, but his eyes were focused on Arcon's entrance. His right hand darted forward, throwing the knife he had been rolling along the tops of his fingers just moments before. Arcon's spell halted the point of the blade two inches from his right eye.

"That's a new one," Mellinda said. *"A scholar that throws knives."*

Arcon dove to the floor, prostrating himself before the gnome, his forehead pressed to the rug at the scholar's feet. "Great Scholar Aloysius! I apologize for the suddenness of my visit. I, your humble servant, wished to see you regarding a matter of utmost importance!"

Arcon dropped the air spell, releasing the steward's swords, and the scholar's knife fell to the floor. The stewards took a quick step forward and their blades pressed into his back.

"What shall we do, Scholar?" asked one of them.

The scholar barked out a sharp laugh and stood. "I must say I'm quite surprised! Humble servant indeed."

"He laughs," Mellinda said in relief. *"If you had tried a trick like this in my palace, I would have sucked the magic from your body, slit your throat, and given the rings to a servant I already trusted."*

"I wished no offense," Arcon said.

"Accosting a scholar is a crime punishable by death," said the other red-sash. He brought his blade up to the back of the mage's neck and jabbed him with the tip, causing Arcon to wince.

"That it is," said the scholar. "So tell me, Mage Arcon, what is it that's so important that you risked your life and . . . mainly your life, to barge in to see me?"

"My current position is inhibiting my ability to be an effective servant, Master," Arcon replied.

"Are you referring to your position on the floor?" Aloysius asked.

"Speak properly and do not show any defiance," Mellinda

said. *"He's thinking about killing us."*

"I am speaking of the pin I wear on my collar," Arcon said.

"I have heard of your request," said the scholar. "You wish access to the libraries."

"It's not just that, sir," Arcon said, hesitating. The words he wanted to say might get him killed. But then again, he had decided to be bold. "I wish to be a red-sash."

"Too far!" Mellinda gasped as the blades pushed in deeper, piercing his skin.

"Stand back, Stewards!" Aloysius commanded and the sword tip was removed from Arcon's neck. "I'll have you know that these two vigilant young men were ready to slay you for speaking such a ridiculous request. I'm thinking of letting them."

He could feel the warmth of his blood sliding down the side of his neck. "Master, having any other position would hamper my efforts on your behalf."

"Call him 'Scholar', you fool," snarled one of the red-sashes.

"Don't overstep your bounds, Steward Madison!" Aloysius warned. He turned his attention to Arcon. "I am curious. Exactly what efforts are you trying to make on my behalf? I have given you no orders."

"I do listen, though, Scholar," Arcon replied. "I heard that you are looking for rogue horses."

The gnome shifted his feet.

"I really wish we could see more than his slippers," Mellinda complained. *"It's much more difficult to read him if I'm just going by sound."*

"I can't say that I like such information being out and about for you to hear," Aloysius said.

"It's the reason I came to you in the first place, Scholar." Blood dripped from his neck and hit the floor with an audible patter. "There is no reason for you to continue to search for rogue horses. I can use the Rings of Stardeon to create new ones for you."

"You? A mere mage?" the gnome scoffed. "You may have the correct tool, but why would you succeed where powerful wizards have been failing for over a thousand years."

"I have with me an expert on the matter," Arcon explained.

"With you?"

"Yes, Master. In my mind are the thoughts and memories of Mellinda, the wife of Stardeon," Arcon said.

"There is no way he's believing that," she said and Arcon had the impression that if she could, she'd be resting her face in her hands right then.

The room was silent.

"If I might explain, Scholar," Arcon said. "Ewzad Vriil was never my true master. I was serving at his side at the direction of Mellinda, though to the rest of the world she was known as the mother of the moonrats."

"So the moonrat witch was actually the Troll Queen. Still alive after all those years," Aloysius mused. "I had wondered if that might be the case."

"Yes, Master. She compelled me into Vriil's service with the use of a powerful eye that she placed into my body," Arcon said. One of the red-sashes groaned in disgust. "When the Mage School's army destroyed her, her essence was trapped in my body."

"Look up at me, mage," the gnome said. Arcon shifted back on his knees and sat up so that he could look into the tall scholar's face. He looked perturbed. "I'm trying to tell if there is any sanity in those eyes. Everything you have done and said so far today is quite insane."

"No kidding."

"I assure you, Master. It is all true," Arcon said earnestly.

The scholar bent down and grasped Arcon's jaw, giving him a long and searching look. Finally, he let go and took a step back. "Even if you do believe this to be true, how does this help me?"

"Because Mellinda was there when Stardeon first began creating the rogue horses," Arcon said. "She worked with him hand-in hand."

"I know more about that era than you might think" Aloysius said. "My own father's writings spoke of it. Mellinda was only around during Stardeon's failed attempts at creating a rogue horse. She left him to join the Dark Prophet months before he had his first success!"

"That's not exactly how it happened," Mellinda grumbled.

"You are correct, Master," Arcon said. "But Stardeon was near his breakthrough when she left. She is certain that if allowed access to the great libraries here at the homeland she and I could discover that missing bit of information and create a new series of rogues horses in your name."

Aloysius raised a hand and thoughtfully stroked his long and pointed nose. "First of all, I must be sure that the thoughts of the Troll Queen are indeed in your head."

"Ask me anything she would know, Master," Arcon said confidently.

"Everything I know was learned through research," said the scholar. "And you were taught at the Mage School, which means that you had access to one of the greatest libraries in the known lands. You would have had access to many of the same books and scrolls . . ." He stopped, smiling. "There is one thing that I can show you that she could know, but you could not."

He thrust his right hand at Arcon, palm out. "She would recognize this!"

Arcon blinked. He couldn't see anything of interest, though he noticed that the ring on the scholar's middle finger had been turned inward, a small opal shining in the center of it.

"*Switch to spirit sight!*" she said urgently.

I don't know how, he said.

"Tell me, Mage Arcon," said the scholar impatiently. "What does she see?"

"*Let me do it!*" she said. "*Give me just that much control.*"

Arcon was struck with fear. Could he do that? Could he dare give her even that tiny amount? What if she tried to take him over?

The gnome started to lower his hand.

"*We don't have time!*"

Fine. He let down his defenses just enough for her to access his mage sight. His vision flared and he saw the elemental realm. Several spots in the scholar's robe shone with various colors of magic, including something long and slender at his left hip. Then it felt as if something thin and gauzy were pulled over his vision and the magesight vanished, replaced by something different, something dark.

"I see you're wasting my time," the gnome began.

"Nothing, Scholar!" Arcon blurted, relieved that he was still in charge of his body. "She sees nothing on your hand. Mellinda says that this means you have not stood before the Dark Bowl."

Aloysius raised an eyebrow. "Truly? How interesting. I was looking for her to remark on the ring I was wearing, but this is perhaps a better proof. That is the sort of thing the Troll Queen would look for on the palm of my right hand."

"*The ring?*" she said. "*What on earth should I have noticed about that ring? Ask him to show it again.*"

"Tell me something, Mage Arcon," said the scholar. "Does Mellinda still hear the dark voice of her master?"

"Not any more," Arcon said without hesitation. "Not since her body was destroyed in the forest. Her connection with the Dark Prophet was severed and all of her power taken away. She lives only as thoughts and memories now."

"*Don't say everything you know, idiot!*"

"Pity," Aloysius said. "Her level of power would have been quite useful for me."

"Please, Master," Arcon said, leaning forward and placing his forehead to the ground again. "I promise you that the power of the Rings of Stardeon mixed with the memories of the Troll Queen can bring you all the power you need."

Arcon didn't raise his head but he heard the scholar's feet shuffle. "I'm not so certain I like having a servant so low."

"Would you like me to stand, Master?"

"No," he said. "I enjoy seeing you as you are. I just don't know how far I can trust someone that acts so subservient."

"I assure you, Scholar," Arcon said. "I may abase myself before you, but I would not do so to any other man. I most definitely didn't do so for Ewzad Vriil. I merely give respect where respect is due."

"*Ooh, well spoken,*" Mellinda said approvingly.

The gnome let out a low laugh. "I must say you excel at telling me things I want to hear. I would have you change your posture, though. I think I would prefer you at a state of readiness. Get up on one knee," Aloysius said and Arcon did so, looking up at the scholar long enough to see the pleased look in his eyes. "Good, now press your knuckles to the floor. Hmm. Now bow your head . . . what do you think, Steward Evan?"

"It is a respectful kneel, Scholar," the red-sash replied.

"*That's the kneel of a knight to a king in my day*," Mellinda said approvingly. "*We've taken a step up.*"

The stewards don't bow or kneel. They obey him and give him respect, but he treats them as people. Arcon griped.

"*One step at a time*," she said.

"I agree with Steward Evan," The gnome said musingly. "Mage Arcon, this posture will be sufficient in the future."

"Of course, Master," Arcon said.

"In addition, it is best that you call me by my proper title. Especially if we are in a public setting."

"Yes, Scholar Aloysius," he said.

From his kneeling position Arcon watched the gnome's feet as he walked over to sit in his chair. "Now as for this thing you ask of me, it is quite ludicrous. Stewards aren't just made. They undergo years of training and you are far older than most beginners. Is that not right, Steward Madison?"

"Indeed, Scholar. I started when I was five, as did my father before me," the steward said.

"True. As did his father. Three generations of men serving me, Mage Arcon. This is why Steward Evan wears the red sash. Only the most devoted and trustworthy are chosen."

"Of course, Scholar. I did not mean to be presumptuous. I just believe that becoming a red sash is the only way I can have the keys I need to serve you to the best of my ability," Arcon said. "What can I do to prove my loyalty?"

"*Now you're being presumptuous*," Mellinda said.

"Enough," the scholar said with an offended tone. "You intrigue me, but you overreach yourself. Red sash indeed. This will I do. I will see to it that you are given the sash of a steward in training. This will open certain doors to you and I expect you will find the position useful."

"A student?" This was ridiculous.

"*Just do it*!" Mellinda said.

"I-. But- . . . Yes, Scholar. Thank you."

"I will have you put under the tutelage of Steward Molly. I believe the two of you are . . . familiar with each other?"

"Yes, Scholar Aloysius," Arcon said.

"What does he do? Peep? Or is she a talker?" Mellinda mused.

"Your mornings shall be spent learning the ways of the green sash. After that I expect you to be working on your rogue horse project. The student sash will allow you access to the libraries, though if you wish access to any particular book that is in the dark section, you must submit a request through Steward Molly."

"Yes!"

"It will be an honor to serve you," Arcon said. He was expected to take classes for the green sash? What was he going to learn about? Feeding schedules for gnomes?

"I find the possibility of creating a new strain of rogue horses quite fascinating. I applaud you for your initiative," the gnome said.

"Thank you, Scholar," Arcon said.

"But in case you get too comfortable, know that I already have my best steward looking for rogues," Aloysius said. "He assures me that he is close to procuring one on his own. I recommend that you outdo him."

"Yes, Scholar. Thank you, Scholar," Arcon said. His knee was killing him. This position was much more uncomfortable than lying prostrate on the floor.

"And one last note, mage. Tell the Troll Queen that I expect her to stay in line. I am well versed in her exploits and if I see anything come from you that could in any way undermine my initiatives . . ." He sniffed. "Let us just say that my protection can be easily taken away. Am I clear?"

"Very clear, Scholar."

"Good, then. Steward Evan will show you out. Your preparations begin on the morrow."

Arcon stood with a wince and forced himself not to limp as he followed the red-sashed steward from the room. From his glare, Evan did not seem amused at Arcon's antics, but he didn't say anything.

Mellinda was still simmering at the scholar's threat. *"Oh we'll show him, sweet Arcon. He may have you on your knees, but the Troll Queen never bowed to anyone. I'll have him bowing to us by the end."*

Chapter Fourteen

Tarah was in a panic. She strained and strained, but couldn't do so much as blink. It was some kind of spell, she was sure of it, though she didn't have enough experience with magic to tell much more than that.

"You got yerself an odd catch there, Boss Donjon." said a gruff voice that approached from the trees.

"These folks were destroyin' our rogue tracks," said the dwarf with the black mustache. He pulled a wooden cylinder from his pocket and swiped the end across his cigar, causing the tip to burst into flame. "We're takin' 'em to Shade."

Shade. A pang of guilt struck Tarah. The man who had hired her in Razbeck had referred to himself by that name. He was the one that had given her the drawing of the rogue horse tracks in the first place.

Why hadn't she been more careful? Riveren had said that the stranger had hired others to find the tracks. She should have been on high alert. She'd had so much on her mind that she'd forgotten all about it.

A short dwarf with a bushy red mustache walked into Tarah's sight. He was peering up at her as if he were a farmer inspecting a new breed of cattle. A wide scar stretched across his bulbous nose and his breath was foul as he leaned in close.

"A human . . . lady. Not bad lookin' fer a human, neither," he said.

Donjon spat. "Don't make me sick, Mel."

"I ain't sayin' I'd go that way," the dwarf said defensively. "I'm just sayin' she ain't bad."

"It's the nose," said the blond-mustached dwarf with a snort. He was giving Tarah that same kind of appraising look.

"Mel's got a thing fer bent noses. You sure she's a woman, though, Mel? She's purty big fer a woman."

"Of course she is, Leroy. Her lady parts might be hid by that armor, but you'cn tell by the rump," Mel said. Tarah felt the dwarf's hand give her a sharp slap. "That's a lady's rump."

She ached to be able to kill him.

"Yer makin' me sick again, Mel," said Donjon before taking a long drag on his cigar. He let the smoke billow out his nose. "That's a weird lookin' quarterstaff she's got."

The red-mustached dwarf took off his hat, revealing a balding head, and took a tinted pair of spectacles out of his shirt pocket. He peered at her staff for a moment, his bushy eyebrows raising. "Never seen nothin' like it, but there's magic to it."

"Lemme see that," said Leroy. He snatched the spectacles off of Mel's face and plopped them on his own. "I'll be dag-gummed. Yer right. There's some protection runes here. Old work too. All them other runes are just gobbledygook to me, though. Don't think that's red paint, though. Gall-durn! It's almost like it was stained with blood."

"Nah, blood would flake off. Bring it here," said Donjon and to Tarah's horror, Leroy pried the staff from her fingers. No one took her staff! She had never felt helpless in her life. Tears streamed unbidden from her eyes.

"Dag-gum it, I'd swear yer right, Leroy. But it can't be. It's part of the wood." He peered closer. "Well, some of these runes look kind of like spirit magic runes to me, but it's hard to say." He tossed the staff back to Leroy. "We'll have Biff take a look at it when we get back to camp."

"Well-well," said Mel, pacing around Djeri. "This-un here's a real puzzle. Look at that beard! What do you think, Boss Donjon? Is he a short, good-lookin' human or tall ugly dwarf?"

"Very funny, Mel," said Donjon, who was peering at Djeri with disgust. "That's Dremaldrian Battle Academy armor on him. Whoever he is, he ain't worth piss."

Tarah's hackles raised as she heard her papa's sword being drawn. Mel let out a low whistle. "That is a dag-gum purty sword. Fine rune-work. This could bring in a bundle."

"Take it off him and bring it in," said Donjon. "Leroy, you grab the lady and tie her to the mule while we-."

"Smugglers!" Shouted Djeri. There was a thud and Tarah saw Mel tumble to the ground, his mustache mussed by a well-placed punch. The Ramsetter clattered to the ground beside him. "Corntown turd-lickers!"

Djeri rushed into Tarah's field of vision. He picked up the sword and charged Donjon, rage on his face. The black-mustached dwarf calmly drew a small dark rod from a holster at his waist and pointed it. A sharp pop echoed from the end of the rod and a wave of magic similar to the one that had paralyzed them earlier struck Djeri mid-swing. The sword fell from Djeri's fingers and he hit the ground, rolling to Donjon's feet.

The dwarf placed a heavy boot on Djeri's chest and puffed on his cigar. "His blood magic's perty strong to break free from that spell. This-un's gonna be trouble. Mel! Get yer lazy arse up off the ground and grab some dwarf shackles 'fore he breaks loose from this spell too." Donjon spat onto Djeri's upturned face. "Come on, boys! Let's load 'em up!"

Tarah screamed inwardly in impotent rage, but could do nothing as Leroy dragged her over to Neddy and tossed her over the mule's back, tying her down on top of their supplies. It was extremely uncomfortable. Her body was bent at an angle and one of their trail shovels jabbed her hip while the dwarves' ropes dug into her wrists and ankles.

Then Donjon walked over to Neddy and pointed the dark rod at him. There was a buzzing noise and the mule stumbled as the spell binding him was released. He turned his large head and looked at Tarah with a worried eye. Unfortunately, there was nothing she could do to comfort him.

Djeri got the worst treatment. Mel punched him in the face a few times just to get even. Then he gagged Djeri with some sort of dirty rag and yanked his arms behind his back. Mel pulled off his gauntlets and clamped some kind of green metal shackles over his wrists. Another set of shackles was placed around his ankles. Then Mel tied a rope to Djeri's legs and used it to drag him over to the others.

They set off away from the stream, heading southward down a path that hugged the edge of a steep ravine. Donjon took the lead and Mel walked behind him, dragging Djeri along by his rope, face down in the dirt. Leroy led Neddy after them and two more dwarves whom Tarah had never gotten a good look at brought up the rear.

A short distance into the hike, Djeri broke free of the spell and began writhing and grunting in anger. Mel put up with it for a few minutes, then let go of the rope and walked back to kick Djeri in the head. That just seemed to further enrage the dwarf and he strained harder at his shackles.

"Fine! You brought this on yerself," said Mel and he shoved Djeri off the trail.

The dwarf tumbled down the steep slope of the ravine, grunting angrily as he bounced off rocks and tree trunks on the way. His plate armor likely protected him somewhat but it also added weight and he picked up speed, rolling faster and faster until he hit the ground with a resounding crash and went still.

The dwarves laughed, finding the whole thing hysterical. All except for Donjon who fixed Mel with a glare.

"What?" said Mel, shrugging. "We'll pick him up at the bottom of the ravine when we get our cart. He ain't goin' nowhere with them shackles on."

Tarah ached to call out. To rush down after him and make sure he wasn't dead. Still, she couldn't budge. The only comfort she had was that the other dwarves didn't seem worried. Djeri was tough, right? Surely his blood magic had helped him survive.

Worry about yourself first, Tarah, said Grampa Rolf sternly. *That's the number one rule. Friends or clients can wait until you make sure you're safe.*

That advice was what caused her to run away in the first place, Tarah thought bitterly. But his words sparked another memory. Djeri had called them smugglers and Corntown turd-lickers. What was it her grampa had said about them? What was it?

She thought back, focusing until the memory bubbled into her mind.

Tarah was standing next to her grampa by the workbench in his room. He was working on her armor, placing a sheet of thin linen on the underside of the moonrat skin. He picked up a painting brush and began slathering a pungent and sticky substance over it.

"I know this is gonna sound funny coming from me, Tarah girl, but there are some folks you shouldn't do business with, no matter how good the coin," he said.

"That is funny, grampa," Tarah had said with a giggle, but he'd given her a serious look.

"I ain't jokin'. Hear me now. Tarah Woodblade should never do business with dark wizards, imps, or Corntown smugglers. They may have good coin and a lot of it, but there never was a deal come from those folks that did a salesman any good. I'm tellin' you this from my own experience."

He turned back to the leather, laying down another sheet of linen and smoothing it out before slathering the whole thing again. "When you deal with dark magic there's always a price. Even if you come out with your skin intact, your reputation will be sullied. If Tarah Woodblade's gonna work, it's all about your reputation, hear?"

Yes, grampa . . . The memory faded away. If these were Corntown smugglers she was in worse trouble than she'd thought.

The dwarves continued down the trail to the bottom of the ravine where they found Djeri squirming and very much alive. A deep gash ran across his forehead and blood streamed from the wound, but he had managed to spit his gag out. He let loose on the dwarves with a stream of profanity laced with creative uses of the word turd.

Finally, they got the gag back on him and dragged Djeri by the rope on his ankles again. They stopped after a short distance and Tarah saw a rather bedraggled looking dwarf with a droopy hat sitting atop a brown painted wagon pulled by two horses. She heard the snorts of several horses and felt the strong hands of dwarves untie her hands and feet from the back of the mule.

She was lifted off Neddy's back and as they swung her around, Tarah saw Donjon and Leroy climbing onto horses of their own. The idea of a dwarf on horseback was funny in her mind, but these dwarves looked at home on the beasts, sitting on specially built saddles that fit them well.

A couple of the dwarves picked up Djeri and tossed him into the back of the wagon like a load of garbage. They were more gentle with Tarah, hoisting her into the back before laying her next to the dwarf. As they did so, she noticed that the wagon was loaded with ropes and canvas. Six steel rings had been bolted to the inside bed and Tarah realized that this rig was set up for the transport of a large beast.

The dwarves had brought the wagon hoping to capture the rogue horse. Idiots. Couldn't they see that the tracks were three weeks old? And how were they planning to get a paralyzed beast from the stream above to the cart below without seriously injuring it?

The wagon started moving and Djeri wormed his way over to look her in the eye. His face was a mess, covered in bruises and cuts and dirt. The gash in his forehead still seeped blood and blood ran from his nose, but he looked at her with clear eyes. Deliberately, he worked his jaw back and forth as he chewed the gag with his teeth. Couldn't he see how hopeless their situation was? But to her surprise, he chewed through the gag and spit it out.

"I have tough chompers, a legacy from my family," he said and smiled at her, something that looked uncomfortable with his split lip. "Are you okay? I know you can't respond. The paralyzing spells these smugglers use are a nasty business. Most of their trade comes in the form of rare animals and the spells are made to last a long time."

Tarah couldn't respond to him in any way, but just the sound of his voice was a relief to hear. He sounded calm and confident and she wished that she were as brave as he was.

Tarah Woodblade is always brave, said Grampa Rolf.

"Listen I know things seem helpless right now, but these smugglers have no reason to kill us. It'll likely be uncomfortable for awhile, but they'll probably let us go a ways from here once they're sure we can't make trouble for them." He shook his head thoughtfully.

"We'll just need to make up a story once they get us to their leader. Something that makes us look like innocent people just out hiking. Maybe we can talk our way out." He frowned. "I wonder who hired them? This is far from their normal territory."

She knew. Tarah struggled to move her mouth but it was useless. Why was he so confident? The dwarves had no reason to kill them yet, but once they found the drawings of the rogue horse tracks in their packs, they'd know they had competition at least. Wouldn't that make them more than enough of a threat for the smugglers to justify killing them?

Djeri noticed the tears of frustration on her cheeks. "Hey, Tarah, I know this is hard. Those paralyzing spells are the worst, especially for someone like you who's so headstrong and used to moving free. Just know it's temporary. You'll make it through it."

A shadow passed over Djeri's face and Tarah saw the driver lean over the seat to look back at them. He had a glass eye and Tarah noticed a few missing teeth as he smiled. "I thought so. Hey boys! This dwarf's talkin' back here!"

Djeri sighed. "I told you this would be uncomfortable. Just hold tight until we can find a way to get free."

The cart stopped for a brief moment and Mel pulled his horse up alongside them. The dwarf jumped from his saddle into the back. He froze Djeri with another spell and sat on his chest. Mel grinned as he slowly took off his boot. Then he stripped off a foul smelling sock and shoved it into Djeri's mouth.

The dwarf tied a new gag in place. "Now pipe down. Next time you'll get my small clothes, see?"

He put his sockless foot back into the boot and jumped back on his horse. The wagon started up again and the dwarves laughed at Mel's humiliating joke. A few minutes later, Djeri broke through the spell and turned to look at Tarah again. She expected to see disgust on his face, but instead the look he gave her was steadfast. He nodded calmly and laid back.

The rest of the journey didn't take long. Perhaps a half hour later they stopped again. A horse thundered up to the side of the wagon, a proud black stallion, and the man astride it wore a long gray cloak with the hood up. He peered over the side. A scarf covered the bottom half of his face, but Tarah caught a glimpse of his eyes, cold and calculating.

It was Shade. He had dressed in a similar fashion when she had met with him in Razbeck, keeping his face partially hidden. Why hadn't his behavior tipped her off back then? Perhaps the truth was that she had been looking for an excuse to return to Dremaldria anyway. Of course the coin upfront hadn't hurt.

What would he do now that he had seen her? Her armor was unique. Surely he would remember hiring her.

He rode away and spoke with Donjon in a low voice. Moments later dwarves came into the cart and tossed Djeri over the side. He was dragged away and Tarah heard the crash of his armor several times as the dwarves hooted and hollered. They must have arrived at the smuggler camp.

Mel climbed into the cart next to her and removed her
papa's bow and her quiver. He took her belt knife and opened her
coin pouch, whistling softly as he checked the contents inside.
Then he gave her a thorough once over, looking for hidden
weapons and binding her hands and feet. For one that said he
didn't like humans, he was pretty handsy while he was at it. Tarah
wished she could strangle him.

When he was finished, he pulled out a strip of cloth and
gagged her, then leaned in and whispered, "Sorry 'bout this, girlie,
but the spell's gonna end soon and we don't want you hollerin'.
Dunno what Shade's gonna want to do with you, but just between
you and me, I think yer a fine filly." He slapped her rump and left.

Mel shouted something and she heard the dwarves
unloading their supplies from Neddy's back. There were a couple
of curses as the mule tried to bite them. A scuffle ensued, but
another sharp pop rang out and the animal quieted. A few moments
later, Leroy shouted at the discovery of the pepperbean wine and
they fought over it for awhile. Tarah held on to hope that they
would kill one another, but Donjon calmed things down.

The sunlight faded to darkness. As the minutes crawled by
Tarah felt the paralyzing spell fade. As soon as she was able, she
rolled to her knees and peered over the side of the wagon. It was a
disorderly camp. Tents were scattered haphazardly along the
ravine and they had several cook fires going in various places.

She couldn't identify their exact location right away, but
she had an idea from the length of their journey. They were
somewhere close to the river, but a ways north of the board bridge.
It seemed that they had camped at the bottom of a dry streambed.

Tarah counted fifteen dwarves and from her position she
could see just as many horses picketed around the edges. There
was one large tent in the center of the camp and she could see a
light emanating from the inside. Two shadows played on the tent
wall, one tall and one much shorter; likely Shade and Donjon.

A tall tree stood next to the tent. A large animal had been
hung up from one thick branch and was being butchered. Its head
was missing and they had already skinned it, but it looked to be a
horse. Why did they kill one of their horses? They hadn't seemed
to be starving. Were they that bad at hunting?

In the shadows on the far side of the tree another figure was hanging from a long rope. Tarah's heart skipped. It was Djeri. He was still in full platemail and was hanging limp with his arms pulled behind his back, his legs splayed.

She worried that he was dead, but then his body rotated slightly and she realized that the rope wasn't tied around his neck. He squirmed a little and she saw that they had strung him up by his elbows. Tarah grimaced. That had to be painful.

"Hey, Boss Donjon!" shouted a gruff voice and Tarah saw a dwarf looking her way. "That lady's spell broke!"

There was movement in the large tent and the shorter figure ducked out. Donjon was clutching his hat in his hands, but he quickly placed it back on his head and headed Tarah's way. While he walked, he put a half-burned cigar in his mouth and lit it again with his fire cylinder.

A couple of the other dwarves followed him. One of them was Leroy. The other one had a full head of gray hair and a silvery mustache.

"I see yer up," Donjon said to her. He took a puff on his cigar and gave Tarah a calculating stare. "Shade wants to see you, so here's what's gonna happen. We're gonna untie yer legs and yer gag, but if you start makin' a ruckus, we'll freeze you again. You hear me?"

Tarah nodded. He gestured to the two other dwarves and they pulled her out of the wagon. While they did so, Tarah weighed how to act. She couldn't fight her way out. Even if she ran and escaped, she'd be leaving Djeri and Neddy in their hands. She thought quickly as her legs were untied and the gag removed from her mouth.

Be in charge, said her grampa. *Tarah Woodblade don't let nothing mess her cool.*

"This was all unnecessary, Donjon," Tarah said calmly. "All you had to do was say you were working with Shade and we'd have come with you."

"Yeah right," the dwarf said and spat, his eyes darting to Djeri as he hung from the tree.

"We're on the same side after all," she added.

The dwarf snorted and Tarah saw that he was not at all convinced. "Then why was you destroyin' the tracks?"

She shrugged. "Yeah, well I gotta admit that we heard

Shade had hired other folks. I wanted to be the only one to find the beast."

"Just follow me and we'll see what Shade thinks," he replied.

Donjon strolled towards the tent. Tarah walked behind him, followed by the other two dwarves. They passed a few cookfires along the way where smugglers were roasting pieces of that butchered horse. Tarah recognized one of them immediately.

"Just a second, Donjon," Tarah said, moving before he could object.

She strode over to the fire where Mel sat with his back to her, busy laughing with two other dwarves while he roasted a spit of horseflesh. Their conversation stopped as other dwarves looked up at her in surprise. Mel turned to look behind him just in time for the side of his face to meet Tarah's boot.

Tarah's arms were still bound behind her, but she put all her weight into the kick. The force of it sent the heavy dwarf sprawling into the fire head first. The dwarf rolled away from the fire, cursing and hollering as he brushed at the burning coals on his face and chest.

Two pairs of rough hands grabbed Tarah from behind. She was thrown to the ground and Donjon stood over her, his black rod pointed at her head. The lit ember on his cigar illuminated an unpleased face.

With a roar of anger, Mel charged at her and had to be held back by two other dwarves. His face was blackened with soot and large chunks of his mustache and eyebrows were singed off. "Blazin' hellfire, woman! What was that fer?"

"That was for taking liberties while you were tying me up, you mangy dog!" Tarah shouted back. She looked back up at Donjon. "I'm ready to see Shade now."

The gray-headed dwarf burst out with a guffaw and several of the other dwarves joined in the laughter. Donjon's expression changed only slightly, though there was a hint of amusement in his eyes. "Listen, girl. You try somethin' like that again and I don't care what Shade thinks, I'll slit yer ugly throat. Hear me?"

Tarah could tell he was sincere. "I do."

They pulled her back to her feet and shoved her towards the tent. Mel complained all the while, cursing his burns and proclaiming his innocence, all the while being ridiculed by the others.

As Tarah neared the tent, she looked up at Djeri's hanging form. The bindings seemed even more painful up close as she saw the two ropes that suspended all his weight by the elbows tied behind his back. But there was no discomfort in his face. His gaze rested on her, his eyes filled with firm determination.

A wave of guilt threatened to rush over her. There he was being so brave and yet he had no idea what was going on. How would he feel when he found out? Tarah pushed the feeling aside. Guilt was a useless emotion right now. There would be plenty of time for that later. She tried to think of something to give him encouragement.

The dwarves stopped at the tent and Donjon gestured for her to go inside. She paused and looked back up at the hanging dwarf.

"Hey, Djeri. Why are turds tapered on one end?" she asked. Djeri's eyes were confused. "'Cause if they weren't, your butt would slam shut."

It was a terrible joke Tarah had heard in a tavern somewhere, but it had the reaction she had hoped. His body shook and she could hear the sound of his muffled laughter. The gray-haired dwarf standing behind her chuckled, but Donjon wasn't amused.

"Shut up and get in!" he said and Tarah gave him a brief nod before walking through the tent flap.

The tent reminded Tarah of a military commander's. The wooden table that sat in the center of the tent was a jumble of maps and pieces of parchment. In contrast, the rest of the space was neat and tidy. The small cot at the back was covered by neatly folded blankets and a set of closed saddlebags was hung over a weathered wooden chest. The whole area was lit by glowing orbs set at each of the tent's corners.

The man she had recognized earlier as Shade sat in a chair next to the table. He still wore the cloak she had seen him in earlier, but his hood had been pulled back. His scarf had been tugged away from his face and hung loose around his neck.

His face surprised her. Shade had seemed so intimidating when she first met him. Now she saw only a mild-looking man maybe in his mid 30's. He had a shock of curly brown hair and was clean shaven. If not for his trail-worn garb and the thin sword at his waist, she would have thought him a tailor of perhaps shopkeeper of some kind. The red sash that he wore across his chest didn't help to break that illusion.

"Good evening," he said, his voice a pleasant baritone. He gestured to another chair that sat facing him. "I must admit I was surprised when the dwarves brought you down from the foothills. Please, sit."

His mildness emboldened her. Tarah grunted and plopped down into the chair. She was Tarah Woodblade, after all. "You know, Shade, no one likes a client that's always hovering over you while you're trying to work."

Shade gave her a disarming smile. "I apologize for that, Tarah, I hope you don't mind me calling you that. My other hirelings weren't aware that you were . . . on the team, so to speak. Your method of capture was terribly unfortunate."

"Right. Terribly unfortunate indeed," she said, returning his smile with one of her own. "Tarah Woodblade does not like being rough handled. There's a dwarf outside with a burnt face that can attest to that. And the way they beat on my bodyguard don't make me happy either."

Shade leaned back in his chair and cocked his head at her slightly. The pleasantness left his eyes. "As I said. I apologize for your rough treatment. As for your academy friend, I really don't care. The question is what do I do with you now?"

Tarah pressed on. "Before you get started, you should know that this little incident is going to increase my fee. If you're still interested in my services, you'll double what you promised to pay and you'll release the dwarf you got hanging from the tree outside. In addition-."

"I'm sorry, there must be some sort of misunderstanding," Shade interrupted, the smile leaving his face completely. "I didn't bring you in here for a contract renegotiation. This is merely an apology for your rough treatment."

Tarah frowned. This wasn't going as she'd hoped. Her grampa urged her to press on. "Sorry, Shade. If you want my help, and believe me you do, you're gonna have to do better than an apology at this point."

Shade cleared his throat. "I wouldn't mind having your help in tracking down the beast we are seeking, but if you wish to be paid nothing and hung in the tree with your associate, I can oblige you. Otherwise, the contract will go on as previously negotiated." A steely tone entered his voice next and his eyes hardened. "Am I understood, Tarah?"

The tone in his voice raised warning bells in her mind. Grampa Rolf now suggested she ease back, but Tarah's rage rose. How dare he? How dare all of them after what she'd been through the last couple of days?

She couldn't keep the glare out of her eyes. "You can quit the tough guy game, Shade. Yeah, fine, put me in the tree, but you'll never find that beast on your own. These dwarfs of yours are idiots. They wouldn't know what to do with a creature like that even if they could find their arses with their own two hands. For nature's sake, they're out there eating one of their own horses right now." She folded her arms. "If you want that rogue horse, you're gonna need Tarah Woodblade."

Mentioning that she knew the beast was a rogue horse was a gamble, but she wanted Shade to know she knew her business. The cool look he gave her told Tarah that she was onto something. Yes, he was frustrated with the efforts of the dwarves all right. He wanted her help or he wouldn't have brought her in.

"I find it interesting that you know the nature of our quarry," he said.

"I'm Tarah Woodblade. I figured it out," she said. "So, what's it going to be Shade? You gonna string me up, or are you gonna renegotiate?"

Shade appraised her for a moment, then whistled. The two dwarves entered the tent and there was a sharp pop. Tarah's body seized up again. As the dwarves pulled her out of the chair, Shade gave a snort.

"Tarah, I am disappointed. Truly I am. I had hoped that you would be less foolish. The rumors I heard told me that you were formidable. Full of confidence. The only thing I've seen from you so far is a scared girl trying to impress." He directed his next comment to the dwarves behind her. "String her up by the elbows next to her dwarf friend. If she's too loud, gag her."

He stood and grasped her chin. Lifting her eyes to meet his, he said. "We move out in the morning. I'll check on you then to see if you've changed your mind."

Chapter Fifteen

The dwarves did as Shade instructed. As they dragged Tarah to the tree, she saw a look of concern in Djeri's eyes. She felt like such a fool. She had ignored her grampa's warning and had antagonized the man. She should have played along for a while instead and focused on getting Djeri released.

At any rate it was too late now. The dwarves had difficulty getting her arms back into the position they wanted, so they unlaced the front of her leather armor to gain some slack, then tied her wrists behind her back. They tied ropes around her arms at the elbows and threw the ropes over the stout tree branch next to Djeri. The position they had her in hurt and they hadn't even lifted her yet.

As they went to hoist her into the air, Leroy grinned at her nastily. "We're takin' this spell off you now. Boss Donjon wants to see how sturdy you are. If you don't scream too loud, we'll let you go without a gag. Hell, who knows. Maybe if you impress him enough, he'll convince Shade to play nicer in the mornin'."

"Bah," said Mel, walking up to them. He'd cleaned the soot off of his face, but patches of his skin were inflamed and flushed red. Tarah would have found the state of his facial hair comical if she hadn't been so afraid. "Look at her dwarf friend. Even he'd be squealin' if we didn't have him gagged. She'll be ballin' her eyes out right away, even if we don't wrench her arms out their sockets just haulin' her up!"

"I think yer wrong about that dwarf, Mel," said the dwarf with the gray mustache. He was giving Djeri a measured look. "I think I know who this one is. If I'm right, he's a Cragstalker."

"He's yer kin?" said Mel. "What the hell's a Cragstalker doin' with a pitiful beard like that?"

"Distant kin," he replied. "Though I don't know who'd claim him. I'd better talk to Donjon."

Mel enthusiastically took his place holding Tarah's ropes. As they hoisted her up, they did so with a jerk. Pain shot from her shoulders down both arms. Tarah's eyes bulged. She gritted her teeth but a cry escaped her lips. As they hoisted her up higher, the pain increased. It felt as if her shoulders were going to tear free from their sockets. She held on, trying not to scream. She was Tarah Woodblade. She was tough. Everyone knew it. She refused to give Shade the satisfaction of breaking her.

Thirty seconds passed. It seemed like hours. She imagined her shoulders slowly tearing free. She no longer cared about toughness. Tarah screamed.

"Let me down! Tell Shade I'll do whatever he asks. Just let me down!"

The dwarves laughed. One of them handed some coins to another one.

"Please! My arms are breaking!" She strained, trying to pull her body's weight off her shoulder joints but there was no way to get leverage. She kicked but each movement just made it worse. She sobbed and moaned. She pleaded. The dwarves in the camp below finally stopped laughing after a sharp order from Shade's tent.

They lowered Tarah to the ground slowly. "Thank you," she said as her feet touched ground. "I'll do whatever he wants, I promise."

Leroy rolled his eyes. "Don't get too excited, girlie. This ain't a rescue. Shade just wants us to shut you up is all."

The dwarf yanked a handkerchief out of his back pocket and shoved it in her mouth. It wasn't clean. Tarah could taste dirt and salt and something a little sour. She tried to spit it out, but his fingers were like iron. He then held it in place with a strip of cloth that he tied behind the back of her head. Tarah choked and retched, but nothing came up.

The dwarf just rolled his eyes. "Yeah, yer tough alright."

They prepared to haul her up again. Tarah panicked, jumping up and down, kicking, trying to stomp their feet. Then she glanced up at Djeri dangling above her. The Dwarf wasn't struggling. Though his face was red with rage, he stayed completely still. His eyes locked on hers with firmness. *Don't let them beat you*, the dwarf's eyes said.

"Don't pretend to be so tough, short beard!" one of the other dwarves said. This one was a female with a downy mustache of her own. She picked something up off the ground and threw it at him. To Tarah's eyes it looked like a dead rat. Perhaps they had killed it skulking around their camp.

The rat would have hit him square in the face, but Djeri jerked his head forward at the last moment, knocking the rat back at them with his forehead. To the dwarf's dismay, it landed in their stew pot with a plop.

The dwarves around the cookfire shouted at the female that threw the rat. Tarah saw Djeri's body quiver with laughter. He fixed his eyes on hers and gave her a brief nod again. She nodded back, forcing down the fear.

The dwarves started hauling her back up. As the rope yanked, she felt a pop in her right shoulder. A muffled cry escaped her lips, but she cut it short, refusing to let them hear her suffering. Once they stopped pulling, she dangled there, squirming until she met Djeri's eyes again.

The dwarf was completely still, his legs spread. Tarah understood. She forced her body to keep still, avoiding any jarring movements. Still the pain was excruciating and though she kept quiet, tears streamed down her cheeks.

Tarah couldn't believe she was reacting to it so badly. She had honed herself to be tough and her grampa had helped her create a persona that would give people confidence in her abilities. She had always imagined that she would be able to handle torture if it ever happened to her. But she'd been wrong. This was a pain she had not prepared for.

It wore on her until the only thing keeping her from kicking and moaning was embarrassment over her behavior. Djeri had seen her screaming like a child. She had shown them the truth she had tried to hide for so long. She was a coward.

Tarah searched for anything to give her strength, pleading for her papa's and grampa's advice, but they were silent. Neither one of them had prepared her for a moment such as this. Why hadn't they prepared her?

It was hard, but she held firm. The night crept by with an

agonizing slowness. Every time she thought she would break, she turned her head to find the dwarf staring back at her, giving her an encouraging stare. Eventually her shoulder sockets went numb. Her arms went numb. She couldn't feel her fingers.

At that point she began to worry about permanent damage to her nerves. Well, that and the dirty handkerchief. It had absorbed all the moisture in her mouth and she struggled not to gag. She focused on Djeri's encouragement for as long as she could. Then she focused on her hate.

She hated the dwarves and their nasty laughter. But even more, she hated Shade. Why had he done this? Why was he hunting this rogue horse and why had he hired dwarves? They were too loud to be good trackers.

She looked at the carcass of the animal that hung across from Djeri, rotating slowly in the wind, most of its meat cut off. Why had they killed the horse? Why kill one of their own work animals like that? She shuddered as a creeping suspicion flowed over her. She hoped she was wrong.

As the night wore on, the ache returned. Tarah drifted into sleep only to wake up with the feeling that hot irons had been stuck in the core of her bones. It was a dull, angry ache that stretched from her back down to her fingertips.

She looked to Djeri, to find that he was still watching her, his gaze warm and understanding. *I'm strong*, his eyes seemed to say. *Take some of my strength.*

How was he doing it? Sure, he was a dwarf, but he'd been strung up much longer than she had and his plate armor was adding a lot of extra weight. Nevertheless, he stayed stoic. Throughout the night, no matter how bad the pain became, Djeri was there hanging beside her, strong and dependable, giving her courage; doing what Tarah Woodblade should have done.

When daylight broke, Shade came out of his tent and stood below her looking up with a calculating expression on his face. His red sash gleamed in the sun and Tarah looked back at him, her face expressionless. He called out to the dwarves and they came over to grasp her ropes.

Gently, they lowered her down and Tarah allowed herself to think on her arms once again. She couldn't feel them, not really. But her shoulder socket was afire with a dull ache. She glanced up at Djeri and he gave her a stoic nod.

When the weight was eased from her shoulders, she was struck again with a sharp pain. Tarah moaned despite her resolve. The dwarves cut her free. She swayed on her feet while her arms hung at her sides throbbing and tingling so fiercely she nearly collapsed.

"Remove her gag," Shade instructed.

Once they had done so, she pushed the nasty handkerchief out with her tongue and grimaced at the taste that remained in her dry mouth. She couldn't even work up enough saliva to spit, much less form words.

"Get her some water!" Shade demanded and as one of the dwarves brought a leather water skin, he said, "Well, Tarah, have you rethought your proposal?"

Tarah worked her mouth but no sound came out. She was really going to fall over soon. When he saw that she couldn't respond, Shade continued.

"I know you think me cruel for the night you just endured. And you would be right. But it isn't something done for pleasure. I find torture quite distasteful myself." He folded his arms. "What you have just learned is that I am a man who does what's necessary to get my point across. You were proud and insolent and I needed you to understand that such behavior wouldn't be tolerated. Now I think you understand me better."

The dwarf with the gray mustache tried to hand her the waterskin but she couldn't lift her arms enough to grasp it. At Shade's nod, the dwarf lifted it to her lips himself. Tarah swirled the water in her mouth and didn't dare spit it out fearing that it would be seen as a gesture of defiance, so she swallowed it down and continued to drink thirstily.

"Here is my proposal, Tarah," said Shade. "I will honor our previous contract as if this uncomfortable evening never happened. You are, from everything I have heard, a gifted tracker. Find this rogue horse for me and the money is yours. Then you will be free to go on your way. Otherwise, I will leave you to our dwarven friends to dispose of as they see fit." He paused to let his message sink in. "What say you?"

Shade's offer was as Tarah had hoped. She had thought long and hard during the night on what her response would be. She had gone through a wide range of decisions, waffling from defiance and anger, to begging for mercy.

"I have a question before I answer," she said.

"Very well," Shade said. He lifted a warning finger. "Just know that further insolence on your part will nullify my offer."

"That animal your dwarfs butchered last night," Tarah said, her voice sounding rough despite the water. "Was it my mule?"

Shade frowned, looking at the stripped carcass that hung from the tree. "Donjon!"

The black-mustached dwarf walked over from one of the cookfires, wiping stew from his chin. "Yeah?"

"Did your men butcher this woman's mule?" he asked.

The dwarf wrinkled his nose. "Like we'd do that. It's a biter, but that'd be a waste of a sturdy pack animal." He gestured at the carcass with his chin. "That there was Merba's horse. Broke its leg goin' up the ravine yesterday. Had to put it down."

Tarah sighed in relief.

Shade turned back to her with a condescending smile. "There you are, question answered. Now give me the answer to mine."

If Tarah had been able to move her arms, she didn't know if she would have been able to keep from punching that smirk off his face. It took all she had just to keep the hatred out of her eyes. She gave him a stiff nod instead. "It's a deal, Shade. We'll do it."

"Very good," he said. Biff!"

"Yeah, Shade," said the gray mustached dwarf.

"Give her one of those healing tonics. We'll need her to be able to move her arms." He turned his calculating eyes back to her. "I am glad you chose to honor our contract. Please know that if you try to run or disrupt my business in any way, last night will seem comfortable by comparison. Do you understand?"

Tarah nodded again, her teeth grit tightly as she forced herself not to run over and kick the man like she had Mel the night before. Soon Biff came back with a small clay bottle. He pulled out the cork and a pungent smell wafted to her nose.

Tarah's papa had taught her how to make several kinds of healing droughts using plants from the forest. She could smell a few familiar herbs but as he poured the liquid into her mouth, she realized that there were far more ingredients she wasn't familiar with. A regular healing drought takes some time to work, but the effects of this one were fast.

She felt her body flush and her arms went from tingling to throbbing. Soon she was able to move her fingers. She winced as she raised her arms, but the pain faded away and she stretched with a groan of pleasure. It felt so good to be able to move again.

As she rotated her shoulders, feeling them ease back into their sockets Tarah realized just how severe her injuries had been. If they had not given her a magical potion like this, she may have had permanent nerve damage. She shuddered. What if she had gone the rest of her life without being able to move her fingers?

She turned to look up at Djeri. The dwarf still hung up on the tree, watching her calmly with something like relief in his eyes. "Can we get my bodyguard down now?"

"I see no need to leave him up there," Shade said. "But I don't need him toddling back to the academy and telling them about us. What do you think, Biff?"

"I won't be killin' another dwarf when he's defenseless like that," the gray haired smuggler said. "'Specially kin. Don't matter how distant."

"What are you saying?" Tarah said in alarm. "You can't kill him. I hired that dwarf for my protection! I paid half upfront."

Shade looked puzzled. "And now you have fifteen dwarves to watch over you. Besides, this way you won't have to pay the last half. What say you, Donjon?"

"Sorry, Shade. I'm with Biff on this one. Aunt Maggie'd have my hide if I started killin' kinfolk." He shrugged. "But it wouldn't be the first time I looked the other way while someone else did it. He's all yours, Shade. We'cn bury him deep so no one'll find him."

Shade sighed. "Fine, get me a crossbow. You can turn away if you'd like."

Mel chuckled and ran towards the horses.

"Wait!" Tarah said, her mind whirring for a way to save him. Djeri, watching from above, grunted, nodding his head at her. His eyes were wide as if he was trying to give her a hint. "I-I said I paid half upfront. If he dies, the academy'll know who he was with. I don't want 'em coming after me."

Shade frowned. "Contracts I understand, Tarah dear," he

said. "But academy warriors are notorious for . . . informing on clients who do things improper. That's why I keep to, let's say, more unsavory help."

"What're you talkin' 'bout, Shade?" Leroy said with a sly grin. "I'm very savory. You'cn ask the ladies." The others laughed.

Shade ignored them. "Warriors die sometimes. It's an academy tradition. If you tell them where the body was buried, they'll believe your story. It's better this way, trust me."

Mel arrived with a heavy crossbow. He had a wicked-looking bolt already notched. Shade took it from him and lifted it with practiced hands.

"Don't! He wouldn't tell! Because . . . because-," she stammered. Tarah glanced up at Djeri and her face colored as she said, "He's my lover."

A hush fell over the camp.

"Yer a humie, academy boy?" Leroy yelled. The dwarves in the background erupted in laughter.

"Lovers?" Shade said, frowning uncertainly. "I find that difficult to believe."

"Runs in his family," said Donjon, his lip curled with distaste. "Just like his granddaddy. Pa Cragstalker'd turn over in his grave."

"He'd never tell the academy about what you're doing," Tarah embellished, an idea coming to her. "In fact, as soon as we found the rogue horse for you, we were planning to take the money and run off to Razbeck together. I-I had a job offer there. A noble gave me his family mark. It was in my coinpurse before Mel took it."

All eyes turned on Mel. The dwarf shrugged sheepishly. "I didn't go through all of it yet, but . . . there was a house mark in there."

"I'll expect all of it back, too," Tarah said. "I know exactly how much was in there. That was gonna be our wedding money."

"You believe her, Shade?" Mel asked.

"We'll see." Shade jerked his head towards the hanging dwarf. "Ease him down, Biff."

To Tarah's relief, they hustled over and began slowly lowering him towards the ground. He grunted as his feet hit the ground, but otherwise, he showed no sign of discomfort. Shade walked over to them and stood in front of the dwarf, his lip still curled. "Take out his gag."

As the dwarves untied the gag, Tarah clenched her teeth in concern, hoping the dwarf wouldn't say something stupid or attack Shade. Djeri coughed as he spat out the nasty sock. He winced at the dryness in his mouth but spoke, his voice hoarse, "Tarah, girl. Are you okay? Are your arms alright?"

She blinked at the tenderness in his voice. He was a better actor than she'd thought. Shade's eyes were fixed on her face, gauging her response.

Tarah knew she had to sell it, so she used a trick her grampa had taught her. She pulled deep on her emotions, focusing on the dwarf's bravery and companionship over the last few days. Tarah looked closely at him. His face was battered and bloodied and his arms were still tied behind his back. She knew he had to be in excruciating pain.

She raised a hand to her mouth, summoning tears. "Oh Djeri, I'm fine. Are you okay?"

Djeri's brow furrowed and for a second she saw a slight look of confusion on his face. "As long as you're okay, I am."

The camp was quiet at this and Tarah noticed that Shade wasn't the only one disturbed by their tactic. The other dwarves seemed to be torn between laughing and gagging at the thought of her and Djeri together.

She could feel Shade's cold eyes on her. "Come over here then, Tarah. Kiss him. Convince me you love this dwarf."

There was a mixture of laughter and groans from the other dwarves.

Tarah swallowed, her heart pounding. She shuffled towards him. Could she do this? She'd never kissed a man, before. Not really. She'd kissed her papa and grampa goodnight, but only on the cheek and a chaste peck was not going to be convincing enough.

"I-I'm afraid I might hurt him," she stammered as she drew near.

Djeri's battered face was red and his eyes were apologetic. "It's just a split lip. I-I'm . . ." His jaw quivered and she could tell he was close to backing down. He could blow the whole thing.

Tarah Woodblade does what's necessary, said Grampa

Rolf.

He was right. Tarah strengthened her resolve. This wasn't about a kiss. It was a mission objective. It was about survival. Tarah Woodblade could fight off half a dozen moonrats with a quarter staff. She could skin a deer in under five minutes and make sausages with its intestines. Dirty work was something she was not unfamiliar with.

Tarah leaned down and grasped the back of Djeri's head. His eyes closed as their lips touched. She held her breath. Not knowing what to do, she called back on memories of watching others kiss and tilted her head, pulling his face hard against hers.

She let her lips part. He tasted of blood and steel and a thick masculine sort of musk. His lips slid against hers in response and if the situation had been different and he had been freshly bathed, the sensation wouldn't have been all that awful.

Finally she pulled back, breathing heavily. She could feel his blood and sweat on her face, but forced herself not to wipe it away. They shared a troubled stare for a moment and she turned back to the others. "Don't hurt him, please."

Shade looked thoroughly disgusted.

"Here," He said thrusting a clean-looking handkerchief at her. "Wipe off your face."

She did so and tried not to let her relief show. Had it worked? Had she been convincing enough. "Will you let him go?"

"Untie him Biff," Shade said in response. "Consider this a show of good faith, Tarah. If either of you betray me or try to run away, I promise we will hunt you down. And hunting is these dwarves' specialty."

"Tarah Woodblade keeps her contracts," she replied coldly.

She watched them release Djeri's arms. He grimaced as they hung to his sides and Tarah knew how much they would be hurting.

"Will you give him a healing potion, like you did me?" she asked.

"Are you aware how much one of those costs?" Shade scoffed. "Just be glad we spared him. He's a dwarf, he'll recover."

"Besides," said Biff. "Them healin' potions are magic. Don't work good on us dwarves anyhow."

"Will you be alright, Djeri?" she asked.

"I'll be fine," he said stoically.

She gave him a dubious look. "Do you dwarfs have any healing potions that do work on your kind?"

Donjon laughed. "You couldn't afford the stuff we got."

"If you returned the purse you took from me when you captured us I would," she said and Mel scowled.

"I had money, too." Djeri added.

"Shade, we would like our things back," she said. "My staff and bow are heirlooms. We also want our pack animal back and-."

"Enough." Shade gestured to Donjon. "Tell your dwarves not to purloin any of their items. They can have their coinpurses and other items back except for their weapons. I don't see any need for them to be armed until they prove they can be trusted."

"There's such a thing as plunder," Mel said grumpily.

"Don't make me kick you in the fire again." Tarah growled. Being separated from their things would make escape more difficult, but Tarah realized she had little room for negotiation. "There is one thing, Shade. I'll need my staff. It has magic that helps me track."

"Like we'd believe that," Donjon said. "That thing's a weapon."

"You have a fifteen dwarf crew and you're afraid of one woman with a staff?" Djeri scoffed. "Maggie's band has gotten soft."

"Fine," Shade said. "She can have the staff. But the rest of their weapons stay in our possession." He fixed Tarah with a glare. "And don't ask me for any more concessions from me today. My patience has worn quite thin."

"Yes, sir," she said. "Thank you."

"And Tarah, clean up your lover there. His face is making me sick." Shade turned and walked back towards his tent. "Now pack up! We leave in the hour. This beast is too far ahead of us as it is!"

Donjon glowered after him and said soft enough that Shade could not hear. "My boys follow me. Not you, you gnome-licker." He turned to his dwarves. "Listen up! Get movin'. Leroy, bring the girl's staff. Peggy, give her some water so she can clean that humie up."

He turned and walked away. The camp became a flurry of

motion as dwarves began taking down tents and putting out campfires. Leroy tossed Tarah her staff and a few minutes later Mel returned and scowled at them as he dropped their coinpurses in the dirt.

"Humie?" she asked Djeri.

"It means a dwarf that prefers humans," he said. "I've been called it all my life. Don't pay it any mind."

Peggy came over with a pail of water and some clean rags. She was a dwarf female with long blond hair and a mustache as thick as any of the men, though it was waxed and neatly trimmed. Tarah hadn't seen her much the night before.

Peggy's voice was gruff as she said "Here, clean him up like Shade said. Then have him wear this," she tossed Tarah a small necklace with a runed crystal pendant on the end. "This'll help him heal a little faster." Her face colored slightly and she handed Tarah a bundle of bandages before she turned and left.

Tarah watched her leave. "Maybe they ain't all bad."

"Believe me. They're all bad," Djeri said. He looked away. "I'm . . . sorry you had to kiss me back there."

"It wasn't so bad." She hung the necklace over his neck and bent down, dipping a rag into the bucket. The water was cold. "They could've made me kiss Mel."

He chuckled, then gasped. "This necklace might be helping but it makes things hurt more." He pulled back when she brought the wet rag up to his face. "You don't need to wash me off. I can do it myself."

"Don't be stupid," she replied. "You can't move your arms." She wiped the dirt and sweat from his brow. He winced when she brushed the gash in his forehead. "Just hold still."

She finished cleaning the rest of his face and neck, then focused on the wounds, cleaning them out as much as she could with just cold water and rags. While she bandaged him up, she said. "Tell me how these dwarves are your kin."

Djeri sighed. "Grandfather Rosco was a Cragstalker. Most of the family line on his side are smugglers. When he married a human it was like a slap in the face to the rest of the family. They've looked down on the rest of us ever since." He shook his head and said softly, "How do you know this Shade character?"

"He came to me in Razbeck a few weeks ago." She told

him the story, emphasizing the fact that she had abandoned the idea of finishing his job to focus on the academy one instead. She worried that he would storm away in anger, but all he did was frown.

"Seriously Tarah? You took a job from a man calling himself Shade. If there's one thing your grandfather should have taught you, it's, 'Never take a job from a man called Shade!'"

"He didn't use those exact words, but you're right. He said something like that," she admitted.

"Alright then. I'll keep my eyes out for ways to escape this, but we should be cautious. They'll be ready for us to try." He looked over her shoulder and Tarah turned to see several of the dwarves watching from not far away.

"There's no hurry," she whispered, turning back to face him. "I think we're working our mission quite well. We're following the tracks like we were told."

"And we're among the enemy learning what they're up to," he agreed with a nod. "But what if we find the rogue?"

"We're three weeks behind," she said. "At the rate these dwarfs move, it'll be a long while before we get anywhere close to finding it. We just need to gain their trust and get the rest of our weapons back. I might even find a way to throw 'em off before we escape."

Djeri strained and she felt his hand on her shoulder. "We can do this," he promised.

"Of course we can," she said with a look of determination. "Tarah Woodblade never leaves a job undone."

Chapter Sixteen

That first day they spent with the smugglers was miserable
for Djeri. The necklace Peggy had given him did seem to speed up
his healing, but it did nothing to numb the pain. Shade ordered
Tarah to go with Donjon and his best trackers by horseback. Djeri,
unable to move his arms without great effort, was forced to sit in
the wagon.

Tarah seemed to have the impression that the smugglers
were stupid, but Djeri knew that was far from the truth. The
dwarves were well organized. They used tactics gained from
thousands of years of collective experience hunting rare game.

While Tarah and the others followed the tracks, Donjon
relayed their findings to Shade by the use of flattened message
stones very similar to the stones the academy used. Shade hung
back, coordinating the rest of the group, sending scouts ahead so
that they could avoid travelers, while keeping the wagon as close
to the trackers as he could. Biff organized the movements of the
rest of the camp and was in charge of provisions.

The mountain terrain was tough and the wagon was
constantly jostled this way and that, sending agony through Djeri's
damaged limbs. He knew that getting away from this group would
be extremely difficult. While he wracked his brain for possible
solutions, one constant distraction haunted his mind.

Tarah Woodblade had saved him with a kiss.

His heart beat faster whenever he thought of it. He had
been in so much pain at the time and was sure his death was
imminent, but the moment her lips had touched his all pain and
worry left. For a few seconds, Djeri had been somewhere else.

It had been an act, he knew, done out of necessity. But in a
way that made it mean all the more to him. Tarah hadn't done it to

save herself. She had done it to rescue him. She had done it despite the humiliation that would come; despite the fear and uncertainty that had to be filling her mind. It was ridiculous, but for him that made the kiss all the more real.

The smugglers stopped the wagon half way through the day and Peggy was kind enough to shove a roll into his mouth. She didn't seem inclined to hold his waterskin for him while he drank from it, though. She just dropped it in his lap and strode away mumbling to herself.

Djeri knew Tarah must have been making progress with the tracks because they got moving again a short time later. The driver mentioned something about their quarry heading over the mountain. The scouts had found a seldom-used wagon trail that curved up the mountainside and Shade had decided to move the whole camp.

The trail was rocky and pitted and sometimes headed upward at such a sharp angle that Djeri feared he was going to tumble right out of the back without the use of his arms to stabilize him. There were many rough stretches where the horses were straining but the wagon barely moved.

That evening they joined up with Shade and found a spot to camp. It wasn't an ideal spot, just a section of the mountainside where the ground plateaued for a stretch. Quarters were tight.

Peggy brought Djeri over to Neddy and told him to set up his own tent if he wanted one. The smugglers had loaded a spare tent on the animal's back and Djeri struggled to lift his arms enough to reach the ties holding it on. The mule actually seemed happy to see him, nudging him and snorting excitedly.

Djeri managed to drop the tent to the ground, but soon gave up on the idea of setting it up himself. He leaned against the mule feeling useless. His arms would need to recover soon or escaping was going to be impossible.

Tarah and the other trackers didn't arrive back at camp until after dark. Donjon took her directly to the command tent where she spent a good half hour reporting to Shade before she was allowed to find Djeri. She embraced the mule and scratched behind his ears, then told Djeri what they had found during the day.

Tarah had followed the rogue horse's tracks all the way to

the peak. The beast had spent a full day at the top before climbing down the far side. There was more, but Tarah couldn't tell him with all the dwarves close by and listening.

Later after they had eaten, Tarah set up the tent. Djeri stood awkwardly to the side feeling nervous. The smugglers were confident enough to let them share a tent but they were wedged between two others. Djeri was worried that they wouldn't be able to talk without being overheard. Luckily the dwarves around them were snorers.

Djeri lay on his back in agony, pain shooting up and down his damaged arms, but all that was forgotten when Tarah turned on her side and leaned in close to whisper her true findings. He could feel the warmth of her breath on his ear and he was grateful that the darkness hid the way his skin flushed red.

As Tarah had touched each track on the way up the mountain, she had discovered something peculiar. The rogue horse had no idea where it was going. The beast took every step with purpose but, unlike with most creatures, she never caught a glimpse of the direction it had in mind. Over time she had realized that this was because the creature was following instructions. This rogue horse had a rider.

They debated the identity of the rider late into the night. Djeri figured it must be a bonding wizard. The other rogue horses he had met had both been bonded. Tarah was unsure. She had looked hard, but had not found any of the rider's tracks.

The next day Djeri awoke feeling much better. Moving his arms still took effort, but the pain was greatly reduced. Tarah had to pack the tent back up, but he was able to tie it to the mule unaided.

Tarah left with Donjon early and Djeri went back to the wagon for the day. This was his method of travel for the next several days while his arms regained their strength. Tarah led the smugglers over the mountain and down into the hills on the west side.

Winter came on with full force as they came down the mountain. A heavy snowfall hampered their ability to follow the wagon trails. Shade was worried that they would lose track of the rogue, but Tarah impressed them all with her ability to find new tracks even in knee deep snow.

The tracks took them quite close to the back road to Wobble and the group had to go out of their way several times to avoid groups of Dremald soldiers that were patrolling the area. Tarah had considered leading them into one of the patrols on purpose, but she realized that the soldiers would have no defense against the dwarves' paralyzing weapons. Not only could they get many innocent soldiers killed, Shade would not react kindly to such a gambit. So she held course with their plan.

As slowly as they moved, held back by the weather, they gained on the rogue. The beast sometimes stayed in one location for a few days before moving on. Most often its resting places were small stands of trees not far from a human settlement.

Several small details about the rogue horse came to light after days of tracking. Some of it was useless. Tarah learned it had a name. The rogue horse thought of himself as Rufus. He enjoyed climbing trees and ate grass and leaves as well as hunting the occasional animal. He ate a lot. In fact, it seemed he liked to try eating just about everything he came across. The dwarves were often finding interesting things in the manure he left behind; strange bones, poisonous berries, small rocks, and one time a silver piece.

In the first week they gained eight days on the beast and Tarah became worried that they would catch up to it. She and Djeri spent their nights whispering about escape plans and contingencies.

It wouldn't be an easy task. Though the smugglers let them have relative freedom within the camp, there were always dwarves keeping an eye on their movements. Whenever Tarah was out with the scouts, Djeri wasn't allowed to go with her.

He began traveling with the main body of the camp and eventually he had enough strength for the smugglers to put him to work. Djeri was called upon to help load horses and carry water and supplies. Through it all, he kept his armor on like he had been trained. All except for his gauntlets, which Mel had conveniently lost.

Shade didn't seem inclined to give them their other weapons back. Tarah asked and each time he declined, telling her he saw no need to take the risk. Djeri began to worry about the Ramsetter. He saw the dwarves passing it around several times examining the blade and one night he watched as Mel and Leroy used it to cut through some heavy chain.

Mel was a constant thorn in Tarah's side. He was one of the company's best trackers and took to following Tarah around while she was working, constantly asking vulgar questions and making suggestive remarks. At night he would sometimes stand outside their tent and listen, breathing heavily.

One night Tarah came back to camp with a swollen black eye. She was limping and holding her ribs. Mel had pinched her behind and Tarah had knocked out two of his teeth with her staff. Donjon had frozen her, allowing Mel to kick her repeatedly before calling him off. She spoke with Shade, but the man had been unsympathetic, saying that she needed to control her temper.

Djeri was furious, but Tarah refused to let him do anything about it. They couldn't afford to do anything that might further compromise freedoms they had been given. Tarah wasn't allowed a healing potion this time, so Djeri put the necklace on her instead. The item seemed to work much faster with her, but Tarah could only wear it for short periods of time because of the increased pain it gave her.

The next day Mel took to wearing the Ramsetter on his back. He claimed that he was holding it for "safekeeping". Whenever Tarah would complain about it, he would turn and grin, showing her his missing teeth.

That evening Djeri and Tarah discussed a plan for getting back at the dwarf. They humored themselves with several very nasty methods of revenge but settled on something much less likely to net reprisals. They followed a suggestion from her grampa. Make allies.

Instead of being stubborn, they became more helpful. Tarah began sidling up to Donjon, calling him sir and complimenting him on his tracking skills. Djeri worked hard and did his best to make friends with Biff who, it ends up, was his grandfather's cousin. The gray-haired dwarf was in charge of the horses and provisions and had the respect of the rest of the smugglers. Djeri found out that Peggy was his daughter and that she sympathized with his and Tarah's plight because she had been caught trying to run away from home with her boyfriend a few years before.

Over time they ingratiated themselves with the crew

enough that they started to get results. Biff confided his concerns about the camp's other leadership to Djeri a few times. One morning Donjon even told Mel to stop giving Tarah such a hard time.

Two more weeks went by and they continued to gain on the rogue. It had been zig-zagging across western Dremaldria, seemingly traveling from town to town always staying on the outskirts. Still there was no sign of the rogue's mysterious rider.

Whoever the rider was, they seemed very careful about staying unseen. This was good because it kept the other trackers from discovering the beast had a rider, but the rogue's tracks left Tarah confused. Rufus was proud, strong, and highly intelligent, sometimes thinking in fully formed words, yet she never found memories of his rider's name or even specific commands he or she had given it.

Eventually they were only days behind the beast. Shade increased their pace, sure that the end of their hunt was in sight. Strangely, almost as if it knew it was being followed, the rogue horse stopped its wandering and made a beeline to the west. The winter weather hampered their ability to keep up. Snowfalls and frozen earth made tracking difficult and Tarah rode a fine line between slowing the other trackers down and making occasional discoveries that showcased her skill.

The cold weather, along with Tarah and Djeri's increased status in the eyes of the leaders, brought out a division in the camp. Mel and a few others, including Leroy and the dwarf woman Melba, whose stew Djeri had ruined on their first night at the camp, began a campaign of harassment.

One night, their tent was pulled down on them while they were sleeping. The next day Djeri found out that someone had peed in his wash pail. After a dead bird appeared in their stew, Djeri began to cook all their meals himself. Tarah identified the culprits by those who where snickering when the discoveries were made.

Biff made some quiet remarks to a few of those responsible one morning, but that just made things worse. When they stopped for the night, Djeri found Neddy carrying Tarah's leather satchel in his teeth. Several lines on the mule's saddle had been cut and many of their belongings had been strewn out along the trail, including their bedrolls. In addition, several long slits had been cut in the fabric of their tent. They spent the night huddled together on the cold ground under some blankets and their hastily patched tent.

Events came to a head the next day.

In the morning, Tarah awoke to find that a horse skull had been placed near her head. She tried to brush off the childish prank, but couldn't help feeling disturbed. The rest of the pranks had been done from a distance at a time when neither she nor Djeri could see it being done. This one had been more bold. How had one of the dwarves snuck that close in the night without waking her? She had been on high alert.

Fearing that the skull had been more a message than a prank, she woke Djeri and hurried over to check on Neddy. The mule was fine, but he was holding her satchel in his teeth again. She took the satchel from the mule and clutched it tightly to her chest.

Tarah opened it, quickly checking to make sure that everything was still there. Sighing with relief, she quickly checked the ground around the mule. Someone had tried to tamper with their belongings again, but there were too many tracks around him for her to tell.

"Did you fight them off?" Tarah said, and stroked his neck. "You're a good mule, Neddy. I don't know how you knew that this meant so much to me, but thank you for watching over it." She thought about it for a moment and pulled the strap of the satchel over his head, leaving it hanging from his neck. "I'll leave it right here so you can watch over it better, okay?"

He snorted, stomping the ground once with one hoof.

Tarah patted his head and walked back to find Donjon. It was time for the trackers to leave and she still felt that disturbing feeling in her chest. As she approached the boss, she saw Mel waiting next to his horse, leering at her. He licked his lips slowly.

Don't abide a bully, said Tarah's papa.

She made a decision. It was time to see if her work with Donjon had made any progress.

"Boss Donjon," she said. "Can I have a word with you?"

The black-mustached dwarf frowned, but stepped away from the other trackers. "'Fore you say nothin', stop callin' me

'Boss'," he said. "That's fer members of the band and you ain't no member."

"Yes, sir," she said. "What I wanted to talk to you about is Mel. He's been getting worse and worse lately and I know he's gonna try and put his hands on me again."

"Ugh," Donjon turned away with a grimace.

"The thing is, sir, I just wanted to let you know that I intend to defend myself if he does," she said firmly.

He looked back at her for a moment and shrugged. "Just don't go breakin' any bones."

"Yes, sir," she said, relieved. This was true progress.

They mounted up and headed back to the last point where they'd seen tracks the day before. Once they reached the spot, they left the horses with one of the dwarves and continued on foot. The tracks continued westward towards the Wide River. Tarah could see the sun glinting on the waters at the horizon line.

It was mid-morning when Mel made his first move. She was inspecting a track and he snuck up on her. Tarah was ready. She whipped her staff out behind her, smacking the back of his hand.

"Gah! Dag-gum biscuit-breaker!" He jumped up and down, shaking his hand vigorously.

"What's that?" Leroy called.

"Nothin'!" Mel said, shooting Tarah a glare.

He left for awhile, but came back again just after noon. He reached out and she smacked his hand aside again.

"Ow! You." He clutched his hand and gave her an evil glare.

"Keep your dirty fingers away from me, Mel," she said.

"Don't you play like that with me," he sneered. "Ever'body knows you like the touch of a dwarf."

"Oh I do." She leaned towards him. "But you're too ugly to be a dwarf. I'd say you're more like a kobald."

Mel snarled and reached into the holster at his side. He drew his paralyzing rod, but Tarah was ready. Her staff whipped across, knocking the rod from his hand. Then she brought in the other end and cracked him in the side of the head, knocking him down.

The blow was hard. A human would have been rendered

unconscious. Dwarves were tougher. He bounded back up, holding the side of his head where a knot was beginning to form.

He reached back and grabbed the hilt of the Ramsetter. His arms weren't as long as Djeri's. He had to pull part of it out, then grasp the blade and draw it the rest of the way.

"You just try coming at me with my papa's sword, you lily-livered nose-farmer!" Tarah said, twirling her staff.

He swung the sword in an overhand chop. Tarah knocked the blade to the side with one end of the staff and brought the other end around to smack him on the side of the head again, just one inch above the last blow.

Mel stumbled back, howling.

"What the hell is goin' on here?" Donjon yelled, approaching them from a few yards away. All of the trackers closed in.

"She attacked me, boss!" Mel said. "Right outta nowhere. Look at my head."

"That's absurd! He was getting all handsy again," Tarah said.

Donjon focused on Mel. "This ain't the first time I told you, boy!"

"C'mon, she's lying. I'd never-!"

"Listen here, you corn-jigger!" Donjon spat, pointing one thick finger at the dwarf's chest. "We all seen it. If'n you can't keep your stinkin' hands off her, I'll tell everbody what a big humie you are."

Mel looked at the others, his eyes wide. "But boss, I ain't no humie!"

"That includes my daddy and Aunt Maggie, you clear?" Donjon warned.

Mel's face paled. "Yer gonna take her side against mine? A stinkin' lyin' girl?"

"I ain't lying!" Tarah said.

"You just get, Woodblade!" Donjon snapped. "Go back to yer trackin' while I finish talkin' to my boy, here."

"Yes sir," she said and turned away. She felt pretty good about how that had gone down. Now she just had to worry about the reprisal she knew would come. Tarah followed the rogue horse's tracks as they continued towards the shoreline, mulling ways to protect herself and Djeri.

Djeri would have to see if there was a way he could keep an eye on Neddy during the day. Then at night, they would just have to take turns on watch. It would be difficult because during the night was their only time to plan. As it was, they barely got enough sleep to make it through the day.

Tarah stopped in surprise. The tracks had disappeared.

She backtracked for a few yards and looked again. The ground had gone fairly hard because of the cold but the beast was so heavy she could make out each print clearly even through the light skiff of snow on the ground. Rufus had come this way and left one last track at the edge of the grass line. Beyond that was an empty stretch of sand that turned to pebbles just before the waterline.

Tarah knelt down and touched the track. As usual, she felt only the strong impression that he was heading forward with strong purpose and confidence. There was no sign that he intended to stop.

She looked at the swift moving water and the big chunks of ice that sped by like large paving stones. Surely Rufus hadn't entered the water. Of course not. The river was so wide here, she could barely see the far bank. Besides, there were no tracks in the sand to show it.

Nevertheless, she followed the path of the rogue horse's last steps straight forward as if he had continued down to the water. Nope. There was nothing. Not even the barest indentation in the sand. Tarah stepped onto the pebbles and shook her head as she approached the water's edge. This was ridiculous. She was going to have to backtrack. Maybe the mysterious rider had fooled them. Maybe he . . .

There at the waterline, in a small patch of mud, was a single human footprint and it was barefoot.

Tarah crouched next to it. What was a footprint like that doing there? And at this time of year? She reached down and touched the print.

For a moment the world stopped. This wasn't like one of the dwarves' paralyzing spells. This was more. Everything paused as if time were frozen. The water wasn't moving. Her very heartbeat stopped.

Tarah felt a warmth on her shoulder as if someone placed their hand there. She heard a voice whisper in her ear; a masculine voice, deep and clear. She heard it audibly, yet at the same time in her mind as well.

"Take them across the river."

Tarah gasped as the water sped past her once more. She looked around, but no one was there. She touched the track again, but this time there was nothing. Nothing at all as if there were no memory attached to it whatsoever.

What had just happened? The experience had been unlike anything she had felt from a track before. That hadn't been a memory. It hadn't been a single thought. It was a message and it was meant just for her. Tarah felt a chill that went beyond the cold air.

Whoever had left the message knew about her magic, knew about the staff. Who could it be? No one knew. No one but Djeri and her Grampa. She thought back to the voice and tried to grasp the tone. Had it been at all familiar? But the memory had already begun to fade. Only the message remained.

"Take them across the river," she whispered. There was only one answer. It had to be the mysterious rider. Somehow he had known they were following.

"Hey, Woodblade!" came Donjon's voice.

She stood and casually stepped on the print as she turned to face him. The dwarves were at the edge of the grass line looking at Rufus' last print. She leaned her weight on that foot and felt her boot sink slowly into the half-frozen mud, destroying the track. "Yeah?"

The black-mustached dwarf was glaring. "Get over here!"

Tarah made a show of taking a wide step, as if over an invisible set of tracks, and walked towards him. He looked angry about the way the rogue horse's tracks had disappeared. Donjon took a few steps onto the sand to meet her. She needed to diffuse his anger a bit if she was going to convince them. Tarah decided to start with some gratitude.

Softly, she said, "Donjon, thank you for helping me back there. I-."

Donjon grabbed the front of her armor and jerked her down to meet him eye-to eye. "Don't give me no gratefulness, girl. I didn't do that 'cause I care one whit about you." His lit cigar illuminated the shadows under his hat, revealing eyes filled with anger and disgust. "I just can't stand the thought of any of my boys lookin' at yer ugly human face that way. If you wasn't such a good tracker, I would've slit yer throat weeks ago. You hear me?"

The other dwarves were staring at her, some of them nodding in agreement. Tarah grit her teeth and clutched her staff tightly to keep her hands from trembling with anger.

Keep a level head, warned Grampa Rolf.

"I hear you, Donjon," she said slowly. "Did you want me to tell you what I think about the tracks?"

He released her armor and folded his arms. "Tell me."

"The rogue is gone. He's crossed the river," she said.

"No way!" said Leroy. "It's too friggin' cold. It probly just backtracked a ways."

"What are you talking about? The tracks end right at the water," she said, pointing at that invisible line.

The trackers looked at each other, frowning. Mel squatted by the last track and peered across the sand with his well-trained eyes. "I don't see nothin'!"

"It backtracked I tell you," Leroy said.

"If it did, you would've seen it," Tarah said. "What do you think the beast did, step backwards perfectly in its own tracks? It's a horse, not an elf. Anyways, its tracks are right here in the sand plain as day."

"I don't see nothin' either," said Donjon.

Show off. Convince 'em Tarah Woodblade knows best, said her grampa's voice.

"The sand was mostly frozen when it made the tracks, that's why they're so light," she said.

"Then how come the tracks in the grass are so deep?" asked Mel.

"Look, the tracks at the edge there are about four days old, would you agree?" she asked. They nodded. "Well we had a cold one that night, remember?"

They shrugged.

"Well I've lived here in Dremaldria all my life and I can tell you that the Wide River gets a stiff wind on cold nights in the winter. The grass will break some of the wind so the ground don't freeze as hard, but the sand becomes hard as rock," Tarah explained.

"Yeah, well I still don't see no tracks!" Leroy said.

She had hoped it wouldn't be this difficult. "Look, I know you dwarfs are all way more experienced than I am. I may seem like just a baby compared to you. But we've been tracking together for near a month now. You've seen what I can do. I've found tracks that no one else could and I tell you I see the durn rogue's tracks going all the way down to the water."

"You know I think I might see 'em too," said one of the other trackers. He was the oldest of the dwarves, more experienced than the rest of them, but Tarah had watched him track. He tried to hide it from the others, but his eyesight was fading.

Donjon shrugged. "Okay, so it went down to the water. But there's no way it crossed. The durn thing would freeze to death 'fore he got half way."

"Then it's dead. And here we tracked it all this way." Tarah shook her head sadly. "I dunno though. He is a rogue horse after all. Maybe he's one of the kind that can take it. He loves the cold. You saw from his tracks how much he likes playing in the snow."

A few of them nodded and she could see that she was winning them over. "You know, Filgren is just a couple miles south from here. There's ferries there that can take us across. Then we can head back north along the coast and pick up its tracks again." Donjon narrowed his eyes at her and she paused, looking abashed. "Of course it's your call, Donjon, sir. I wasn't trying to talk out of place."

"She's talking too sweet to you," Mel said suspiciously.

"Shut up," Donjon said. "All of you, split up. Head up and down the bank a ways. Make sure she's right and there ain't no more tracks."

"Yes, boss," Leroy said.

As the trackers scattered, Donjon reached into a satchel at his waist and pulled out the message stone that he used to communicate with Shade when they were out of camp. It was a long thin piece of rock that he wrote on with a piece of wood. He started to write a message, then paused and cocked his head in Tarah's direction.

"You better be right, girl. 'Cause if we cross this thing and don't find no tracks on the far side, I'm paralyzin' yer arse and tossin' you in the water."

Tarah nodded. She hoped that trusting this mysterious rider was the right thing to do.

Chapter Seventeen

Filgren was a prosperous city, not so large as Sampo, but a major stopping place for people traveling from Dremaldria to Razbeck. The ferries were run by the Roma Family, one of Dremaldria's high noble houses, and they levied a tidy fee for transport.

Shade rode into Filgren alone to make the arrangements. Getting the band across the river was going to be more difficult than usual. Most times of the year the ferries worked all day long, but usually closed down when the ice chunks were this large. The boats were made to be tough, but an impact at just the right spot could cause a lot of damage.

In addition, the noble family could not be seen making such a dangerous exception for a troupe of dwarves with handlebar mustaches. Dwarf smugglers were in ill favor with the capitol at the moment. Lord Commander Demetrius had passed a law against doing business with them in any form.

While Shade made his case with the Romas, the rest of the camp traveled down the river bank and stopped just outside of the nearest farm. Tarah updated Djeri on the situation while they waited. Once again, he was impressed by her ability to think on her feet. The message she had received was strange, though. How could the rider have known such a message would work?

Donjon went through three cigars pacing back and forth as he waited for Shade's go ahead. The boss was in a foul mood, berating anyone and everyone he came across. Peggy was slapped across the face when she asked if they should start cooking dinner.

"Donjon takes this hunt personally," Djeri said to Tarah as they watched Peggy walk by with a glower.

"I've noticed," Tarah said.

"I was talking to Biff today and I think I know why," Djeri added with a whisper. They were standing next to Neddy, but some of the other dwarves were just yards away and they were watching.

Tarah stepped closer to Djeri and put her arm around his shoulders just as a lover should. She whispered back, "What did you learn?"

"Donjon's family is familiar with this rogue horse. They had captured it once before, but it escaped." he replied. "Thing is, they already had it sold to a gnome scholar at the time and it gave the clan a black eye when they couldn't deliver."

"How long ago was this?" she asked.

"It was a couple hundred years ago," he said. "They've been on the lookout for the rogue ever since."

"Two hundred years is a fairly short time when you're talking business deals between gnomes and dwarves," Tarah said in understanding.

"Exactly. Shade came to them representing some hoity-toity gnome scholar that's looking for a rogue horse for some kind of research," he said.

"The same gnome as before?" she asked.

"I don't know, but Maggie Cragstalker is the clan boss and she sees this as a way to save face after their last mistake. She's put a lot of responsibility on Donjon for this, so he's under a lot of pressure."

The sky had grown dark before Donjon finally received a message from Shade. It had been a difficult sell, but Shade's silver tongue and purses of gold had persuaded the nobles to let them cross. The Romas had made a stipulation, though. The crossing would have to be taken in the deep of night after most of the city had closed down. The fewer people who knew of this particular ferrying the better.

Two ferries were in use; one docked at the port in Filgren, the other docked at the port on the far side of the river in West Filgren, their sister city in Razbeck. The two ferries were connected by heavy steel chains that were pulled by giant water wheels on either side of the river. Because of the way they were interconnected both ferries ran at the same time, passing each other in the very center of the river.

Just after midnight passed, the band headed into town.

They stayed to the riverbank, avoiding the major roads and entering Filgren on the north end of the docks. They led their horses along the wooden planks in this relatively dark side of the city, careful to keep their mustaches covered by bandannas or scarves. The trip went smoothly. There was the occasional raucous sound from dockside taverns, but it was quiet otherwise.

Because of the size of the smuggler's group it was going to take two ferry trips to get everyone across. When they arrived, ferrymen were already hard at work prepping the boats and de-icing the chains. Most of them were droopy eyed and none of them looked excited to be making the trip. They knew it would be dangerous. Where each boat normally had a crew of four, they had crews of six tonight.

Tarah and Djeri were in line to be part of the first ferry across. The dwarves started walking their horses onto the deck and tying them in place. While Tarah and Djeri waited for their turn to load, they discussed what to do once they reached the far side.

"This vision you saw, did it show you what to do on the other side of the river?" Djeri asked, a bit unnerved that they were following instructions from a complete stranger.

"It wasn't a vision, just a voice," she whispered. "It said, 'Take them across the river.' That's all. There were no further instructions."

"Are you sure the rider meant everyone. All the smugglers?" he asked.

"I don't see how it could have meant anything else," she said giving him a frown.

"What if it just meant for you to take Neddy and me?" Djeri asked. Tarah's brow furrowed and Djeri knew that she hadn't considered that possibility. "I don't know how we could have done it that way. I'm just saying. We have no idea who they are or what they-."

"Get in, lovers," Leroy interrupted with a frown. "Come on. Don't slow us down."

It was their turn. Tarah walked across the wide plank and onto the deck of the ferry first. Djeri followed, pulling Neddy's lead, but when he stepped onto the plank, the mule wouldn't budge.

"Come one, Neddy. Come on up," Djeri said. Neddy dug

his hooves in at the edge of the dock, refusing to move. What was wrong with the animal? He hadn't been a problem since day one of their mission.

"What is it?" Tarah asked, looking back at them.

"I don't know," Djeri said. "He won't come up."

"I'll get him up fer you," said Mel, walking up from behind the mule. Two large knots bulged on the side of his head from Tarah's blows earlier that day. He swung the Ramsetter, delivering a stinging blow across Neddy's rump with the flat of the blade.

Neddy's eyes bulged and he let out a startled squeal before clattering up onto the deck. Tarah comforted the animal, bringing him over to tie him with the horses. Djeri fixed Mel with a glare.

"What? You ain't gonna give me no thanks?" the dwarf said, sheathing the sword.

As far as Djeri was concerned, any time the dwarf touched the sword it was an insult to Tarah's father. What he really wanted to do was throw the fool into the icy water. Instead, he said nothing and stepped aside to let Mel board. Sooner or later they were going to have a reckoning and Djeri was looking forward to it, but for now he just walked over to stand by Tarah.

The ferries were circular boats, wide and flat with stocks for up to ten horses and room for more to stand unsupported. Most of the regular band members were on the first ferry, while the wagon, supplies, and rest of the group would wait for the second ferry to arrive.

Once everyone was aboard, one of the ferrymen raised the plank and signaled the powerhouse to get the ferry moving. On both sides of the river great signal lamps flashed. Two men at each dock turned heavy cranks lowering the enormous water wheels into the river. As soon as the swift-moving water hit the paddles on the wheels, the ferry jolted forward, breaking through the thin sheet of ice at the bank. Huge gears moved the chains, propelling both boats into the water towards each other.

Djeri had crossed the Wide River using the ferry system several times over the years and this was the part he hated the most. As they left the dock and moved further away from the bank, the currents of the river caught the boat and pulled it southward. The undersides of the ferry were shaped like smooth saucers to offer as little resistance as possible as they went. This reduced the drag, but also led to an awfully bumpy ride as the large chunks of ice hit the hull and either slid under the boat or were pushed to the side.

The only lighting on the ferries were great lanterns pointed outwards in four directions so that the ferrymen could keep an eye out for obstacles. The further out they went, the more isolated Djeri felt. The wind wasn't very swift this night but snow began to fall. Big fluffy flakes clouded up the lights of the lanterns until the only thing he could see was the heavy chain attached to the prow arcing into the darkness.

Soon the lights of Filgren faded to a muted glow, obscured by the falling snow, and Djeri saw the lights of the second ferry approaching. As it came closer, the ferryman rushed to the southern side of the deck with long poles to make sure the two boats didn't come too close. The lanterns on their ferry illuminated the ferrymen on the north side of the otherwise empty second boat with poles of their own. Keeping the boats from colliding was a group effort. When the ferries crossed paths without incident, Djeri let out a relieved breath. The crossing was half way over.

Tarah clutched his arm. "Djeri, we might have a problem."

Confused, Djeri turned and immediately understood her concern. The light of the passing second ferry illuminated their deck in the falling snow and Djeri could see the faces of their fellow passengers. The only dwarves on the boat with them were Mel's friends and co-conspirators. Several of them were giving Djeri grim looks. Mel was smiling.

Djeri swore softly. He should have noticed that all of their supporters had waited for that second ferry. He and Tarah had been so focused on their plans that he had let Leroy and Mel herd them onto this ship alone. It would be another fifteen minutes before they reached the far shore and at least another thirty minutes longer before Shade and the leadership arrived. That was plenty of time for Mel to stage something and no one on the boat would tell the truth of what happened.

"Be ready," he whispered. Tarah nodded, both hands gripping her staff.

As the second ferry's lights faded to the east, the deck of the boat was plunged back into darkness. Djeri grabbed a short pole from the edge of the deck and moved with Tarah to stand by

Neddy. Tarah crouched to make herself less of a visible target.

"Hey lovers," came Leroy's voice from the darkness to Djeri's left. "Where you at?"

Tarah and Djeri glanced at each other, but said nothing.

"Yeah, I think its time we had us a good chat," said Mel, somewhere to their right.

"I think they're over by their stupid mule," said Merba.

Djeri brought the pole down low, his muscles tense. The question was what to do? Should they try to talk their way out of this? If he and Tarah struck first, they could take down many of the smugglers by surprise. But they were outnumbered eight to two and dwarves were hard to subdue. One shot from a paralyzing rod and Tarah would be out of the fight. Djeri was pretty sure he had built up enough of a resistance that he would only be subdued temporarily, but it wouldn't take long for someone to bind him.

Tarah suddenly stood, taking the choice out of his hands. "What do you want, Leroy?"

There was a shuffling in the darkness as eight pairs of boots walked their way.

"Well here's the thing," Mel said, stepping close. "We don't like you two."

"I was talking to Leroy," Tarah replied.

"I agree with Mel," Leroy said.

The only thing Djeri could think to do was try to delay the confrontation. He decided to try being reasonable. "I'm sorry you don't like us. I can see that's partially our fault. I know we haven't tried too hard to be friendly."

"We don't want to be friendly," Leroy said.

Being reasonable was going to be hard. "Then what do you want from us?"

"We want you gone, humie," Mel said. Djeri could just barely make out the hilt of the Ramsetter sticking up over his shoulder. The lights on the western bank were coming into view. "Just havin' you 'round makes the rest of us look bad."

"I don't think Shade will let us leave," Tarah said. "Leastways not until we find our quarry."

"Maybe not," said Merba, her voice almost as deep as the men. "But if you tried to escape and got yerself killed, he wouldn't care too much."

"We don't need you," Mel agreed. "We can find it all on our own."

"They'll know," Tarah said, her voice full of contempt. "Shade and Donjon both. They ain't stupid. They know you have it in for us. No matter what story you concoct, they'll see right through your plot. If we die, you'll have to answer for it."

"Dag-gum it, she's right," said one of the others. "If'n we don't find the rogue, the blame'll fall on us."

Good, Tarah, Djeri thought. *Give them doubts.* "Hey, you don't have to like us," he said. The lights of the dock were getting closer. Just a few minutes more and they would be off the ferry. "You just have to put up with us long enough for us to catch the beast and then we'll be gone. You'll never have to even think of us again if you don't want to."

"We can call a truce," Tarah said, building on what Djeri was trying to do. "From here on out, until we get the rogue, we stay out of each other's hair. What do you say?"

There was a moment of silence.

"Nah," said Mel. A sharp pop rang out and Tarah stopped moving.

Djeri jumped forward, swinging his pole up from the darkness. He felt the end catch Leroy in the side just as another pop sounded. Djeri's body seized up and he fell to the deck.

"You son of a dog!" Leroy said, wheezing. "My rib!"

"What's that sound?" asked one of the ferrymen. One of the lanterns turned slightly and Djeri saw the narrow, droopy-eared face of a gnome standing precariously on the railing. His voice sounded slow, like the voice of a drunken man. "Hey, you all right? I heard a pop-pop."

"We're fine," said Merba. "Just a scuffle's all. We're just messin' around."

"Leave them alone, Cletus," said another of the ferrymen. "It's none of our business."

"Okay," the gnome said slowly and he moved agilely down the rail.

They were close enough to the eastern bank now that the dock lights were starting to illuminate the deck. Djeri watched with dismay as Mel walked up to Tarah. Djeri strained against the spell, willing it to break. He could feel the strands of the magic start to give.

Mel tore Tara's staff from her hands. "Well, filly, you won't be needin' this anymore." The dwarf took two steps and launched the blood red weapon like a spear, sending it overboard and into the icy water.

Djeri leapt up from the deck, swinging an armored elbow at Mel's head, but Leroy was ready for him. Another pop dropped Djeri before he could land the blow. He crashed to the deck and strong hands shackled his feet and hands.

"I've been saving this for you," Mel said and shoved a stained piece of cloth in Djeri's mouth before gagging him.

"What do we do?" Merba asked.

"We wait until the ferry pulls away. No witnesses," Leroy said. The three of them moved off, huddling together and planning.

Djeri broke through the spell again. He sat up and scooted back until his shoulders were against the railing. He ignored the taste that filled his mouth, focusing on escape. Unfortunately, there wasn't much he could do besides kick out at his captors.

"Hey, pretty dwarf, you okay?" said a slow voice beside his ear.

Djeri turned his head to see the face of the gnome ferryman peering right at him. The gnome's body was bent in an impossible manner. His feet were on the rail and his lanky form was crouched, his body hanging over Djeri at an angle, his weight suspended by a thin silvery chain that he held in one hand. Djeri couldn't see what it was connected to.

"What's in your mouth?" the gnome asked. "You still messing round?"

Djeri made a muffled sound and shook his head violently indicating that he wasn't okay. The look of vague concern left the gnome's face, replaced by a tense focus.

"These dwarfs," said the gnome, his voice losing that odd slowness. "Are they with Shade?"

Djeri blinked in surprise, then nodded fiercely.

"Cletus, get over here!" shouted another ferryman. "It's docking time!"

"Docking time?" the gnome said, looking over his shoulder. The focus left his face, replaced by a vacant smile. "Okay." He pulled on the silvery chain, bringing his tall body back into a standing position and he was off, running along the top of the rail towards the prow.

Merba and Leroy walked back across the deck. Djeri kicked out as they reached for him, but they dodged his legs and Leroy punched out with a meaty fist, knocking him in the head. The two of them grabbed him by the arms and pulled him across the deck.

Djeri saw Mel and another dwarf dragging Tarah towards the front of the boat. Mel reached down with one hand, giving her rear a wicked pinch. Djeri struggled, grunting loudly and Leroy cuffed him again.

The docks reared before them as the ferry cut through the ice. Signal lights flashed and a whistle pierced the night. A great set of brakes were pulled, halting the water wheel so that the passengers could disembark. The ferrymen opened the front side of the rail and the plank was dropped into place.

The dwarves started leading their horses onto the deck, one of them pulling on Neddy's lead. The mule looked at Tarah with wide eyes, but there was nothing the beast could do. Once the horses were off, Djeri and Tarah were dragged down the plank and across the dock, before being pulled into the darkness, out of view of the dock lamps. They were leaned against the outside wall of a tavern and Leroy and Mel went back to talk to the other dwarves.

Soon the signal lights flashed again and another whistle rang out. The plank was pulled up and the brakes released. The ferry moved back off into the river and for a brief moment, Djeri saw the thin outline of the gnome standing on the back rail watching them.

He looked over at Tarah. She was staring off into the night, glassy eyed, tears streaming down her cheeks. Her hands reached out into empty claws, clutching air where her staff should be. Djeri swallowed. Mel would likely kill him quickly, but Tarah . . . surely Mel couldn't do anything too vile, not in front of the other dwarves.

Djeri shook the thought from his head. He scooted over until he was next to Tarah and laid his head on her shoulder. He hated this helpless feeling. There had to be a way to save her. He just didn't know what it was.

The lights of the ferry dwindled into the darkness as the

dwarves argued their course of action. Djeri couldn't make out what was being said, but it looked like there was a division in the ranks between Mel and Leroy and the others. Djeri let his hopes rise. There was a difference between pranks and murder, after all. Maybe some of them were having second thoughts.

The snow fell like cascading flakes of gold in the lamplight and, as the conversation ended, Djeri saw grim looks on the faces of the opposition. These were veteran smugglers, Djeri realized. Murder wouldn't be something they were unfamiliar with. Sure enough, the dwarves seemed to reach the same conclusion. Five of them walked aside to stay with the horses while Mel, Leroy, and Merba returned with a gleam in their eyes.

Mel drew the Ramsetter while Leroy tapped a thick cudgel in his palm. Melba lifted a bow and notched an arrow and, for the first time, Djeri realized that she was carrying Tarah's father's bow.

"What we was debatin' was whether to let you loose and then kill you or kill you first and then pose you like you was tryin' to escape," Mel gave him an evil grin. "I chose number two."

Out of the corner of his eye, Djeri thought he saw movement on the river, but the sword tip coming at his chest was of far greater importance. Mel rested the tip of the Ramsetter on Djeri's breastplate and pushed slowly. The magic blade pierced through the armor like it was made of wax. Djeri could feel the cold steel rest against his chest.

"I guess we just need to figger out how long to tell Shade this fight took. Was it over quick, or did we have to wound you a lot first?" Mel said.

"They're perty tough," Merba said. "I say it took lots a hits to take 'em down." She fired an arrow into Tarah's shoulder pauldron. The tip pierced the leather, but bound up in the material underneath and hung loosely. "Dag-gum! What's that ugly armor made of?"

"Next time do a full draw," Leroy advised.

A shout echoed along the river and Djeri's eyes moved back to the dock where to his astonishment, he saw a figure approaching out of the snow-filled gloom. A tall form was running towards them along the top of the icy chain. Djeri's eyes widened. It was the gnome ferryman.

Cletus was bent over, his arms sticking out straight behind him as his legs churned. His progress was slowed because the chain was moving in the opposite direction, yet he didn't look winded. His face was filled with focus and determination.

"What're you lookin' at, humie?" Mel said with a snarl. The dwarf whipped the blade out to the side, tearing through Djeri's armor and cutting a narrow furrow in the skin of his chest. Mel turned to look at the river and gasped as the gnome ran up the chain and jumped onto the wooden planks of the dock. "The hell?"

The gnome went into a flurry of motion. He spun a long silvery chain in one hand and Djeri saw that there was some sort of metal ball on the end. Cletus darted towards the cluster of dwarves and horses. With a flick of his wrist, the chain shot forward, the ball burying itself in the back of one of the dwarves' head.

The dwarf dropped and the gnome was among the rest of them. He was a flurry of fists and palms and knees and elbows. Dwarves cried out, staggering to the side, one of them falling unconscious.

The gnome slung the chain around one dwarf's head and yanked downward, bringing his knee up to collide with the dwarf's face. One dwarf swung an axe at the gnome's back. Cletus leaned to the side, dodging the blow, and sent the chain towards the dwarf's neck. There was a splash of blood and the dwarf dropped his axe to clutch at his ruined throat.

Djeri realized that the chain was two weapons in one. There was a ball on one end and a blade on the other. Cletus was a gnome warrior, and he was brilliant.

The dwarves backed away warily now, some of them limping. They brandished weapons and Mel and Leroy went to join them. Merba drew an arrow back on her bow.

The gnome stayed in motion, but he left the dwarves alone momentarily. With two spins of his chain, he sent the bladed end out, hamstringing two of the horses. The animals screamed, kicking and jerking. One of them fell, knocking another horse into the water. The other horses scattered, running into the city, all except Neddy, who trotted a short distance away before working his way towards Tarah and Djeri.

"Stop him, dag-blast it!" Leroy cried.

Merba fired an arrow. The gnome's spinning chain caught

the missile in mid-air, sending it spinning off into the snow.

"No arrows!" the gnome exclaimed.

He darted towards Merba, who was hastily trying to notch another arrow. Leroy stood in Cletus' way, his paralyzing rod aimed at the gnome's chest. The dwarf fired with a loud pop.

The gnome was unaffected. He flicked his wrist and the ball end of his chain struck Leroy in the forehead. The dwarf dropped to his knees, his eyes rolling up in his head as he fell backwards.

Cletus contorted, wrapping his chain around his own body in a complex knot, then turned and thrust out his arm. The chain shot away from his body, the bladed end darting out straight like a spear.

Merba jerked as the blade pierced her throat. Djeri saw the tip burst out the back of her neck before the gnome yanked it out again. Merba fell hard to the seat of her pants. She gurgled as her hands clutched her throat in a vain attempt to stop the bleeding.

"Cletus! What are you doing?" cried an anxious voice from up in the watchtower.

The gnome looked up, his face momentarily losing its focus. A series of pops rang out through the night as the three remaining dwarves repeatedly fired their spells. Unfortunately for them, all that did was jolt the gnome back into action.

Cletus spun the bladed end of the chain in ever widening circles as he weighed the three remaining enemies in his mind. Then, making a decision, he sent it out in a quick slash, taking one dwarf in the knee. The dwarf began to scream, but before he fell to the ground, the ball end struck him in the head, silencing him.

The other dwarf, not wanting to come in close, threw a spear. The gnome wrapped his chain around the pole and yanked, jerking the weapon aside. The dwarf turned and ran. Cletus whipped his chain around and sent the spear spinning back at him. The pole caught the dwarf in the back of the legs, tripping him up and sending him tumbling off the dock with a splash.

Mel was the only one left. He charged, bringing the Ramsetter in a wide sweeping stroke. Djeri winced, knowing the blade would shear right through the gnome's chain. But Cletus didn't try to grab the blade as he had the spear.

The gnome sucked in his gut and leapt back, avoiding the

strike. He sent the bladed end of his chain around to strike Mel's hand on the backswing, causing the sword to spin out of his fingers. The sword clattered to the deck at the edge of the dock, stopping just before it slid over the edge.

The gnome swung the ball end, striking Mel in the hip. As the dwarf doubled over, grunting, the gnome spun the metal ball in two quick arcs. Crack-crack! The ball hit Mel twice in the side of the head, leaving indentations in the swollen knots Tarah's blows had caused. The dwarf dropped.

Cletus surveyed the dock. The only thing still standing was Neddy. The mule was taking slow, cautious steps toward Tarah. Cletus focused in on him, walking forward, the blade spinning.

Djeri grunted loudly, chewing on his gag as hard as he could. The gnome slowed, cocking his head at the shadows where Tarah and Djeri sat. Djeri felt a twinge of pain in his jaw as he finally chewed through the gag. He pushed the filthy cloth out of his mouth with his tongue and tried to speak, but all that came out was a disturbing, "Don'th hurd 'im!"

Cletus took a tiny sphere out of his pocket and rolled it along the dock towards the shadows. The sphere lit up as it rolled, illuminating Djeri's bruised face.

"Pretty dwarf!" Cletus exclaimed, rushing over. The gnome touched his face. "Are you okay?" He gasped and looked at Tarah. "What happened to the pretty lady? Is she dead?"

"No," Djeri said, finally working up enough saliva to talk. "She was just hit by a paralyzing spell. Can you undo these shackles for me?"

"Sure-!" The gnome drew back, his expression suspicious. "Wait, pretty dwarf, are you with Shade? Scholar Tobias said to kill all Shade's men. Kill-kill! And-uh, disa . . . dissarup his plans?" He stuck out his bottom lip, trying to think.

"No," Djeri said earnestly. "We're not with Shade. He captured us. Letting us go would really disrupt his plans."

"Oh! Okay," the gnome said happily. He took a small rod out of his pocket and quickly picked the locks on Djeri's shackles with practiced hands. "Click-click! All done!"

Djeri stood and rubbed his wrists in awe. This gnome had to be both the most slow-witted and the most skilled fighter he had ever met. "Thanks . . . Who are you?"

"I'm Cletus of house Set!" the gnome said proudly. "I like you, pretty dwarf! You're Battle Academy, right? I like your armor. And I like the pretty lady!"

"Her name's Tarah," Djeri said, confused. What was with this gnome?

Cletus knelt down beside Tarah and pulled back her hair, reaching out one hand to stroke her cheek. "Oh, pretty Tarah. Why are you crying?"

Hurried shouts rang out from main street leading up to the docks. The gnome stood, his expression alert. "That's the watch. I'll talk to them."

"No, wait," Djeri said, concerned that the gnome who saved them was about to get tossed in jail. But Cletus didn't stop. He spun his chain and walked around the corner, his eyes narrow and focused.

Djeri swallowed. They needed to leave and fast. Before Shade and the others arrived.

He lifted Tarah from the ground. She was still paralyzed. He pulled her over to Neddy and shoved her up to lay face down over the pack saddle. He began tying her down. "Sorry, Tarah. I know this has to be uncomfortable, but we're in a hurry."

He rushed over to Merba. The dwarf was limp and her wound had stopped bleeding. Djeri picked up Tarah's father's bow and pulled the quiver from her lifeless shoulders, then he went to Mel's still form and removed the sword sheath.

The dwarf's chest was still moving. Crazy as it seemed, even with all the blows to his skull, Mel still lived. Djeri stood over him for a second. The dwarf was helpless, but it might be best to kill him right now while he could. Djeri grimaced. There was no time to debate it. He ran for the Ramsetter.

As he picked up the sword, he heard shouts and cries from several streets away. Djeri wasn't sure why the gnome was doing it, but whatever distraction Cletus was causing was a help. Djeri had no desire to be captured by the watch at that moment.

He paused for a moment, looking out over the river. He could see the lights of the approaching ferry. Shade was on that boat. So was Donjon and the wagon and the rest of their men and supplies. When they arrived, they would likely come after him and Tarah. Even if they didn't, they would definitely keep tracking down that rogue.

Djeri eyed the heavy chain that pulled the ferry. He set down the bow and quiver and grasped the hilt of the Ramsetter with both hands. Closing his eyes, he muttered a quick apology to Biff and Peggy and the ferrymen manning the boats.

It took three heavy chops to sever the chain. A cry of dismay echoed from the watchtower above as, with a deep groaning sound, the water wheel began to spin out of control. The man at the signal light began sending a frantic series of flashes across the river.

The lights of the ferry bobbed and shifted in the snow, no longer moving forward, but floating downstream at a fast pace. The force of the river would take the ferry in a wide swing back towards the eastern shore. Likely, unstable as it was, the boat would flip.

Djeri took a few steps backward, his heart pounding. He may have just killed all of them, the guilty and the innocent. He had known it when he made the first cut, but as he watched the light of the lanterns jerking wildly in the darkness, the weight of what he had done hit him.

Numbly, he picked the bow and quiver and walked over to Neddy. He grabbed the mule's lead and started northward out of town. Djeri reached back and stroked Tarah's hair, but he felt no pleasure as he said, "We're free, Tarah. They won't be coming after us now."

Chapter Eighteen

Djeri stayed off the main road, heading north along the riverbank. He knew where he was going. There was an academy outpost several miles to the north. He had been stationed there once when he first graduated from the academy. But thoughts of his destination were far from the forefront of his mind.

He weighed the events of the night over and over, wondering what he could have done differently. If he had just noticed what Mel was planning, the whole thing wouldn't have happened. Then again, if they had stayed back with Shade, they would still be captives and Mel would have tried something another time.

He would have talked to Tarah about it, but she was still paralyzed, so Djeri kept walking, beating himself up until the sky began to lighten. Tarah didn't break free of the spell until just as the sun broke the horizon. When she did so, it was with vigor.

"Down! Down! Let me down, Djeri!"

He hurried over and untied her from the back of the mule, easing her to the ground. "I'm sorry, Tarah there was no other way I could get you out of there I-!"

Tarah's fist connected with his nose. "What are you doing? Why are we going this way, you jerk!"

Djeri looked back at her in surprise, his hand held to his nose. "What?"

"My staff! Blast it, we have to go find my staff!"

"It was lost in the river," he said.

"I know that! I was there," she said. "But it won't stay in the water forever. It floats, so it'll wash ashore. We can find it."

"You've been wanting to say this for awhile, haven't you?" he said.

"The whole friggin' time you had me strapped to that mule while you walked in the wrong direction!"

Djeri frowned. "I'm sorry. I had no way of knowing, but even if I had, the river's wild right now. Your staff could be anywhere. It could be miles downstream or it could get hung up on an island or trapped in a piece of ice. That staff could end up in the swamps of Malaroo, for all we know."

"Or it could be hung up on the shoreline just outside of town," she insisted.

Djeri held out his hands defensively. "I know it's important to you, but going after that staff is the worst possible thing we could do right now. The town is riled up and I'm pretty sure the gnome left some of the smugglers alive."

"I have to have it!" Tarah declared.

"No you don't," he laughed, throwing up his arms. "Look at us arguing here. We're free! For the first time in a month, we aren't prisoners. We completed our mission. The rogue horse is safe and we're arguing about . . ." He sighed in understanding. "An heirloom. Yes, I know it's important to you and that's a legitimate thing to be upset about. But look! We're free!"

She smiled back briefly, but the smile faded. "You don't understand. Without that staff I'm . . . I'm not me."

"What do you mean?" he said.

"I didn't tell you everything." Tarah bit her lip. "I've been thinking about this too and I think you should know. My . . . those powers aren't really mine. Back at my house I told you they were, but the tracking abilities I have come from the staff. Without it, I don't see any memories."

Djeri nodded slowly. He had suspected as much. At least in the beginning. But that had stopped mattering to him long ago.

"Hey. Hey, come on," Djeri said, putting his arm around her shoulders. "That magic is just one small aspect of who you are. Power or not, you're still Tarah Woodblade. You're calm. Tough. Never flustered."

"No! I'm not!" she said, jerking out of his grasp. Tarah turned from him and took a couple steps away, putting her face into her hands. "Tarah Woodblade isn't real. She doesn't exist."

"What do you mean?" he said, confused.

"I'm a fraud! That's what I mean. My name is Tarah

Beraldi," she said. "This armor . . . my abilities, all of it is something made up by my grampa and me."

Djeri stood there for a moment, flummoxed. "How can that be true?"

She sighed, dropping her hands from her face, but still refusing to look him in the eye. "Grampa Rolf was a . . . traveling merchant of a sort. He was always looking for some new big thing or other that he could sell and make it rich.

"He was big for awhile up in Five Hills. But he made a few bad business deals and lost it all. After that, he went from town to town, peddling things like potions, tinctures, and cure-alls. Problem is, most of it didn't work or at least enough of it didn't that he got a bad name for himself. Every time some town booted him out, he'd reinvent himself with a new name and go somewhere else."

"A swindler," Djeri said, shaking his head in surprise.

"He didn't mean to be," Tarah said, her eyes catching his firmly. Then her shoulders slumped and she looked away again. "Leastwise, Grampa Rolf said he never sold stuff that didn't work on purpose. Papa didn't believe him, but I always did. I guess I'm not that sure what to think anymore.

"Anyways, when I turned twelve, grampa came to the house to see us. Papa didn't like it, but Rolf said he had a present for me. He gave me the staff. He told papa he'd tried to sell it at the Mage School, but the wizards just told him it was painted fancy. There was just a couple of runes making it strong. Nothing worth their time.

"But then when papa wasn't looking, Rolf took me aside and told me that he'd just told papa a story so he'd let me have it. He told me that the staff was really high magic. It was ancient, made of a wood that don't exist no more. Then he made me promise to keep it secret."

"And you think he was right?" Djeri said.

"I felt the first memory from a track only two days after grampa left. I practiced and found that it only happened when I held the staff. Once I knew how to make it work, I could track better than anyone. Papa thought I was a tracking genius but I never told him the truth.

"I didn't see Grampa Rolf again until I was sixteen. It was

the day after papa died. Rolf showed up and told me that papa had sent for him, asking him to take care of me. Grampa Rolf was getting old and he wanted to teach me everything he knew before he died. It was his dying mission in life to make sure I knew how to make a living.

"First he taught me how to fight with my staff. Grampa Rolf was real good. Said a good salesperson had to learn to fight so he could to protect himself when business deals went bad. His staff and his wits were what kept him alive through the hard times."

"Well, he did a good job teaching you," Djeri said.

Tarah shook her head sadly. "He said I was a natural. He saw how good I was with the bow and the staff and he came up with an idea. He said he had a sure way to help me survive. He'd make me a legend.

"That's when he came up with the name, Woodblade. He said that Beraldi meant wood sword in Khalpany. Tarah Wood Sword sounded silly, so he changed it to Woodblade. I didn't feel right at first, calling myself something I wasn't. Papa said a name was earned. Grampa Rolf disagreed. He said a name was something you claimed. He said if I called myself Tarah Woodblade long enough, people would start believing it."

"I see," Djeri said, feeling a little disappointed. It wasn't the honorable way, but then again she wasn't the first warrior to declare their own name.

"Grampa came up with a set of rules for Tarah Woodblade and he made me recite them back to him every morning. Tarah Woodblade is wise. Tarah Woodblade is strong. Tarah Woodblade never cries . . ." She swallowed. "I guess he figured if I said 'em enough they'd come true.

"Problem was no one would believe it. First few times he sent me out to get tracking work, I got laughed at. Womenfolk wanted a strong man to hire. Men didn't want to pay no 'ugly girl.'"

Djeri winced at the pain in her voice. Her story was starting to make him feel ill. "You're not ugly, Tarah. You're beautiful"

She growled as if he had bit her. "Don't even try to cheer me, Djeri the Looker! I know the truth. I've heard it all my life, ever since I busted my nose. Grampa Rolf said that my looks could work in my favor. He said that I was a growing to be a big girl and if we enhanced that, folks would hire me anyway.

"That's when he got the idea for my moonrat armor. He had me go out and hunt a mess of moonrats and bring 'em back home. He had this special armor recipe, you see. It was his last big find. His 'grand achievement,' he called it. His special resin could make any cheap leather as strong as heavy armor."

"That's the recipe I found back at your house," Djeri said.

"That's right. Rolf said this armor would show the world that Tarah Woodblade was brave and tough. Who else would face down the scariest creatures in the woods and spit in their eye like that? No one, woman or man. That's how I'd show 'em."

She was right, Djeri thought. No one else was crazy enough to send their teenaged granddaughter out in the world dressed in armor like that.

"It worked too. I started getting jobs. Then he made me recite new phrases. 'Tarah Woodblade is tough.' 'Tarah Woodblade is meaner than a herd of bears.' 'Tarah Woodblade could out track the prophet hisself.'" She laughed softly to herself. "Folks started believing me. Everyone except the folks in Pinewood. They knew who I was. Tarah Beraldi, the ugly little daughter of that ex-berserker. Even after the Sampo Guidesmen Guild let me in, Pinewood didn't accept Tarah Woodblade. They knew I was a fraud."

Djeri was staggered. His heart told him that this wasn't right. He knew Tarah. Whatever she thought of herself, he knew that wasn't true. Or did he? "But the people of Pinewood are proud of you. They bragged about Tarah Woodblade all summer long during the siege."

"I guess I fooled 'em in the end then, didn't I?" she said, her voice harsh.

"You saved them. All fifty of the survivors had stories," he said.

"So I saved fifty!" She laughed bitterly. "Tarah Woodblade could have saved them all! You don't know me Djeri. Not the true me. Tarah Woodblade is brave, but I'm scared spitless most of the time. That night in Pinewood, the magic of my staff was on fire. My tracking senses were doing things they didn't normally do. Tarah Woodblade knew where the rats were coming from. Tarah Woodblade could see the trolls from a mile away.

"I snatched the folk as they ran from town and took 'em to escape trails. I went back for more and more. Then she caught me." Tarah's face went white as she fell into the memory. "An orange-eyed rat looked me in the eye and that witch saw my soul. She told me I was marked for death and I knew she meant it. She intended to hunt me down."

"That would have scared anyone," Djeri said.

"Not Tarah Woodblade. Tarah Woodblade would have gone back into the town and kept saving folks until there was none left to be saved. She could have done it! That night, she could have guided the whole forest out from under the moonrat mother's nose!"

"Then why didn't you go back?" Djeri asked.

"Because Tarah Woodblade doesn't exist! There's just me, Tarah Beraldi. And Tarah Beraldi ran!" Her voice was shaking and tears poured from her eyes. "I ran as far and as fast as I could. I left those folks I saved up in the mountains to die for all I knew. I ran for the border. I crossed the river and hid in Razbeck, ignoring the voices of my papa and grampa saying I should be brave. All I could hear was the witch's threat.

"I stayed in Razbeck like a coward with my fingers in my ears until Shade found me and told me the war was over."

"Tarah, of course you were scared. Everyone was scared during that war," Djeri said, but the words sounded hollow in his ears. The person she was describing didn't sound like the Tarah he knew.

"But not everyone ran," Tarah said. "I did. I could have been an asset in the war. As Tarah Woodblade, I could have saved lots of lives. But I'm a coward." She turned and looked him straight in the eyes, her hands balled into fists. Her voice quivered as she said, "So now you know me. You know the ugly truth. What do you think of me now?"

Djeri looked at her, his jaw dropped open and his brow furrowed. For one brief moment, she convinced him. In that moment he saw her as she saw herself. A regular human girl, small and frightened. She searched his eyes and, though he immediately regretted it, Djeri looked away.

"That's what I thought," she said and moved to Neddy's side. Tarah took the quiver and bow and slung them over her shoulder. Then she grabbed her father's sword and started back south down the riverbank.

"Wait, Tarah. Don't go down there yet," Djeri said weakly. He needed time to think about what she'd told him. "Come with me to the outpost. We'll find out how everything turned out back at the dock and once we know it's safe, we'll go back and look for your staff together."

She paused. "No, Djeri. I think it's best we part ways here. I'll go down the bank and hunt 'till I find my staff and then I'll go back to pretending to be Tarah Woodblade. You can . . . tell folks what you want. You've every right to."

"But Tarah," he said numbly. "The smugglers could find you."

"I may not have my magic anymore, but I can hide my tracks well enough to fool those idiots," she said and continued walking.

"Wait," Djeri said, his voice trembling. His mind was blank. He couldn't think, but he was sure of something. "I can't let you go like that. I . . . I care for you."

Tarah turned on him, anger in her eyes.

"Don't make me sick," she said and strode away.

Chapter Nineteen

Tarah kept walking, her back stiff, until Djeri was out of sight. Then she stumbled. Overcome by weakness, she sat down and planted her face between her knees.

Don't make me sick.

Had she really said that to Djeri? That was terrible. Those were Donjon's words, not hers. Why had they come out of her mouth?

She hadn't meant it that way, of course. Djeri didn't make her sick. If anything she felt . . . well whatever she felt about him, that wasn't why she'd said it. What made her sick was the thought of the dwarf taking pity on her. She had seen the look of shame in his eyes. The thought that Djeri would stay around her out of some sense of duty, all the while knowing how terrible she was . . .

No. She stood and started walking forward. As horrible as she must have made him feel with that remark, it was for the best. Now Djeri would leave her be and she could go on with her lie of a life without his knowing eyes watching her do it.

Tarah shook her head. Those thoughts felt hollow. She was lying to herself again.

Djeri cared for her. He'd said it out loud and the thought scared her. He cared for her and he knew her for what she was. Those were the two most frightening things she could think of.

So Tarah ran like the scared girl she knew she was. Without the staff and the mantle of Tarah Woodblade to hide behind, there was nothing else she could do. At least that's what Tarah told herself as tears streamed down her cheeks.

Tarah Woodblade doesn't cry, reminded her grampa.

"Shut up!" she yelled.

You have been doing a lot of crying lately, her papa agreed.

Tarah slowed. "What?"

For almost a month, you've been crying non stop, Grampa Rolf said.

Bawling, her papa said.

"Don't say things like that." This wasn't the way things worked. The words she heard in her head were memories, things her papa and grampa had told her when they were alive. They never said something new.

Maybe it's time we started, papa said. *Old advice is old.*

Sure. Listen to us babble. You might as well go full on crazy, Grampa Rolf said with a snort. *Forget Tarah Woodblade. You can become Tarah, the Crazy Hag that Lives in the Woods of Razbeck.*

Not bad, Her papa agreed. *The name's a little long, but-.*

Tarah laughed and the voices vanished. They were correct. Or rather, she was correct. They had been her thoughts after all. She was driving herself crazy. She had gone through a long and traumatic month and she wasn't thinking right. She just needed to calm down and think rationally.

Poor Djeri. Tarah winced. Oh, why was she so stupid? Djeri had been right. Completely right. The staff didn't matter. Not with everything else that had happened. Maybe she would find it some day. Maybe not. But for now . . .

She leaned against a tree and a powerful memory entered her mind. A beast had brushed against this tree not long ago. A great and beautiful beast.

Her heart thundered. A beast had been here. She had felt its memory without her staff!

Tarah began looking around for more signs of the creature. There was one not far away. It was just the slightest indentation in the ground, but her practiced eyes found it. She crouched down and touched the track. This memory was just as strong as the last. The creature was big. It was strong. And it was scared.

Tarah felt a shiver go down her spine. The power of the memory was the same intensity as the memories of the rogue horse she had been following, but this wasn't the same beast. It was different.

She walked forward, following its path through the woods, touching every trace of it she could find and each one brought a powerful memory. Oh, this beast was clever. It moved quietly, softly, afraid of being seen. And its tracks were fresh.

The traces of its passing were minor, so faint that most trackers would miss them. In fact, Tarah may have been the only one that could find them. She saw the littlest things, the bent leaf, the slightest scuff on tree bark, and they brought a picture up in her mind.

This rogue horse was a she and she had been around a long time. Centuries for sure, and she had survived all this time on her own. Alone in the world and she had done it by hiding. This beast could hide, often times in plain sight. Tarah didn't understand how she did it, but she did. This rogue horse, her fear is what kept her alive.

"Esmine," Tarah said. That was the rogue horse's name. Her father had given her that name long ago. Esmine's memory of him was very faint; just a pair of kind eyes and gentle hands that would stroke her scales and sometimes comb her mane. Yes, the memory was faint, but she held onto it. She thought of him all the time.

Tarah continued following the tracks. She didn't know for how long. She didn't eat, she just kept tracking. She crossed a wide road at some point and climbed over a farmer's fence. A dog ran at her barking and snarling. It wanted to bite her, but she just waved her hand and it ran away. She had no time for dogs or any other fears. There was just the horse. There was just Esmine.

Esmine was gentle. Her teeth were sharp and her hoofs were hard, but she didn't like to fight. She stayed away from violent things. She hid from danger. She ate leaves and berries and bugs and sometimes the carcasses of dead things she found. She also hunted from time to time. Elks, foxes, the occasional orc perhaps if she was hungry enough. But she didn't hunt anything that was dangerous. There was that giant once, but it had been asleep and it had been easy to tear its throat out.

Esmine loved to run. She loved to jump and frolic. Sometimes she would watch people. Human people like her father, or short people, or the skinny elves. But none of them saw her. Esmine was too careful. She was too fearful to let that happen.

As Tarah closed in on her, Esmine discovered something strange. There was a human following her. A human woman with a filthy armor was walking behind her and touching the places where she had stepped.

Esmine found it frightening, but interesting. She had learned to be careful with her tracks. She was careful not to leave a mark. A thousand years of experience had taught her how to stay hidden, yet this human continued to follow.

Her instincts told her to run, but this human was so intent on her tracks it made her curious. From its scent the human was a female. It had the weapons of a human; the hunting bow, the biting sword. Yet she didn't believe it was hunting to feed its young. There was no urgency. No hunger to its movements.

How strange, Esmine thought, her curiosity overwhelming her fear. The human followed her no matter what she did. She began to walk in circles, staying just outside the human's grasp. Circle. Circle. It kept going. It hadn't even realized that she was playing with it. A strange thought occurred to her. What would the human do if she were to stop?

Tarah's fingers touched something warm. She breathed slowly for a moment as she came back to herself. Tarah had been tracking the rogue horse for so long her thoughts had been blending together with the rogue horse's memories. It took her a moment to understand that she was touching Esmine right now.

The strange thing was that Tarah couldn't see her. The scales under her fingers were translucent. If she focused very hard, she could just make out the slightest shimmer. Tarah smiled. Now that she knew what she was looking for, she could just make out its shape. Esmine was similar in size to the horse Tarah had been riding with the smugglers. In fact, from the vague outline she could see, Esmine's shape was very much like a regular horse.

Tarah looked towards the vague shape of the rogue horse's head and knew that as equine as it seemed, there was a mouthful of teeth there waiting to bite her if she did anything stupid. She swallowed, realizing how strange it was that Esmine was allowing herself to be touched.

"H-hello," Tarah said softly. "I'm not going to hurt you, Esmine."

The rogue horse snorted in surprise and Tarah forced herself not to flinch. That had been surprise at hearing her name from a human's mouth. The rogue was likely a hairsbreadth from running away.

"Shhh," Tarah said, softly running her hand down the rogue's flank. "It's okay. I learned your name from your tracks, Esmine. It's a power I have. I can't explain how it works. In fact, I understand it even less today."

Esmine didn't move and Tarah carefully, gently, leaned forward to lay her ear against the rogue's chest. Esmine's heartbeat was loud and strong. With each thump, Tarah felt like she understood the rogue a little better. Esmine had been created. Somehow her father had taken the best parts of many animals to create a new one. Esmine had been designed for stealth.

Tarah opened her eyes and had the incredibly strange experience of watching her body disappear. The rogue horse was enveloping her in its magic. "Oh, Esmine, you are perfect aren't you?"

She felt the rogue horse's hot breath on her face. Tarah reached out and felt the underside of Esmine's neck. She ran her hand up to the underside of the rogue's chin, feeling the sharpness of her pointed teeth.

"What do you look like?" she asked. Esmine exhaled loudly and Tarah felt somehow that the rogue horse was making a decision. "Show me. What do you look like really?"

Slowly the translucence faded and milky white scales began to appear. Esmine's body was shaped just like Tarah had imagined. She looked like a horse, though her tail and mane were fiery red. But that was where the equine ended and the strangeness began.

Esmine's ears were very un-horselike, curling into pointed spirals. Her eyes were a solid red, matching the color of her mane. Her snout was long and covered with bony spikes and her teeth were pointed, protruding from her jaws like those of a great reptile. Tarah smiled. To most people that face would be a nightmare, ugly and fearsome, but Tarah saw something beautiful. This was a face that showed the rogue horse could defend itself.

Esmine seemed to be taken aback by the lack of fear in Tarah's eyes. She had been prepared for Tarah to run away in terror. Instead, the human had smiled. The rogue horse felt an urge she hadn't felt in centuries. Esmine had been created to hide and to sneak. But there was one purpose she had been made for that she hadn't done since leaving her father's herd.

Esmine gave Tarah a gentle nudge and a single simple word entered Tarah's mind, a word that all rogue horses knew. *Ride.*

"Yes!" Tarah said. She had never tried to ride bareback before, but somehow she knew that it wouldn't be a problem. Deep down Tarah understood that this was the horse she was meant to ride. She reached up, preparing to swing her leg up and over the horse, but something went wrong.

Esmine jerked. At the same time, Tarah felt something sharp pierce her shoulder. She looked down and saw a long crossbow bolt protruding from the rogue horse's neck. It had gone all the way through the horse and pierced her moonrat armor.

Blood spurted from Esmine's neck. It splattered Tarah's face, filling her open mouth. Esmine's blood tasted of salt and metal, but there was also a strong sweetness. Tarah fell. She swallowed the thick fluid as she hit the ground. She tried to climb back to her feet but there was no strength in her legs. The best she could do was roll to her back.

Esmine let out a piercing scream of fear and rage. Blood continued to pour from the rogue horse's neck, coating Tarah's chest and arms. Esmine turned, standing protectively over Tarah's prone form as gruff voices came from the woods around them. Dwarf voices.

At that point Tarah couldn't move. She hadn't been hit by a paralyzing spell like before. It was something else. She was pretty sure that the crossbow bolt had been poisoned. That made sense, but she was finding it hard to think right.

I'm sorry, Esmine! This is my fault. Tarah wanted to say it out loud but she couldn't form words. Esmine's blood was thick in her mouth and she could barely swallow to keep from breathing it in.

Esmine let out another scream. She snorted and stamped her feet. Then when the dwarves started appearing out of the trees, she turned translucent again, or tried to. The poison in the bolt was somehow disrupting her magic and the camouflage was spotty. Her legs quivered and Tarah knew that she was having trouble standing.

"Holy hells, that's an ugly one!" said a voice Tarah

recognized as Mel's. Why was he still alive? She had hoped he
was dead.

"All rogues are ugly, you con-founded idjit! And you shot
it in the dag-blamed neck!" This was a voice Tarah didn't
recognize.

"I-I didn't mean to, Ringmaster Blayne," Mel said in a
pleading manner. "It's this blasted wound. I was aimin' fer the
shoulder."

"I didn't friggin' say to shoot its shoulder!" said the
ringmaster. "You was supposed to shoot its rear!"

A dwarf dressed all in black with a wide-brimmed hat
walked into Tarah's field of view. He twisted the tip of his black
handlebar mustache with thick fingers, a scowl on his face. Mel
had called him Blayne. Tarah recognized that name. He was
Donjon's father, one of the higher-ups in Maggie Cragstalker's
band.

"Robert, stop the bleedin'!" Blayne said and glared towards
the trees "Mel, if this thing dies, I'm cuttin' off yer babymaker and
turnin' it into a coin purse."

Esmine staggered to the side, nearly stepping on Tarah's
hand. Her skin pulsed, splotchy patterns of translucence ebbing
and fading as she fell to her knees. Several dwarves rushed in from
the trees, one of them kicking leaves and dirt all over Tarah in his
haste to get to the animal.

Esmine reared and tried to bite, but one of the dwarves
threw a thick sack over her head. Another one rushed over and
yanked out the crossbow bolt while the one called Robert jumped
on the rogue horse's back and packed blue powder into the wounds
on either side. The bleeding slowed and stopped.

The dwarves backed up and the rogue horse screamed
again. She tried to stand, but kept collapsing.

"Is it gonna live, Ringmaster?" Mel asked, sounding
worried. He stepped into Tarah's line of sight and she saw that the
dwarf's head was bandaged up heavily, as was his hand.

"You'd better hope so," Blayne replied.

Mel swallowed. "Then why'd you have me shoot a
crossbow? Not that I'm sayin' it's yer fault Ringmaster. But why
didn't we just pop her?"

"Paralyze spells don't work on rogues, you idjit!" Blayne

said. "This stuff does the trick, though. You'cn see the poison's got her now. She'll be sleepin' soon."

Tarah could feel the effects on her body as well. She felt tingly all over. Her eyes drooped.

"What about scars?" asked another dwarf. "She's gonna have some nasty ones when that wound heals up. Will that take down her value?"

Blayne snorted. "The gnome won't care about scars. What shape it's in don't matter as long as it's alive when it gets there. After that? Well if we're lucky, he'll let us take the body home."

"Hey, where's the girl?" asked one of the dwarves.

"I dunno," said the one Blayne had called Robert. His head was shaved, but for the mustache. "I tell you I done saw her head this way. She walked right across the road like she had no clue anybody was lookin' fer her. Did you see anythin' Mel?"

"I thought she was there when I shot," Mel said. He looked right at Tarah. "She must've run off."

What were they talking about? Tarah struggled to comprehend it through her clouded mind. She was lying out in the open after all. Then Tarah noticed something strange. Move her eyes as she might, she couldn't see her nose. Somehow the rogue's blood was making her invisible. Oh poor Esmine. Tarah was so sorry.

"I watched that girl walk right up to the rogue," Blayne said. He shook his head. "I dunno how she tracked it here. I didn't see no tracks."

"She's a real good tracker," said another voice that Tarah recognized as Leroy's. "When we was tracking that other rogue in the snow we almost lost it a few times, but she always found it."

"Want us to chase her down, Ringmaster?" Robert asked.

"Naw. Why bother. Shade hired her to find us a rogue and lookee here, she found us a rogue." Blayne spat. "Far as I'm concerned, the deal's done. Send some boys up the riverbank, though. See if they can find the other rogue's tracks. Maybe we can make this a twofer."

Esmine had stopped struggling and laid on the ground, breathing slowly. Her large red eyes seemed to be pleading with Tarah to do something. The dwarves pulled out a long piece of canvas and pulled Esmine onto it. As they pulled her away, a shadow fell across Tarah's face.

"Hey," Mel whispered, his lips close to her ear. "Yeah, I know yer here. I'm keepin' that to myself though. I just wanted you to know I'm coming back for you later."

Tarah's vision darkened. She barely saw the dwarf stand and walk away with the others. Everything went black.

Chapter Twenty

Tarah's parting words struck Djeri like a punch to the gut. He watched her walk away, his outstretched arm slowly falling as she disappeared from sight. He leaned against Neddy, breathing heavily.

"I make her sick?" His mind was numb. Stunned, he replayed the moment over and over.

Neddy reached around and bit his hand just hard enough to get his attention.

"Ow! What?" He glared at the mule. Neddy snorted and jerked his head in Tarah's direction. "No, she doesn't want us going after her." The mule rolled his eyes and Djeri glared back at him. "She'll be fine. There's not one of those smugglers she couldn't out track."

He pushed off of the mule and stepped away, looking at the river rush by. In the far distance he could barely make the wooden buildings of Filgren on the Dremaldrian side. The great water wheel had been lifted out of the water and stood still. He wondered what had happened to the ferry. He remembered the violence of the river and didn't see how anyone could have survived.

Clasping his hands behind his head, he turned away and looked into Neddy's accusing eyes. The whole conversation with Tarah had been surreal. Was she truly a fraud? He didn't know what to think.

He stood there for a long time, his mind going in circles. How could she say that to him? How could she leave after all they'd been through together? Maybe she really was a coward. After all, she had run away. She had run away from the war and now she had run away from him.

"Come on, Neddy," he said finally. He grabbed the mule's

lead and pulled him towards the academy outpost. "If we stay here any longer, we're just begging to get caught."

The mule resisted for a little while, but eventually he gave up and followed along. Djeri shook his head, mumbling to himself as he went. What had he been thinking, telling her that he cared for her? He was a stupid, stupid fool. How had he expected her to react? Sure she had kissed him. Sure she had saved his life. That didn't make her beholden to him.

He continued to mull things over in his mind as he walked. The going was slow. This section of the riverbank was only sparsely forested and wind had blown the previous night's snow into drifts that were sometimes waist high. He growled in anger at the weather. Why was it still winter? It already felt like the longest winter of his life and there were still two months of it left to go.

He pushed on until noon. He was pushing through a particularly annoying snowdrift when it occurred to him that he had let Tarah go without taking any supplies. She took her bow and sword, but he had their blankets and provisions. Djeri stopped, his emotions torn. Surely she'd be fine. She was a survivor after all. She'd been living on her own in the wilderness for years. Still, the thought of her shivering without a blanket, huddled by a small fire made him anxious.

He almost turned around and went after her. Then his nose caught a savory scent in the air. Someone was roasting meat. His stomach rumbled and Djeri realized that he hadn't eaten since the night before. He looked around and saw a wisp of smoke curling up from the center of a small stand of trees.

Cautiously, he followed the smell until he found the source. Sitting on a rock by the fire was a nondescript man in his middle years. He wore plain traveler's clothes and a winter cloak of fur. He was roasting four small spits of meat, turning them slowly. He had brown hair and kind eyes, but a forgettable face. In fact, Djeri was sure that as soon as he looked away, he would be completely unable to remember what the man looked like. He frowned. That's what always happened when you met the Prophet.

Standing behind the Prophet, standing two full feet taller than Neddy, was the rogue horse they had been following for so long. He looked just as Valtrek had described. His front end was that of an enormous gorilla, his rear end that of a great cat, and he currently had one enormous finger up his nose.

"Come, Djeri the Looker," said the Prophet without looking up from the skewers. "Sit and eat for a spell. We have things to talk about."

"Of course it was you. Who else could it have been?" Djeri said, his brow knit in frustration. This was just like the Prophet. Wandering around, nudging people here or there, changing their lives, but never telling them what he was up to.

"You look displeased to see me," the Prophet said, his eyebrows raised. He held out one of the skewers. "Don't be too mad. I cooked you some squirrel."

"Why didn't you tell us it was you?" Djeri asked. "I mean, you could have left Tarah a single footprint message on the first day. 'By the way, it's me, the Prophet. I'm the one riding the rogue horse around.'"

"Sit. Eat," the Prophet said. "And call me John. We've certainly known each other long enough."

"Fine, John." He sat on a tree stump across the fire from the man and accepted a skewer of meat. He was in a foul mood, but when he bit into it, he moaned in spite of himself. The meat was tender and had the perfect amount of spice. He could taste salt and curry and something else he couldn't quite identify. "You de-boned this? Who de-bones a squirrel?"

"There's a trick to it, but it's not so hard with as much practice as I've had," John said with a shrug. "How is it?"

"I'd say it's just about the best squirrel meat I've ever had," Djeri said, chewing the last piece. "Strange, I never pictured you cooking."

John handed him another laden skewer. "Why is that? Do you think I go around with a maidservant?"

"Nobody knows what you do," Djeri said with a shrug, as he filled his mouth. Wow, it was good. "Some people think you don't eat." At the Prophet's raised eyebrow, he added. "You never ate with us during the siege."

"Djeri, I find that a meal is a fine time for private reflection. I have some of my greatest moments of understanding while filling my belly." he said. "This is one of the reasons I'm feeding you right now."

Djeri frowned. What reflection did the Prophet want him to

make? "I asked you a question before."

"Ah, the tracking. Well to tell you the truth, I didn't know you were following me," John said. "At least not right away. You were almost on our heels when I realized what was going on. As for why I didn't tell you, I ask, would that knowledge have changed anything?"

"Perhaps not, but it would have at least been a simple courtesy," Djeri said, wiping his mouth.

The Prophet handed him a third skewer before claiming the fourth one for himself. "I apologize. At my age courtesy is something easy to forget."

Djeri gave him a wry look. John always spoke like an old man, yet he looked to be no more than forty or fifty in human terms. Then again, maybe that's what happened when one lived for thousands of years.

They chewed in silence for a moment and Djeri's thoughts turned back to Tarah. It felt strange that she wasn't sitting there with him. "It's a shame that Tarah's not here. She would have liked meeting the rogue horse she's followed for so long."

"Me?" The rogue horse looked at him and smiled, showing him an enormous mouth full of plate-sized teeth. Neddy had walked up to the rogue and was sniffing him suspiciously.

"Yes," Djeri said, surprised to hear the thing talk. "And, uh, I'm sure she would have liked to meet you too, John."

The Prophet swallowed a mouthful of food. "So why isn't she here?"

"Oh. She, um . . ." Djeri leaned forward, staring into the fire. "I don't know what happened. We had this talk and she tells me she's not who she is and for a minute there, I didn't know who she was . . . The truth is, I think I screwed up. I don't know."

"Come on now, you're Djeri the Looker!" John said in mock surprise. "You're supposed to figure out these things. Why do you think I coined that name for you?"

"Because you have a sense of humor," he replied dully.

"No. It's because you have a particular talent. You have eyes that see the soul."

Djeri snorted. "That's not what people think when they hear that name. I've allowed everyone to call me it out of respect for you, John, but come on. Most folks hear 'Djeri the Looker' and either assume I'm vain, or just a peeper."

"Indeed?" the Prophet laughed. "To be honest, I hadn't thought of it that way. I thought it was a clever bit of wordplay, myself."

Djeri sighed. "So what are you saying?"

"I'm saying use that skill," John said. "What do those 'peepers' of yours tell you about Tarah Woodblade?"

"I don't know," Djeri said, clutching his hair. "My brain is all jumbled up when it comes to her."

"That's called love," the Prophet said. "Look past it."

"Love? But-." He sputtered a bit, then sighed again. Arguing with the Prophet was useless. He knew too much. "Alright. Give me a minute."

Djeri closed his eyes and cleared his mind. He tried to think about Tarah logically, pushing all his emotions aside. He took all his theories he'd come up with about her over the last month and added the information she had told him that morning. He frowned. It didn't make sense. It was like she was two different people. He re-examined their conversation and stripped out all of her own opinions about her actions, looking only at the facts.

Suddenly, everything fell into place.

"Oh." Djeri opened his eyes.

"Do you see now?" John asked.

"I've got to go now," Djeri said, standing up. "I've got to find her."

"Yes, I think it's about time that you did. But before you do, there's something I must give you." He leaned back. "Rufus?"

The rogue horse grunted and picked something up from the ground. He stretched out his enormous arm and Djeri saw Tarah's red staff clutched in his hand. John took it from the rogue and leaned it across his knee.

"Where did you find that?" Djeri asked.

"Floating downstream," he said. "We saw it early this morning caught in an eddy. Rufus swam out to get it for me. He's a great swimmer. Loves the cold water."

Rufus shivered. "Cold!"

Djeri laughed. "And she ran off looking for it. Oh if only I had been able to convince her to come with me."

"These things happen," John said. "People part ways. You

needed to think. She needed to think. But now that's done." He spun the staff through his fingers with practiced hands, then held it out with a slight frown on his face. "You know, this blood staff is a distasteful tool in many ways. In the old days people went so far as to call it evil." He shook his head. "But in the end, the value of a tool has more to do with the user than the tool itself. I suggest you take it to her."

"Blood staff?" Djeri said, taking it from the prophet's hands. "What does it do? She thought it was giving her tracking powers."

"Well, I suppose it may have enhanced them a bit. Magic this old seems to have that effect on spirit magic powers. As far as what it's designed to do, well . . . that's old news, I'm afraid," John said with a sad smile. "And you know me, Djeri. As frustrating as it is, there are things I like to keep close to my chest. I've learned over these long years that the right bit of information at the wrong time can ruin everything."

"So we should just take it on faith?" Djeri said with a scowl. "That's what you always ask us to do, isn't it?"

He shrugged. "It's the way my master works and therefore part of my job. Now go. I have the feeling that it's important you leave right away."

"Right," Djeri said. "Neddy!" The mule was standing in front of the rogue horse. They were looking at each other very closely, staring into one another's eyes as if they were having some kind of contest. "We need to go find Tarah!"

Djeri looked at the Prophet. "But how do I find her? She'll have hidden her tracks."

John frowned. "That would make it difficult." He stood and walked over to Djeri. "Would you like my help finding her?"

"Yes." he said. Of course he would. Why even ask?

"Very well, then. Hold tightly to her staff." He gave Djeri the staff and placed his hands on the dwarf's head. "This is more difficult to do with dwarves, but hold on."

A strange warmth gathered under the Prophet's hands and descended over Djeri's body causing a shiver to run up the dwarf's spine. Then the warmth focused in his head. The heat increased, becoming hotter and hotter until Djeri thought his brain must be cooking.

The Prophet finally removed his hands. He stepped back. Wisps of steam rose from his fingers.

Djeri swayed for a moment. He felt the heat inside his mind, almost as if like a hot coal had been left just behind his eyes. It didn't actually hurt, but there was a dull throbbing. "What did you do to me?"

"More than I intended when I started," John said, looking at his hands in surprise. "I placed a link between the two of you."

"Like a bond?" Djeri asked, thinking back to Sir Edge and the other bonding wizards he'd met.

"No. Not exactly," John said. "You won't be hearing each other's thoughts, but . . ." He bit his lip. "Hmm. This may have some unintended consequences." He slapped Djeri's shoulder. "Oh well, it's time you got going. In fact it's past time. I'm afraid I've delayed you too long already."

Djeri blinked. "But-."

"Go." He turned Djeri around and gave him a shove. "Mule, go with him. Tarah needs you. I would go with you, but I have somewhere to be." He picked up a small shovel and began burying the cook fire. "Evidently I have a gnome to speak with."

"A gnome?" Djeri said. His mind was muddled and there were strange afterimages in his vision. Neddy chose that moment to bite his hand. "Ow!"

Djeri jerked, startled as if awakening from a dream. John was right. Tarah needed him. He turned away from the Prophet and his enormous rogue horse and hurried away. Tarah was almost directly to the west. He could feel it.

He clutched her staff in both hands and began to run. He didn't bother pulling Neddy's lead, knowing the mule would follow. At times he was slowed by drifts of snow, but he plowed through as fast as he could. Tarah was somewhere straight ahead.

It made so much sense now. During their argument that morning, he hadn't understood why she'd run away from the war. He'd been so fixated on the twisted chains of logic she was spewing that he'd looked right past the truth. Tarah hadn't run because of fear. She'd run because of unbelief. She didn't run because she feared her death. She ran because she actually didn't believe herself capable of winning.

Djeri imagined what his life would be like if he'd believed

all the foul things people had said about him over the years. Oh, what that must have done to her. And the guilt afterwards . . . He knew how he would have felt about himself if he had run from the war.

He began letting out a constant stream of curses. He cursed Tarah's grandfather. He cursed the people of Pinewood. He cursed all the other men and women throughout Tarah's life that had made her feel unworthy of her name. Then he cursed Tarah herself. Why had she let them do it? Why had she held on to the belief that she was a fraud for so long? The only thing he could think of was that her grampa had left out a key piece of information in her training. She didn't understand the meaning of courage.

He stopped at the edge of the East King's road. It was one of the major arteries of Razbeck, running from the capitol city of Beck up the bank of the river to the farmlands and holds of the north. It was a heavily traveled road, but right now it seemed busier than normal. Djeri gritted his teeth as he waited for wagons and horses to go by, most of them traveling south.

Tarah was somewhere across that road, but Djeri needed to cross unseen. The man in the watchtower had seen him cut that chain. People would be on the lookout for the murdering dwarf in green plate armor and it would do Tarah no good if he were arrested before he could reach her.

Finally the road cleared and he stepped out onto the packed dirt. He made it two steps before he heard the thundering approach of horses. Swearing, he ducked back into the trees and watched as three dwarves rushed by, heading southward. All of them wore wide-brimmed hats and all three had handlebar mustaches.

Djeri didn't recognize these dwarves. That meant there was another band of smugglers nearby. It was too soon for these new riders to be there in response to the events of the night before and it was too coincidental that they would just happen to be in the area. Djeri frowned as he considered the possibilities.

He hurried across the road and into the forest beyond. Tarah was closer now. He could feel it in that place behind his eyes. It was as if there was a rope pulling him towards her.

He increased his pace, running through the snow and leaves. Djeri was no tracker, but he saw obvious signs of horses among the trees. The soil was churned up and a wide swath of snow was flattened as if something heavy had been dragged along the ground. The track was coming from the direction Tarah was in now.

He came upon a farmer's field. A long fence line blocked his path. The horse tracks curled around the outside of the fence line, but Djeri didn't have time for a detour. He climbed the fence and cut across the pasture, running straight for Tarah's position. The pastureland had been cleared of trees and as he ran, he saw another set of prints in the otherwise undisturbed snow. His heart skipped a beat as he realized these were Tarah's tracks.

A large snarling dog came over the hill, barreling towards him. Djeri glanced at the animal and knew it had been trained to attack. Knowing it would go for his arms, he gripped Tarah's staff and waited until the last possible second. As it leapt towards him, he turned and struck it behind the ear with the tip of the staff, slamming it to the ground. The dog rolled through the snow a short ways before lying there unmoving, Djeri ran on, hoping he hadn't killed the beast.

He followed Tarah's tracks to the far side of the pasture and at the edge of the fence saw two more dogs. They were standing at the fence line, paralyzed, their jaws open, frozen mid-bark. The smugglers had been this way.

Djeri climbed over the fence and found the long drag-mark running along the fence line for a short distance. Then it turned and led into the forest right towards Tarah. Djeri started down it and heard the approaching clomp of hooves. He stepped off the trail and ducked behind a tree just in time to see Neddy approaching at a gallop. Being unable to jump the fence with Djeri, the mule had followed the smuggler's trail around the fence line.

Djeri stepped in front of the mule, stopping him. He grabbed Neddy's lead. "Shh! There are smugglers somewhere up ahead. Follow along behind me, but do it quiet, okay?"

The mule snorted in agreement and Djeri jogged ahead. Tarah was very close. It wasn't long before he saw two horses tethered to a tree on the side of the tracks. He slowed down, being as stealthy as he could in his damaged platemail. One of the tears in the metal caused it to creak.

He crept between some trees and saw two dwarves come into view. Both of them wore bandages under their hats. Djeri's lip curled as he realized they were Mel and Leroy. They were squatting over something on the ground. Djeri had a hard time making out what it was. The object on the ground was . . . blurry.

"What're you planning on doin' with that?" Leroy was asking.

"What do you think?" Mel replied. He was pulling on some kind of lacing. "It's invisible armor! It'll sell real good."

"It's only invisible on the front side," Leroy said skeptically. "'Sides, we don't know how long that magic will last."

Mel stood, folding his arms and Djeri noticed that Tarah's bow and quiver were lying on the ground next to him. A few feet away, Djeri saw the hilt of the Ramsetter, seemingly extending out of solid air.

Mel scowled. "We'll find out, then, won't we?" He continued pulling at the laces and then yanked at some invisible material, exposing the pale yellow of a woman's undershirt. The body inside was limp as the dwarf tried to remove the armor.

Djeri snarled. It was Tarah. He had no idea why he couldn't see the rest of her, but that place behind his eyes was screaming that she was right there. More importantly he knew that she was alive.

"Boys!" Djeri announced, coming out of the trees towards them. He held Tarah's staff at the ready. "I'm here to kill you!"

They took a step back, startled. Then Mel let out a laugh. "So there you are! When we woke up on the dock and you wasn't there, I was hopin' that gnome'd tossed you in the river."

"Idjit," said Leroy. "I told you he just scampered off."

"I was out retrieving this," Djeri said, spinning the staff in his hands. He charged them, his jaw set, his eyes blazing with anger.

Leroy reached into his holster and drew his rod. With a sharp pop, Djeri was frozen. "Man are you stupid!"

Mel laughed and reached down to grasp the hilt of Tarah's father's sword. He drew the long blade out of an invisible sheath. "I wanna cut him in two."

"Naw, Mel, you wait," Leroy said. "I got this."

Djeri concentrated on breaking the spell. Leroy was right. He had been stupid. Instead of announcing his intentions, he should have ran straight in. He cursed his love of theatrics.

Leroy approached him, his paralyzing rod in one hand, his thick cudgel in the other. The cudgel seemed like a crude weapon to be in the hands of a smuggler as experienced as Leroy, but Djeri had seen the runes carved into its haft. They were air runes. Whatever they did, Djeri knew he didn't want to be hit by that thing.

He shoved at the paralyzing spell as hard as he could. Then, as if by some unknown trigger, he felt that place behind his eyes flex. The spell dissolved.

Leroy's eyes went wide as Djeri suddenly surged forward, extending the staff in a savage swing. The smuggler brought up his cudgel just in time to block. When the two weapons met, there was an explosive flash of energy from the cudgel, but that wasn't enough to stop Djeri's attack. The staff knocked the cudgel aside and struck Leroy in the chest, sending him stumbling backwards.

Another pop rang out, this one from Mel's rod. Djeri was frozen again, but he focused on that spot between his eyes and flexed again. He burst through the spell and walked towards Mel.

"Hah! You don't scare me, academy boy," Mel said, hefting the Ramsetter and giving him a gap-toothed grin. "Yer tough, but that ain't yer weapon and I been fightin' with greatswords fer a hunnerd years."

"You don't know me very well," Djeri replied, twirling the staff.

Mel came at him, swinging the sword. Djeri knocked the blow aside and sent the staff down low. Mel had to jump backwards to avoid being tripped up and Djeri thrust the staff forward like a spear, jabbing the dwarf in the sternum and knocking him back further.

Leroy chose that moment to charge in at Djeri's back, but Djeri sensed the attack coming. He spun, his hands in the middle of the staff. One end collided with the cudgel, igniting another explosion, and the other end shot up, cracking Leroy in the jaw. The dwarf stumbled back again, this time falling on his rear.

"I might not be as good as Tarah Woodblade, but I'm more than good enough to drop you two," Djeri said.

Djeri had a large collection of weapons back home and he'd had an even bigger one back at the academy. A defensive specialist, he was well-versed in the use of polearms, especially in the pike and halberd. The quarterstaff was much easier to use than any of those.

"We'll hit him together, Leroy," Mel said, wincing as he rubbed his chest. "C'mon, Leroy, get up!" The blond-mustached dwarf tried to get to his feet, blood streaming from his lips.

Djeri glanced down at Tarah. Her body was mostly invisible, just blurring at the edges, but where the dwarf had opened her armor, he saw her chest rise and fall with each breath. He also saw blood staining the side of her undershirt. His hands tightened on the staff.

Djeri didn't wait for the smugglers to regroup. He charged at Mel and knocked the dwarf's hasty attack to the side. Djeri struck him once in the chin, knocking his head back, than struck him twice in the hand, causing him to drop the sword.

One more crack to the side of the skull and Mel went down. Djeri bent and picked up the sword, then turned to see Leroy coming up behind him, pointing his paralyzing rod. Djeri dropped Tarah's staff and raised the sword over his head.

Pop! Djeri was frozen just long enough for Leroy to bring his cudgel to bear. The magic weapon struck Djeri's weakened breastplate. The explosion of air that accompanied the strike tore his breastplate open, pieces of metal scattering into the snow.

Djeri felt like he had been punched in the chest. His mind flexed and as the spell broke, he launched his body forward and kicked Leroy in the chest, sending the dwarf reeling.

Leroy recovered quickly, but Djeri didn't give him time to fire the rod again. With a growl, Djeri rushed ahead and slashed the Ramsetter diagonally across the smuggler's body. The blade cut deep, opening Leroy's torso from collar to hip.

The dwarf's bloody jaw dropped open and he gave Djeri a look of shock. Then he fell face first, blood pooling beneath him.

Djeri stood there for a moment, breathing heavily. Then he bent down and picked up Leroy's cudgel.

"Stop!" said Mel behind him and Djeri turned to see that the dwarf was kneeling over Tarah. The dwarf's bandages were blood-soaked, but his eyes were clear. He was holding his belt knife over her chest, its sharpened point aimed at her ribs. "Put yer weapons down or I'll kill her!"

In one quick motion, Djeri twisted his body and threw the

cudgel. Mel raised his hands defensively, but he didn't react in time. The weighted end struck him right in the nose. An explosion of air sent blood and flesh flying and Mel fell to his back.

Djeri grunted and pulled at the leather straps holding his breastplate in place. With a creak, it fell from his body. He looked down and saw a piece of metal sticking out of his chest. Gasping, he pulled it out to find that it was a jagged shard almost two inches long.

Djeri tossed the metal to the ground and knelt at Tarah's side. He reached out and touched her invisible face to find that something sticky was covering her skin. Concerned, he pulled back her armor and found the shoulder wound. A sigh escaped his lips. He didn't know how long she'd been laying there, but the wound was no longer bleeding and it didn't look to be infected.

"It's okay, Tarah. I'm here," he said. He gently patted her face, but she didn't wake. "Hey, I brought your staff." He reached for her translucent hand and placed the staff in her palm. "See, it's right here. It's . . ."

Djeri's eyes widened. He could see her hand. The runes on her staff glowed briefly and the strange invisibility that covered her began to flow into the red wood. In moments, all of the translucence was absorbed and Tarah was completely visible again.

"Tarah," he said. "Can you hear me?"

There was no response. Her eyes were closed and her face peaceful as she continued to breath slowly. He touched her face gently and felt her neck. Her heartbeat was steady and strong. What to do now? His fingers trembled as he laced the front of her armor back up.

He called for Neddy and the mule walked up to them. He sniffed at Tarah and looked up to Djeri with concerned eyes.

"I know, boy," Djeri said. "We've got to get her out of here, but I hate to move her with a wound like that. Do you think you can carry her without being too rough?"

A cough rang out behind them and Djeri turned to see Mel stirring. The dwarf let out a pained moan. Djeri picked up the Ramsetter and strode over to the dwarf, placing the blade against his neck.

"Mercy . . ." said Mel weakly.

Djeri glared. "Tell me what happened and I'll spare you."

"B-Blayne . . . Blayne came to meet us at F-Filgren, but only three of us was alive," he said with a gurgle. "We . . . saw yer girl she was pettin' a . . ." His eyes became unfocused. "We . . . They . . ."

Mel drifted into unconsciousness and Djeri stood over him for a moment, his eyes searching the dwarf's ruined face. Mel's nose was gone, his skull likely fractured. Still, Djeri knew if he left him there, the dwarf would probably survive, even though he'd be scarred for life.

Djeri sighed. He had always believed in giving quarter to defeated foes. Enemies that were shown mercy rarely came back looking for revenge. But as he looked into Mel's unstaring eyes, that new place in Djeri's head flexed. He saw deeper into the dwarf. For a moment he saw into Mel's soul.

Djeri flinched, taking a step back. He'd seen a small glimpse of the future. Mel wouldn't let them go. He was too proud and too vicious. The scars on his face would drive him to chase after them again and again. Djeri thought of Tarah and the humiliations Mel had already forced her to endure. He thought of the further cruelties the dwarf had planned.

Mel stirred and groaned. He blinked his eyes and saw Djeri swinging back the sword. He saw the disgust in Djeri's face. He extended his arm, pleading, "Wait! I said mercy!"

"Not for you," Djeri said and brought the Ramsetter down, lopping off the dwarf's head.

Chapter Twenty One

It was monsoon season in Alberri. Torrential rains pounded the normally arid hills and desert dunes that surrounded the capitol city. The small rivers and dry beds quickly overflowed, turning the area surrounding Mallad into a huge floodplain.

"This happens twice a year here," Steward Molly recited as she led Arcon down the corridors of the king's palace, following behind Scholar Aloysius. "The farmers count on the rains. The country would starve without them, but as a whole, the scholars abhor this time of year. The air becomes humid, making the care of ancient documents difficult. Their robes get wet and heavy. For years, the scholars searched for a way to stop the rains."

"A difficult problem," Arcon said, though her lesson bored him. He followed behind the steward at a respectful distance, his shoulders hunched and head bowed.

That's how life as a steward in training had been over the last month. His mornings were full of listening to Molly's inane prattle regarding stewardly duties. Hardly any of it was interesting. The only positive development had been her reluctance to summon him to her rooms at night now that he was her student.

"*No kidding,*" Mellinda said. "*It's the first time in hundreds of years that I've found propriety an advantage.*"

Then again, without the green and white striped sash he wore over his robes, he wouldn't have been allowed anywhere near the palace. Scholar Aloysius had been right about the advantages of his position. As a steward-in-training, no one looked at him twice. He had access to most areas of the Homeland and he was able to read in the libraries at whatever hours he wished. If he had been a full steward, his duties would have kept him away from studying most of the day.

Scholar Aloysius paused and looked back at him, causing the entourage of stewards to stumble to a halt. "Indeed, Student Arcon? Do you find the rains a difficult problem?"

"No, scholar," Arcon said. "The solution is a simple one. I was merely saying what I thought Steward Molly wanted me to say."

Molly shot him a withering glare.

"Oh?" Aloysius said. "Then what is your simple solution?"

"*Careful*," Mellinda warned. "*With him there's a fine line between humor and blasphemy.*"

"Perhaps it is just simple to me because my parents were farmers," Arcon replied. "Rain is a necessity. It's not something you stop. You simply find ways to work around the moisture."

Fortunately, the scholar laughed. He turned and continued down the wide hallway, his retinue following at his heels. "Precisely. This is a fine example of the ridiculousness of our culture, Arcon. Carry on, Molly."

The steward cleared her throat and continued on, red faced. "As stewards it is our duty to keep the scholars comfortable in these seasonal times. We cover them with parasols and make sure that they wear water resistant boots.

"Of course it is much easier to deal with now than it used to be. The streets of the homeland used to flood each monsoon season. Water depths of six feet or more were not uncommon. Twice a year, the stewards had the responsibility of sealing the scholar's basements and bringing all their texts to the upper levels of their residences."

Arcon nodded. He knew this part of the history. It was still built into the architecture of the homeland. Every residence had high stairways leading to their front doors and many of the older residences didn't even have a ground level. They were just built atop high columns.

"Indeed," Scholar Aloysius said. "Twice a year the stewards would shoo us up to our attics to huddle over candles, waiting out the storms, doing all they could to make sure we didn't walk outside and drown ourselves."

Mellinda laughed. "*I love it when he does that. Look at Molly. She has no idea how to react.*"

She was right. Molly and most of the other stewards looked

vaguely offended at having their efforts belittled. The only stewards that didn't were Evan and Madison. The red-sashed stewards wore green sashes in public and walked at the Scholar's side, their weapons hidden.

The scholar turned down a hallway and headed towards a heavy steel door. Four bulky palace guards were standing watch in front of it. A black-sashed steward ran ahead and presented a note to the guards signed by the king himself. By the time Aloysius arrived at the door, the guards had already pulled it open.

The scholar paused at the doorway. "Evan, Madison, and Student Arcon, come with me. The rest of you wait for my return."

"But-," Steward Molly said.

"Thank you for your history lesson, Molly," Aloysius said. "I shall take it from here."

Her face colored again and she gave him a short bow. "Yes scholar."

The gnome entered the doorway and began climbing the stairwell within. Evan and Madison followed closely behind while Arcon took the rear.

"*Aloysius continues to surprise me,*" Mellinda said with excitement. "*I've never seen a scholar be able to order his stewards around like that. Usually they treat the gnomes like children.*"

As you've said countless times, he's different, Arcon replied. The longer they were stuck together, the more the dead witch talked. He understood that there was nothing else for her to do, but at times it really grated on his nerves.

The scholar climbed the long series of stone steps without pause, his breath never laboring even after the red-sashes had begun to tire. Arcon would have tired as well, had he not used a new trick Mellinda had taught him. Muted shafts of air magic lifted his body in multiple places, greatly reducing his weight.

"So, Student Arcon," said the scholar as he climbed. "Now that Molly is no longer with us to give you her rather slanted official view of history, why don't you tell me what you know about the events that happened two-hundred-and-twenty-seven years ago?"

"I believe you're referring to the day when High Scholar Abernathy created the Abernathy Barrier?" Arcon said.

"That is the event," said the scholar, raising a finger. "Do you know how the barrier was created?"

"No, Scholar," Arcon replied. "The texts describe the artifact in great description, but they don't say how it was made."

"*I have my suspicions*," Mellinda mused.

The gnome stopped at the top of the stairwell, standing in front of another steel door. "Don't you find that strange, Student Arcon?" he asked. "After all, is not the purpose of scholarly pursuit to bring knowledge to light? Why hide the means of creating such a powerful item? Would the world not be better served if such artifacts could be created and used all over the known lands?"

Arcon hesitated. What did the scholar want him to say? "I follow your logic, scholar. Though I understand why he would want to keep it a secret."

"Do you?" he asked.

"Well, I was just thinking that once an artifact becomes common place it's no longer special. As long as it was unique he could ride high on his fame for centuries while people waited on him and asked him how he did it," Arcon said.

"But isn't a scholar's life's work to build a legacy?" Scholar Aloysius said. "To leave something behind that would benefit the known lands in the future?"

Arcon paused. "That's true, but Scholar Abernathy was a gnome. He was expecting to live over a thousand years, why let the secret out while he was still young? He could wait until his old age, then release his memoirs and still have his legacy."

"Ah, now you see the right of it," said Aloysius. "Another of the failings of my people. We are too patient. That's why most of the innovations in the world these days come from humans. Their shorter life span makes them eager. Now come, see Abernathy's miracle."

Steward Madison opened the door. Arcon could hear the pounding of the rain and saw a flash of lightning. The smell of ozone filled the air. Steward Evan went out first, Aloysius next. Hesitantly, Arcon followed them. He walked through the door and stepped out onto the highest point in the capitol city, the Barrier Tower.

Just outside the door was a wide balcony that overlooked

the city below. The contrast between the Mallad half of the city and the Gnome Homeland was obvious here. The streets and buildings of Mallad were sort of dingy, while the residences and libraries in the homeland were brighter and well-maintained.

Arcon walked to the center of the balcony. The air was thick and humid here but no moisture fell. He looked up at the roiling clouds, his jaw dropping in awe. It had been an impressive view from the streets below, but here it was even more so.

Water fell in torrents above him, but it didn't touch the city. A massive dome of energy held back the rain. From Arcon's perspective, it was like being inside a glass orb and watching water being poured over it. The barrier began just above the tower and covered the entire city, encompassing both Mallad and the Gnome Homeland.

"*Amazing!*" said Mellinda.

Arcon had to agree. The barrier's construction truly was a miracle. Air was let in, as was sound and the occasional lightning bolt, but the water stayed out. The land around the city was immersed in water, but the raging floods parted around the city, keeping everyone inside dry.

"The sheer power of the barrier is stunning, isn't it?" Aloysius said, looking up at the dome. He had to speak loudly to be heard over the rain. "Are you ready to see the source?"

"Yes, Scholar," Arcon said.

He followed the scholar around to the back of the tower where a fifteen-foot statue stood. It was shaped like a hill giant and was carved out of solid onyx. Its mouth carved in a defiant roar, it held one arm into the air. Something was clasped in its fist.

Aloysius climbed the stone staircase that curved around the statue, ending at its fist. Arcon joined him to stand in front of the artifact that generated the barrier. Clutched by the statue's fingers was a polished brass scepter. It was about three feet in length and covered in intricate runes. The head of the scepter was shaped into the likeness of a joyful gnome with an open mouth.

"*For all the build up, I think it's quite ugly,*" Mellinda said. Arcon couldn't help but agree. He found the end result underwhelming.

"Strange, isn't it?" Aloysius asked. "Such a small thing and yet it creates so much energy."

"It seems rather unprotected, Scholar," Arcon remarked, looking around. "There are no guards here. What if someone were to scale the tower on the outside?"

"Impossible," said Evan. The red-sashed steward was peering over the tower's edge, looking at the smooth stonework below.

"To obtain an item this powerful, people would find a way," Arcon replied. "Can you imagine what a dark wizard could do if he stole the artifact? He could hold the entire country hostage."

"He's right, Evan," Aloysius said. "But the barrier is not as unprotected as you think. Look at the statue that holds the scepter."

"Yes?" Steward Evan said, eyeing the onyx sculpture.

"That is a golem," the gnome said. "A living construct of magic. It rests now, but if anyone save the king himself were to try to remove the artifact, they would not make it down alive."

Arcon looked at the statue and swallowed, thinking of the plant golem he and his friends had made at the Mage School and how easily it had destroyed half the grounds. How much more deadly would it have been made from solid rock?

"Oh, but I could wreak so much havoc here, dear Arcon." Mellinda giggled and Arcon caught the brief image of this enormous golem punching its way through the palace.

Aloysius let out a great sigh. "Every time I see this I shake my head in shame. All of this power, yet when all is said and done, Abernathy, one of the greatest scholars of our day, left us with very little. Do you know why Abernathy's work fell short?"

"In part, I would say it's because you killed him," Arcon replied.

"Silence, you idiot!" Mellinda warned. *"You go too far."*

He likes boldness, Arcon reminded her.

"Boldness, yes. But that was just a guess on my part. If we're wrong, you made an even larger mistake."

Scholar Aloysius turned, giving Arcon a tight glare. One hand was tucked into the pocket of his robes, clutching the handle of the sword Arcon knew was hidden within. It was an oddity that neither he nor Mellinda yet understood. Scholars didn't wear swords. Only the guards and the house warriors were allowed them.

Arcon kept his eyes averted, his expression respectful. "I'm sure it was a necessary step, Scholar. Otherwise his research would have remained sealed. This way you could take up his research and you have the knowledge necessary to recreate his feat."

"Student Arcon, sometimes I think your perception is far too dangerous," said the gnome. He withdrew his hand from his pocket. "Was this your epiphany or Mellinda's?"

"Hers, Scholar. It's what she would have done in your place," Arcon replied.

"Hmm . . . well, she wouldn't be wrong, but that was not the answer I was looking for," Aloysius said. "The reason Scholar Abernathy fell shy of true greatness was that he was short-sighted. He discovered a way to make an item of such immense power and decided to use it to keep a city dry." He shook his head. "Ridiculous, isn't it, wasting such a marvelous power to fix something that, as you pointed out earlier, was a minor inconvenience. An inconvenience, by the way, that we gnomes had worked around for thousands of years."

"I agree," Arcon said. "Truly a waste."

Aloysius sat on the edge of the stone golem's fist and smiled. "You must be wondering why I went through all this trouble to bring you up here."

"The question had crossed my mind, Scholar," Arcon replied.

"Because I wanted you to see what it is that you are going to help me create," Aloysius said.

"Me, Scholar?"

"Of course," the gnome replied. "You see, the secret to the creation of this item, the secret that I had to kill Abernathy to get, is the soul of a rogue horse."

"*Of course!*" Mellinda said. "*This makes so much sense now.*"

"Scholar Abernathy had powerful binding abilities," Aloysius explained. "He had already created a small personal rain barrier for himself using the soul of a large beast, but it fizzled out after awhile. He needed a more powerful soul to achieve a greater effect."

"*And a rogue horse was a perfect choice,*" said Mellinda. "*Their souls are not only extremely powerful, they are also docile,*" *eager to serve."*

"So you want me to create rogue horses just so you can kill them?" Arcon said.

Aloysius laughed. "You have such a blunt way of putting things. I wouldn't kill all of them. After all what leader doesn't need an impressive steed. However, can you imagine what I could do with multiple artifacts of power of this magnitude?"

"By the gods, he really would rule the world," Mellinda gasped.

Arcon's face went pale. "It is an honor to serve you, Scholar."

"I received word this morning that my man succeeded in the task I sent him on. I already have one rogue horse on the way," Aloysius said.

"Might I inspect it before you put it to use, Scholar?" Arcon asked. "With Mellinda's help I might be able to discover what Stardeon did to make them stable."

The scholar frowned. "Could you 'inspect' it without destroying the beast?"

Can I? he asked Mellinda. The majority of rogue horse deaths through the years were caused by wizards trying to understand how they were made. Magic tampering tended to cause them to melt down.

"If you're wearing the rings you might be able to," she said. *"Though other men have tried to use the rings to discover the Stardeon's secret and failed."*

"Mellinda says I can, Scholar," he said.

"Good. Then prepare yourself. It will take a few months for the beast to arrive," Aloysius said. He stood and began to descend the stairs. "I will be expecting results from you and the Troll Queen."

Arcon tarried by the artifact for a moment. He gazed at it, inspecting the workmanship. The scepter had been carved into a rictus of joy, but its expression was a lie. He looked into its hollow brass eyes and winced, unsettled. The only thing he felt from that face was sadness.

Chapter Twenty Two

Tarah rode Esmine and it was glorious.

Riding horses wasn't her best skill. She preferred the feel of her own two feet on the ground. But her papa had taught her and she rode when necessary for particular jobs. Tarah had just never enjoyed it. Until now.

She rode without a saddle, sitting further forward on the horse than she was used to. Tarah held on with two fistfuls of her red mane and let Esmine do the work. The rogue knew what to do. Esmine was made for this. It was exhilarating. Tarah moved with the horse, the wind blowing through her hair, the sun warm on her back as they glided over verdant green plains.

Suddenly, bursting out of the side of the hill before them was the head of the enormous giant. His eyes were intense and his mouth wide open, but instead of teeth he had spinning blades. Tarah was riding right towards him.

Tarah cried out. She pulled back on Esmine's mane, but her inexperience as a rider confused the rogue horse. Esmine increased her speed, continuing to run towards the open jaws of the giant as if she didn't see that it was there.

They rode closer and closer until there was nothing else Tarah could do. She jumped off at the last second and watched in horror as Esmine rode right into the whirring blades of the giant's mouth.

Tarah's eyes opened. She winced, her eyes stinging from the brightness of the sunlight that streamed in through uncovered windows. She was lying on something soft. She was in a narrow bed, covered with blankets. What was she doing here? She needed to help Esmine.

Tarah sat up and groaned. Her shoulder throbbed with the

pain of a recent wound. She was wearing a long white sleeping gown. She had been recently bathed and her shoulder was covered in fresh bandages.

She looked around to find that she was in a long room with stone walls. The whole place had been painted white. Where was she? There were several other beds but all of them were unoccupied but one. It took a moment for Tarah to realize who the occupant was because one arm was wrapped over his face, covering his eyes to keep the sun out.

Her heart thumped. It was Djeri. She knew it even though the dwarf wasn't wearing his armor. Nor did he have a shirt on. She had never seen him bare-chested before. His wide arms were heavily muscled and he was covered in hair. Two large bandages were wrapped around his chest.

Tarah smiled. She didn't know where she was, but she knew she was safe and if she was safe, she knew that it was because of him. Somehow Djeri had found her and taken her here, she was sure of it.

She swung her legs out of the bed. Her vision swam as she stood and she took a moment to steady herself before walking over to him. Tarah sat down next to him on the little amount of the bed his body didn't take up. He was deep in sleep.

Gently, Tarah reached out and touched his arm. "Djeri! Djeri, wake up," she whispered. He shifted a little, but didn't wake. She raised her voice and nudged him harder. "Djeri!"

He swung his arm away from his face, his nose wrinkled in irritation. One eye was blackened, but his neck had been shaved and his beard neatly trimmed.

"What in the dag-gum turds, waking me up afte-!" His eyes widened and he wrapped her up in a big hug. "Tarah, you're awake! They said you'd be fine, but I didn't know what to believe."

Tarah froze in surprise for a moment, then she joined in, hugging him right back. Her shoulder twinged with pain, but she didn't care. The hug felt good. It felt really good. She hadn't been held this tightly since her papa died. At that thought, Tarah began to cry.

"Are you alright?" Djeri said and tried to pull back, but she just held on tighter. He rested one heavy arm on her back and reached up with the other to stroke her hair. "Hey. Hey, it's okay."

"I didn't think I'd see you again," she said, not letting go. She buried her face in his neck. He smelled like soap and cleansing alcohol, but under that was just a hint of steel and the masculine scent she remembered from the day she'd kissed him. Her face colored a little but she didn't let go. "I'm so sorry for what I said. I didn't mean it like that. I didn't. You don't make me sick. You make me . . ."

"I-I'm sorry too," he said, his voice thick. "I shouldn't have doubted you and I sure as hellfire shouldn't have let you doubt yourself,"

Tarah finally broke her grip on him and leaned back, looking into his tear-filled eyes. "What do you mean?"

"You are Tarah Woodblade," he said with conviction. "Girl, I thought about it over and over after you left. I realized that I was letting my thoughts be clouded because the woman you described to me wasn't the woman I knew. Then I understood that you had described yourself that way because you didn't know that you really were the woman I knew. Do you understand?"

Tarah pursed her lips, but decided to let go of the fact that he'd called her 'girl'. "I have no idea what you just said."

He grimaced. "Okay, let me put it a different way. You spent your whole life believing that you weren't what you were. Your grandfather told you who to act like, but you never believed that was who you'd become. Then you let other people tell you bad things about yourself and you believed them instead. What I'm trying to say is that your actions make you who you are. You are Tarah Woodblade!"

Tarah squinted at him, totally lost. "Djeri, I don't know what you're trying to say, but I'm not Tarah Woodblade," she said. "I realize that now. I'm just Tarah Beraldi. I'm a good tracker, but I'm not all those other things and I can't keep lying to everyone."

"Just, dang it, girl! Just . . . Here!" He picked up the pillow from his bed and shoved it over his face with both hands.

Tarah leaned back in concern. Had he struck his head at some point? He seemed all jumbled. "Djeri? What're you doing?"

He held the pillow there for a moment longer, then pulled it down, his face strained as if he had been concentrating very hard. "There," he said breathlessly, holding the pillow out to her. "That's all I could put into it. Touch that and understand me because I haven't been good at saying it."

Tarah frowned, but she reached out and touched the pillow like he asked. She gasped as a clear set of thoughts entered her mind. She saw herself through Djeri's mind, watched through his eyes as he met the fierce-eyed woman, brave and stern. She watched herself save him in the icy river. Then a few images of her standing naked before him flashed by. Tarah saw her bravery as she faced down the goblinoids that had invaded her home. She felt his admiration for her as she told him of her powers, then as he watched her burn her childhood home down.

She felt his worry for her as they were captured by the smugglers. She saw how impressed he was with the way she had handled herself that night, the way she overcame the pain. She experienced his emotions as she had been forced to kiss him in order to save his life. Then a couple images of her naked flashed by again. Tarah felt his admiration for her grow as they spent that month together as prisoners.

Then came that morning after the gnome had saved their lives. She felt his pain at her harsh words, his confusion, then watched as Djeri saw the rogue horse and the Prophet gave him her staff. Finally, she experienced his revelation about who she really was.

When Tarah withdrew her hand from the pillow, her fingers were shaking. She cocked her head at him. That was really how he saw her?

"Now do you understand?" he asked, his expression earnest.

"I do," she said, numbly.

"Good. And another thing. I-I shouldn't have told you I cared for you. Not the way I did. That was going too far," he babbled. "Especially since I'm a dwarf and you're. . . You're . . ." he paused, confused by the expression on her face. "What?"

Tarah was gazing at him intently as if she were memorizing his face. "I think I'd like to kiss you again," she said.

Djeri swallowed. "You would?"

Tarah nodded and leaned towards him, wrapping her arms around his neck. This time as her lips met his there was no fear about having to perform, no worries about hurting him, no concerns about it being done against her will. There was just the moment. And it was a good one.

Tarah didn't know how long the kiss lasted, but when they pulled apart, both of them were breathing heavily, their faces flushed. Neither of them said anything for a few seconds, just searching each other's eyes. Then Djeri cleared his throat.

"That was nice," he said.

"Very," Tarah replied. She swallowed. "Thank you. Thank you for believing in me when I couldn't. Thank you for bringing me here, however you did it. I . . . where are we, anyway?"

"We're at the Eastern Razbeck Battle Academy Outpost," he said. "As for how I got you here, well it's a long story." Djeri told her about how the prophet had told him to go after her and how he had fought and killed Mel and Leroy.

"I'm relieved that they're gone," she said.

"After that, I bandaged you up as good as I could and put you on Neddy's back. It took us almost a full day to get here," he explained. "When we came in, Healer Anaria took over. She's a local woman and takes care of all the wounded here at the outpost."

"How long have we been here?" Tarah asked in concern.

"A day and a half," Djeri said. "Anna said you were lucky that the amount of poison in your wound didn't kill you. She said that it might take you another day to flush all of it out of your system."

"And you have my staff?" she asked, standing up.

"All of your gear is over there in the corner," he said, pointing to the back of the room. "Your clothes and armor are in the wardrobe."

Tarah walked to the corner and picked up her staff. She sighed in relief as she held it in her hand. Now she felt more like herself. She pulled open the wardrobe and smiled as she pulled out her underclothes. They had been cleaned and folded.

"Get up," she said, looking at Djeri. "we need to go."

He was still sitting in the bed, the blankets pulled up around his waist as he watched her. He looked embarrassed. "Uh, I kind of don't have anything on under here. I don't know why it is that healers put clothes on the wounded women, but the men get stripped bare."

Tarah rolled her eyes. "Oh come on!" She tossed him the large shirt and pair of pants that she found in the wardrobe. "I think these are for you."

She pulled the sleeping gown off over her head, wincing at the pain in her shoulder, and started putting on her own underclothes. Then she grabbed her shirt and pants. "That's enough, Djeri the 'Looker'," she said. "Avert your eyes and get dressed."

Djeri cleared his throat and pulled on the pants she had given him. They didn't fit him quite right. It looked as if they were made for a tall guard and the legs had just been cut short to fit him. The shirt fit him better. Though as he buttoned it up, she saw that it strained to fit him. She felt that he filled it out quite well.

"Where's your armor?" she asked as she pulled on her boots.

"It was too badly damaged for repair," he said looking disgusted. "The captain here said he'd try to procure me some dwarven armor, but he couldn't promise anything."

"I'm sorry to hear that, Djeri," she said, knowing how awkward he felt without his platemail.

"They wanted to throw your armor away too, but I wouldn't let them," he said.

"Thank you." Tarah pulled her armor out of the wardrobe and lifted it up.

She could see why they would want to trash it. She'd had it for years and moonrat leather didn't hold up all that well. There were multiple scratches and tears and it was cracking and splitting in wide patches. The only thing holding it all together was the cloth treated with Grampa Rolf's resin. Tarah shrugged and put it on anyway, knowing she would have to replace it sooner or later, but not wanting to think about it.

Tarah slung her bow and quiver over her shoulder. Then she grabbed her staff and her papa's sword. As she touched the handle, a flash of memory entered her mind. She felt the sense of justice in Djeri's heart as he lopped off Mel's head. Tarah clutched the handle tightly. Then she walked over to Djeri, who had just found and put on his boots.

"What are you in such a hurry to leave for?" he asked.

"I want to kiss you again," she said, ignoring his question

and he didn't object.

They didn't pull apart until they heard the uncomfortable sound of a man clearing his throat. Tarah looked and saw a tall man with a long face standing in the doorway, holding his knuckles to his lips. He wore standard-issue academy leather armor and had the largest bow Tarah had ever seen slung across his back.

"Captain Djeri," said the man with a deep monotone voice. "I-uh, thought you might want to hear what I found?"

"Yeah," said Djeri, looking embarrassed. He gestured to Tarah. "Tarah, this is Swen the Feather. Swen, this is Tarah Woodblade."

"Ma'am," Swen said and Tarah thought he might have one of the most expressionless faces she had ever seen.

"Swen here headed down to West Filgren for me to see what news he could find," Djeri said. "I needed to know if they were looking for me."

Tarah frowned in concern. "What would you do if they were?"

"I would probably have to turn myself in," he said.

"No you wouldn't," she replied.

"I can't have the academy taking the blame for my actions," Djeri said. Tarah's frown turned into a glare.

"I don't think you'll have to do that," Swen said. "There was a lot of confusion going on at the docks. All the talk is about a crazy gnome that used to work on the ferries. The tower man said that he suddenly attacked a large group of dwarves, killing most of them, then he ran on and attacked the town watch. He somehow managed to knock most of them unconscious without killing any of them and then he disappeared."

"I see. And the ferry chain?" Djeri asked, his eyes troubled.

"The man in the watchtower didn't get a good look at the man who cut it because of all the snow, but he said he thought it was one of the dwarves the gnome attacked. The Town council and the local nobles are planning to meet with House Roma to discus how to repair the ferries."

"Any survivors?" Tarah asked.

"The westernmost ferry hit the rocks, but everyone survived," Swen said. "The strangest thing though, was the easternmost ferry. It swung all the way across the river and people were sure that everyone had been killed, but just before I left, they got word that a miracle happened. There was a man on the boat that took charge and somehow with everybody's help, they kept the boat stable. When they reeled the ferry into the docks, they'd only lost one ferryman and one dwarf passenger."

Djeri swallowed, both relieved and disturbed at the same time. "Then Shade lived."

"Somehow I knew it. It seemed too easy for him to be dead," Tarah said. She chewed her lip. "It sure would be nice if Donjon was the dwarf that fell overboard," Tarah said.

"We can only hope," Djeri said. "Well at least our part in this is over. We can find our way across the river and report back at the Mage School."

"I'm sorry. We can't. Or at least I can't." Tarah said.

"Why?" he asked, frowning.

She told Djeri about how she had tracked Esmine and how the dwarf smugglers had taken the rogue horse away. "She was free for a thousand years and it was my fault she was captured! Just before I passed out I heard the one they called Ringmaster Blayne say they were taking her to her death. I won't let that happen. I won't!"

Djeri paced back and forth, thinking about it. He ran a hand through his black hair and finally gave her a decisive nod. "Alright. I'll send a message to Captain Commander Riveren telling him that I'm taking a leave of duty. He'll understand. Still, I don't see how we'd be able to take down Blayne Cragstalker's group by ourselves. We'll need help."

"I've been thinking about that, Djeri," Tarah said. "I want to hire the academy."

"You want to hire us?" Swen asked, his wooden eyebrows raised in surprise.

"I've decided. Tarah Woodblade has been hoarding her money for too long. Now I know what I want do with it."

"Tarah you don't have to do that," Djeri said. "I might be able to rustle up some volunteers."

"I want to do this," she said, her eyes intense. "Besides, we don't have time to try and gather up support. The dwarves are taking Esmine to Alberri and they already have a head start."

"We have a little time," Djeri said. "They're still wasting

time looking for the Prophet's rogue horse. Chances are they won't get moving until Shade rejoins them anyway."

"How much money do you got?" asked Swen.

"Six-hundred-fifty gold," she said and Swen whistled.

"You won't need that much," Djeri insisted.

"You could hire a whole division with that kind of gold," Swen said. "The only problem is we don't have that many troops at the outpost. The academy is stretched thin right now with the rebuild. Even if we take staff down here to a minimum, we could only spare maybe five men and I don't know if our captain would go for that."

"I'll take all I can get," Tarah said firmly.

"The captain will have to okay it, but I'd be happy to go with you," Swen said. "I can also pick out the best of the rest to go with us."

"Even if he'll give us all five, that won't be enough," Djeri said, frowning.

"If you want to pick up some volunteers real quick, we could head over to Coal's Keep," Swen suggested. "Your uncle Lenny's still there last I heard."

"Uncle Lenui is there?" Djeri asked in surprise. "I thought he and Bettie would have headed back to Wobble for their wedding by now."

"Naw, the baby took longer to come than they expected," Swen said. "Lenny's been raring to leave, but Bettie's been wanting to wait awhile."

Djeri scratched his head. "That's good news, but I don't think he could come and help us. There's no way Bettie would let him."

"Maybe not, but Master Tolivar and his bonded are there. Since this is about a rogue horse, I'm sure they'd want to help," a smile split his wooden face. "Especially Willum. He's still on the academy payroll and he's been looking for excuses to keep clear of Dremaldria."

"Willum Oddblade, huh? That sounds like a plan to me," Djeri said with a relieved chuckle. "Tarah, it sounds to me like you're going to be my client. Though I hate that you're spending so much money to do it."

Tarah nodded thoughtfully as her Grampa Rolf provided

her an angle. "I don't know. It sounds to me we're still a little short handed. As your client I demand you bring along a tracker."

"We . . . don't have any here at the outpost," Swen said, confused. "But aren't you-?"

"I agree," Djeri said grinning at her as he understood. "Well-well, that is a dilemma. Lucky for you I happen to know one the academy can hire."

"I think I know who you're talking about," she replied with a wry grin. "But I'll warn you now, Tarah Woodblade don't come cheap."

Epilogue

Justan grunted, his muscles straining under his heavy winter jacket as he pulled a heavy cartload of rubble up the hill towards the dumping point. "This is a lazy way to train me, Jhonate!"

"I finished my training this morning while you were meeting with the dwarves," Jhonate replied. She was sitting on top of the rubble as he pulled it, seemingly unconcerned with the cold, her arms folded over her knees. "Besides, if Gwyrtha can do this kind of work, you can."

"That isn't fair," he said through gritted teeth. He was pulling the two-wheeled cart by the two handles that protruded from the front and a leather strap that he had slung across his chest. "She's a rogue horse. She loves to do this kind of thing!"

I'm helping! Gwyrtha sent as she rushed by them, pulling a wagonload. It was a two horse wagon, but the rogue horse had increased her size so that she would be able to pull it by herself. *You're slow, Justan.*

Yeah, thanks. She had been getting better and better at transforming herself and strangely enough, her intelligence seemed to be increasing too.

The workers had been frightened by her appearance at first, her sharp teeth and patchwork mix of fur and scales bringing nightmares to mind, but they had quickly learned she was sweet and a hard worker. A few of them even called out to her and waved as she passed.

The construction of the new Dremaldrian Battle Academy was going faster than expected. The wizards sent by the Mage School were making the cutting and transport of new building stones much easier and the new contract with the dwarves of

Wobble meant that they had no shortage of tools and equipment.

The most painstaking part of the process was the removal of the rubble caused by the old academy's destruction. This was something the wizards weren't as keen to help with. It was a huge undertaking and somehow Justan's father had convinced him to be part of the group in charge of the removal. He wished that he had been able to go out on scouting missions with the academy graduates like Deathclaw had.

"Stop griping, Edge," Jhonate barked from atop the cart. "Deathclaw needs that type of work. You have let your training regimen become far too lax lately."

"You've . . . picked up a bad habit of monitoring my thoughts, Jhonate," Justan said as he was almost to the top. Of course he knew that meant she'd just make him go down and bring up a new load. "If you don't stop it I might just have to take off my ring."

"You would not," she said, but he could feel through the link that connected them that she was concerned. The matching Jharro wood rings they wore allowed them a connection that was similar to the bond, but it was weaker and its range was much more limited.

"I would not," he said with a sigh as he reached the top. She was the most self-confident woman he knew, except when it came to their relationship. Then she seemed almost fragile. He didn't know what she was worried about. Their connection through the rings should have made it obvious to her just how much he loved her.

Fragile, am I, Justan? she sent, and Justan winced. "Once we dump this load, I shall make them stack the next one higher."

At the top of the hill, the ground leveled off and Justan waited in line for the dump-off point. The wizards had cut an enormous quarry out of the ground in the first two months of the rebuilding process. Looking down into the pit, Justan found it hard to believe that all the rubble would fill it, though the dwarves on the planning committee had assured him it would.

When it was his turn, Jhonate jumped down and helped him back the cart to the edge and dump it out. There were a few tricky moments as he tilted the edge of the cart over the precipice. The ground was icy in places and they had lost two carts over the edge in the last week. Luckily no one had been hurt, but the loss of equipment slowed them down. The carpenters could always build more, but they were overloaded with projects as it is.

"Alright. Back for the next load," Jhonate commanded.

"You know that I outrank you, right?" Justan said. "If I chose to, I could put you on caltrop duty."

One of the biggest problems with the cleanup project was dealing with the thousands of iron caltrops that the academy had catapulted into the hills during the war. People and animals were constantly stepping on them, and it happened even more often when they were covered with snow. Most of the workers found scouring the countryside for the sharp metal pieces a nice respite from their heavier labors. Jhonate found the work tedious.

She raised an eyebrow at him. "Get moving, Edge."

Jhonate jumped into the back of the cart and he started pulling it again. He made it as far as the top of the incline when he saw two familiar figures walking up the hillside towards him. He smiled and came to a stop.

"The longer you take, the heavier that next load will be," Jhonate warned.

"That load will have to wait," Justan said, setting the cart down. "We have visitors."

She jumped from the cart and joined him as he approached the two men. One was tall and broad shouldered, the hilt of an enormous sword rising from behind his shoulder. That was Justan's father, Faldon the Fierce. The second man was the bigger surprise. He was slighter of build and wore a sword on each hip.

"Sir Hilt!" Justan called. The man smiled and greeted him with an embrace.

"It's good to see you, Edge!" Hilt said, and as he pulled back, Justan noticed a wide scar that ran from just behind Hilt's ear and down his neck to disappear into the collar of his coat. He didn't have that scar the last time he'd seen him. "You know, as much as I have fond memories of this area, the part I miss the least is the winter."

"Why are you back so soon?" Jhonate asked.

"Where is Fist?" Hilt asked, ignoring her question. "Beth sent me with a present for him."

"He's back at the Mage School with my mother," Justan

explained. The ogre couldn't leave until Darlan was finished with her projects there. "She's eager to join us here, but they still haven't filled all the spots on the high council."

"Wizards," Hilt said with a snort. "How long did it take the academy?"

"Once the war was over?" Faldon said. "A week."

"So why isn't Beth with you?" Justan asked.

Hilt gave an embarrassed laugh, "Well that would be because she's home with the baby."

"Baby? That's impossible considering we just saw you four months ago," Justan said. Not to mention the fact that Beth was barren.

"We sort of, uh, 'adopted' one on the way back to Malaroo," he said. "She's sweet as can be. Beth named her Sherl-Ann, after your mother."

"Wow. I'm sure mom will be flattered," Justan said.

"I'm planning on sending her a letter about it today," Faldon said.

Jhonate's frown increased the longer they talked. "Why are you here?"

"I'm glad to see you too, Jhonate," Hilt said, embracing her as well.

She patted his back dutifully but when he pulled away her face was serious. "I mean it, Hilt. What does my father want now?"

He grimaced slightly. "We always do seem to meet this way, don't we? Yes, I am here at your father's request. Only this time I brought several envoys with me."

"Envoys?" Jhonate said suspiciously.

"Yes. A few of your brothers and Yntri Yni came with me as well," he said.

Gwyrtha chose that moment to thunder past. Justan felt a rush of glee coming from her through the bond. She had a rider.

I like this elf! Gwyrtha sent. *He's really old!*

Clinging awkwardly to her back and looking concerned was Yntri Yni. Like the last time Justan had seen him, the ancient brown-skinned elf didn't seem to feel the cold. He wore nothing but his loincloth and the bow and quiver that hung over his shoulder. He was making a rather frantic series of clicks and whistles as they rode past, but Gwyrtha continued on down the hill without stopping.

Hilt watched them go by with a bemused expression on his face. "Your brothers are back at the camp getting some proper winter gear. I warned them about the winter, but they figured if Yntri could handle it, they could. Did you know they had never seen snow up close?"

"Why are all of you here?" Jhonate said. "I am not going back home until my contract is up, I told you that when you left last time."

"Your father disagrees," Faldon said. He gave her an apologetic smile. "He sent his delegation here with an offer. He wants to create an alliance between the Roo-tan and the academy. They arrived late last night and have been meeting with the council all morning."

Jhonate gave Hilt a glare for not telling her. "An alliance?"

"That's great news," Justan said. An alliance with their people would make his marriage to Jhonate happen so much easier. But his connection to Jhonate told him that her thoughts weren't nearly so enthusiastic. "Isn't it?"

"As part of the agreement, two of your brothers will stay here with us and you will return to your father's side," Faldon said.

"Oh," Justan said, understanding her anger.

"I will not allow him to break my contract," Jhonate said with a glower.

"He's not breaking anything. The council is," Faldon said. "I'm sorry, Jhonate, but the alliance is too valuable for us to throw away just because you want to stay for a few more months. Your contract has been ended as of this morning."

"We leave in two days," Hilt said. He looked at Justan with something akin to pity in his eyes. "Xedrion is also quite anxious to meet the famous Sir Edge his daughter is betrothed to."

"That's good," Justan said nervously, feeling Jhonate's worry rising. He put an arm around her. "That means we won't have to wait so long to get married, right?"

"Perhaps," Jhonate said. She pointed to Hilt's neck. "Did Father do that to you, Sir Hilt?"

"This?" Hilt said, reaching up to trace the scar with his fingers. "Well, let's just say that Xedrion was none too happy with me for okaying your betrothal."

Jhonate's face paled. "Father is that angry?"

"He wounded you?" Justan said, concerned. Hilt was the best swordsman he had ever met. If he could do that to Hilt . . .

"It's alright now," Hilt assured them with a hesitant smile. "He and I patched things up."

"That's something I wanted to talk to you about, son," Faldon said, placing a hand on Justan's shoulder. "When you get there? Try not to get killed."

The Bowl of Souls series will continue in

The Jharro Grove Saga: Book Two

Protector of the Grove

Summer 2014

Keep an eye on the Trevor H. Cooley Facebook page, Twitter @edgewriter, and trevorhcooley.com for updates.

Please keep the comments coming and tell your friends. Book reviews are always welcome.

Preview Chapter
Protector of the Grove

As far as winters in Dremaldria go, this was a mild one. The rubble that remained of the city of Reneul and the Battle Academy was covered in a thin blanket of snow and ice. The area was a hive of activity despite the chill. Laborers in winter clothes climbed over the site, clearing rubble and rebuilding important areas.

The workers were a mix of war refugees and tradesmen from all around Dremaldria. The mood of these people was high. The academy paid well and the rebuild was moving along far quicker than anyone had hoped. With help from Mage School wizards and the dwarves from Wobble, the structures of the new academy buildings grew at a rapid rate.

Justan ran around one completed structure at the edge of Reneul's ruins. The long rectangular building would eventually be a town government office. For now it was just in his way as he hurried to catch up to his future wife.

"Jhonate, wait!" Justan shouted as she came into view. Jhonate wasn't wearing her usual hide armor, but was instead dressed for the cold, with a stiff coat over a thick woolen sweater and padded leather pants. Her breath frosted in the air and her cheeks were flushed pink. With the determined way she was walking, Justan was surprised she didn't slip. It took him several long strides to catch her. "Where are you going?"

Jhonate didn't answer right away and he fell in at her side, noticing how tightly she gripped her staff. Justan could feel the slow burn of her anger through the Jharro ring she had given him. The gift was a precious one, for it allowed them to communicate privately over short distances. Unfortunately it also meant she could listen in on his thoughts, something that had led to many uncomfortable conversations.

Jhonate's strides were leading them through what used to be Reneul, heading down one of the roadways that had been cleared of rubble. He was pretty sure that she was heading towards the main camp, but Justan didn't push her, content for the moment to walk along beside her. A smile touched his lips.

She was as fierce as ever, their betrothal hadn't changed that. Her jaw was set in determination, her lips pressed into a thin line. A smile broadened Justan's face. Ah, but she was beautiful. Her green eyes were striking even when they were burning holes into the world around her.

Those eyes darted at him to show that she was not in the mood to be admired. "I must speak with my brothers," she said.

"Why didn't you just tell Sir Hilt and my father that?" Justan asked.

"Must I tell them every thing I am thinking?" she replied.

"Well, no. But you did turn and leave while Hilt was mid-sentence."

"I was done speaking with him on the subject," Jhonate said, but slowed down, her glare turning to a frown. "Do you think I was rude?"

"Incredibly," Justan said, though his smile didn't fade. Jhonate was straight forward and honest in her conversations, a trait which often led to rudeness, but those that knew her were used to it. In fact, Justan found it endearing when it wasn't complicating things. "He did come all the way here from Malaroo to speak to you, after all."

"Hilt came to undermine me and deliver an ultimatum," she clarified, picking her pace back up.

Less than a half hour earlier, Justan's father had shown up with Sir Hilt at his side to announce that the Roo-Tan people were forming an alliance with the academy. As part of the agreement Jhonate's contract was being severed. Her father had commanded that she was to come home with Justan in tow.

"He was your father's messenger, yes. But you know that he didn't have to come." Justan replied. Sir Hilt was friends with Xedrion bin Leeths, but he didn't work for him. "The only reason Hilt would come back so quickly, leaving Beth and their baby at home, is because of the affection he feels for us both."

They quieted for a moment as they strode past a large

group of workers. The men were laboring to clear the center of Reneul where the large arena had once stood. Justan had tested to join the academy in that very arena. Little but the foundation remained now. Justan felt a shiver as he was reminded of the sheer power of the explosion that had destroyed the academy. He had been working at clearing the rubble for four months and still it affected him.

"This is the third time he has come on my father's request to fetch me," she replied finally. "He has reasons beyond simple affection to come all this way."

"Maybe," Justan said, though he didn't know what Hilt's other reasons could be. "Listen, I know you are upset, Jhonate, but to tell you the truth, I'm relieved. Finally we can go to your father and get this over with."

"Get this over with?" she asked, dumbfounded. This time she stopped completely and planted her staff into the ground before turning to face him, her hands on her hips. Several workers stopped their work to observe the conversation.

"Yes," Justan replied, not backing down despite the intensity in her eyes. "We have been betrothed for over half a year now and I'm tired of the threat of your father looming over us. Now we can face him and get on with our lives."

"Do you think I am foolish, Edge?" Jhonate asked, her eyes narrowed at him. She usually called him Justan when they were alone, but she found it disrespectful to call him anything other than his title when in public.

"No," Justan said slowly, realizing that he was treading a thin line.

She raised an eyebrow. "Do you consider me a coward?"

Justan winced. "Of course not. Why would you-?"

"I am well aware of how much time has gone by," Jhonate said. "And I am also fully aware that I could have cut my contract short at any time just by asking. Each delay I have made has been deliberate."

"Okay," Justan said, confused at where she was going with this. As far as he had known, her contract was the only thing keeping them from traveling to Malaroo. He had assumed that her reasons for staying out the year at the academy and fulfilling her contract was out of a sense of honor.

"No!" Jhonate said and Justan was reminded that her close proximity to him allowed her to sense his thoughts through the ring. "My original purpose for coming here was brought to an honorable conclusion months ago."

"Then why have we been waiting?" Justan wondered. Everyone seemed so fearful of her father's wrath.

She turned and strode forward again. *I have not delayed out of a fear of my father!*

Justan scratched his head and followed. Why hadn't she talked to him about this earlier? Why couldn't she just come out and declare her reasons instead of keeping them bottled up for so long?

"There is still just so much that needs to be done," she said.

Justan still had no idea what she was talking about, but he let it go for now. If they were traveling all the way to Malaroo, there would be plenty of time for talk along the road.

Where are you going? Gwyrtha asked through the bond. The rogue horse sounded confused. Justan sensed that she was still back at the work site where he had left her and there was a bit of a commotion. He sensed laughter around her as well as frantic cries.

Gwyrtha, why is someone beating you about the head? he asked.

This old elf is tired of riding. Gwyrtha replied with a very un-horselike chuckle.

Justan rolled his eyes. *Then let him down, for goodness' sake!* When he had last seen her, Yntri Yni had been clinging to her mane for dear life as she galloped past. Justan felt guilty for letting her continue her little joke. The elf truly was ancient; little more than wrinkles and bones. Surely such a rough ride wasn't good for him.

He is stronger than he looks, Gwyrtha replied, but she slowed down enough that Yntri was able to leap down. She sent Justan an image of the elf tumbling quickly to his feet and shaking his fist at her, all the while berating her in his language of clicks and whistles. Gwyrtha chuckled again. *This elf really likes me.*

Justan sighed. She had changed a lot over the last few months, her mind sharpening quickly as if, by learning to transform her own body, she had somehow overcome some great hurdle in her development. *Be nice. I'll get back to you later.*

She sent him an irritated grunt. *I'll see if Hilt wants to ride then.*

Justan turned his attention back to Jhonate. He had fallen a few steps behind her and hurried to catch up. "You have to admit that this alliance between the Roo-Tan and the academy is a good thing."

"Perhaps." Jhonate's brow furrowed. "I would never have believed father would agree to such a thing. At least not so quickly. My contract with the academy was a starting point, but I had imagined that, even with steady negotiations, our children would be fully grown before my people consented to an alliance with outsiders."

Justan stumbled. "Uh, how many children did you expect we would have?" She didn't answer the question.

They were quickly approaching the main camp. It sat at the base of what used to be the academy's main gate and consisted of a long cluster of winterized tents and hastily constructed buildings. Smoke rose into the air from hundreds of cook fires and burning piles of scrap.

The partially-built walls of the academy rose high above the camp. Stoneworkers set large blocks of stone hewn from nearby quarries into place while wizards runed the completed sections with earth and fire magic. The dwarves and wizards had approved the plans together and everyone was confident that the new academy would be far superior to the old one.

Soon they were at the barracks; a long hall erected by the wizards when they had first arrived at the site. The building was two stories tall, its walls made from stone pulled up from the ground directly beneath it. The different coloration of the various layers of strata in the walls made it stand out from the buildings built by regular means.

Jhonate spoke to a guard and was directed to the room on the second floor where their new guests were housed. They headed up right away, but Jhonate stopped Justan just outside the wooden door at the top of the stairs.

"Before we enter there are things we should discuss," Jhonate said, her eyes focused.

"Okay," Justan replied.

She pointed a finger at his chest as she spoke. "I have

things to say to my brothers and you are not to interfere. I wish I could ask you not speak to them at all, but unfortunately my brothers are likely to ask you questions."

Justan smiled and shook his head. "You're that worried about what I might say?"

"My people can be . . . prickly. It will be all too easy for you to say something that could offend them or bring down my father's ire."

"Jhonate, I have spent enough time around you to learn how to deal with someone 'prickly'," Justan said.

"That may be true, but I am easy to talk to in comparison," Jhonate replied and Justan frowned at the implications. She added, "My siblings do not like the way my father dotes on me. They have often enjoyed finding ways to make him angry with me in the past."

"Very well," Justan said. "Then why don't you just use the ring?"

"The ring?"

"Yes. If they ask me a question, simply tell me what to say to them," he explained. "That way I won't offend."

Her eyebrows rose and she gave him an approving nod. "I had not thought of that. It is a good idea, Justan."

"Thanks," he said. She still had much to learn about the way their connection could be used.

Jhonate opened the door and they stepped in to a wide open room. The first half of the floor was taken up by rows of bunks and small chests where the academy soldiers could store their goods. Most of the soldiers were out working but there were multiple guard shifts during the day and several men were sitting at their bunks in various stages of undress. A few smiled as Jhonate brazenly strode through, but the ones that recognized her scrambled to cover themselves. Some of them saluted Justan. He smiled and nodded in return.

At the end of the main room was a short hall leading to the officer's quarters. The rooms were small and consisted of little more than what the rest of the soldiers were given, but at least there was a bit of privacy. Jhonate's brothers were being housed in the back, for the time being, in rooms that were held for visitors. These were more spacious, but just as starkly furnished.

Jhonate moved to the last door on the right and knocked. It opened a moment later and a tall man answered the door. He looked slightly older than her, but Justan could tell right away that he was one of Jhonate's brothers. He had the same long black hair and his braids were interwoven with green ribbons, though they were pulled back from the side of his face in a different style than Jhonate's. He wore an academy-standard winter coat but looked uncomfortable in it. The laces in the front were tied unevenly.

His chiseled face formed a frown. "There you are, sister lost."

"Fullbrother Jhexin," she said, returning his look. "Are you the best father would send?"

She strode past him into the room. Three other men were inside sitting on cots, each of them wearing similar clothing as the first.

Jhonate raised an eyebrow. "Qurl and Xendrol. I thought this was a joke before, but now I see that father is serious about this."

One of the brothers uncurled, coming quickly to his feet. He looked to be older than Jhonate and wore black ribbons in his braids. He darted forward, his hand lashing out to deliver a ringing slap across her face. Jhonate didn't bother to block. Her head was rocked back, but she did not stagger.

"You bring us dishonor!" he declared.

The blow caught Justan by surprise. His hands balled into fists and he took a step forward, his arm swinging.

Stop! Jhonate demanded through the ring, halting Justan's fist inches from her brother's face. *I deserved the blow.*

She stepped in front of Justan and met her brother's angry gaze. "Are you one of those staying behind, Xendrol?"

He glared and shoved past her towards the door. Justan stood in his way, his bulky form crowding the door. Xendrol snarled and his hand moved to the wooden hilt of a Jharro sword belted at his waist. "Move, 'dry foot'!"

Justan, several inches taller than the man, refused to back down. He ached to strike at this Xendrol. Brother or not, how dare he slap Jhonate?

Let him go, Jhonate sent to Justan and she said to her brother, "This school will be good for a man like you."

Reluctantly, Justan stepped aside. Xendrol brushed past him and stormed down the hallway, muttering something about 'father's pet'.

"Who else did father bargain away?" Jhonate asked, looking at the others. "Sir Hilt says that two of my brothers are remaining behind to join the academy. Surely not you, Qurl. Father would not send away both his fourth and fifth born sons. Or have you fallen from his favor?"

"Your tongue is sharp as ever, Jhonate," the man replied. Qurl looked to be the oldest of the brothers and had the bulkiest build, stretching the seams of his winter coat. Red ribbons were woven into his braids. "Father sent me here to make sure you don't find a way to slither out of this." He glanced at Justan. "Is this your betrothed?"

Jhonate turned to look at Justan and he saw the red welt that was already forming on her cheek. "Yes. This is Sir Edge, named at the Bowl of Souls. He is a great warrior and bonding wizard."

Qurl stood, giving Justan an appraising look. He was just as tall as Justan and carried a Jharro staff slightly smaller than Jhonate's in his right hand. "I have heard that you have a Jharro bow, Sir Edge."

"I do," Justan replied.

"May I see it?" Qurl asked.

"It is in my quarters," Justan said, knowing instantly that he had already made the kind of mistake Jhonate had warned him about.

"Do you often let the tree's gift gather dust?" Qurl replied, his voice tinged with contempt.

Justan saw Jhonate's jaw clench. He realized that he had never seen her without her staff at her side. Justan kept his voice level. "I usually keep it with me, but I was clearing rubble when we heard of your arrival. I haven't had time to retrieve it."

"You leave your bow behind when you labor and yet you carry your swords?" Qurl snorted and gave Jhonate a wry look. "How low. Are you always so lax when teaching your pupils?"

Jhonate winced. *He is right. I am sorry, Justan. I should have prepared you better before coming in here.*

What should I say? he asked, wanting to make things better.

Nothing, she replied.

"You are being harsh, brother," said the youngest of the brothers in the room. He was lounging on his cot, his winter coat unlaced down the front revealing a simple deerskin shirt underneath. His hair was more dark brown than black and he wore ribbons the same shade of green as Jhonate's. "The trees do not require this."

"This is true," Jhonate said. "Father may require that the Leeths Clan keep our weapons at our side, but Sir Edge is not of our family."

"It is about respect!" Qurl said through gritted teeth. He shot a promising glance at the younger brother.

Justan wanted to say something but kept his jaw shut. Instead he folded his arms, making sure the rune on the back of his right hand was clearly visible, and gave Qurl a level gaze.

"He is my betrothed," Jhonate said. "I would not be with him if he did not respect his gift."

Qurl snorted. "Perhaps. We have a long road ahead of us in which to determine the manner of your betrothed. Come, Jhexin. Let us see what these 'dry foot' warriors have to eat at this time of day."

Jhexin nodded and the two Jharro wielders moved past Justan into the hallway.

"Wait, Qurl," Jhonate said. "I have questions for you!"

"Ask the yearling," the other brother said with a dismissive wave and they continued down the hall.

"Yearling?" Justan wondered.

"They are remarking on my youth, dry foot," said the youngest brother, still laying back on the cot.

"Dry foot?" Justan said, confused.

"It is a derogatory term," Jhonate said, frowning. "My people come from the marshes and most outsiders that come there fear to get their feet wet."

She nudged her brother's leg with her staff. "Sit up, Pelgroth, and show my betrothed more respect than the others!"

Pelgroth sighed and swung his feet over the edge of the cot. He leaned forward, resting his elbows on his thighs. "Sorry, fullsister. And I apologize, Sir Edge. If Jhonate likes you, your feet must be at least partially damp."

"And do I not warrant an embrace, fullbrother?" Jhonate said, raising an eyebrow.

A cautious smile appeared on her younger brother's face. "Well, I suppose the others are gone." He stood and wrapped his arms around her. "I missed you, Jhonate."

"And I you, Pelgroth," she said with a smile, returning his embrace. She placed her hands on his shoulders and pushed him back at arms-length. "You have grown much since I last saw you."

"That happens when one is gone for over three years," he said reproachfully. "With you gone, the clan's clod-head ratio has been out of control."

Jhonate's smile faded a bit. "My one regret has been leaving you and Trincy behind."

He shrugged. "We were quite angry with you about it at first, but that was just because we wished we could do the same."

Justan found himself smiling. He liked this brother. "So you're the other one staying behind here at the academy then?"

"I am," he said, turning an appraising gaze on Justan. "And I am glad of it, too. Anything to get out from under father's thumb."

"Pelgroth!" Jhonate said reproachfully. "Do not disrespect father."

"Come on," he said. "It is not about respect. It is about freedom. You of all people should know that." Jhonate pursed her lips, but didn't disagree with him. Pelgroth spoke to Justan. "So, Sir Edge. You are the one who won my sister's heart. How did you do that when she does not have one?"

Justan chuckled. "We both know that isn't true."

Pelgroth raised his hands and tucked them behind his head. "I think I like you, Sir Edge. Too bad. I think father plans on killing you."

Justan's smile faltered. Jhonate grabbed Pelgroth's arm and sat, pulling him down to sit on the cot next to her. "You must tell me what has been going on since I left."

"What do you want to know?"

"Everything."

"You mean over the last three years?" Pelgroth looked incredulous. "Do you know nothing?"

"Very little, fullbrother," she replied. "Sir Hilt told me a few things but I did not ask for more."

"What does it mean when you call him fullbrother?" Justan asked.

"We share the same mother as well as father," Jhonate replied.

Pelgroth wrinkled his nose. "Have you told him nothing of our people?"

"Just tell me what has happened," Jhonate said, refocusing him. "All I know is that father is still Protector of the Grove and that he has refused to take another wife from the Prath Clan."

"The Prath Clan is pretty soaked about it, too," Pelgroth said, shaking his head for emphasis. "But they never have liked father anyway and he says he is done taking wives. I, for one, am glad of it. Our clan is enough of a snake pit as it is with seven surly women about. Besides, father has become too fixated on Tayle women. Can you imagine the outcome if he took on another wife from their Clan?"

"The Prath might take up weapons against us," Jhonate said.

Pelgroth laughed. "Sure, they would arrive just in time to find that our other mothers had killed him in his sleep."

"Do not be ridiculous," Jhonate said dismissively, but her brow was knit in thought. Justan could sense her mind churning. "I suppose that means no more siblings then."

"Did Hilt not tell you?" Pelgroth said. "Liz had a daughter about six months ago. Father named her Lizbeth."

"So you have another sister?" Justan asked. That made twenty six children. When you had that many did another one even matter? Being an only child, he found the concept of having twenty five siblings a difficult one to grasp.

"Possibly two," Pelgroth replied. He looked Jhonate in the eye. "Our mother is pregnant again."

"At her age?" Jhonate said, her eyes wide. "Is that safe?"

"The nurses were worried, especially after what she went through with Trincy. The other wives wanted to stop the birth, but Listener Beth said she had a vision that both mother and the baby will live," Pelgroth said. "The baby will be born some time this spring."

Jhonate sighed in relief, one hand on her chest.

"Your people seem to have a lot of respect for Beth," Justan remarked.

"She did save the grove, after all," Pelgroth said. They gave him surprised glances and his nose wrinkled in confusion. "You are Hilt and Beth's friends are you not? Did you not know?"

"I saw that she had a Jharro dagger, but I never asked her why," Justan replied. "What did she do?"

"What did she-? She only fought her way to the top of the highest mountain and brought down a bag of Jharro seeds!" Pelgroth said, his face animated. "You should ask Hilt about it. Both he and Yntri were there when she did it."

"New seeds . . ." Jhonate raised a hand to her mouth. "Then-."

"A whole new section of the grove has been planted! Over a hundred saplings have grown and the old trees have wakened with new life! If not for the Roo-Dan, life couldn't be better!" he said enthusiastically.

"The Roo-Dan?" Justan asked.

"Rag-tag villages to the east of the grove, full of witches and sorcerers," Jhonate said, pulling on her lip thoughtfully. "A constant annoyance, nothing more."

"More than an annoyance now," Pelgroth said. "There are rumors that they have been banding together. Even father is worried. People are going missing."

Jhonate dropped her lip and looked right at her brother. "Witches' work?"

"Maybe," he said with a shrug. "No one knows for sure, but whole villages of our people have disappeared. There is no sign of battle. It is as if they just wandered off."

"That would take one powerful witch. Even Mellinda couldn't do that," Justan said. Bewitching magic could control lesser minds, but for a witch to take over a human mind, the victim would have to be a willing participant.

"Is this why father is making the alliance with the academy?" Jhonate asked.

"I do not know," Pelgroth said with a shrug. "Father acts as if he is not worried about the Roo-dan, but he sent Xeldryn and Sen along with two score warriors to investigate."

"Then he is worried," Jhonate said. She looked at Justan.

"Xeldryn is the first-born son. Father prefers to keep him at his side."

Justan shook his head. "If he was setting up this alliance to get the academy's help right away, this is a bad time to do it. There is little we can do. We are stretched far too thin as it is with the rebuild. Besides, if he was sending for help, father and Hilt said nothing about it."

"Then why would he go to such lengths for the alliance?" Jhonate asked. "Why send four of his sons away at a time like this?"

Pelgroth gave her an incredulous look. "Seriously, Jhonate? After all that father has gone through to bring you home, you still don't believe?"

"What are you saying?" she asked, squinting in confusion.

"It is about you!" Pelgroth shouted. "By the marshes, why else do you think our brothers are so angry? With each successive time you rebuffed his requests to come home, father has gotten more and more angry. You saw what he did to Hilt the last time he came back empty handed."

Justan swallowed at the thought of the new scar that ran from Hilts ear down his neckline. The dread he'd been feeling grow in his stomach at each mention of Xedrion's fury reached a new depth of intensity. Jhonate was worth any obstacle he would have to overcome, but he was realizing just how much he didn't know about the situation he was about to walk into.

"I am just one of his daughters and an unimportant one," Jhonate said, though her voice was uncharacteristically weak and unconvincing. "He has ten now, after all, and I am number six."

"You are and always have been his favorite, and you know it. Everyone knows it!" Pelgroth said. "Among all of us, besides maybe Xeldryn, he loves you best."

"I don't understand," Justan said to Jhonate. "If he wants you home so badly, why did he send you here in the first place?"

"You have not told him?" Jhonate looked down sheepishly and Pelgroth laughed. "Father did not send her here. She stole off in the night and came on her own."

Made in the USA
Lexington, KY
09 December 2014